ABOUT 1

Ben Gardener is a writer a
London.

RYDON HALL

Ben Gardener

www.heddonpublishing.com
www.facebook.com/heddonpublishing
@PublishHeddon

To My Father,

who also wrote

Vera Taggart, if you're out there... this is what I meant.

RYDON HALL

PROLOGUE

Exhausted, filthy, rigid with fear, the crew of the cargo ship *M.V. La Belle Hélène* blinked and scowled into the cold white light of the camera. A week into their captivity, they still looked shocked to find themselves so powerless. Anyone watching these images must have felt relief at seeing them alive, mixed with terror that they were being paraded like booty – or prepared for a horrific death. All four men were, by now, heavily stubbled; two wore woolly beanies instead of the trawlermen's regulation hard hats. Their pale skin contrasting vividly with their orange jump suits, they knew about withstanding the rigours of high seas and storm-force winds, but this new reality – captured by pirates off the coast of the Horn of Africa – had caught them unprepared. They huddled together, without any furniture to support them, in front of a wall which looked so pitted and, in places, moist, that an observer could have thought they were in a cave. Then a chair scraped, and someone could be heard to clear his throat.

'*Vous... sont français, oui?*' The interrogator phrased his question as if it had taken careful thought, and yet the grammar, in the space of so few words, was very wide of the mark. The accent was also indisputably non-French. If anything, it sounded British, and considerably younger than any of the individuals in shot.

'*Où est... où est vous sommes... allez?*' Normally, such men would have reacted with scorn at hearing their national tongue so abused, but they must have been in too much of a stupor. Their thick eyebrows lifted, perhaps, but little more.

'*Vous savons que je me suis...? Vous savons?*' The juvenile accuser appeared to be trying to ask them if they knew who he was. Maybe they hadn't understood the question because it had been expressed so badly,

1

or because they were overcome with fear, or exhaustion, but really they should have known. After all, there were few distractions on a ship, and the story of the young hostage all alone in the most dangerous country on earth had been global news for weeks. Had he been forced to ask the questions or was he now on the same side as his captors? The crew might not have realised it right then, nor have been in a mood to identify their interrogator on camera, but they were about to become headline news.

PART ONE

CHAPTER 1

(Six Months Earlier)

Beneath a grey October sky, the garden of Rydon Hall Preparatory School For Boys – bustling with cyclamen, pansies and polyanthus – was a spray of colour. The walk from the bus stop had taken Charles Goldforbes precisely six minutes, just as Mrs Portal, the receptionist, had assured him it would, and the throb of cars from the Upper Churley Road was soon replaced by the threep of blackbirds. Churley was an affluent but architecturally conservative suburb of south-west London, and the closer Charles got to the school, the further the houses stood back from the road.

The gate buzzed and the lock sprang away. The path Charles stood on was a crazy-paving art project. Each slab formed part of an inter-planetary rocket by the Junior School. It was one of headmaster Dr Raymond Ironsize's favourite initiatives, Charles read as he flicked through the school's glossy brochure, "to encourage our young students to take ownership of their surroundings". Charles had prepared for the interview by downloading a copy from the school website, but he preferred holding the real thing, in the topaz and magenta school colours, stapled and with a nice stiff cover. He was a classicist, after all, and he had a natural sympathy with threatened forms of media such as the printed word.

Mrs Portal was making a cup of tea as he walked in. The mug that she raised to her lips bore the inscription, "Is it a bird? Is it a plane? No it's Mrs Portal!"

Charles had already drunk two cups of tea that morning but when she offered him another, he felt it would be a career blunder to refuse so he sat, cradling it in one hand while staring at a photograph from the prospectus in which some Year Five boys had very

3

nearly kept still for long enough to make it look as if they were balancing the Eiffel Tower on their heads. He was trying to think of an intelligent question when Mrs Portal asked him if he had taken the H14 bus. Charles - sandy haired, two inches shorter and a stone heavier than his ideal dimensions - nodded, and wondered what a teacher would say about the local bus network, but she had moved on.

'The forecast said look out for rain today,' she said, shaking her head and pursing her lips. 'I always knew it wouldn't. Ah, here's Dotty. She's the deputy head.'

'Mr... Goldforbes, is it?' said Dotty, stretching out a hand. She had nut-brown hair in a little bob, and a fresh contact lens look that still seemed to be adjusting to life without glasses.

'Yes, I'm...'

'Interesting name,' said Dotty, as Charles followed her across the playground.

'Well it's actually...'

'I hope Mrs Portal gave you one of our prospectuses,' she said. As they walked, she explained that she was called Dhoti de Souza, but that everyone called her Dotty. 'Or is it prospectae? I expect you'd know that, being a Latin teacher.'

'It sort of depends what declension it is,' said Charles, trying to draw a veil of scholarly ambiguity over his own uncertainty. 'But I thought the boys looked like they were enjoying themselves on the France trip.'

'They like their trips,' she said. 'If you get the job, you might get to go on one.' As she said this, she smiled, tipped her head down and looked at him through her fringe, which he found rather attractive.

'You're not a formally qualified teacher, Charles, are you?'

'Not formally,' said Charles. 'But...'

'And you went to Cambridge.'

'Yes, er...' He didn't want to sound hesitant, but somehow it always managed to creep in, as when shaking the headmaster's hand a few minutes later.

'Qualifications,' said Dr Ironsize. 'They're useful, don't get me wrong, but if you've got what it takes, you can always get your NQT later, once you've settled in.'

They were sitting in his office, which was a small, bright room packed with more files than books. At one end was a framed watercolour painting - perhaps another instance of the school's strength in the arts - of an item of bakery that appeared to be bouncing on a ruler. Charles looked again and realised that the image was of a diver, preparing to spring.

'I never studied Latin but I wish I had,' the Head continued. 'It's the foundation for so many other subjects, isn't it?'

'Yes...'

'And yet, no one really speaks it, do they..?'

'No,' said Charles, as if, come to think of it, Dr Ironsize had a point. He looked across the low table at Dotty, who smiled at him.

Dr Ironsize was nodding. 'It's not just the language, is it? All those gods and goddesses, they never lose their fascination, do they? I mean, take, um...'

'I think your predecessor was more interested in the language than the stories,' said Dotty, to move the conversation along.

'I suppose most teachers are linguists first,' said Charles, trying to stifle a blush as he recalled confusing Orpheus with Oedipus in his last Finals paper. Obviously he had been tense, and a pub session the night before, unnecessarily long and featuring his best friends Milo and Penny, who had already finished their exams, hadn't helped, but even so, it was a shocking oversight. Charles had covered up ever since by professing a lordly lack of interest in the 'chatty' side of classical studies, preferring the black and white certainties of grammar.

'Well,' he said with a smile, 'it's hard not to be a bit down on Classical Civilisation because it does feel rather, um, light; somewhat insubstantial, compared to...'

'Compared to declining all those irregular verbs!' said Dr Ironsize.

'Exactly,' said Charles. 'Although strictly speaking, you conjugate verbs and decline nouns.'

'Just as well it's the boys taking the exam, not us,' said Dr Ironsize.

The job vacancy had arisen because the previous incumbent, Mr Norringham, had left just a few weeks into the autumn term.

'We shall miss Geoff, obviously,' said the headmaster, with a sniff. 'But those teaching jobs in the Gulf come with such a salary that we can't really compete.'

He spoke as if implying that they all knew that there was more to teaching than making money.

'And do you know the area?' asked Dotty. 'Churley?'

'I must admit I don't,' said Charles. 'But obviously I'm looking forward to getting to know it.'

He meant that: he liked its deciduous leafiness and the casual sprawl of its streets. He was less drawn to the large cars, mostly driven by nannies or young mothers at particular times of day, which seemed to throng the roads. When they tried to get past each other, they looked like dogs sniffing each other's bottoms. But he liked the poster at the bus stop, which read: "Alight here for Close to the Hedge and all your gardening needs".

'It's quiet,' said Dotty. 'A lot of net curtains on the windows, that sort of thing. I don't know what they get up to behind them: probably all bonking each other like crazy but we try not to get involved in that sort of thing.'

'Glad to hear it,' said Charles.

'We like to think of ourselves as a friendly school, don't we, Dotty?' said Dr Ironsize as, contrary to Mrs

Portal's prediction, rain began to drum on the louver window overhead.

'Hundred per cent yes. Friendly, but not too friendly if you know what I mean,' said Dotty. 'And small, but not, you know...' she raised her eyebrows warily, 'diddy.'

Charles nodded and smiled. He had noticed that Dr Ironsize's hair was thinning slightly on top, and the thicker layers to the side were a darker colour. The combination reminded him of a coral reef, viewed from above.

'We are a confident school, though. Wouldn't you say that we are confident, Dotty?' Dr Ironsize appealed to his deputy for support once more.

'We are indeed. And it's a great chance for you to develop as a teacher,' said Dotty. 'Building up your C.P.D.'

'C...?'

'Continuing Professional Development,' she said. 'Using every lesson to grow as a teacher. Even when you're up against...'

There was a slightly uncomfortable pause, during which Dotty and Dr Ironsize seemed to exchange a wary look.

'Are they well-behaved?' asked Charles.

'They're little angels, aren't they, Dr Ironsize?' said Dotty.

'Absolutely,' said the headmaster. 'All except for the ones who aren't.'

'Or the one who isn't,' added Dotty, and showed Charles a very even set of pearly teeth as she smiled.

Charles managed to add what a "privilege" it must be to be entrusted with a child's education, and that he was "passionate" about teaching. He said this because, deep down, he felt it very strongly but also because, just to be on the safe side, he had typed "Top interview tips for teachers" into *Google*, and those were the first two words that had come out. At college, he had tried

7

to avoid using fusty old classical terms. But during the interview for Rydon Hall, they just spilled out. When summarising his decision to become a teacher, he could feel the siren pull of *alea iacta est* and did not resist it. When discussing the changes to the syllabus as a case of *mutatis mutandis*, he had hesitated for a moment about whether to translate it, but Dr Ironsize was already nodding and smiling. He had definitely said "*ipso facto*", and he may well have said "*sui generis*" twice, but did that matter? Latin, he was allowing them to infer, welled up out of him like oil from Kazakh turf. Squeeze him and he bruised in Latin.

'We get so many words from Latin, don't we?' said Dotty. 'But it's all Greek to me! Though I suppose in your case that means you've understood it perfectly.'

They parted with more firm handshakes, which Charles interpreted as sympathetic and regretful. He maintained his composure until the iron gate shut behind him, at which point he sloped off, convinced that he would never see any of them again.

Charles' instincts were usually wrong, and this was no exception. He was back home, trawling through some unappetising website called *Classical Openings* when his phone rang. It was Dr Ironsize, asking if he could start the following Monday. Charles punched the air. Then he wondered how on earth he was going to teach Latin.

CHAPTER 2

As he neared the advanced age of 29, an age at which most professional footballers are beginning to think about managerial posts, Charles Goldforbes had been forced to question whether acting really was the career for him. His joint best friend from university, Milo Lobel, had said as much during the prolonged drinking bout that followed the first night of Charles' "sensitive, well-drilled" success as the second lead in the classic 1954 weepie *Will It Be Long?* at the Catshole Theatre, Pembroke. Without gainsaying the *South Wales Evening Star*, Milo asked Charles to spool forward five years – to what?

A few days later, his other best university friend, Penny Crowthorne, the woman he had almost but never quite dated, used a verbal formula so similar to Milo's that Charles had begun to wonder if they had been discussing the subject behind his back. It occurred to him that their friendship might be developing without him.

After a further week of polite but unpacked audiences, the question implicit in the title of *Will It Be Long?* was answered, negatively, and Charles returned home to find an embarrassed email from Milo and Penny who were indeed entwined and about to go off for a year, travelling around the world.

The shock of losing two friends, and the feeling of stupidity that, beset by his own issues, he had never seen it coming, had made Charles feel isolated, but also determined to do something different. Abandoned by undergraduate friends, it was to his undergraduate course that he turned for support, to transform his undistinguished II.2 into the stuff of teaching – not acting - legend.

Standing outside the door of the Year Eight form room, Charles could hear Madame Allardyce approaching the last moments of her lesson. There seemed to be a background ripple of desk-to-desk chat: Charles knew he must quell this straight off, or the lesson would never belong to him. Engaging with young minds: what could be more inviting?

Madame Allardyce, her arms weighed down with books to mark, pushed past him with a thin smile.

'Latin?' she said.

'Yes, I'm... Charles,' he said.

'Don't take any crap,' she said, under her breath but in an accent that sounded pure Burnley, or Rochdale, or somewhere in between.

Charles had found out more about Year Eight earlier that morning in the staffroom, when he had met Charmian Thirst, the art teacher. Charmian was tall, slender and sensual, with a mass of reddish hair steepled up one side and flecks of green paint down her smock. As she was introduced to Charles, she lifted both hands and, in a soft southern Irish accent, declared, 'Hail Caesar.'

'Hello,' said Charles. 'Hail, I suppose, or *salvē*.'

'Those about to die salute you, or something, is that right?'

'That's it,' said Charles. 'But I'm sure you won't.'

'Salute you? Or die?'

'Well, er, yes, who knows?' said Charles.

Then the door was wrenched open and a small man with knotty veins in his forehead stood on the mat, looking at the door frame as if surprised he hadn't wrenched it off its hinges. He saw Charles and almost stood to attention.

'Bill Drummer,' he said in a softer voice than Charles would have guessed. 'I teach English. And rugby, yeah.'

'I'm the new Latin teacher,' said Charles.

'*I know*,' said Bill. 'I've heard, they told me. News gets around fast in this place, I can tell you. I love Latin.'

'Do you?'

'Don't know a word of it, but... *always* loved it.

10

Wish I'd learnt it at school but, you know, common as muck, me.' Bill stopped again and raised a quivering finger in the air: '"I come to *bury* Caesar, not to praise him." Yeah...' He shook his head and wiped his mouth with the back of his hand. 'Not to *praise* him, you fucking idiot, I've come here to bury him. It doesn't come much better than that. Anyway, know what? We should go for a drink. Do you know the Four Horsemen, round the corner?'

'I didn't,' said Charles. 'Is it the beginning of the end?'

'It's our local,' said Bill. 'We call it the Four Hoarse Men. Four teachers with sore throats, you see? From shouting at the kids. Kind of a joke, yeah.'

'Sounds great,' said Charles.

'Twat - sorry!' Bill flashed a dazzling smile. 'Sorry, a bit Tourette's this morning.' He grabbed a mug that read "Historians Are Good On Dates" and said, 'Teaching can be a lonely profession at times.'

'Everyone seems very friendly,' said Charles.

'Oh, yeah,' said Bill. 'Oh yes!' The second time was much louder, needlessly so in fact. He shook himself and let out an immensely loud belch. Charles nodded and tried not to breathe in. 'But there's one of you, and there's 20 of them. You're outnumbered: totally outnumbered.' Bill suddenly looked ravaged, as if the shock of this imbalance had only just struck him.

'And how were the terrible two?' asked Charmian. Charles looked blank. 'Raymond and Dotty.'

'Oh, fine, fine,' said Charles. 'She was very friendly: we talked about...'

'Sex?'

'I don't think so,' said Charles.

'Really? It won't take her long,' said Bill. He corrected himself over-energetically. 'I mean talking about it! I don't mean doing it.'

'She's never asked you, has she, Bill?' said Charmian.

'No,' said Bill. 'She's tried most of us, not me.

11

Scared of my virility, I expect. My man-wand.'

'That'll be it,' said Charmian.

'My rod of love,' said Bill. He looked back at Charles. 'Sorry, are we going on a bit?'

'Not at all, I just, um...'

'Stop scaring him, Bill,' said Charmian. 'He's only young.'

'Wondered if anyone wanted some tea,' said Charles.

'Good idea,' said Charmian. 'Do you like a drink? I don't mean, like, do you drink too much, do you have a drink problem or anything like that.'

'I'd probably want to keep that sort of thing private, on my first day,' said Charles.

'But if you do, you know you can get help for that.'

'That's very reassuring,' said Charles.

'Your first teaching job,' she said.

'It is? Yes, it is,' said Charles.

'The fuck it is,' said Bill. 'Sorry: sorry! Don't mind me.'

'Don't mind Bill,' said Charmian. 'He's quite friendly really, aren't you, Bill?'

'Course I am,' said Bill, a little more calmly now. He gave Charles another brilliant smile. 'You'll be fine,' he said. 'My office is by the Art block next to the Hall. If you ever want a chat, just come in. Got my own coffee machine!'

'Well done on getting the job,' said Charmian. 'Interview must have gone OK?'

'Any tough questions?' asked Bill.

'I, um, well it was stuff like, "What do you want to get out of teaching?"'

'Oh yeah, me too,' said Charmian.

'Sorry?'

'Get out of teaching. I'll drink to that!'

'Me too!' said Bill. 'Get out and stay out.'

'Retire to a cottage in the country. With a caravan and a lake. Just paint all day. No kids! Just me and a brush, some acrylics, nice book of cartridge paper.'

'Yeah,' said Bill. 'Rent a cottage by the road, and just play with my knob all day. Just, you know, get up, crack one out straight after breakfast. Back to bed, watch TV, drink all day, wank all night.'

'I don't think I'm quite ready to think about retirement yet,' said Charles.

'Wait until you've had your first lesson with Year Eight,' said Bill. 'Bunch of, yeah...'

'Wait until you've met Florian Bavington,' said Charmian. 'You'll be quite ready for retirement then.'

'You can't put me off that easily!' said Charles, trying to sound breezy.

The others had gone out and Charles had picked up a mug. He was staring at the inscription, "When I Come Back, I Want To Be An R.S. Teacher", when the door opened again and a woman with crisp, almost pink blancmange, hair walked towards him, holding out a hand. She must have been in her mid-50s. Tall, very well-preserved, she could have been umpiring an early round on one of Wimbledon's outer courts.

Charles stretched out a hand to greet her. 'Hello, I'm...'

'You're the new Latin teacher,' she said, with what was left of an Edinburgh accent. 'You look a lot younger than Geoff, but I don't suppose Latin grammar changes much.'

'That's right. And you are...'

'Joy Hughes-Howard. I teach Maths,' she said. The smile she gave him was slightly jaundiced, as if that were her best defence against an otherwise suffocating disappointment.

'Maths?' said Charles, unable to think of any other question. 'That's...'

'Mostly just numbers,' she said, as if the concept needed no further unpacking. 'Although I should probably teach Music, with a name like Joy.'

'Oh, what...'

'What with Beethoven writing an ode to me. I

expect you'll get that, being a Classicist.'

'Oh yes, that was nice of, of Ludwig,' said Charles, trying to join in the slightly forced tone of levity.

'All set?'

'Well I thought I'd start off with...'

'So long as you're not introducing them to fifth declension verbs!' She rocked back on sturdy, uncomplaining heels.

'Ah, well, you see the conjugations are for the verbs, and the declensions are...'

'Did I get it wrong?' she said, folding her arms. 'Just as well I'm not taking the exam! Well, best of luck. They're not bad boys, most of them...'

'Are there any I should...'

'Look out for?' He was wondering if teachers built solidarity by finishing each other's sentences, but the door opened and a man with crisply spiked hair came in.

'Come and meet Charles, the new Latin teacher,' she said. 'Charles, this is Colin *Woo*.'

'Ah,' said the man. He was slightly podgy, with a pair of wafer-thin rectangular glasses. 'The name's spelt N-G-O, pronounced Woo. I teach I.T.'

'That's computers and the internet,' added Joy, helpfully.

'Yes,' said Colin. 'I like to think I put the S.H. into I.T.'

Charles wondered how hard it must be to teach teenagers to play on a computer, but he resisted the thought: it was only his first day, after all.

'Obviously they hate being forced to spend any time on a computer,' said Mrs Hughes-Howard, her voice undulating with mild sarcasm. 'Which is one reason why Dr Ngo is the most popular teacher in the school.'

'Perhaps they could do extra Latin in the I.T. Room,' said Charles.

'Now there's a thought that would have had Geoff reaching for the bottle,' said Joy. 'Colin, Charles just asked if there are any boys he should look out for.'

'Well...' Dr Ngo's eye-brows rippled, as if totting up whether to hold onto privileged information.

'Colin's also the Year Eight form teacher so he knows them pretty well,' said Mrs Hughes-Howard.

'Most of them are just tiresome,' said Dr Ngo. 'Apart from...'

'Oh, don't,' Joy groaned. 'Not on his first day. He's got his whole life ahead of him.'

'You might as well tell me,' said Charles. 'I've got to meet them some time.'

'Well, the main offender, really the only genuine culprit... is called Florian Bavington,' said Colin. 'He has his cronies, but he's the one to watch.'

'Florian...?' Charles thought this was the name he'd already heard from Charmian.

'You'll find out soon enough,' said Mrs Hughes-Howard. 'He's fairly unmistakable. Face like an angel: heart like a mini-Satan.'

'Just go in hard,' said Dr Ngo, 'and don't let them get away with anything.'

'Right,' said Charles.

'Show them who's boss,' said Joy. 'And don't take any...' she trailed off.

'Any shit,' said Colin.

Charles could feel the mood becoming more confrontational, as if they were all steeling themselves for an onslaught.

'It's like riding a horse. If they feel you're not in charge, they'll take off. So you've got to impose that straight away.' Colin thwacked his mug down so hard on the table that the sound was still rattling in Charles' ears as he looked out across the desks of his new students, an hour or so later. 'And if you don't get it right first time, you'll never get it back.'

Charles rested his hand on the door and prepared to push it open for his first lesson at Rydon Hall. He had read, or tried to read, several handbooks about teaching in preparation, but he suddenly felt alone, exposed – as if Bill Drummer's words about one teacher confronting 20 pupils had seeped into him.

He let the door close after Madame Allardyce. Then, grasping his copy of the school textbook *Now That's What I Call Latin!*, together with an elderly Loeb Latin-English edition of Caesar's *Gallic Wars*, to be read from in English when all else failed, he flung it open and – perhaps a little too shrilly – shouted '*Salvete, pueri!*'

'Good-morning-Mr-Goldforbes,' they chanted slowly. He was surprised that his surname had been trotted out as monotonously as if it were just any home-grown species. He couldn't hear it spoken without recalling his immigrant grandparents' optimistic but flawed attempt to anglicise Goldfarb, which still left him feeling like an outsider, two generations later. People sometimes commented with surprise that he was the first Goldforbes they had ever met. He knew why.

'And I am your new Latin teacher!' said Charles, surprising himself at the relish with which he had invested this subject. This must be why he was a natural teacher. He strode to the board, vaguely conscious that several pairs of eyes were glancing up at him from beneath an array of hairstyles that, ten years from now, they would surely look back on with unconcealed embarrassment. Aged 12 or 13, Year Eight were the senior year in the school. After this, they graduated to secondary school, taking with them – Charles had been assured in the staffroom – agreeably vague memories of prep school, most of which would fade to nothing within the first term.

'So, Year Eight, who knows about Latin adjectives?' (Perhaps too open-ended a question: his first mistake.)

'I do,' said a boy in the front, without putting up a hand.

'Good,' said Charles, without cautioning him first: his second mistake.

'Mr Norringham said no one ever got adjectives right,' said another voice from the back.

'Oh really?' asked Charles, joining in too readily with playground gossip. 'Now...' He paused in front of an empty desk. 'Is somebody missing?'

'Rohan Shapcott's in Dubai, sir,' said a boy in the front row, indicating an empty desk. 'He's in a skiing competition but he'll be back on Monday.'

'Thank you for telling me that, but you did not put up your hand, did you...'

'Excuse me, sir, that's Arthur,' said the voice from the back. 'He's the head boy. And may I say that I hope you'll be very happy in our school.'

'Thank you,' said Charles. 'And your name is..?'

The boy stood up, holding out his hand. 'Yes sir, I'm so excited that you're our new Latin teacher...'

'Good, well...'

'Because I really love Latin, sir.'

'Thank you.'

'*Amo... amas... amat.* See, I'm good at it too. I love it.'

The class was beginning to stir.

'You'd better tell me your name.'

'I loooooove La-tinnn.'

'Your name?' said Charles, though he had a feeling he didn't need to ask.

'Florian,' said the boy, holding out his hand. 'And I know some people think Latin is for weirdos but I don't.'

The two boys either side of him - one with a fringe as low as a visor, the other with an army crew-cut - nodded gravely and repeated the words quietly, to muttered giggles from around the room.

Florian's desk was in the back row. He had sandy-brown curly hair, a dusting of freckles on his nose and cheeks, a slightly chipped front tooth and preternaturally blue eyes. His expression, though, was entirely unsubmissive. In fact it seemed to be spoiling for a fight.

'OK,' said Charles. 'Now listen. Some of you may have felt that you could get away with having a laugh with my predecessor...'

'I liked Mr Norringham,' said Florian, with a sweet smile. 'I didn't think he was a loser...'

For a moment, Charles just stared at Florian. He had never anticipated this level of insolence, even when speed-reading those pages which the author of *What A Way to Behave?!* had assured him were all he needed to guarantee classroom discipline. Some sat neatly behind their desks, waiting for education to descend as if queuing for a car wash. Others were still wedded to infant school throwbacks, from blu-tac sculpture to plastic-ruler origami. Two, on either side of the room, might as well have been twins, since Charles looked in vain for signs of physical variation. He had been given a list of names, and his eyes had swept down a list of Hamishes, Tristans, Maxes, Duncans and Joshes. There was even a boy called Archie whose only distinguishing feature – apart, he had been told, from a weakness for unsuitable piano pieces played badly – was the unfortunate surname of Neeples. And there was a strong smell of fish-oil in the room, which Charles eventually tracked down to a boy with a skull as tapered as a Ku Klux Klan hat, dead fish eyes and yellowing Halloween teeth. When the boy put up a hand, it was with a sense of urgency.

'Sir, I have to go to the toilet,' he said.

Here, thought Charles, was an example of rudeness on which he could take a stand. '

Oh, you *have* to, do you?' said Charles. 'Now, that's exactly the sort of...'

'Sir, he has to go,' said another voice.

'Please can I go, sir? I'm really desperate.'

'Sir, he's called Adrian Purvis and he's got irritating bowels,' the voice said. It was Florian again. 'If you don't let him go he'll piss in his pants.'

'Shut up, Florian!' the boy shouted. It was the only opposition to Florian that Charles had noted.

'He probably has already,' said Florian. 'I swear he's a total weenie.'

'Florian...'

'He'll want to be your friend, though,' said Florian. 'Cos he doesn't really have any friends, do you, Adrian?'

'Florian!' Charles could think of no way of silencing someone who refused to endorse the silencing process. The boy called Adrian turned, glared ineffectually at his abuser and ran from the room before his teacher could say anything.

A boy had his hand up.

'Sir? Why do people still learn Latin?'

'An interesting question,' said Charles. 'Hello? I am waiting for silence!' He raised a fist into the air and extended his fingers, counting down loudly, a trick he had read about in the first chapter – which was as far as he had got - of a book called *Teaching With The Body*. There was still a buzz of chatter when he reached zero but he decided to press on. 'And you must be... Duncan?'

'I'm Josh,' said the boy.

'And I'm Duncan,' said a voice on the other side of the room.

Charles looked at them both in turn, convinced that they must spend half the week being dropped at each other's houses after school.

'Sir, I don't know if you know this...' Florian said, lowering his voice as if imparting a secret, 'but I actually do have an offer from Thickett Lodge. So I don't really need Latin, to be honest. But the way you describe it makes it sound so interesting...' He bounced back in his chair, as if he could only keep this level of sarcasm up for so long.

'So why do people learn Latin? That sounds like a Classical Civilisation question,' said Charles, speaking louder. 'But we're not here to learn Classical Civilisation: that's for people who aren't learning Latin. In fact, Class Civ is for dummies. It's for people who

19

can't read this...' He waved his Caesar's *Gallic Wars* in the air – 'in the original. But we are here to learn... Latin!' For a moment he could imagine that he had the attention of every member of the class.

'Have you met Dylan?' Florian broke in. The boy to his left stood up. 'This is Dylan,' said Florian. 'He is my really best friend.'

Charles decided that this attempt to start a discussion – a ruse inspired by the Acknowledgements page (he hadn't managed to read any further) of a book with the truly lack-lustre title of *Planning Memorable Lessons* – had failed.

Then Dylan, his eyes barely visible through his overhanging fringe, lifted one finger into the air. 'And this is Yedverd.'

The boy on the other side of Florian stood and held out his hand. 'Pliss to meet you,' he said in what must have been a Polish accent. He had a badly mangled shirt collar, perhaps due to the circumference of his neck, which appeared to be twice the size of any of the other boys'.

'My name, Yedverd Zygnwycyz. This my third year Latin and still I can not translate basic Latin sentence.'

'Dear me,' said Charles. 'Well, I'm sure we'll get beyond that very soon.'

'I doubt it,' said Dylan. 'Mr Norringham said Ed was so bad at Latin it made him want to yak.'

Charles knew that Florian and his pals were staging a hold-up, but what tools did he have to fight back? He recalled a chapter called "Anti-Distraction Distractions" in a needlessly jaunty volume called *Please May I Be Excused?* but he couldn't remember the contents.

'Sir, irritable bowels is really terrible isn't it?' asked Dylan.

'Shut *up,* Dylan!' said Florian with a grin. 'Can't you see Mr Goldforbes is trying to get on with the lesson!'

The two boys grinned at each other, delighted at their ability to achieve the opposite.

'Purvis is a weenie,' said Florian, suddenly looking almost chastened at the admission.

'You must not call someone by that word,' said Charles, trying to appeal to the boy's nascent adult sensibilities.

'It's a song by Eminem, do you know it?' Florian tried. 'I'll sing it for you.' He began to tap out a rap beat of mouth, cheeks and fingers.

'NO!' Charles shouted, ignoring the friendly advice proffered in *Teaching Without Losing Your Voice!*

Trying to find a calmer tone, he declared, 'I will not tolerate this sort of behaviour,' but he may as well have been miming. Little skirmishes were breaking out and scores were being settled across the classroom: chair tussles, ruler rivalries, desk-lid vendettas, anything but the lesson plan. Charles' presence was mere wallpaper. What had become of his passion for teaching?

'Right,' said Charles, in a loud, stern voice. 'Florian Bavington, I am going to write your name on the board.'

'Oh no sir, please don't *write my name on the board*,' Florian said, with mocking emphasis.

'Well, I am going to, and then you will...'

'I think that's really cruel. No one likes to see *their name* written *on the board*.'

'If his mum finds out...' said Dylan.

'Yeah, cos my parents are divorced? But if my mum finds out I'll be in serious trouble?' said Florian, looking suspiciously close to tears.

'I am not going to discuss this any further.'

'But you might need this.' Florian had come to the front and was waving something at Charles.

'What is that?'

'It's a pen, sir. I'm trying to help you?' The boy smiled.

Charles checked his pockets, then the desktop. He had forgotten to bring a pen, and there were no others. Charles felt it odd that the boy was conniving in his

21

own exposure, but he took the pen and started to write. As he did so, the room became even noisier, but he was so incensed that it was not until he had written the letters "F-L-O" on the board that he realised they were telling him he should not be writing on an interactive board with a normal board marker. He tried to rub the letters off with his finger but could not. The ink gripped the surface like Araldite, standing out from the surface like a shard of newly excavated Thessalonian pottery.

'Oh no, sir,' said Florian, who, Charles now saw, obviously didn't mean a word he said. 'I was trying so hard to help you, I gave you the wrong pen. That ink will never come off and Dr Ngo will be so cross. Oh sir, I'm gutted for you.'

Then Adrian Purvis walked back in and Yedverd tripped him with his foot. Dylan and Florian joined them on the floor, on the truly specious grounds that Adrian had tried to trip them. While the boys tussled, Charles turned away and looked out through the window, across the back gardens of Lower Churley, most of them chequered with industrial-sized, safety-netted trampolines. It was his first day, his first lesson, and it had been a disaster.

'Oh... shit,' he said.

'Sorry, sir?' said Florian.

'I said... shit!' Charles paused. The room was nearly silent now. Had it been his first successful attempt at stamping his mark on the class? Then he turned around and saw Dr Ironsize standing at the back of the room. Charles recalled scanning a page at random from a teacher-training book called *Look Who's Talking!* about classroom-inappropriate language. The only sound in the room came from Adrian Purvis, wheezing noisily on the coarse grey carpet.

'Florian, are you at the bottom of this?' asked Dr Ironsize quietly.

'Well, sir, strictly speaking it's Adrian Purvis who's at the bottom of it...' the boy began as he stood up.

'Be silent,' said Dr Ironsize. He was speaking, Charles noticed, in just the sort of hiss which the author of *Look Who's Talking* must have had in mind, and it appeared to be working. 'Year Eight, this is completely unacceptable. Sort this mess out. Mr Goldforbes, would you come and see me at break-time?'

'Of course,' said Charles, but Dr Ironsize had already left.

He took a deep breath. 'The next lesson will not be like this. We will revise some first and second declension adjectives and...' Charles began, but the bell had gone and, within seconds, all the boys had rushed for the door.

Charles sat down heavily on a chair. There was a tap on the door and Dr Ngo walked in, smiling. 'How did it go?' he said.

'Not bad,' said Charles. 'Some of the class were a bit jumpy.'

'Hmm,' said Dr Ngo. He ran a hand through his spiky hair.

'Actually, it was a complete disaster, and I said "shit" in front of Dr Ironsize.'

Dr Ngo snorted, but it felt an oddly supportive gesture. 'Well, don't beat yourself up about it,' he said. 'Just blame Bavington: that's what everyone else does.'

Charles stood up. Then he remembered a statistic from the dust jacket of a book which he hadn't managed to open, called *Teaching Magic*. 'Is it true that children's attention spans last one minute longer than how old they are?'

Dr Ngo blinked. 'I must admit I'd forgotten that one.'

'Read it somewhere at the weekend,' said Charles. 'But I can't remember where.'

Dr Ngo pointed at the shaky whiteboard letters. 'Did you write on the board?' he said with a half-grin.

'Er...'

'With that pen?'

'Well…'

'We'll get the cleaners onto it,' said Dr Ngo. 'You learn from your mistakes.'

'Well I must have learnt a shit-load that time,' said Charles.

'Language,' said Dr Ngo.

'Sorry. It's only my first day. I wish I felt a bit more cheerful.'

'Did you spot Archie Neeples?'

'I don't think so. Why?'

'No reason. He's completely forgettable, but when I'm a bit down, I just say Archie Neeples to myself. Usually gets a laugh.'

Charles tried it, without great success. 'Oh well: up before the Beak, I suppose.'

Dr Ngo pointed to Charles' unopened copy of *Now That's What I Call Latin!* 'Why not slip one of those down your trousers?' he said.

'Good idea,' said Charles.

CHAPTER 3

'No need to ask who was behind this disturbance, I suppose?' said Dr Ironsize. Charles shifted uncomfortably in his seat. The headmaster's office had been built out of a bathroom and it still had something of the air of the urinal: most male teachers, he learned later, preferred to stand.

'Well,' Charles said, after a pause, 'is it really necessary to name names?'

'Not if you are teaching Year Eight,' said Dr Ironsize. 'Unless Florian Bavington happens to be away that day, which of course he isn't.'

Charles shrugged. 'It wasn't just him,' he said. 'Dylan, and Yedverd… they were at it too.'

'Of course they were,' replied the headmaster. 'He always does that. He lures the feeble-minded and they fall for it every time. Actually I feel that Dylan is quite a bright cookie, even likable in some ways. But Yedverd is just a thug: like his father I suppose.'

'What does Yedverd's father do?'

The headmaster looked away. 'I try not to ask in too much detail, but put it this way: I'd rather he owed us money than we owed him.'

'And what's Florian like, outside the classroom?'

'Oh,' said Dr Ironsize, gripping the bridge of his nose. 'Perfectly charming. Just like, um, his mother. But I shall let your other colleagues enlighten you about the Bavington family. My job is merely to remind you that we must be very firm about language. They look to you, you see.'

'Really?' said Charles. 'On the basis of this morning's lesson I find that hard to believe.'

'I mean,' said Dr Ironsize, 'that if they hear you say words like "shit", they'll end up saying words like "shit" too.'

'I see what you mean,' said Charles.

'You might go and see Dotty. I think she's out this

afternoon, at a seminar on, uh, web resources for R.S. teachers.'

'That should be useful,' said Charles.

'It'll be a miracle if she gets anything from it,' said Dr Ironsize. 'Ha ha! Rather good. But do try and catch her. She's a mine of information on the subject.'

Charles nodded again. He heard the bell go for mid-morning break, followed by the clatter of feet as if a class were trying to kick their way through the ceiling above.

Dr Ironsize swallowed another mouthful of tea. 'Other than that, Charles, we do hope you are settling in well.' He appeared to look to the side, as if missing Dotty's reassuring presence. 'I hope you are. Are you?'

'I… Well, it's early days,' said Charles.

'Of course,' said Dr Ironsize. 'But there are many opportunities to make yourself part of the fabric of life at Rydon Hall. Have you been told which house you are in?'

'Er, no I don't think so.'

Dr Ironsize explained the system. Central to the philosophy of the school was that being 'first' or 'best' or 'number one' was not the sole aim in life. This was a school that had chosen for itself the motto "*Vincere Non Superando*" - "Winning Isn't About Beating". And so, the houses were named after four British Olympic athletes from the early 20th century who had all done their best, tried their hardest – and ended up with a silver medal.

'No bronze?' said Charles.

'Well, no,' said Dr Ironsize. 'We don't want to back a bunch of losers, after all.'

They both laughed. Charles was told that he would be in Halswelle (1900, 400 metres) while his colleagues were in Rangeley (1928, 100 metres), Ferris (the 1932 Marathon) or Webb (various long distance walks between 1908 and 1912 in which the Gold had constantly eluded him).

'You may also like to take up the reins of one of

our many lunchtime activities.'

'Oh, yes, of course,' said Charles, with forced conviction.

'Do you sing?'

'Not much.'

'Play chess?'

'I've never really learnt.'

'Drama?'

'I don't go to many plays,' said Charles, wincing as he thought back to the final, lifeless curtain call for *Will It Be Long?*

'All teachers are actors at heart, Charles. Or maybe you would enjoy something practical, like clay modelling...'

'A bit arty for me...'

'Bill Drummer could always do with a hand with his swimming club.'

'I've never really seen myself as a sports coach.'

'Oh...' Dr Ironsize puffed his cheeks out in consternation. 'How about debating?'

'Debating?'

'Yes. The school...' Dr Ironsize scratched his cheek with one ringed finger. 'The school used to have a very proud tradition of debating. Weren't the Romans big on debating? Socrates and all that sort of thing.'

'Greeks,' said Charles.

'Exactly,' said Dr Ironsize. 'At some point you just have to dive in. Or...' Dr Ironsize paused. (As he did, those spinning the strands of Charles' fate must have grabbed an extra ball of wool.) 'Or travel. Now here's a thought. How about joining one of our school trips?'

'I don't ski much, if it's...'

'Wouldn't have to be skiing,' said Dr Ironsize. 'Best thing to do is have a chat with Dotty. Chance for you to spread your wings. It really helps with your C.P.D.'

'C.P.D., that's...'

'Continuing Professional Development.'

'Of course. Will Florian be going on one of these trips?'

'He'll be on the Year Eight trip to Egypt, straight after the January Mocks,' said Dr Ironsize. 'I must admit: we've had some tough kids over the years but he really is in a class of his own.'

'Is he?'

'Yes. Or he should be. Preferably without windows. Or doors.'

It took Charles about a week to tire of the gamey pasta, fishy shepherd's pie and sugar-free fruit crumbles that Rydon Hall's chef, Dorotea, served up at lunchtime in the school hall. Within the same period of time, and even having failed to turn up for one lesson, Florian Bavington had received three minus house-points and two lunchtime detentions for humming in class, losing his books, fusing the projector by repeatedly switching it on and off, squirting glue into the wall-heater and inscribing the words "Purvis est gayus" on the cover of Adrian Purvis' Latin book. But at least, unlike the teachers, Florian couldn't leave school during the daytime, which explained why, one lunchtime and a mere week after he started, Charles Goldforbes could be seen walking out, down leaf-strewn Windrush Avenue towards Lower Churley.

There was a gentle eccentricity to the area's front gardens that had quickly won him over. (His favourite housed a swarm of wire-sculpted aphids.) As he walked, he wondered about his status within the school. If some of these boys knew him as the fun-filled Lunchtime Debating Club Chairman, or that adventurous teacher from the school trip, would they respond more readily to his attempts to make Latin come alive?

He was still wondering how to make more of an impact upon the school as he reached the high street. Here, any self-respecting Classicist (or pedant) had to tread warily. There was a hairdresser called - or rather spelt – *Mark & Anthony*, which may have been true for the proprietors but was a slur on Roman history, and, in the newsagent window, a notice for a Bible group called *Creedo*: he wondered if the faithful realised that they had grafted an 'e' onto an unsuspecting verb. Worst by far, though, was the brass sign to the first-floor office of some sort of management consultancy called – with a brazen disregard for the genitive third declension ending – *Omnius Business Solutions*.

Charles tried to register these little snubs to his classical heritage without displaying too much emotion, but they hurt nonetheless. Halfway along he came to the Fire Station, the words chiselled into its solid, Victorian fascia. He had studied it before but never gone in. It was now a café but every few seconds a coffee barista slid down the fireman's pole, armed with a mug, plate or tray. As he walked past, he heard nannies and au pairs exchanging Slavic syllables, and very few recognisable vowels. He hovered near an empty table, and wondered whether to claim it with his pile of books for marking.

'Are you the new Latin teacher?' said a woman's voice. He turned. A hand darted out, fingers waving animatedly. The eyes were hidden by a pair of monstrous black sunglasses. 'At Rydon Hall?'

'I, er, yes,' he said. At first, all he could see was a tangle of blonde-streaked hair, tied up with a pale blue scarf. A yellow pullover, possibly cashmere, was slipping off one of her shoulders, revealing a swirl of tiny freckles against tanned skin.

'Yes,' said Charles. 'And you are...?'

'Natasha Bavington,' she said.

CHAPTER 4

Charles took one look at Natasha Bavington and knew straight away that this was a woman for whom he was unlikely to fall, even though she must once have been rather beautiful. He couldn't tell what her natural hair colour was. Her arms were bony, almost scrawny – perhaps from eating less heartily than she should. She sat on her own, her BlackBerry lying on the table beside a tall glass of milky coffee. She had smile lines curving round the corners of her lips, which he never normally found attractive. Her forehead had a stave of tiny wrinkles creasing it and yet she looked as if she knew that someone, somewhere, was looking at her, which Charles found laughable until he realised that, in fact, *he* was looking at her. Or rather, at those freckles on her shoulder, like a dusting of fine dew on a meadow. It wasn't that he found them sexually attractive, but they was interesting to note.

'Are you... Florian's mother?' he said, smiling.

'So you've met Florian,' she said. Her voice had a floating quality. Charles began to think that ten years earlier she would have been quite a catch.

'I've only had a few lessons with him,' he said. 'I'm not sure that we've quite hit it off.'

'Oh dear, is he being a monster?' Natasha motioned to Charles to sit down.

He perched on a chair carved from a lacquered coil of fire-fighter's hose and wondered how to phrase his answer. 'He's certainly very lively,' he began.

'He was such a beast to Mr Norringham. No wonder the poor man shot off to the Gulf.' She had a rather conspiratorial giggle.

'Well, he has a very strong, um, personality, doesn't he?' said Charles. As Mrs Bavington removed her Ray-Bans, Catullus' phrase about honeyed eyes – *mellitos oculos* – came to mind.

'He probably needs extra lessons,' she said. 'Geoff

30

Norringham gave him a few after school but it didn't really work. It's his father's fault really.'

'His father... Not your...'

'Not my husband, Mr Goldforbes. Long story: I shan't bore you with it now.'

'Maybe another time.'

'Or maybe I should be the one having lessons. Do you teach adults? Would it be rude to offer cash?'

'No, I'm... You'll have to try harder than that to offend me, Mrs Bavington,' said Charles. 'Which days are good for you?'

'Most of my afternoons are busy, Mr Goldforbes; I lead the life of a busy Churley mother. Tennis, pottery, Pilates, yoga...'

'You must be rushed off your feet.'

'It's never-ending.' She took a sip of latte. 'Still, I'm sure you have better things to do than sit around chatting to a sad old housewife.'

'I'm, no, er... Is this your local?' he tried.

The question seemed to amuse her. 'Yes, I'm the sad loser in the corner they can't get rid of. They tip coffee down me all morning until I go away. Actually I love it here. I'm a great people-watcher, Mr Goldforbes. I like to study faces.' At which point she put her sunglasses back on and flicked her newspaper as if the interview were over.

As he rose from his chair of coiled fire-hose, Charles wondered if she liked to study backsides too. He tried to make his movements as lithe and sexually charged as a leopard. In truth, he had never been described as that before. Pigeon-toed and bandy-legged, if anything. He walked back to school, and wondered, since it obviously wasn't going to come from Mrs Bavington, where his next love affair might arise. He longed to feel inflamed and regretful, and to sense once again the heroic urgency and desperate sadness of infatuation.

'Wanker. Tosser. Prick. Dickhead. The c-word. Arsehole, bastard, fuckhead, shithead, dickhead. Knobhead. And twat, obviously.' Ms de Souza the deputy head counted the words off her fingertips as she spoke. 'We use them all in everyday conversation, don't we, but you can't use them in school. Whereas "Dipstick"...' Dotty curled her face into a mass of scowling wrinkles. '"Harry, don't be a *dipstick.*" See?' Her features relaxed into a warm smile. 'See what I did to that word? I invested it with all the loathing and resentment that I normally use when I'm talking to my boyfriend.'

'Oh... I suppose, I mean...'

'Well, that was when I had a boyfriend. But...' she smiled brightly. 'Doesn't mean I can't try out a few candidates!'

Charles smiled. 'I hope you don't get too many dipsticks.'

'You're going to be really good, Charles: hundred per cent sure of that. You just need to learn a few tricks. Fancy a cup of tea?'

'Good idea,' said Charles. 'If you know how to make Florian Bavington sit down for longer than about 30 seconds...'

'He is a bit unusual,' said Dotty.

'Shouldn't he be in a... you know, a specialist school?'

'Possibly,' said Dotty, as they arrived at the staff room. 'Have you seen the I.C.T. Suite yet, by the way?'

'The what...?'

Dotty flicked the kettle and, while teachers drifted in and out, started to tell the story of Natasha and Hugh Bavington, once one of Churley's most glamorous couples. When Florian was born, Hugh was still making a huge profit from trading Third World debt, but it was only after his employers decided to downsize that Hugh went solo and found his métier: selling huge American cars to rich Britons. As his business expanded exponentially, so did his appetite for sexual conquests far beyond Natasha. By the time

Florian had started at Chumblebumbles, the most expensive nursery in the area, Hugh and Natasha were in the middle of divorce proceedings.

Hugh left Natasha and the Jacobean elegance of Churley House, and moved to Monaco, to a house you could land a helicopter on, as he proceeded to do, several times a week. Hugh was said to have a monstrous temper which, even though it was often directed at Florian, did little to staunch his son's longing to spend more holiday time with his father. Florian – the name was his mother's idea, and one of the few battles which Hugh had not won – was a horribly spoilt only child, and he was every teacher's nightmare. Worse still, other adults adored him because he looked angelic, and the children worshipped him because he was so unruly.

'I suppose,' said Dr Ngo, flicking through a copy of the *Times Educational Supplement*, 'that if your parents were tearing lumps out of each other, it would tend to make you a bit self-centred. But Florian gives the very strong impression that he just doesn't give a toss about school. And that, of course, is deeply threatening.'

Charles nodded. 'But is he clever?'

'Yes, in an unconventional way,' said Ms de Souza. 'Or, to put it in less academically cautious language, no.'

'But, deep down,' said Charles. 'Underneath all that attitude?'

'I beg to differ,' said Dr Ngo, raising a bony hand. 'Best, most left-field I.T. student I've ever had. Apart from exams, which he invariably contrives to cock up, being dyslexic or whatever he is.'

'You see what we mean,' said Mrs Hughes-Howard. 'Total wash-out at everything except one subject - if you can call I.T. a *proper subject!* She waved a hand at Dr Ngo. 'Oh look, he's going to kill me now: sorry, Colin!'

Dr Ngo brushed the apology aside. 'And brilliant on

the sports field, of course. We'd lose every match without him. But effing naughty, and effingly badly behaved.'

'Why did the school take him?' said Charles.

'Good question,' said Dotty.

The explanation was simple. Even aged six, Florian's hostility to authority was plain. In what should have been a fairly routine interview, the boy refused to read out of a book, answer any questions, look up, or speak to (or even acknowledge) Dr Ironsize. But when, later, the headmaster told Mr and Mrs Bavington – separated from each other by two empty chairs – that this might not be the best school for their son, Hugh interrupted to say that he saw things rather differently. The meeting was said to have ended with smiles and handshakes all round.

That September, on the first day of the following autumn term, Florian turned up, in his topaz and magenta blazer and cap, for his first day in Year Two. By a neat coincidence, the builders had, just the day before, finished working round the clock to complete the Henry Bavington I.C.T. Suite, named after Hugh's late father and rippling with 25 computers, all equipped with the latest version of Microsoft Vista.

'So you see,' concluded Mrs Hughes-Howard, massaging the tannin-stained insides of a mug with a square of J-Cloth. 'It's no wonder he feels like he owns the place.'

'That's what we're up against, Charles,' said Dotty de Souza.

'But don't worry,' said Dr Ngo. 'We're all in this together.'

'Oh did I tell you?' said Charles, trying to appear casual. 'Mrs Bavington asked me to give her some private lessons.'

This produced a throaty braying from Bill Drummer, who had just walked in, and expressions of regret at the absence of a Latin oral.

'She should invite you over,' said Charmian.

'Churley House is the nicest house in Churley. If I lived there, I'd never leave it. I'd just stay indoors all day. So pretty...'

'She should definitely have you over there,' said Bill, nodding vigorously. 'And you should have her! Sorry – wanker! Sorry, not really. But obviously you're not going to...'

'Well he's not going to shag her, is he, Bill so it's not a problem,' said Dotty sharply.

'No,' said Bill. 'Well, you can't, can you? Sackable offence and all that.'

'It's her mind I'm interested in,' said Charles. 'I'm just there to give her Latin lessons.'

'Well, give her one for me,' said Bill. 'And while you're at it, give her a lesson too. Only joking: wanker! Sorry.'

A micro-rump of top students – Rohan Shapcott, Roley Yousuf, Cato Wang and Des Muireadhaigh (pronounced Murray) – had scored well in the autumn Mocks paper, but most of Year Eight had barely grazed the 50 per cent barrier. Florian Bavington's score was not the lowest: that distinction was shared between Josh (or was it Duncan?) and the unfortunately-named Archie Neeples, but Florian had probably brought about their demise, as he was said to have wasted a lot of time asking if Adrian Purvis could be moved, and at one point his phone had gone off, to the tune of Eminem's *Big Weenie.* The colossal degradation in concentration spans caused by these actions was such that no single punishment could serve as a corrective. Various teachers made comments about bringing back the birch, or the stocks, or forcing him to undergo a week in solitary confinement, but in the end, he got away with a stern letter to his mother, after which he returned to persecuting Adrian Purvis, which seemed to be the only classroom activity at which he really excelled.

Charles decided to seek Natasha out. He increased

his casual strolls down to Churley High Street, and within a few days he was again waved over to a chair, this time made from several up-ended fire buckets.

'You see,' she told him, 'Florian needs Latin so that he can get into whichever school his father is paying for him to attend next – otherwise I'd have probably hoiked him out years ago, stuck him in front of a computer, and given the others more of a chance.'

'Oh but I'd hate to lose him,' said Charles.

'Really?' she said, re-knotting her blue *Hermès* scarf. Charles was beginning to enjoy looking at her greeny-blue eyes. He assumed she was in her early 40s, but in pretty good shape.

'He could always benefit from some help at home,' he said. 'You see, I was thinking...'

She suddenly sat back. 'So go on then,' she said, arching her shoulders. 'Teach me Latin.'

It was one of the most sensual things he had ever heard.

Fortunately for Charles, he had a triple free period every Wednesday morning which he now dedicated to a grammatical analysis of Natasha Bavington's face, via the filter of *Now That's What I Call Latin!* Halfway through their first lesson she tapped the cover of the book.

'Beautiful woman, isn't she?' she said, pointing to the photograph of a statue of Diana. 'Amazing how vivid that expression is.'

Charles nodded. 'I was thinking the same thing.'

'Fabulous boobs, too,' Natasha added. 'Wish mine were still like that.'

Charles nodded again. 'I'm sure they were – I mean, the woman's...'

'Grapey,' she said.

'Did you say grapey?' said Charles.

'Her boobs,' she said. 'Firm. Bouncy. Probably not the sort of thing you discuss in your lessons, though, eh, Mr Goldforbes?'

'Not for Common Entrance,' said Charles, unable or unwilling to prevent a genital stirring. He began to look forward to being surprised by her again.

Charles did his best with the interactive whiteboard, but the educational resources he felt most comfortable with harked back to an earlier era, of lollipop sticks (useful for verb and noun stems), Post-it notes and tracing paper. In a bid to enliven his lessons he had once walked into a Year Five lesson wearing a Roman toga, but two boys had burst into tears, which he took as an indictment of Classical Civilisation more eloquent than any he could have composed himself. He knew that he was irretrievably old school but his energies were being pulled apart by two members of the same family: Natasha and her son.

In class, Florian's demeanour was so etched with sarcasm that his every comment had to be read in reverse. Whenever Charles walked in, it was to the words, "Oh good, now we've got Latin with Mr Goldforbes." Every word of that exclamation was insincere, but it set the scene for every lesson. "I've done my homework" was untrue. "I understand" was a lie. "I've got the book open right here" was a brazen distortion of the facts, yet this was how Florian operated. His inability to understand Latin was staggering. He liked to declaim "*amo, amas, amat*" as if, simply by pronouncing those 11 letters, he had done enough to take his place alongside the giants of classical scholarship. He would say, 'I hope we're having a vocab test today,' when he knew there wasn't one, and would get almost none right when there was.

'There's basically a giant NO over everything he says,' said Madame Allardyce one day. 'If he says "Oh this is fun", it isn't, and if he says "I get it", he doesn't.'

'And if I said I like him,' said Charles, 'I don't, because he's an annoying little prick.'

'Ooh I don't know if I'd go that far,' she said.

'Oh come on,' said Charles. 'Live a little.'

By contrast, Charles looked forward to his weekly Latin coaching sessions – "Latin fire-fighting", as Natasha teasingly called it – more and more. Her one-shoulder-exposed look was making him wonder if he might one day discover the real reasons for her separation from Mr Bavington. Was it, perhaps, that they were not sexually compatible? Had the vigour, the audacity, the sheer inventiveness of her demands drained the somewhat older Mr Bavington? If so, perhaps what she needed was a younger man. Charles cast around for someone to take on this role and began to wonder, almost wistfully, if that candidate might be himself.

The few times he went for a drink to the Four Horsemen with Bill Drummer, they talked briefly and amiably about their colleagues' quirks, and – more earthily – about which Rydon Hall mother was the most attractive. It was usually not long before the name of Mrs Bavington came up, but the Latin teacher left most of the talking to the English teacher. Charles' track record with women had been less than impressive. He had always treated sexual desire as something to be nursed in private, like an animal licking its wounds in anticipation of being savaged. But perhaps all that was about to change.

His other sightings of Natasha were rare. There had been the morning when he had nearly been run over by her colossal Lexus as she was driving Finzi, the family Shih Tzu, for his shampoo and blow dry at Paws for Thought. Another time, he had heard a shout from a helmeted figure as he paced through the leafless glades of Churley Old Park and realised that she was calling him. He tried to chase her, but she was being dragged backwards by a stiff breeze. He felt like Orpheus pursuing his beloved, though this Eurydice was standing on an oversized skateboard connected to a huge kite. Yet even her one-armed greeting contained, to Charles' increasingly fevered mind, an intimation of sexual promise. Alone at night, he sought to embellish these fantasies, imagining the moment at which, in a nook of the café, Natasha swept the mugs off the table, beckoned to him in a *huc veni!* voice and began to slip out of her cashmere shirt, shoulders first.

The Fire Station was a good enough venue for humdrum chat. As a study base, though, it was too noisy, and there had been cases, albeit rare, in which a coffee waitress had not timed a slide correctly, resulting in a mess of cappuccino and croissant on the floor. They would have tried Churley Old Town Library, but a sign went up at the beginning of December that it would close, to reopen as an internet café, crèche, wi-fi and leisure centre within two years.

'Well, I suppose we'll have to stop meeting like this,' said Natasha.

Charles felt his insides begin to defragment in a way he had not expected. 'Oh dear, and you were doing so well.'

'I know,' she said. 'Not sure if I'll be able to do without my weekly fix of Latin.'

That was definitely encouraging. How could he leave it at that?

'Unless,' she went on, 'you were able to come to the house. Could you be persuaded?'

Charles tried to look as if he were weighing up this one option.

'I live in Churley House,' she said. 'It's not much further from the school than the Fire Station. Do you have any objections to plunger coffee?'

'That's taking me to places I've never been before,' said Charles. This was what he most enjoyed about teaching.

'Well, you'll never know if you've never tried it,' she said.

Charles' landlady in Embury Park was a middle-aged divorcee called Julia Annersley. She had once been happily married, up to the point when her husband had decided to buy an eternity ring to celebrate their

20th wedding anniversary. Having booked an appointment at *Tiffany* in Bond Street, he became hopelessly infatuated with the sales assistant – whose name happened to be Tiffany – and the two ran off together.

Mrs Annersley's response had been to wage war, in her own words, on monogamy. She chose to rummage for men opposite her house, in a former spit-and-sawdust pub once known as the King's Head and now, with wearisome Franglish innuendo, called Le Coq And Bottle. From struggling pub to mediocre wine bar, it attracted a steady stream of under-performing home and overseas students from the nearby Forest Vale Language School. These were the objects of Mrs Annersley's pursuits, and, being in pretty good shape herself, she rarely came away empty-handed. But her moral register operated on a different set of points as far as her tenant was concerned.

'I don't like the sound of all this,' she said sternly as they sat in her kitchen one evening, a squalid assortment of pots, pans and plates obscuring the sink area.

Their rooms were at opposite ends of the kitchen – his modest, hers large – and they had lived together in this way for two years. Apart from her wrecked marriage, and her voracious appetite for one-night stands with much younger men, Charles knew almost nothing about her, but he could never keep any secrets from her.

Mrs Annersley rarely kept her views about Charles to herself. 'You need a woman your own age, my lad.'

'You're a fine one to talk.'

'What on earth is wrong with you, trying to get into the pants of your own students' mums? Is that why you went into teaching?'

'But this is different,' he reassured her. 'It's not just a...'

'They all say that, my lad,' she said, drawing heavily on her regular half-pint wine glass.

'How was your assignation last night?' he changed the subject.

'Oh...' She eased some wine down and pushed the bottle towards Charles. 'Pedestrian,' she said at last, 'but hardly worth crossing the road for.'

Mrs Annersley's verdicts on her sexual conquests were rarely flattering.

It was early December when Charles Goldforbes paid his first home visit to Mrs Bavington. Churley House was built from rusty orange bricks in a herringbone pattern, their corners picked out in creamy stone. Charles crunched up the twisting gravel drive. As he did so he had to duck to avoid the water jets which were, even in winter, sprucing the velveteen lawns. He admired the lozenge-shaped Japanese rock garden and lake, amidst which three flamingos squatted contentedly. Species of turtle and peacock gambolled 'twixt grass and water, a whole habitat at ease with itself. And out of all this tranquillity, Charles reflected, the horror that was Florian Bavington had emerged.

The door was opened by the same Filipina maid who occasionally emerged at school from the hog-sized Lexus to deliver some offensively tiny object like Florian's mouth-guard. She introduced herself as Linda and led him into a side room. The walls were decorated with red and blue-tinted pages from a post-war French cartoon series featuring pipe-smoking yokels in berets. At the end, a biplane crashed humorously into a hayrick.

'Meesis Babbington, she come soon,' said Linda. 'You can seat here, wait. You want tea-coffee?'

Charles didn't know what to ask for, but as he contented himself with a glass of water, he heard a squeak on the dark green carpet, and Natasha Bavington's head appeared from behind the door.

'I won't be a second,' she said. She was dressed in a thick white bathrobe. 'I was just having my morning dip.'

41

Charles puffed his cheeks. 'Oh, you've got a...'

'It's barely a paddling pool, but it's better than nothing.'

She turned to go. The top edge of her bathrobe slipped to reveal the rest of the dragon's tail tattoo on the swell of her left shoulder. Charles put a hand out to the wall to steady himself.

The lesson, in the regally neat front room, went well. She made a mistake at one point and when Charles corrected her, she looked so vulnerable that Charles wanted to reach out and grasp her by the shoulder. She seemed to be attempting a ponytail at the back, which she was forever re-tying. At the end, she stood up and took a step towards Charles.

'So tell me, Mr Latin teacher. Do you think it's worth it?'

Charles' mouth opened again, wordlessly, but she looked straight at him. 'Because you do know what's happening to us, don't you?'

Charles fought hard. Was this the moment, the Rubicon of their love? Was pretence now pointless? If he took a step forward, or held out a hand, would she tumble toward him? At first he had just wanted to hold her in his arms and whisper what he hardly dared say – that her son was crap at Latin – but now there was so much more than that. Maybe she had picked him out, from that first day she had seen him outside the Fire Station. She was still young, after all, still hungry for love. What better contrast could there be with her foul, car-fixated ex-husband than a man who could glance at a Wasteminster Scholarship paper and barely need to look up a single word in a dictionary? Having struggled all term, was she now at the mercy of feelings which it was pointless to try and control?

Charles looked at her and smiled sadly.

'With me and Hugh, my... ex-husband?'

Charles' smile changed to a different kind of sadness. He coughed, clearing his throat. 'Yes, that must have been... difficult.'

'It still is, very, at the moment,' she said. 'And I know that it's having an effect on Florian. I mean, I won't go into details but if you knew his father, it wouldn't surprise you that Florian can be a bit of a monster at school. Still, I hope he isn't disrupting your lessons too much.'

'No, no, not a... no, I mean... no,' said Charles.

'So could you bear to come back next week?' she said at the end.

Charles nodded, and smiled again, and decided, on the basis of absolutely no evidence - none of which he needed anyway - that she was becoming as interested in him as he was in her.

He was like a latter-day Schliemann, misguidedly inventing a whole city from some shattered remnants of stone and bronze. He could no more read her feelings for him than he could read her son's appalling handwriting. But he was indifferent to one, and at the mercy of the other.

The staff meeting that changed Charles' life occurred shortly before the end of term. Mrs Hughes-Howard was the only other teacher there when he arrived, and he could hear the foamy splash of freshly poured tea that was her refrain. She picked up a mug that read "My Friend Went To A Ceramics Factory And All I Got Was This Lousy Mug", filling it to the top.

'How are you settling in, Charles?' she said. 'Is it all a bit of a shock?'

'Well, I suppose it is, kind of. But...'

'You know what they say: Rome wasn't built in a day,' she re-applied some thick red lipstick as she flicked her hair back.

'Dr Ironsize put it rather well, I think,' Charles added. 'He said something like, "It's a long plunge but you'll soon surface."'

'Yes, well he would, wouldn't he?'

'I love the way he uses diving imagery all the time.'

'Imagery?'

'Yes, the diving metaphors: boards, shallow pools, head first. Very colourful.'

'My hat,' she said. 'It's just the way he was trained.'

'I thought he had a D. Div,' said Charles.

'Yes,' said Mrs Hughes-Howard.

'Doctor of Divinity?'

'Diploma in Diving,' she said with a sniff. 'I'm told they're very hard to come by.'

The other teachers began to file in.

'It's like a support group, isn't it?' said Charmian Thirst, rocking on her chair. 'Hi, I'm Charmian. Yesterday I taught for five hours, non-stop. Like Alcoholics Anonymous,' she explained.

There was one procedural matter, in which Dotty de Souza asked if any boys were being especially good or bad, Florian Bavington excepted (this seemed to go through on the nod). Mrs Hughes-Howard suggested that "the unfortunately named Archie Neeples" should be put on report card for not handing in his homework. There seemed to be some informal rule that Archie's surname had to be mentioned, just to raise a laugh.

'So. Report card for... Archie Neeples.' Dotty waited for the obligatory giggle to fan out across the room. 'And finally, school trips. Still a few gaps, so... Good opportunity for new members of staff... Charles?'

'Well...' said Charles. 'What's... what's available?'

Dotty flicked through her iPhone. 'Let's see... Madame Allardyce's French party is fully booked, as is Mr Drummer's bard-lovers' day out to Stratford upon Avon next term: standing room only on that one. So that leaves...' She puffed out her cheeks. 'Well there's the Year Four trip to the Aberdaffy Flint Museum which is always...' Dotty tapped at her phone, 'always a popular one, not that you teach Year Four. And then of course, it's rather late in the day but there is still space for one teacher on the *legendary* Year Eight trip to Egypt at the end of January, straight after Mocks, taking in Cairo, Luxor and Alexandria. Your predecessor Geoff Norringham was a regular on that but now that he's, you know, upgraded to the Gulf, we've kept a space open just in case. For many boys it's the highlight of the school year, so let me know if you're interested.'

'Will it be just me in charge..?'

Some of the teachers laughed, perhaps a little too freely. Dotty coughed, 'Er, no, Mr Goldforbes. You've made a very encouraging start, and we admire your attitude one hundred per cent, don't get me wrong, but you're perhaps not quite ready for an entire party of Year Eight boys running riot on the Nile. That trip has been organised for some years now by Dr Ngo and Mrs Hughes-Howard.' (Both acknowledged the name-check with a slight bow.) 'And they both do a fantastic job, they really do. It's hard work, I've done it myself with them once, but their organisation is one hundred per cent watertight. And also...' She leant forward on the chair. 'It's very good for your...'

'Continuing Professional Development?'

'C.P.D., exactly,' Dotty gave him the thumbs up.

'Such an exciting part of the world,' said Dr Ironsize, ' and relatively stable, too, in these uncertain times. I remember when I was, er, taking part in a, um, convention at the Red Sea, and the people there were *so* friendly. And, of course, it's a very interesting time to be undertaking a visit to the Arab world.'

'So long as Florian Bavington doesn't get everyone arrested,' said Dr Ngo.

'Let me know either way,' said Dotty.

'OK,' said Charles.

'And let's be honest, it goes down very well with the parents,' Dotty added. 'I love seeing the look on their faces at the end of a trip. So long as you bring their little ones back safe and sound, some of those mums would do almost anything for you. I mean, literally. Do you want to have a think about it?'

'Is there any other business?' asked Dr Ironsize.

'Actually, I think I'll do it,' said Charles.

CHAPTER 5

Towards the end of the Autumn Term, Christmas lights were twinkling in every retail outlet in Lower Churley. Even though Charles was distracted by the prospect of not seeing Natasha for three weeks, he managed to concentrate enough to post a revision guide on the school intranet, which the boys could study in preparation for their Common Entrance mocks in late January. Charles printed a few copies on demand, too, but most of these were found on the floor of the cloakroom that same afternoon, scuffed and foot-soiled. There were some minor bits of extra news, such as the announcement – no secret to most – that Rohan Shapcott had to leave school two days early, as he was spending a week at a Plexiglas-ceilinged indoor skiing tournament in the Maldives. In the last week of term, Charles went up to Joy Hughes-Howard in the staffroom as she was about to drain a mug that read "Stolen From the Department of Comparative Ethical Studies".

'I'm glad you'll be coming on the trip, uh, Charles,' she said.

'Me too,' he said. 'I'm looking forward to it.'

'Geoff Norringham loved Alexandria. Of course there's so much there for you classicists to enjoy. Doesn't it have one of the Wonders of the World?'

'Yes, the Ancient Ones, yes. That was the lighthouse of...'

'Alexandria, that's the one,' she said. Charles had even slowed down, anticipating that she would interrupt him at some point. He was getting to know her. 'And I hope it'll help you more broadly. It does help the boys to see a different side of you, you know. Do you know Egypt?'

'No,' said Charles. 'But I've heard the museum in Cairo is...'

'What, the Egyptian Museum?' she said. 'Oh, well,

spectacular doesn't do it justice. We could spend all week there, to be honest, but I think some of the boys might get a little restless.'

'Lucky to be there at all,' he said.

'Oh I agree. Because the holidays can feel a little flat, can't they, after Christmas? But I like knowing that I've got the trip to look forward to. My Ivor always says to me, around New Year's Day, "You've got your Sphinx face on, Joy."' She patted Charles' arm, a little self-consciously. 'He gets a bit lyrical at times.'

Charles had a quiet Christmas break. He had a drink with Milo and Penny who had run out of money and flown home from New Zealand for a few days. Mostly this consisted of Charles indirectly rebuking Penny for running off with Milo, or Milo with Penny. He then spent a few days with his parents, mostly hidden in his old bedroom while he slogged through Caesar's *Gallic Wars* with the help of his Loeb Latin-English edition. As he read, he tried to see himself as Caesar, and Florian as a wimpy, irritating Vercingetorix, forever eluding the greater man's clutches by withdrawing to natural fortifications, to the horror of generations of school pupils.

He also tried to revitalise his knowledge of Classical Civilisation, or, as he viewed it, the safety flue for students too stupid to conjugate verbs. His eyes glanced across pages rich with descriptions of Roman baths or gladiator fights, but none of the words stuck in his brain, and by the end he couldn't tell a *laconicum* from a *lanista*. He accepted that the subject had value, but he still felt that it was a back-entry – the Greek term he came across was *opisthodomos* but there was no guarantee he would remember it – to a higher-status subject, much as Community Support Officers contented themselves with removing drunks from doorways while real police officers got on with the business of hunting terrorists and arresting criminals.

And then it was the New Year and he could get

back to Embury, and school – and private Latin lessons with Natasha Bavington. It was difficult to know which was exerting the greater spell on the boys: the January Mocks or the trip to Egypt which immediately followed them. Charles tried his best to prepare entertaining lessons, but he was distracted too, disproportionately interested in his Wednesday morning free periods, and most of his research went into those.

Rydon Hall boys traditionally took their Mock exams at different times to most other schools, and traditionally achieved lower marks at them, probably for the same reason. The results brought few surprises. Florian's mark had sunk several percentage points while Josh and Duncan (or Duncan and Josh) did slightly better. The results were read out, and analysed as much as was thought to be fruitful, but by now all were thinking about the following week, and the Egypt trip.

That Wednesday morning, Charles stood on the pavement outside Churley House at five minutes to ten, for the last lesson before half-term. The air was damp, with mossy overtones, and the sky was as grey as a stone mausoleum. He rang the doorbell and waited.

'It's... the Latin teacher,' he said to the intercom. Then he pressed it again. The Latin teacher always rings twice.

'Hello, Mr Latin teacher,' Natasha said as he walked in. She was wearing a plain white T-shirt and jeans. A slightly skewed vein of blue underscored her eyes, as if she disdained vanity but couldn't quite do without it. 'So you're taking my horrible son to Egypt?'

'Yes,' he said. 'I dare say you'll be glad to get rid of him for a week.'

'Sort of,' she said.

Charles remembered what Dotty had said in the staff meeting. 'And even more glad to get him back.'

'Of course,' she said, smiling with what Charles

felt, or had convinced himself, might be a hint as to the erotic *quid pro quo* of a safe return. 'I'm very jealous of you all. It's such an exciting time to be going to that part of the world.'

'Oh yes,' said Charles. 'The Middle East is such a fascinating region.'

'I saw something about a demonstration in... Tunisia?'

'Yes, but I'm sure we'll be a safe distance from any political unrest,' said Charles. 'I was talking to Mrs Portal and she said she and her husband have a holiday home in Sharm El Sheikh. She says Egypt's the last place on earth where there'd be any trouble.'

'Someone set himself on fire or something?'

'Really? How horrible. I hope it wasn't a school-teacher.'

She smiled. 'Shall we go and sit by the pool? It's more comfortable there, when it's cold outside.'

'Nice idea,' said Charles. She pushed a thick wooden door onto a part of the house that he had never seen before. A blue-tiled walkway skirted a 15-metre swimming pool. Verdant foliage filled the walls, tumbling out of concrete pots and the ground itself. The waters were wriggling, perhaps from the ripples left by Natasha's most recent immersion. Charles spotted two curvy bamboo chairs at a slight angle to a taffeta-fringed hammock. There was also a blue tile-topped table and matching cocktail bar, with Hawaiian-style ice bucket, beakers and coasters.

'My husband's choice,' said Natasha. 'I should have known we weren't compatible. Look at these!' She waved two orange-tinted glasses, each dimpled halfway down, in the air.

'Very tasteful,' said Charles, perching on one of the bamboo chairs.

'Now, Florian was talking about the non-linguistic side of the exam. You know, daily life and all that sort of thing.'

'Oh yes,' said Charles, feeling the classicist's

snobbish detumescence at the mere mention of Classical Civilisation.

'I mean, I'm going to the gym today. But that's actually a Greek word isn't it?'

'Yes it is. In fact it means...' He paused, checked himself, then carried on. 'Well, basically, you wouldn't have worn a lot of clothes in a Greek gymnasium.'

'Right,' she said. 'I suppose that tells us something about the Greeks, doesn't it? They let it all hang out, didn't they, all arms and legs and bits in between?'

'Maybe it was warmer in Athens in those days,' said Charles.

'I mean,' she said, emptying the contents of a tiny bottle of Tibetan sparkling water into two glasses, 'I think we've lost touch with a part of ourselves, going around all wrapped up. Perhaps we should have a lesson about what they wore. Or didn't wear...'

'Daily life in a Greek gymnasium? That sounds interesting.'

Natasha grinned. 'And we could get into the spirit by sitting here stark naked, freezing our tits off!'

'Good idea!'

'In the middle of January!' she said, laughing even harder.

'I'm sure we'd learn a lot from the experience,' said Charles.

'Like how cold it is in England!'

'Exactly,' he said. 'Me completely starkers, talking about gladiators and athletes.'

'That would be so funny!' she said, tossing her head back. 'A naked Latin teacher in my house. How would I live it down? It's like a porn movie, but with...'

'With better dialogue,' Charles added.

'Yes! Oh, it's so funny.'

'Because, you know,' said Charles, 'the ancient Greeks used the most disgusting language.'

'Really?' she said. 'Hardly surprising, I suppose. All those naked statues and...'

'And the plays: the comedies, of Aristophanes,' he

said. She looked interested. 'Like the *Lysistrata*: that's the most famous one. Do you know it?'

'Know it? I don't think I could pronounce it if you wrote it down,' she said.

'It's about the women of Athens who get so fed up with their husbands, for fighting all the time, that they go on strike, on a sex strike.'

'Ah,' she said. 'So that's what I've been doing all these years! I never knew I was so political.'

'Some of the lines are quite, you know, full on. Would you like to see? I might have the book here.' Charles reached into his bag, which he had packed with a graphically thorough selection of classical texts.

'Don't worry, Charles, a few racy words won't scare me.'

Charles turned the pages. 'I'm just looking for the line where one character says something like, "My cock is bursting out of its skin."'

'Oh God..!' Natasha raised her top lip, revealing a set of not quite white teeth, not quite straight, but which any greater evenness would have ruined.

'It's incredible; I must show you.'

'In a play written, what, two thousand, three thousand years ago?'

'Somewhere in between,' he said. 'It's amazing, isn't it?'

'Incredible... I never knew you could talk dirty in ancient Greek. I suppose, being a single mum and living in Churley, that's about as near as I'm going to get.'

'And the male characters are all going on about what massive hard-ons they have.'

'I'd love to see that!' she cooed.

'Would you?' he said. He could barely focus on the lines. 'Give me a second.'

'How hilarious. A massive hard-on. And, "my cock..?"'

'My cock is bursting out of its skin.'

'Oh my God, that's hilarious!'

51

'Would you like to see? I can show you.'

'I definitely want to see that. But we must have some more drinks. All this talk about sex! It's making me thirsty. Do you want a drink? Hot, cold, fizzy?'

'How about a massive… Coke?'

'I think I've got that. Hold on! I won't be long.'

'And then do you want to see my…'

'Yes, you must show me your "massive hard-on",' she said. She definitely said it. 'I can't wait.'

'I'd love to,' he said.

The door swished shut and Charles was left on his own with nothing but his *psōlē*, which his 19th century dictionary would have translated as a *praeputio retracto*, rather than a "hard-on", for company. There were plenty of other such expressions, which he had found during a fascinating but all too brief revision session on Aristophanes earlier that week. Charles felt sodden with erotic juices. His *psōlē* was fully engaged, scraping against the roof of his pants like an over-active fern in the hothouse at Kew. It all seemed so jocular, so facile and light-hearted, that surely anyone could have come to the same conclusion as Charles did, and behaved as he did next, which was why, ten minutes later, as he waited in cenotaph-like silence for the H41 bus to pitch him back to the ignominious suburbs of Embury Park, he was still trying to work out how events could have looped off into such a disastrous anti-climax.

'Oh no, Mr Goldforbes,' she had said. Over and over again, Charles tried to block out her next few words. His subconscious could only deal with his response.

'I'm, I'm so sorry, er, I...' he said as they reached the door. 'A... misunderstanding.'

'Forget it, Mr Goldforbes,' she said, a minute later as he stood at the front door.

'Forget it? I mean...'

'As far as I'm concerned, nothing happened between you and I.'

Charles had to correct her there.

'Between you and me,' he said.
'I'm sorry?'
'Between... you... and me.'
'That's what I said.'
'Well, you said I, but it's me.'
She stared at him.
'It's the grammar, I mean.'
'Whatever.'
'Between us, anyway.'
'Nothing happened between us.'
'Yes, I mean, no, I'm very sorry.'

'Goodbye Mr Goldforbes,' she said, and closed the door behind him, leaving him to wander sadly down the driveway. He pressed the gate-release button, pushed it open and was nearly flattened by a *Harvey Nichols* delivery van.

Greek expressions borrowed from tragedy dominated Charles Goldforbes' thoughts as he retraced his steps towards school and slid back onto his chair in the marking room. With what misapplied optimism had he eased himself out, just an hour or so earlier. The phrase "*en aporia*", meaning "in utter distress", is used by most of the major classical Greek authors to describe a mind at the end of its tether. Charles felt just this way that Wednesday, and for the next three days until the end of term: reduced to ceaseless but vain internal probing, unable to turn elsewhere yet charging, with manic energy, at the same locked door.

Among the many questions that thrashed around in his head, the first was the question of whether or not he would be sacked from his job. The second was whether he would face criminal proceedings, or whether the teaching union he had just joined would side with him after only a few monthly payments. The third was whether, during the inevitable disciplinary hearing, he dared advance the argument that this had been a genuine attempt to explore attitudes to clothes and clothing in pre-fourth century Greece. The next thought was a twinge of remorse at what the expression on the face of his great ally, Dotty de Souza, would be when she heard the news. When she talked of Continuing Professional Development, this was clearly not what she had in mind.

Other questions fluttered around his increasingly perturbed mind. Would he ever work again? Should he, *in extremis*, try and contact his predecessor, Mr Norringham, who seemed to have found a well-paid job in the Arabian Gulf? But could there be any school sufficiently liberated (or desperate) to offer him alternative employment? No: it was all because of the intellectual vacuousness of Classical Civilisation, since he would never have been thrust into such discomfort if they had stuck to sentences such as, "For a long time the Romans were attacking the town." And above all these, his mind lurched forward, with nauseating clarity, to the post-Mocks trip, now only a few days away. As, red pen in hand, he confronted a stumpy pile of overlooked Year Eight homework, each relating, in a variety of spidery scrawls, some misconstrued summary of Jason's search for the golden fleece, he fought to resist the awful image of his own genital ascendancy.

How on earth could he have interpreted her mild toleration as a green light? And even if, for reasons best known to herself, Mrs Bavington did not denounce him to the senior management of Rydon Hall, did he seriously think that she would allow such a man to accompany her son and the rest of his class on the annual Year Eight trip to Egypt? Could he really be so shameless?

PART TWO

CHAPTER 6

(January 2011)

Charles had been warned that central Cairo was likely to be lively, but as the crocodile of Year Eight students edged its way around Qasr al-Ayni Street on its approach to Tahrir Square, he was taken aback by what he saw. At first he felt as if they had walked into a full-blown rock festival, except there were no bands playing. Hundreds, thousands, of people were walking, as if drilled, across the roads, and hardly any cars were present. What surprised him more was that he couldn't see anyone in uniform. It wasn't scary, but it did seem somewhat skittish. He aimed what was intended to be a minatory glance at Mrs Hughes-Howard but she was in no mood to be put off.

'I told you it could be like Oxford Street, didn't I?' she said, clutching her handbag. 'Watch where you're going, boys! We don't want any of you ending up as museum exhibits.'

Charles had no knowledge of Arabic, nor had he studied the Egyptian political scene in any depth, so he spoke as any tourist would.

'It seems a little turbulent, wouldn't you say?'

'I expect it's some sort of show,' replied Mrs Hughes-Howard, looking genuinely insouciant as some women unfurled a large banner that read "Freedom Not Tyranny".

There was a camera crew nearby, filming everyone. In fact, there seemed to be more camera crews than people in some sections of the square.

'I can understand that,' said Arthur. 'It's in English.'

'I thought it was going to say "Egypt welcomes Rydon Hall",' said Mrs Hughes-Howard, 'but they won't feel like welcoming us if Rufus Coe-Haine is having an arm wrestle with Roley Yousuf. Settle down, boys, please.'

'I swear there's like a rally going on?' said Florian.

'Oh lovely, is there a tennis match?' said Joy, waving at Dr Ngo up ahead to check that the party was still together.

'If I were the president, I think I'd stay away,' said Dr Ngo as the boys lined up against the red stone walls by the main entrance to the Egyptian Museum.

'I thought everyone liked him,' said Charles.

'So did he, it seems,' said Dr Ngo.

'Miss, I think this is all about, like, freedom?' said Dylan, as if he had held up a finger to the wind and thus diagnosed the collective will of the people. 'They all want to be free.'

'I don't blame them,' said Mrs Hughes-Howard, 'and we'll be the same when we get down to the Red Sea in a couple of days. It's lovely down in Hurghada. The water's so clear.'

'It's getting very noisy,' shouted Dr Ngo.

'Oh but you know what they're like,' said Mrs Hughes-Howard. 'Any excuse for a party, this lot.' She turned to Charles. 'Obviously they can get a little excitable at times but it's all perfectly harmless.'

'Miss, are they having a demonstration?' asked Arthur Clough.

'I don't know, Arthur. What sort of demonstration?' said Mrs Hughes-Howard. 'Cosmetics or cookery?'

'Let's go into the museum,' said Dr Ngo. 'We're five minutes late as it is.'

Somewhere a car horn was punching the air with a series of sharp bursts. Now the bands of people were merging, and they seemed to be uttering some enormous burst of collective, guttural will which none of the tourists understood.

Mrs Hughes-Howard smiled brightly at the tour party. 'Right!' she said. 'Who wants to meet a mummy?'

The last few days of January had not been a comfortable period for Charles Goldforbes. He feared it was only a matter of time before the facts about his mortifying encounter with Mrs Bavington became the stuff of Churley backchat. Every cracked smile of Florian's, every suppressed giggle at the back of the classroom between Dylan Cristiano and Yedverd Zygnwycyz, every exchange of notes between Josh De Burgh and Duncan Moyne – unless it was the other way round – held the threat of imminent exposure. He had managed to keep the secret to himself at first, but after four nights of jerking sleeplessness, even Mrs Annersley had felt moved to ask him what the matter was. When he told her, rocking back and forth on a wooden kitchen chair, his voice thick with self-loathing, she gurgled.

'Well, dear,' she said, stroking the stem of her glass in which a lagoon of red wine still trembled. 'It's like we used to say: Don't let the winkie do the thinkie.'

'I don't really understand that,' said Charles, trying to ignore the comment.

'Yes you do. But you're not the first,' she emptied and immediately re-filled her glass, 'and you won't be the last.'

'I thought she wanted me,' said Charles. 'But when she came in, it was like… it was like seeing a deponent verb and thinking it's passive, you know what I mean?'

Mrs Annersley's lips made a smirk of displeasure. 'I don't know what the bollocks you're talking about, dear,' she said. 'Anyway, you didn't know what *she* wanted: you knew what *you* wanted. Or what Mr Winkle wanted.'

'What do I do now? How do I apologise?'

'Put it behind you, lad. I don't mean put your winkle behind you.' She laughed more gruffly. 'Although if you can, I'd like to see it.'

Mrs Portal had assured everyone that the sun would be shining, but as the coach pulled away from the playground, waved on by a chorus of parents and chained dogs, the windscreen wipers were beating time like a deranged conductor to counter the sheeting rain. A few hours later, as the Jumbo rose into the air, Charles was still considering his options. He had thought about resigning from the tour, or even from the school but, since no accusing finger had been pointed at him, was it not just possible that he could redeem himself by putting in a flawless performance as a master in charge? If Florian and the rest of his class returned home, all raving about what a fun teacher Mr Goldforbes was, and how far removed he was from the image that they had built up of him, surely Mrs Bavington would not want to spoil things by pointing out that he had behaved disgracefully in her house. Or, as Mrs Annersley had said, 'It's a private bloody school, dearie, not an inner city academy. People like that know how to keep a lid on things: that's what the whole system's built on.'

Charles wanted to prove her right. When they returned in just over ten days, grubbier, darker and a bit thinner from some minor digestive tract irritation, he was hoping that their shared experiences of discomfort and pleasure would have forged a new bond which would extend beyond Year Eight, transforming relations all through the school. No longer could Florian be said to be holding Charles like some sort of hostage: they would be all for one and one for all and no one would be left behind – least of all Charles himself.

The Rydon Hall tour party were met at the entrance to Cairo's great Egyptian Museum by a nervous tour guide called Ali, who swore he had met Mrs Hughes-Howard the previous year. ('I bet he says that to all the ladies,' she whispered to Charles.) Ali did his best to give a shouted introduction to the boys of the wonders that awaited them inside the museum, but even beyond the Security desk there seemed to be a great deal of random coming and going. They went with Ali as far as the Tutankhamen exhibits on the upper floor. They walked past the very gold leaf coffin that Howard Carter and his team had found in 1924. While Ali was pointing out the winged Wadjet cobra and the Nekhbet vulture, Charles did a head-count and found one missing. He walked around the room until he came to a figure in an orange hoodie, slumped on the floor, head down. A momentary flash of concern was replaced by revulsion.

'What on earth are you doing, Florian?' he said angrily.

The boy looked up. 'Oh sir, I'm just...'

'Come on: give it to me.'

'But sir, this game's, like, nearly over?'

'It's not, like, *nearly* over, it *is* over. We said no iPods this morning.'

'I know but...'

'Give it, now...'

Florian huffed, and handed it over. And yet Charles knew he couldn't win. The greatest art in the ancient world was as nothing compared to the attraction of a computer game. As he put it in his pocket, he looked at the screen and tried to adopt a more conciliatory approach. 'I mean, how angry do birds need to be?'

'There's 26 levels,' said the boy. 'And each level you get ten games. It's amazing, I swear.'

'But we're in Cairo in the Egyptian Museum of Antiquities. Does that mean nothing to you?'

The boy looked up. 'Course it does,' he says. 'I just got onto level 18. I'll never forget what I was doing when I got there.'

'What were you doing?'

'I was sitting here, on the floor.'

'Pathetic. You really are pathetic,' said Charles. 'Did you know there are 120,000 objects in the museum? Don't you want to see some of them?'

'Did you get that off the website?' said the boy.

Charles gasped in exasperation. 'We had about an hour and a half when we came in. There's only an hour left.'

'I'm pretty hot, sir, to be honest.'

'So am I. We all are.' It wasn't that hot, but it was warmer than London. And the square had felt not just hot but moved with some extra emotion.

'I could smell this weird smell, and I thought it was from one of the statues...'

'They're mummies, actually...'

'Yeah, mummies, but now I think it's Adrian Purvis and it's making me feel a bit uncomfortable, to be honest.'

Here we go again, thought Charles; same old stories. But then Dylan came running up.

'Sir, can we go to the gift shop? It's massive. I swear I just saw someone buy this, like, chocolate pyramid.'

'Museum first, then shop,' said Dr Ngo, coming to Charles' rescue. 'Now go and find a leopard. Go!'

Charles marvelled at his ability to motivate the students. Even the reluctant ones rose to the challenge. Mo Hegarty and Josh de Burgh attempted a crude pencil sketch of the goddess Sekhmet. Roley and Tyler stood back-to-back, pushing their chests out to resemble Nubian and Asiatic prisoners, feet bound together to represent Egypt's supremacy over its two old enemies. For a moment, an almost scholarly calm hung around the display cabinets. Cato Wang broke the mood.

'Sir, can we go to the café?' Cato could always be relied on to bring the subject back to food.

'Oh dear,' said Dr Ngo, resplendent in the Legendary Pyramid-print shirt that he always wore for this trip. 'Next you'll be telling me that Adrian Purvis...'

'Sir, I really need the toilet?' said Adrian, as if in answer to an unwanted prayer.

Dr Ngo rolled his eyes. The pyramids of many shapes, sizes and colours bounced up and down as his rotund tummy quivered. Was the design an ironic master-stroke or something simpler? Charles still wasn't sure. 'Do you know, if it had been left to you lot, I doubt those pyramids would have been built at all. Does anyone else need to go?'

'Is this ancient enough for you, Mr Goldforbes?'

asked Mrs Hughes-Howard, leaning forward to give him an affectionate little swipe with her programme. 'I bet you wish you were an Egyptologist now.'

'Sir I need to go too,' said a voice behind Charles.

'Must you, Josh? You could have gone with Adrian.'

'It's Duncan, actually, sir,' said the boy matter-of-factly, 'but I'll be very quick. I'll probably catch him up.'

Charles was saved from apologising to Duncan as two museum guards walked in briskly and made what sounded like a very solemn announcement in Arabic. As they did so, some people began to move away, quickly. The guards spoke again, in English. 'The museum have to close,' they said. 'We are sorry but is close: please, you must to leave.'

'Oh no,' said Mrs Hughes-Howard. 'We've come all this way.'

'I am sorry, madam,' said one of the guards. 'Is big demonstration in the square. Is better for you to leave. You are staying in Cairo?'

'Yes, but...'

'Please go back to hotel. Is better for you.'

'Good timing by Purvis,' said Dr Ngo as they fell in step behind the exiting masses. 'How are we going to find him in the crowds?'

'Eddy and I'll go and get him,' said Dylan. 'He's got a very sensitive sense of smell.'

'We don't want to lose you too,' said Charles.

'Actually,' said Dr Ngo, 'come to think of it...' But Adrian's bobbing head was soon visible, as were his feet, moving as if pulled from above by strings.

'Well, this is all very dreary,' Mrs Hughes-Howard was saying. They were trying to pick their way through the crowds to where their tour bus was parked. An array of stalls had suddenly appeared. Mrs Hughes-Howard adjusted her enormous macaroon-shaped hat as they pushed past what appeared to be a man lying flat upon the caterpillar tracks of a tank. 'I do love the way they fill these spaces with these spontaneous, er, gatherings,' she said.

'Comes from not relying too much on Health and Safety policies,' said Dr Ngo.

They could hear a rap song being strummed on a guitar, and the name "Mubarak". Charles' guess was that it was less than flattering towards the president. As the party twisted between the crowds, he could only just make out Dr Ngo and his swirling pyramids. Then, Florian approached Charles with an uncharacteristically contrite expression on his face.

'Sir, my bag?' said the boy.

'What about it?' said Charles, who was holding the rear of the line, but Florian had already turned around.

'I left it in the museum?' he said. 'In the cloakroom?'

'But...' said Charles. 'Mrs Hughes-Howard!' His voice rang out to the first in command.

'It's got my passport,' said Florian.

'Oh shhhhh...' Charles began, but Mrs Hughes-Howard had halted the group before the banned expletive had detonated on Charles' tongue. He explained what had happened. In the long run, it probably wouldn't have mattered if he had said "shit" anyway.

'Right, Florian,' she said, with an edge to her voice that could have ripped through a tin of tomatoes. She crossed her arms with a gesture of magnificence. '*You* will walk to the museum with Mr Goldforbes while *we* all stand here under the midday sun until *you* have returned. And *when* you're back, *I* shall expect an answer as to *why* you brought your passport with you when you were all very deliberately told to hand them in.'

'I thought I gave it to Mr Goldforbes...' he began. As ever with Florian, anyone but himself would do.

'Now go!'

Charles was tight-lipped on the walk back. For one thing, he couldn't quite remember if he had collected Florian's passport or not. This was his first trip, after all, and there were so many other things to think of, but he had the uneasy sense that part of Mrs Hughes-Howard's venom was aimed at him. He was also uncertain about the mood in the square, as they walked past a series of tents, put up by demonstrators, offering foodstuffs or pharmaceuticals, or wet shaves. A bunch of people who looked like students approached them. Charles waved at them and asked if they spoke English.

'This is demonstration for freedom,' they said. 'Against president.'

'What do you want him to do?' asked Charles.

'He has to go,' they said. 'Leave! Now! You must go!'

Charles wasn't sure if the latter comment was aimed entirely at the president or partly at them, but he wished them luck and they continued walking. Along the way, Florian looked puzzled. 'What I don't understand is, what are they complaining about?'

'I think it's a question of political freedom,' said Charles.

'So that's why there's all that, like, tension, in Giza?'

Charles hesitated. 'In Giza?'

'Yeah, like, with that wall...'

Charles sighed. 'No, Florian. That's Gaza, not Giza, but let's talk about that another time.'

'Sweet...' said the boy, with not even a semblance of concern.

When they finally reached the museum entrance, it seemed to be shut. When they explained their predicament to one of the guards, with many protestations about passports and British embassies, he shrugged and let Florian back in, but as Charles was wearing a backpack, he had to stay outside.

'I will wait right here, Florian,' said Charles finally, trying to sound like any reasonably competent teacher would. 'You will come back to this exact spot, won't you?'

'Course sir, don't sweat.'

'Don't make me.'

Florian ran off. Charles briefly wondered how he would explain to Florian's mother that her only son had disappeared under his watch, but then he shelved the distasteful thought. She was hardly likely to fall sobbing into his arms, so he had better just sit there and wait. He wished he were taller so he could have a better view, but he was fairly sure that he could see some camels being drafted in to try and keep the peace. Charles felt a fleeting but sincere surge of pure hatred towards the boy who had kept the whole group waiting. For all he knew, the police were about to put on a show of brute force. If their shooting was as accurate as their driving, Year Eight of Rydon Hall were as liable to be victims as anyone.

The heat suddenly felt oppressive. Even the car horns sounded alien and guttural compared to the first few days when everything had been so exciting and strange. The chanting drummed against his head menacingly. Charles saw that a stretch of wall was covered with newspapers, perhaps to spread the word of whatever was going on. He smiled at one or two people and tried to strike up a conversation, but few seemed interested in talking to a lone western male without a camera or microphone. From the scraps that he picked up, he gathered that freedom was good, the president was bad, and that if he needed more water, there was a stall in the centre of the square where they were giving it away, so long as he could brush past the seventy five thousand people in the way. He tensed, wondering if he could smell tear gas. Was something happening under one of the bridges? No, it was just a Camel cigarette. He took another sip from what was left of his bottle of Baraka mineral water, and realised with relief that he had not thought about Mrs Bavington for several minutes. Perhaps he was getting over it. But then he realised that he *was* thinking about her, which was hardly surprising. His mind ticked back guiltily to the last time he had seen her, just after she had offered to go and get the drinks.

'You must show me your "massive hard-on",' she had said. 'I can't wait.'

As he waited for her to come back, Charles was wondering how closely her breasts would correspond to the outline they made against her running top, once he had coaxed them out of her bra. He tried to rationalise with himself but he was so bloated with lust, he worried that he was becoming incoherent. He would, of course, ask first if he could touch them. One must always remember one's manners, at least until animal disinhibition takes over.

She smiled and left the room. Charles continued with what could best be described as lesson preparation. Suddenly, the world of Classical Civilisation – or Classics for Dummies as he had previously thought of it - had opened up to him the most amazing range of extra-curricular activities. He was so grateful to it. And grateful, too, to this woman for having the presence of mind to realise that fusty school rules requiring staff and parents not to become entangled only existed in a world of Platonic ideals. If truth was an abstraction, as Charles thought he remembered Plato arguing, then it was separate from the external world. So, perhaps, in the world of Platonic (or was it Socratic?) truth, a Classics teacher might have to exist in an ideal world. But the world that he and Natasha were about to discover was a world of the particular. And things happened differently there. Once they had done it for the first time – he half-remembered a line from Sappho: "What frenzy in my bosom raged...?" – how could they stop? Would he be receiving texts from her all morning at school? "Another lesson! And another! More Class Civ! Come! See me!" He could barely wait. He had never known that there was so much to Classical Civilisation.

'Here come the drinks!' She was almost singing as she pushed the swing door open. Then she stopped, and the door slip-slopped silently behind her. Charles saw the retreating figure of Linda, pushing a trolley away, and realised with a shudder that, in Churley, getting the drinks meant asking the nanny or au pair to bring them. Natasha let the pool door close against her legs. The tray which she had quickly put down contained two glasses, two bottles of Coke, a bucket of ice and some lemon slices – not that any of that mattered as Charles was hardly likely to be staying for his drink.

'Oh, no,' she said.

Charles measured her disapproving stare. It moved from the edge of the pool, to the chairs, to the pile of clothes which he had hastily slung onto the tiled floor, until it rested like a follow-spot on that point just below his waist. Charles stood, entirely naked, penis perched at a rakish angle.

'Oh no...' she said. 'No... That's not what I meant at all.'

From her choice of words, Charles could tell that this was not a sexual invitation. In any event, his *boubonia* - one of many humorous terms coined by Aristophanes to describe a bulging groin - was now definitely wilting. He couldn't tell if it was merely the presence of the thing (the *qualis*, as he might have taught in a classroom), or the dimensions of it (the *quantus*) – that so displeased her.

'Why... why have you taken off all your clothes?'

'I...' he started to say, then stopped. The question struck him as rather apt. Why on earth had he taken off all his clothes?

'I...' he stammered. 'I thought, you wanted, to see... my... massive...'

'Oh God...' she said, crossly but peremptorily, as if the paperboy had left a *Times* (or a *Guardian*) instead of a *Guardian* (or a *Times*). Then, picking up the tray, she walked back into the house. The door banged behind her.

Charles dressed hurriedly, and made what excuses

he could. But the thought that burned away at him, needlessly, endlessly, unanswerably, was this: as he stood there, his nether regions proclaiming "*estuka gar*" (I am horny) and expecting the response "*binētiōmen*" (We need a fuck), had she nothing of the sort in mind, or was she hoping for something on an altogether bigger scale?

With another shiver of remorse, Charles returned to the present. He looked at his watch: what was the matter with the wretched boy? This part of Tahrir Square seemed to have taken on the feel of a picnic. Primus stoves had appeared, and those present seemed determined to cook their way towards democracy (suggesting that Mrs Hughes-Howard's joke about cookery demonstrations might not be that far off the mark), but Charles was concerned that a breakaway movement might ignite the wrong sort of spark. It would have been just his luck if Florian Bavington's idiocy had led to him having his head knocked off in a stream of water cannon spray. So it was with mixed feelings of revulsion and relief that he greeted Bavington junior as he swung his legs over one of the metal railings outside the museum.

'Job done!' Florian said with that infuriating blend of bravado and cultural ignorance which he brought to everything, and immediately started walking away from the museum.

'Florian,' said Charles. The boy kept walking, looking behind and beckoning at Charles. 'Florian!'

'What...?' It was as if Charles were holding him up.

'Can't you see I am waiting for something?'

'What's that, sir? You'll never get a bus now, not with all these crowds...'

'I have been out here for, what, half an hour.'

Florian stopped. The retrieved backpack was fuller than before: he had more than a passport in there. 'Oh, sweet. Yeah, sorry, but there was, like, such a queue there, I thought I'd never get it back.' He turned and set off again.

Charles had to hurry to catch him up.

'What's in the bag?'

'Oh nothing,' the boy said, raising his voice against a wave of impassioned chanting that, again, included the president's name and which did not feel like an oath of undying loyalty. 'I left all this other stuff in the locker.'

As Charles and Florian jostled their way back across the square, it seemed that they might never reach the corner of Qasr al-Ayni street. The undertow of the crowd was so strong that it seemed constantly to be pulling them further away from the edge into the centre. The mass of humanity was so huge, and its focus so strikingly at odds with the needs of the school party from Churley, south-west London, that for a few truly nerve-racking moments Charles was fighting to control the fear that he might somehow never manage to reach the rest of Year Eight. And he entertained the thought – which he would soon have more time to pick over – that it really was a huge responsibility to be in charge of a party of schoolchildren, or even one schoolchild, in a big and complex country, far from the parochial certainties of London. But eventually they fought their way through, with most of the Egyptians friendly or distracted enough to let them pass without comment, and he was both relieved and delighted at seeing, high over most people's heads, the peak of Mrs Hughes-Howard's creamy-coloured walnut whip hat, and to be told that they had been delayed because Adrian Purvis had had to dash into a handily-located café to use the toilet.

'My goodness, you took your time, Mr Goldforbes,' shouted Mrs Hughes-Howard over the buzz of pro-democracy chatter. 'And Florian, what is that bulge in your bag?'

'Something from the gift shop. For my mum, you know.'

'I see,' she said. 'Well, for now, I think we'll just

make our way back to the coach with as little chatter as possible. But I will be writing to your mother by email when we get back to the hotel, Florian. Perhaps Mr Goldforbes should too.'

'No Miss, it was just a...'

Mrs Hughes-Howard held up an uncompromising hand. 'There's no point protesting. Mr Goldforbes, will you be writing to Florian's mother? I'm sure there's something you wish to say to her.'

Charles felt his mouth becoming dry. He smiled weakly at her, trying to overcome the brilliance of the noon sun, but she was wearing her tortoiseshell sunglasses, and Charles could discern no expression.

When they got back to the Ramses Happy Nation hotel, the expression on the faces of the staff mirrored the drawn look of the bus-driver.

'This situations is vary tanse,' said Mr Mehmet, in surprisingly well-judged language. 'I think Cairo is difficult now, so you will see not so many good things. Maybe you can come back when is safer, *inshallah.*'

The teachers discussed their options over dinner. It seemed that "Mother Cairo", which was in so many ways the heart and brain of the nation, was experiencing the ripple effect of the political convulsions also taking place in Tunisia, Algeria, Jordan, Oman and elsewhere. More to the point, and whatever their long-lasting effects, these events had proved that Mrs Portal's grasp of geo-political developments was as unreliable as her meteorological skills.

'Maybe we should make a run for it,' said Dr Ngo, helping himself to a second dish of cream caramel.

'I'm sure it'll all blow over,' said Mrs Hughes-Howard. 'You probably don't remember the Brixton riots but I do. It was awful at the time but Ivor gets all our dry cleaning there now, and he says it's perfectly friendly.'

'Maybe we should go straight to Hurghada,' said

Charles. 'Escape to the Red Sea.'

Dr Ngo paused. The distant sound of Florian Bavington beating down on Adrian Purvis' skull with a dessert spoon could be heard. 'I've got another idea,' he said at last.

'Share it with the group, Colin,' said Mrs Hughes-Howard.

'Let's leave Florian behind.'

Mrs Hughes-Howard smiled. 'I don't think Mrs Bavington would be very happy about that. What do you think, Charles?'

Charles smiled back at her and wished he was still wearing his sunglasses, like his two more experienced colleagues.

CHAPTER 7

It was Dr Ngo who spotted the two men first. As Year Eight of Rydon Hall dragged their bags off the bus at the Blue Turtle Leisure Resort, Hurghada, with a distant but alluring prospect of sea across the Safaga Highway, most of the boys and staff were looking forward to nothing more than a dip in the waters after an uncomfortable seven-hour drive. Dr Ngo came up to Charles and tapped him on the elbow. It was a rare moment of physical contact, and Charles was on the alert straight away.

'Seen those two?' he said, making a gesture behind his back. Charles peered past Dr Ngo's Ray-Bans at two men in, he guessed, their 20s, who seemed to be hanging around the periphery of the hotel.

Charles squinted. It was very bright at midday.

'Keep an eye on them,' said Dr Ngo, and turned around to help some of the others with their bags. Charles was given the job of assigning boys to their rooms. Perhaps to make up for the possible passport oversight with Florian, he took this very seriously, basing himself in an annexe off the main Reception area. The boys were given their room keys – each attached to a bulky, blue plastic turtle to match the name of the hotel – and then went off to their rooms. All seemed to be going fine until Florian walked past with a small plastic bag in addition to his backpack.

'What's in there, Flo?' said Charles, venturing an abbreviated form that suggested that even these two were drawing slightly closer together on holiday.

'Oh it's nothing,' said Florian. 'It's fine. I just had to re-pack some stuff.'

'Is that what you got in the gift shop?'

'The what? Oh, the... yeah,' said the boy.

'Could I have a look?' said Mrs Hughes-Howard, cradling a cup of tea in one hand. 'Since you were the only one to get anything, you lucky beggar.'

'Oh, no, it's OK...'

'Oh come on Florian, don't be shy,' she said. 'Your mum likes scarves, doesn't she? I bet it's a nice cotton scarf.'

'No it's not that.' He was looking uneasy, perhaps because all the other boys had now gone upstairs to their rooms.

'Well now you're going to have to show us,' she said, smiling. The boy held on to the bag tighter, but she started tugging it. 'Let go of the bag, Florian!'

'Don't, Miss,' he said. He seemed, to Charles, uncharacteristically edgy.

'Come on Colin, we need you!' she called, as both teachers now joined in what they were both still treating as a light-hearted tussle.

'No..!' yelled Florian but it was too late. The bag ripped open and something large, and solid, and about the size of a football, arched through the air. Charles stepped forward, rather athletically he thought, to catch it. He held it in his hands for a moment, staring at it. Then, with a feeling that he couldn't yet express in words, he laid the item very gently on the table, and a silence fell as the two teachers studied it.

It was the head of a falcon, and its eyes, which were perfect black ovals, seemed to burn into anyone who looked at it. It was too heavy to be made simply of wood: bronze inlay perhaps, and the dark shimmer of the face was produced by a shade of gold to which no mass-production could do justice. The hooked nose must have been formed by many patient man hours, and by a set of craft skills long forgotten. The bird had a fluted gold collar, with a sequencing pattern of green, perhaps from some dye made from copper. Bold, expressive lines criss-crossed the face, formed by a chisel and hammer. It stared at them with a disdain that could only be thousands of years old.

'Well, this is rather nice,' said Mrs Hughes-Howard, calmly. 'I didn't know you had such good taste. Your mother will love this.'

'Yeah, 'snice,' said the boy, trying to take it from Charles.

'Is it a hawk? Or an eagle perhaps..?' Mrs Hughes-Howard said. Charles couldn't tell if she was humouring him or not.

'I dunno,' said the boy. 'I thought it was like a pigeon or something.'

'I don't think it's a pigeon,' Mrs Hughes-Howard said. She was looking more serious now. She flicked a finger at the falcon and addressed Dr Ngo, who had just appeared.

'Florian's souvenir of the Egyptian Museum,' she said. 'What do you think?'

Dr Ngo stared at it. He took off his glasses and let out a low whistle. He crouched down, put on his normal glasses and examined it close up. Then he got to his feet. When he spoke, it was almost in a whisper. 'I didn't know they sold stuff like this at the gift shop,' he said.

'That's what we're trying to work out,' said Charles. 'Just how it came into Florian's hands.'

The screen on the other side of the Reception area was showing the crowds from Tahrir Square, even larger and angrier than they had been the day before. Charles thought he ought to get in on the interrogation too. 'How much did you pay for this?' he asked.

'Oh...' Florian stroked the tip of his nose, a gesture which reminded Charles of a paragraph subtitled "Jones Minor's Whopper!" from his very brief excursion into *The Body of a Teacher.*

'Florian,' he said, 'I think you're lying.'

'I'm not,' the boy said, twiddling his nostrils more agitatedly. 'I just, you know, I can't remember paying, I mean, how much I paid.'

'Where's the price tag?' said Mrs Hughes-Howard. 'And what's happened to the packaging?'

'Oh, yeah...' Florian seemed to be playing for time. 'Well it was like they were, sort of, getting rid of them, you know.'

The three teachers clustered more tightly around Florian. 'Florian,' said Dr Ngo. 'What... is... this?'

'I told you. It's a statue,' he said. 'I got it at the museum.'

'From the gift shop?'

'From... nnyeah,' he said, nodding earnestly. 'I think so, yeah it was.'

'What do you mean you *think* so?' asked Charles.

'Well, like, you know the gift shop, right?' They continued to stare at him. 'Well, just there, just... yeah, near it.' He was beginning to look edgy.

'What do you mean *near* the gift shop?' said Mrs Hughes-Howard.

'Can I go now please, Miss? I have to put my stuff away.'

'Where did you get this?' asked Dr Ngo, with a sharpness in his voice that Charles had not heard before.

Florian held up a hand, as if the matter were really too wearisome to go into. 'See, what happened, right? I went in, and Mr Goldforbes said he was waiting, and he was, like, get a move on, yeah? So I'm under all this pressure...'

Charles waved away the attempt to offload the responsibility.

'So I go in and there's all these guys running around, and alarm bells going off, it was crazy. But I had to get something for my mum, cos she's divorced from my dad...'

'We know that, Florian,' said Dr Ngo.

'And I'm near the gift shop, but, I swear, there's people just grabbing stuff and running, it was mental. And one of the cases was, like... the glass was broken? And there was stuff there you could just... I didn't do anything wrong, did I, cos everyone else was... was grabbing stuff too.'

'Was this from the gift shop?' asked Mrs Hughes-Howard.

Florian was almost looking tearful now. 'I don't

know, I just... There was this charity box by the till. I left some money in there.'

'Did you? That's nice,' said Dr Ngo.

'Yeah, 50 Egyptian pounds. That's like...'

'That's about a fiver. Well I suppose it's a start,' said Dr Ngo.

'Was that wrong?'

'Florian...' began Dr Ngo. Suddenly, words seemed to fail him. He went very pale, sank to his knees and, for a moment, buried his head behind his hands. Then he reached forward and, deliberately but with great care, removed the statuette from Florian's unresisting hands and put it back inside the plastic bag. 'I don't think this is from the gift shop,' he said in a low voice.

'I was beginning to wonder myself,' said Mrs Hughes-Howard.

Dr Ngo stood up. 'Florian,' he said, holding the bag out in front of him as if it were about to explode. 'This is not good.'

An hour later, the three teachers emerged from a crisis meeting held in an area marked "Privates Dining Room". From the window, the Red Sea was full of happy swimmers, but the mood among the staff members of Rydon Hall was anything but carefree. Dr Ngo had taken to the internet and established, with reasonable certainty based on a further cross-examination with their teenage tomb-raider, that they had boarded a tourist coach outside their hotel and driven the long route from Cairo to the Red Sea - the passengers watching a double-bill of *Romancing the Stone* and *The Jewel of the Nile*, while occasionally sipping from water bottles, listening to their personal stereo systems or munching on crisps – with, tucked inside Florian's backpack, the obsidian head of a falcon, made of beaten gold, from the temple at Helikonopolis, one of the predynastic capital cities of Upper Egypt, lovingly crafted 2,300 years before the birth of Christ, its height just under 12 centimetres, and discovered by the great Egyptologist Sir Flanders

Petrie in 1897. From its resting place in cabinet J.E. 35128 on the ground floor of the Egyptian Museum in Cairo, it had now been relocated to room 14 on the first floor of the Blue Turtle Leisure Hotel, Hurghada which had been rated at three stars ("Has its own internet café but the corridors are noisy and don't go there for the food") on an Egypt online travel forum.

Mrs Hughes-Howard broke the silence. 'I mean, what an absolute honking great first-class cock-up. That boy should be locked up. Well, I mean...'

'He probably will be, now,' said Dr Ngo.

The two men whom Dr Ngo had spotted earlier had been joined by a few more, from which the teachers drew the unwelcome conclusion that they were under observation. These men must be recovery agents from the museum, their task to round up lost or stolen objects, but Mrs Hughes-Howard had given them a most glacial smile, and they had approached no further. Upon further interrogation, Florian had denied absolutely that he had mentioned his Egyptian Museum souvenir to Dylan, Yedverd or any other of his friends, but as, shortly after, he had been found trying to stuff a pillow down the throat of Adrian Purvis, this had provided a convenient premise to isolate him in his room.

The other boys were allowed to wander around the hotel but given strict orders not to leave the grounds or talk to anyone they did not know. The teachers checked all the news sites: one of the breaking stories was indeed that various artefacts had been stolen from Egypt's – possible the world's – most famous museum. So far, though, there was no evidence to incriminate a Year Eight boy from Rydon Hall.

'So we've been cavorting around this country for a whole day with one of the world's great antiquities in a 13-year-old's rucksack,' said Mrs Hughes-Howard. 'I mean, it's unbelievable. I don't believe it.'

'I should have known,' said Charles. 'If only I'd asked to see inside his backpack.'

'Oh, don't blame yourself, Charles,' said Mrs Hughes-Howard, though from the expression on her face she didn't seem too far from doing just that.

Behind them, the television was broadcasting more images of the ever more violent commotion sweeping Cairo. Every time Tahrir Square came into view, they all shuddered.

'We'll contact the museum,' said Mrs Hughes-Howard, 'and arrange for them to transport this... this piece back to Cairo.'

'Perhaps if we tell them it just turned up in our bags one morning they'll say, "Oh thanks very much, have a free Tutankhamen key-ring",' said Dr Ngo.

'But if Cairo isn't safe...' said Charles.

'You're saying it might be safer here, with us?' said Dr Ngo. 'A sort of mobile Elgin Marbles?'

'Well, you never know...'

'I mean, who would suspect a bunch of innocent English school kids?'

'Innocent?' Mrs Hughes-Howard snorted, needlessly underlining, as she often did, Dr Ngo's sarcasm. 'Florian?'

With Churley's very own Howard Carter confined to his room and Dr Ngo patrolling the corridor, Mrs Hughes-Howard and Charles led the rest of the tour party down to the aptly named Seagull Beach. The town seemed to have been built, or adapted, into a pleasure ground for wandering Russians, who stomped grimly from one source of amusement to another, sunglasses clamped to their reddening necks.

Mrs Hughes-Howard led the group towards a ritzy little shopping arcade. 'Retail therapy,' she said breathlessly. Everywhere offered opportunities to buy desert perfumes, papyrus rolls – "Oldest paper in world", as all the clamorous salespeople promised – and elaborate smoking apparatuses.

After only a few minutes scudding in the languid

waters of Hurghada, Charles got out and started patting himself dry. The water was lovely, and the change of scene should have done them good, but Charles seemed to see museum recovery agents behind every tree, table and car. He went up to Mrs Hughes-Howard, who was guarding the clothes on the beach and drinking tea from a paper cup with the logo "Pyramid Selling".

'I'm going back,' he said. 'I can't get that falcon out of my head.'

'So long as it stays in your room, dear,' she said. 'That's the main thing.'

It was hot, but Charles almost ran back to the hotel. Everywhere he looked, he saw cheap imitations of birds' heads, and men in sunglasses staring at him.

'Please, sir, you want souvenir?' said one man. 'We have many. Very old.'

'Thanks,' said Charles. 'We already have one.'

When he reached the hotel, the men were still there, but they didn't try to approach him. Perhaps one reason was that Colin Ngo was sitting in a hammock on the hotel forecourt, wearing a truly garish pair of crocodile swimming trunks.

'You're back early,' he said.

'I came to help you,' said Charles. 'I thought you might be under attack from those...'

'No, they're just drinking tea,' he said. 'Same as me.'

'Had any brilliant ideas about what to do with a priceless wooden falcon?'

'Nothing apart from *eBay*,' said Dr Ngo. 'But if you want to take over for a bit, I'll go and find Joy and the boys. Do you want to go and check up on the captive?'

Florian was sitting in his room. The curtains were drawn, the light was off, and he was flicking at TV channels

'What are you doing?' asked Charles, switching the light on.

'Nothing,' he said. 'There's nothing to do, is there?'

'Why not?'

'You've got my phone.'

Charles did not even try to keep the loathing out of his voice. 'Just stay there,' he said, trying to keep his voice as low as Colin Ngo's. 'And think about what you can do to make it up to the group.'

Charles closed the door and walked back to the hotel's terrace bar. His legs felt very heavy. He took his copy of Caesar's *Gallic Wars* and sat on the hammock where Dr Ngo had been. He started reading about Vercingetorix's attempts to resist Caesar, but he suddenly felt Mrs Hughes-Howard dabbing at his shoulder. He glanced up. The book lay face down in his lap.

'Hello Snoozy,' she said.

'I, er...'

'Adrian was feeling the sun so we came back early,' she said. 'Poor boy, he has very sensitive skin.'

Charles was about to claim, without knowing for sure, that Florian was fine, but a whoop from the first floor had them all dashing inside. Florian was still in his room. However, what didn't bode well was the jubilant look on his face.

'Hey guys!' he said, knuckle-clipping Roley, Tyler and Cato as they trouped in. 'I've had an amazing afternoon. You won't believe this.'

Charles felt sure that they might not, but he wanted to be the first to know.

'We have the trip of a lifetime lined up. And it's all for free!' Florian pointed to the two men who had been loitering in reception, who were now standing in the hotel garden. They waved back merrily.

'We told you not to leave the hotel,' said Mrs Hughes-Howard.

'Miss, I never did. I stayed right here. They rang me on the, you know, the landline!'

The men were wearing long black trousers and

sleeveless shirts. They looked shifty, but maybe museum recovery agents had to blend in with whichever group they were tracking.

'They're called Id and Moo,' said Florian. 'They, like, run this travel company?'

'Why were you speaking to strangers?' said Charles but he was out-shouted by Dylan.

'Where do they wanna take us?'

'Man, guess what: free trip! Free food and drink!' said Florian.

'When you say free, Florian...' began Mrs Hughes-Howard.

'I mean...' said Florian. 'It's on me. I talked to them and I told them what a hard time we'd been having...'

'You didn't mention...'

'Course not,' said Florian sharply to Charles.

Perhaps these gentlemen had some time on their hands, Charles speculated. Maybe, given the country's current paroxysms, some of their clients had dropped out.

'And,' said Florian with a grandiloquent flourish, 'it's on me, it's my treat.' He was obviously feeling guilty for leaving his passport at the museum and keeping everyone waiting while Cairo was in such a tumult but his age, temperament, gender, personality – everything about him, in fact – prevented him apologising. Maybe he had even heeded Charles' exhortation to do something positive.

'And what are they offering?'

'Well,' said Florian, 'we pick up the rest of the programme tomorrow, right? So just this afternoon, they're going to take us all for a drive to this, like, mountain near Hurghada? It's called, like, Mons or something. Is that..?'

'That's "mountain" in Latin,' said Charles, feeling a surge of interest. 'I hadn't intended to get into third declension nouns on this trip but, there you go, you just can't keep those Romans out of the picture, can you?'

'Yeah,' said Florian. 'And I checked it with the hotel, and it's totally cool. We'll get there late afternoon when all the crowds have gone, and we can just stroll around. How about it, guys?'

The ruin that Florian was referring to turned out to be Mons Porphyrites, an ancient quarry about 70 kilometres from Hurghada. The two men drifted over and, smiling broadly, shared their plans with the teachers. They didn't seem nearly as suspicious now. On consulting a local guide book, it was explained in better English than the men were capable of that the site had been much in favour with Rome's imperial families as a source of a white and purple crystallite stone that was used in sarcophagi, temples, and other decorative constructions.

At other times, Charles would have discarded this sort of information as suitable only for Classical Civilisation malingerers but out here, it felt topical and exciting.

Mrs Hughes-Howard tried to issue a cautionary note. 'Our Red Sea programme starts tomorrow, you know. We don't have to do this now.'

'Yeah, Miss, but this is free,' said Florian. 'And he'll take us to all the best places along the way. And we're kind of bored.'

At the sound of the dreaded B-word, all three teachers became a little uneasy. Florian and the others were sent away, and the discussion continued. There was no denying that this was a generous offer. Free food and drink were promised, and the whole package had the comforting stamp of the Egyptian Tourism Ministry, which was surely too established a body to be swept away by the political ephemera of events in Tahrir Square.

After a brief but guttural grilling by the men on the hotel Reception desk, they were pronounced proficient and some basic amenity bags, consisting of water, sun cream and jackets, were loaded onto the large bus that, with surprising efficiency, appeared almost immediately. And Florian, king of all he surveyed, appeared, imperious and unapologetic, at the head of the caravan.

Id and Moo sat on their own at the front of the coach. They were both short, and both thin, but one – Moo, Charles thought, though in the end it hardly mattered – was slightly shorter than the other. Their skin was very dark and hair tightly scrolled; perhaps from being born further south into Africa, Charles thought. He sat near them and tried to make pleasant conversation, but the engine was extremely noisy, and their English was functional but pedestrian. Eventually he gave up and sat on his own, looking out of the window at the distant coastline until the bus turned inland and the land began to get more bumpy.

After about 30 minutes, during which Charles had seen no other vehicles, the engine appeared to suffer a coughing fit and then cut out. The stretch of road which they were on was deserted, but the air conditioning still rattled and there was plenty of time left in the day so nobody was too concerned. Most drivers in this country seemed to be able to whip an engine into life with their bare fingers and several lengths of cat-gut, so they didn't imagine they'd be waiting too long.

Charles was despatched to the back of the bus by Mrs Hughes-Howard with instructions to organise some on-board entertainment. Florian, in no way abashed at the setback to his grand plan, suggested they sing a song.

'Good idea, Florian. What'll it be?' said Mrs Hughes-Howard. 'Something to cheer us all up?'

Florian, unapologetic as ever, started to sing. 'The wheels on the trip have come right off, come right off, come right off, the wheels...'

'Thank you Florian, that's enough of your wit for now,' said Mrs Hughes-Howard.

Half an hour later, the engine was still only making a feeble burping noise. Id and Moo were sitting by the roadside, sharing a cigarette, while the driver wiped his hands with a cloth, scratched his head, and let out the odd curse. The sun was starting to sink but the boys were still hiding inside the coach.

'I'm not sure if my AA Roadside Assistance stretches this far,' said Mrs Hughes-Howard, who was standing outside with the other two teachers, all of them trying not to worry about this delay. Then, from far away on the horizon, came the throaty wheeze of an approaching vehicle.

'Moo said they could fix it themselves but I was beginning to wonder,' said Dr Ngo.

The bus, which looked much bigger than theirs, was flashing its lights at them and was obviously going to stop. 'It's marvellous how other drivers come to one's aid, isn't it?' said Charles. 'There's such a sense of community out here.'

'A bit like school teachers,' said Mrs Hughes-Howard. 'Always drifting over to see what the problem is.'

'Or sharks,' said Dr Ngo, straining his eyes towards the bus.

'Yes,' said Charles, not sure how to take Dr Ngo's last remark. 'Should we tell the driver that help is at hand?'

'I think he's seen it,' said Mrs Hughes-Howard.

'Yes, he's working faster than ever,' said Dr Ngo.

'It was just the same when we broke down on the M3 coming back from Winchester,' said Mrs Hughes-Howard. 'Ivor just sat there at first: I think he was in shock. But as soon as we knew the RAC were coming he was under that bonnet with his sleeves rolled up.'

'He does seem to be working extra-hard,' said Charles.

'Almost urgently,' said Dr Ngo. His eyebrows had narrowed to a single V as the bus slowed down and stopped opposite them. It was empty of passengers. A man with even darker skin, and more tightly curled hair than Id's and Moo's got out of the driver's door and smiled at them. There were three other men with him. They were wearing black T-shirts, denim jackets and jeans.

'They don't look much like tour guides,' said Mrs Hughes-Howard.

'I don't think they're tour guides,' said Dr Ngo.

'Do you think they're from the museum?' asked Charles.

Dr Ngo gave him a forced smile. 'Do you really think so?'

'Please,' said one of the men, walking over to them without removing his shades. 'Here is bus. You come with us.'

The three teachers looked at each other. Charles was beginning to feel nervous.

'Sir, who are these men?' Arthur Clough, doubtless goaded by the rest of his classmates, was fixing them with one of his most appealing, and irritating, grins.

'We're just going to find out what's going on, Arthur,' said Dr Ngo. 'You get back on the bus now and we'll...'

'Yes, plizz,' said the man. 'You all get on ziss bus.'

There was something about the man's expression, which, unlike Id and Moo's near-constant smiles, discouraged resistance. Either it was getting hotter, or Charles was feeling nervous, but he could feel his palms sweating. There was a brief but tortured exchange of eyebrow semaphore between the three teachers, and then a gutting compliance.

'Plizz,' said the man. 'Is no problem. You get on the bus, we can to go.' Charles decided that this was not the time to explain to him the workings of the prolative infinitive. Taking a few boys with them at a time, the teachers got on the bus. The driver ground the gears, and within seconds they were moving off. But, to general astonishment, the bus commissioned by Id and Moo burst into life at the same time, and zoomed away in the other direction.

'What was wrong with our bus, sir?' asked Dylan.

Charles was going to answer that he didn't know either, but the man sitting beside him allowed his jacket to fall open and Charles saw, from the contents of his inner pocket, why further resistance was now unwise. A flicker of pure terror transmitted itself to his heart, stomach and buttocks. He looked to the side, where Mrs Hughes-Howard was sitting beside another man. She was looking nervous too.

'He's got a...' Charles tried to mouth the words to her. He couldn't see Dr Ngo, who was on the seat behind, but to judge from Joy's expression, she seemed to have seen the same thing he had.

'If this is about the falcon,' said Mrs Hughes-Howard, 'we can explain every...'

'Plizz,' said the man, placing his hand inside his jacket, which had her springing back in her seat.

Something about the looks on their teachers' faces must have affected the boys, because they stopped complaining that the bus wasn't as comfortable as the smaller one. Even Florian stopped claiming credit for the free trip.

Then, terrifyingly, the men began to work their way along the bus, tying the boys' hands with plastic tags, as if they were criminals. They did the same to the staff. A few cries of 'What's going on?' began, but then the gun that had been hiding in Charles' neighbour's pocket was made evident, and the man put his fingers to his lips for silence. The results were instantaneous. Charles had not heard Year Eight as silent as this since he had sat in on one of Mrs Hughes-Howard's lessons and watched in amazement as they all attempted a past paper without anyone whispering to anyone else. But there was something more eerie about this.

He knew how bad things were when he looked at Archie Neeples, and didn't find his name remotely funny. The trip had foundered disastrously and, although this was no time to point the finger – which he could still do, even though his hands were tied – it was all Florian Bavington's fault.

Charles stared at his bound hands for a few minutes and wondered what sort of men these might be. Was Joy right: were they vigilante curators? But the falcon was back at the hotel. Then again, they might be from the government, but trained to work in undercover ways. Well, he pondered, a country like this could not afford half-measures with the stewardship of its national treasures. His own tour party was in possession of stolen property and so the museum authorities had initiated a daring raid to return what was rightfully theirs. Fate had caught up with the boys – and teachers – of Rydon Hall.

'*Moira*,' said Charles to himself, invoking the Greek for "fate".

A man passed down the aisle of the bus. Short but wiry, with narrow, rectangular sunglasses, he was handing out bottles of mineral water. He gave Charles one, then sat down next to him. He didn't look like an obvious Egyptologist, but then who did? Try as he might, the only image Charles could come up with was Sophocles Sarcophagus from *Cigars of the Pharaoh*. This Egyptologist looked nothing like that Hergé character: no top hat, no umbrella. And now, he assumed, they were going to be driven somewhere to face whatever punishment Egyptian law had to impose. It seemed harsh that the men were armed, but this was the national museum of Egypt, and clearly there were a lot of very desperate people around. The man motioned to Charles to open the bottle.

'We are sorry, sir, about the... the falcon,' whispered Charles, dignified but remorseful. The Egyptologist looked bemused but did not reply. Charles decided to try again. 'Are you from the museum?' he asked in a low voice, taking a swig of his water. It tasted very sweet.

The Egyptologist said nothing. He was clearly still

very angry about the theft of the falcon, and why not? This man had probably been to the Egyptian Museum several times with his own children, taking the trouble to point out to them, with tears of national pride in his eyes, the falcon of Helikonopolis. And then some fool of a teenager – a foreign one at that – goes and snatches it, squirreling it away in his backpack along with sticky sweets and snotty tissues. No wonder he was angry.

'I am very sorry,' said Charles. He thought they seemed to be getting on quite well; at least, he hadn't been shot yet. He considered whether he could incriminate Florian sufficiently to exonerate the rest of the group, though obviously he didn't want Florian to be stuck in an Egyptian jail: Natasha would not be happy about that.

'Bad to take the falcon,' Charles said. 'Are we going to the hotel?'

The angry Egyptologist seemed not to understand, perhaps because he did not speak English. It must make attending international conferences very difficult, Charles thought. But then they probably had those headphones they could use. Or maybe he spoke German. The Germans were great archaeologists, after all.

Charles lowered his voice again. He didn't want to irritate him. 'You are from the museum? Yes?'

The man wobbled his head, as if he hadn't quite understood.

'The falcon.' Charles tried to stick out his elbows, which was all he could move, like a bird – more like a chicken – but the man gripped his arms and the look on his face changed. Suddenly he didn't seem to have a background in museum conservancy.

They drove on in silence for a few more minutes. The Egyptologist got out a packet of cigarettes and lit one. The smoke was shockingly acrid. Charles wobbled his head. Amazingly, the man offered him one.

'Thanks,' said Charles. He turned his head,

cigarette in mouth. Mrs Hughes-Howard looked horrified to see a teacher smoking, but he attempted by his expression to suggest that he wasn't inhaling; this was just a ruse to win the Egyptologist's trust.

Maybe they were going to drive straight to a museum warehouse along the way, where other treasures were housed, but as Charles asked the words, for the first time, he began to feel light-headed. He took another swig from the bottle. A few minutes later he felt even more light-headed. He looked around: one or two of the boys seemed to have fallen asleep too.

'Charles,' said Mrs Hughes-Howard. 'I think the water is...'

She didn't finish her sentence as another man had taken a gun out of his inside pocket. He motioned to her to finish the bottle which, with an expression of pure thunder, she did.

'Where are we going, sir?' Charles asked.

The man removed his cigarette from his mouth and looked at Charles, so he repeated the question. In response, the man put his face so close to him that Charles could smell the tobacco on his breath, and saw an impressively clean expanse of uneven white teeth. Feeling a curious mix of panic and sleepiness, Charles began to change his mind about the man's profession.

'Where... we... going?' The man, who Charles now realised was almost certainly not an Egyptologist, repeated the question, word for word.

'I was just wondering,' said Charles, his drugged lips barely able to form the words. 'Would you tell me?'

'We go to... Democratic... Republic... of... Smilia,' he whispered, pronouncing the name as "Smilier".

They came to a junction, the engine revved up, and the bus shot off, heading south, in the opposite direction from the Blue Turtle Hotel.

PART THREE

CHAPTER 8

The bus journey into captivity consisted of endless potholed roads and occasional road signs in Arabic, which none of them could read. The only available drink was doped mineral water, which sent the lucky ones back to sleep. There was no pretence about this from their captors, nor any choice, so the days collapsed one into the other. If there were border posts, they were either unmanned, or the guards had received instructions – or money – to let them through. The kidnappers had been merciful in one respect, by not going to the trouble of strapping all 20 students' mouths with masking tape, although they had at various points been required to slip cotton masks over their heads, so that they could not see where they were – not that they knew anyway. This of course terrified them all and, worse still, left them to their own private thoughts. No one was allowed to talk, and the guards were spaced between them so that, by and large, no one did. The only concession was that the bus had a WC, or at any rate it had a doorless booth with a hole in the floor, so bladders, and even bowels, could be drained when absolutely necessary. This was obviously a particular relief for Adrian Purvis.

It was on the third night after their removal from Hurghada that they found themselves in mountain territory. The air felt thinner and a little cooler. They drove up through a narrow, twisting ravine, until the engine came to a complete halt and a man clutching a fearsome-looking rifle pulled the door of the bus open. One of Charles' few coherent thoughts was that kidnapping people might be like the old teachers' maxim about not smiling until Christmas. They might go in hard, in other words, to create a mood of fear, but loosen up later. For now, though, no one in the tour party knew where they stood, and that was doubly terrifying.

They were standing in front of what looked like a vertical slab of rock. The welcoming party, dressed in scuffed, western clothes, all held guns. Many of them looked about the same age as the teenagers they were guarding. Rufus Coe-Haine tugged at Charles' sleeve.

'They've all got Kalashnikovs, sir,' he whispered.

Charles nodded.

'The AK-47 isn't as accurate as the M-16 but it's a lot more reliable. I've got a picture of one on the desktop of my P.C...'

'That's enough, Rufus, thanks,' said Charles, firmly but quietly. He could hear several boys crying from nerves or exhaustion. With his hands still tied, he turned his head very slowly. A dim light seeped through a square hole in the rock face. It was a window, set into a metal door. The door swung open. After a little prodding from the nozzle of a rifle, Dr Ngo went in first, followed by the crocodile of grizzling Year Eights. Charles was left to bring up the rear. He wanted to tell someone holding a gun that he had suffered from a life-long fear of being locked inside a cave, but he didn't feel that he had caught them in a listening mood. And making a run for it was clearly suicidal. Whether or not that was the more sensible option remained to be seen, but all the others were moving forward and so, it seemed, must he. They entered the cave and the door closed with a sickly metallic squeak.

The cave was pretty large, to judge from the echo of sobs bouncing off the walls. Illumination was provided by a necklace of low-watt lightbulbs, hanging above them. There were a few straw mats on the ground, and several buckets dotted about. A moment later, the door was opened again, and all their bags were thrown into the room, as if unloading the minibus at the fields on a games day. Then the door opened a third time and some plates with a kind of pancake were brought in.

'OK, sit,' said a boy with a gun. He wore torn-off jeans and a tattered vest, enlivened with a picture of a Kung Fu warrior. The whole class sat down on the bare earth. The air was cold, and the light was grainy.

'This, bread,' said the boy. '*Anjara*. Bread.' He put some in his mouth and began to chew. 'Good.' He smiled, and gave it the thumbs-up. Then he twisted a corner, and threw it to Dr Ngo who, despite his hands being tied, caught it in his lap then brought it up to his mouth. The boys waited. Cautiously, Dr Ngo's jaws began to move. The guard-boy took some more handfuls and threw them to the seated boys, as if it were catching practice. After a few seconds, as tufts of anjara bread flew through the air, a sound could be heard. Someone was making a performing-seal noise.

'Was that you, Florian?' asked Mrs Hughes-Howard softly.

'Yes, Miss.'

'I'd keep your animal impressions to yourself for now, if I were you.'

'Sorry Miss.'

The guard smiled. 'Good?' he pointed to the bread.

'Very good,' said Charles, convinced that flattery could save them all. He hadn't even had a chance to discuss their possible location with his two colleagues. 'Thank you. *Shukran*, er...'

'Excuse me but where are we?' asked Dr Ngo.

'I think I know,' Charles began, but Dr Ngo ignore him and repeated the question.

'Welcome to my country,' said the boy. He had a wide open stare, and he was not smiling.

'But where are we?' asked the teacher.

'Smilia!' said the boy, flashing some large and unevenly spaced teeth.

Smilia! Silence. Uproar.

The realisation that they were being held in Smilia, a country widely regarded as the most unstable, violent, lawless, volatile country in the whole of continental Africa, if not the world, inevitably came as something of a blow. Charles, together with Dr Ngo and Mrs Hughes-Howard, had seen, heard and read about the desperate situation in which the country had been languishing for decades. Pooling their resources, they established that they were in a region which, for at least three decades, had had no recognised central government, no national currency, no army, no police force beyond the mob rule of local fiefdoms, no functional national legal system, no centralised transport structure, no industrial centre that was safe from clan-based gun or mortar attack, no healthcare system, and no nationwide educational system. No feature, in other words, that could be applied to a normal country. What authority there was lay with smaller semi-autonomous states and rival warlords, one of whom, they presumed, was responsible for their current plight. They had heard, read or seen that these warlords were brutal, gun-toting buccaneers whose supporters, eyelids bolted open with drowse-resistant drugs or loaded up on the unnatural high of imminent death and the misleading reassurance of fire-arms, would as soon shoot someone dead as stop them for a bribe.

It was into this hell-hole that the 2011 Post-Mocks trip to Egypt, undertaken by Year Eight of Rydon Hall, and organised with unstinting detail (and a near-perfect safety record for the last six years) by Mrs Hughes-Howard and Dr Ngo, had unwittingly stumbled.

Had their view through the frosted glass window been coastal, they would probably have seen a steady stream of oil tankers or private yachts being boarded and then towed away by hooded Smili pirates. Charles assumed there must be dozens, hundreds, of kidnap gangs jostling for space, each with its own piratical bolthole. Doubtless all the other gangs knew about the latest arrivals too: He and his fellow teachers, in one of their whispered late-night conferences, muttered that they didn't know if they had more to fear from their own captors, or from being harmed in the crossfire as a rival gang attempted to re-kidnap them.

Whatever happened, it put the school's major holiday trauma to date – Oliver McKember succumbing to a nasty bout of diarrhoea on the coach to Luxor four years earlier – very much in the shade.

After a few days of unbearable tension, the teachers came to the conclusion that their captors' motives had nothing to do with the falcon of Helikonopolis. They were being held in a grotto, and they didn't know why. The straw matting had increased, they were given sheets to lie on at night, and a bucket to wash in when they awoke, but that didn't do justice to how basic their living standards were. It was cold in the cave, they were frightened, and everyone was hungry. It was not long before Cato Wang began to obsess about food, and to stare at Rufus Coe-Haine with such appetite that the poor boy looked even more like a frightened sheep than he did normally. The food compared poorly even with Dorotea's lunchtime efforts back in Churley, and scarcity – some days they ate virtually nothing – did little to enhance its flavour. In appearance it usually suggested a potage of maize, with occasionally banana, mango or grapefruit segments thrown in, but it was an alienating experience, producing many trips to the buckets, which should have been private. Mrs Hughes-Howard and Dr Ngo's First Aid skills were called on many times a day. The cave interior was either chilly or stuffy and hot, but it wasn't always easy to tell if the fetid odour came from their conditions, or from Adrian Purvis' sweat glands.

Adrian, in a wheedling voice, drawing barely any sympathy from his teachers, voiced loud concerns that his allergies would not be taken into account by their captors, but there seemed little chance that the cook, whoever and wherever he was, would sneak a pinch of sesame – let alone peanut butter – into their dishes.

The boys had to learn a new routine, trying to adapt to their confinement. For example, when the door was flung open, it had been made clear to them that they must all sit on the floor cross-legged with their heads down. The first few times, they had scurried to adopt the right position, their faces tight with fear. But, after a couple of days, this too became just another wearisome and reluctant gesture of deference, and Charles was pleased to see that they obeyed this edict as half-heartedly as when standing to greet each teacher's entrance between lessons in Churley.

The nights were awful. Mrs Hughes-Howard's shoulders were sore from rubbing the backs of sobbing boys. Charles and Colin – Charles was still not that comfortable referring to Dr Ngo by his first name – were, by nature or in deference to the school handbook, more restrained in their physical gestures, but they had done their best to calm the pupils' nerves, while feeling exactly the same way as their charges. The screech of a nocturnal beast testing its vocal strength in the hills outside was often matched by displays of emotion from the boys as they gave in to their fears and simply cried themselves to sleep. Charles once overheard Mrs Hughes-Howard, mid-slumber, murmur tenderly, 'Oh no, Ivor...' to herself, somewhere between a sob and a sniffle.

The three teachers took it in turns, torch in hand, to patrol the back of the cave while everyone else slept (or tried to), in case a snake might suddenly appear, but so far it was mainly spiders, and they kept to their own side of the cavern. Charles didn't mind admitting to his colleagues that there were times when he could have done with some nocturnal comforting too: he wasn't sure if he spoke in his sleep, but if he did, he hoped that the name "Natasha" didn't slip out.

The teachers were bombarded with questions all day. Would they be rescued? Had a ransom been demanded? Did the school know where they were? Was the SAS coming to save them? Would they be killed? Shot? Tortured? Starved? Beaten? All these questions met the same cheery reply that there was nothing to worry about, and that everything possible was being done to negotiate their release. Charles tried to look positive, but he was sure that his face looked as terrified as he felt.

By about the fourth or fifth day, hopes had begun to fade that there would be a knock on the door to reveal a smartly-dressed British consular official, apologetically explaining that the whole thing had been a terrible mistake, and asking them if they wouldn't mind boarding the air-conditioned bus parked around the corner. A new reality set in.

Mrs Hughes-Howard told the boys that she wanted them to treat this experience as if they had all got into a rather unusual boarding school – similar in some ways to those that many of them were applying to – and that they must simply buckle down to this new regime.

Despite their night-time terrors, and apart from the general withdrawal of freedom, no one had been mistreated. The guards, who all wore the same style of tatty jeans and ripped T-shirts, spoke very little English, but they didn't seem eager to exact physical punishment on any of their captives. The knock on the door to produce the night-time bucket came at about seven, and it was usually accompanied by a polite 'G'mahning' and even a half-smile, as if acknowledging that nothing personal was intended, and that the Rydon Hall party were merely innocent players in a larger conflict. Mrs Hughes-Howard had tried asking if they wouldn't mind swapping the duvet covers, or re-stocking the mini-bar, but this hazy attempt at cross-national humour fell away within two or three days. The guards never let it be forgotten that they were armed, and none of the school party behaved as if it had slipped their minds.

Leaving aside the fact that the cave had not been fashioned by Nature with teaching in mind, it was amazing how effective lessons could be crafted from the least promising materials. Since writing tools were not provided, at first it was Dr Ngo who had been charged with producing these. His negotiating tactics – drumming on the locked door and shouting, 'You are in breach of the United Nations Convention on Human Rights!' – generated little except a physical rebuke from one of the guards, who strode in and slapped the outspoken I.T. teacher on the face, leaving him white-faced and speechless for several minutes. Mrs Hughes-Howard tried an alternative approach, speaking in slow, simple English mixed with methodical French and skeletal Italian. (The teachers were still struggling to piece together the complex strands of Smilia's colonial legacy.) She had gambled that she might one day catch someone in a softer mood, and it worked. On the third day, a quantity of coarse paper and some blunt pencils appeared.

In a bid to raise morale, the teachers decided that the boys should stand and sing the school song every morning before their anjara breakfast. The anthem, *Rydon Hall, Rydon Hall,* had been composed in that burst of emotion-drenched patriotism which led into the First World War.

"Rydon Hall..." rang out the first phrase, the first two words taking up the best part of two bars. As if the matter were in any doubt, the verse continued, "Rydon Hall..." Then the poet, who went on to win second place in a 1917 national poetry competition, took up his theme in the second line:

"Born to pride so lightly worn, never were we bound to fall.
Holding hard upon the field, R.H. boys will never yield.
Ends the day or fades the term? Rydon boys are standing firm."

The second verse was packed with equal dollops of sentiment.

"Ry-y-y-y-don Hall, Ry-y-y-y-don Hall,
Youthful shapes are ours today, growth to manhood far away,
Yet in time we know that we, will achieve maturity,
Till that time comes, hear our cry, hearts extended to the sky."

There was a third verse, but that had not been sung for some years. The anthem, with its maverick rhymes, barefaced jingoism and preference for sporting heroics over academic pursuits, ended with a further blast of "Ry-y-y-y-don Hall!"

It was one of those experiences which, though mocked in freedom, became emblematic in captivity, and Mrs Hughes-Howard, who was used to hearing it sung on speech day, rarely completed the second verse without dabbing at the corners of her eyes with her hankie. Charles earnestly wished – prayed, even - that he would be able to hear it sung *in situ*.

The teachers had agreed – or rather, Charles had agreed with Dr Ngo and Mrs Hughes-Howard – that they stood a better chance of retaining their sanity if they tried to impose a routine on the day. For that reason, the school timetable was followed, to a larger or smaller degree. Half-hour lessons were carved out of what would otherwise have been an empty period of festering apprehension, the uncertainty heightened by shouts from outside in a click-clacking tongue. The chalk scraps which the guards tossed into the room looked as if they had once been used to roughen pool or snooker cues, and seemed to hark back to an era of serenity that few of Smilia's population could even remember. A stretch of rock had been declared dry enough to serve as a writing surface for the teachers. It was far from perfect, of course, but Charles felt that he had made the easiest transition to a life without electronic wizardry, simply because he had almost never relied on it before.

'We used to laugh at your lollipop sticks, Charles,' said Mrs Hughes-Howard one day. 'If only I'd known: I'd have brought some of my own.'

Unwelcome and unbearable though it was, confinement presented Charles with his best opportunity yet to focus his captive audience's minds on the Common Entrance Latin syllabus to which few had, so far, shown much application. Charles was grateful that he still had his Loeb Latin-English edition of Caesar's *Gallic Wars*. He could never quite get to the end of it, but just feeling it inside his jacket pocket gave him a comforting connection with home, and he knew that the boys who had brought books with them felt the same way. On the other hand, he didn't at all miss the school's own Latin textbook, the garishly illustrated and (in tone) over-familiar *Now That's What I Call Latin!* which Geoff Norringham, in one of his occasional emails, had assured him, correctly, he would come to hate.

Given that the Romans were such authorities on attacking, capturing and guarding, there seemed little reason to avoid those topics merely because they themselves had been attacked and captured and were now being guarded. He encouraged the boys to translate words like "terrify", "punish", or even – yes, why not? – "kill", thus fleshing out the outlines of conjugations two, four and three. Emboldened, Charles encouraged them to enact the scene from book nine of the *Odyssey* in which the wily Odysseus outwits Polyphemus, the huge but mono-focal Cyclops. Although this was, as Charles acknowledged, 'Classical Civilisation by any other name', there was now an obvious reason for them 'to do something as stupid as this'. So when Cato Wang stomped around the cave, looking to devour more of Odysseus' men, Rufus Coe-Haine really did have the look of an about-to-be-eaten prisoner as he emerged, blinking, from a dark corner. In another surprise, it was Adrian Purvis who had a brave stab at the role of Odysseus. Even when it later emerged that he had been under the impression that Odysseus was the giant and Polyphemus the Greek warrior, Charles did not assign blame. Being stuck in a cave, they would have time to iron out such misunderstandings.

Of course, their enforced detention was, in other ways, not ideal for teaching Latin. In a normal school year it would not have been until the Summer term before even the top set could contemplate the Olympian heights of constructions like "We *have been* captured *for* four months." Here Charles struggled to master his emotions as he contemplated the possibility that he might still be there, grafting away at the perfect passive or expressions of time, four months down the line.

The teachers made valiant efforts to teach subjects not their own. Dr Ngo had been on a lot of camping holidays, and so knew several geographical terms. Mrs Hughes-Howard, on the other hand, proved unexpectedly proficient at spoken French. ('Ivor and I used to love taking the caravan down to the south of France,' she said, stifling a sob.) And Charles dredged up what he could remember of the Crusades, Henry VIII's "Great Matter" and the Great Fire of London, and dealt as graciously as he could with Roley Yousuf and Cato Wang's frequent corrections. All three teachers had a go at Religious Studies, but there was precious little agreement on what one was meant to do in a Gurdwara, or what Siddhartha's quest was, or what "The message of Islam" – a syllabus topic, they were assured – really was.

Another unexpectedly positive by-product of being locked in together was that Charles could act on Ms de Souza's suggestion of watching his colleagues in action. He particularly admired Mrs Hughes-Howard. Even here, and under such duress, her organisation was faultless. He noted how meticulously she prepared each lesson while the boys were getting changed, or washed, bumping into each other in the morning's half-light. Her sense of discipline never left her. At the very moment that she was making them solve linear equations with whole-number coefficients, her eyes were scanning the room to detect the first hint of insurrection in any part of the cave. Somehow, a red ballpoint pen had remained lodged in one of Mrs Hughes-Howard's inner pockets, and this was passed from one staff member to another. Marked work was handed back, if anything, more efficiently than in Churley.

There were very few comforts. Occasionally a tatty undergarment was produced by one of the guards, which was pounced on by the teachers and then handed out to the boys in strictly alphabetical order. Toothbrushes were present in abundance, but there was some anxiety about when the toothpaste would dry up. Charles, in particular, was terrified of suffering a gum infection, knowing the likely distance of the nearest dentist – let alone the fact that he wouldn't be allowed out. This was Mrs Hughes-Howard's cue. She assured the others that she was "cultivating" one of the guards, and before long, several lengths of African chew-stick were delivered. Charles plied the twig between his teeth cautiously.

'You see, boys?' said Mrs Hughes-Howard, angling the bendy stick against her sharp incisors. 'This is how real Smili people live.'

'That's right,' said Dr Ngo. 'You couldn't buy an experience like this.'

After the first few days, the guards allowed groups of four boys at a time to venture outside for 15 minutes or so, watched by one teacher. It was like lunchtime playground supervision, except that they were also guarded by a teenager with an AK-47. As soon as they were in the open air, they behaved much like any group of children in break-time: sliding about, knocking into each other, their chief concern to score a goal. As in Churley, Charles' presence was peripheral, merely there to remind them what they couldn't do, which was to kick the ball too far to be returned. Whenever possible, he allowed his eyes to travel away as far as the distant hills of a foreign land called Freedom. The clouds were high, and the rocky landscape a series of meditations in dark brown earth or rock. The guards didn't even mind when they took photographs on their phones, which had now been returned to them. Apart from the utter terror, it was strangely beautiful and, as far as the eye could see, totally uninhabited.

'Let Joy be unconfined,' Mrs Hughes-Howard muttered to herself. It sounded like a private joke between herself and Ivor, but Charles decided not to ask for an explanation.

The teachers took pains to point out that they should not blame the Smili people for their own sufferings. Mrs Hughes-Howard reminded them that they knew at least one person from that area.

'You know,' she said to Charles on the fourth or fifth day, 'there's that young chap who works in the kitchen. Manual, isn't that his name? Always smiling. I think he's from Enitenia or somewhere nearby. Always gives me an extra potato for lunch.'

'I think it's Emmanuel,' said Charles.

'That's what I said: Manual,' she said, raising her voice to address the boys. 'Because this country, let us not forget, has not had a functioning government for many years now. It is, essentially, lawless.' She folded her arms to emphasise the severity of the situation.

'It's like when Mr Scamage was sick and we didn't have a caretaker for the first week of term?' said a voice from the side. 'That was so rank.'

'In a way it is exactly like that, Duncan,' said Mrs Hughes-Howard. Later, to her two colleagues, she said, 'The key thing is not to let them see that we're scared.'

'But we *are* scared,' said Charles. 'I'm terrified.'

'Don't be silly, Charles,' said Mrs Hughes-Howard. 'Anyway, we've got something that they haven't got.'

'What's that?'

'Florian Bavington,' said Dr Ngo.

The teachers had to admit that the vast majority of boys had responded to this calamitous deprivation of freedom by finding an inner strength which verged on nobility. Rufus Coe-Haine and Mo Hegarty had buried their differences and no longer thumped each other whenever a teacher's back was turned. Harry Beamish had stopped humming in lessons, and Des Muireadhaigh had ceased to roll blu-tac into balls – though, in all honesty, this was only because there wasn't any blu-tac for him to fiddle with. But in the face of all this impressive progress, one boy remained as surly, apathetic and reticent as ever: Florian Bavington.

Even in a cavern of mud and rock, Florian was still the major irritant. Break times had been cut back to five minutes because Florian had repeatedly kicked the ball too far from the patch of scrubland where they were allowed to play. Meal times had been reduced from just under two a day to one because Florian had flicked a spoonful of soup, then more, and finally the whole bowlful, at Adrian Purvis, in alleged retaliation for an offence that he refused to reveal. The paper ration had been cut off for a day when Florian had "forgotten" to stand up when the teenage guards entered the cave one morning. In numerous little ways, Florian's selfishness had deprived them of the few liberties they still had.

Another was his attempt to appropriate the entire hostage process as if it had been organised with the sole purpose of discomfiting Florian Bavington. Thus, if he were being accused of handing in a completely inadequate piece of work, his eyes would well up with tears and he would say, 'I'm sorry, sir. It's really difficult, because I'm, like, a prisoner?'

And if the teachers dismissed such self-centredness, he would add, 'But it's worse for me cos my parents are, like, divorced..?'

And if any teacher told him to think of others for once, not just himself, he would throw in the fact that he was finding it hard to concentrate, 'Because I have to sit next to Adrian Purvis? And he really, you know, smells bad?'

The persecution of Adrian was pathetic and childish but mostly harmless. On one occasion Charles almost admired Florian's quick thinking as Adrian was about to sit down, and Florian deployed a pencil directly below his buttocks so that Adrian almost spiked himself on its tip. All the others laughed, and Charles allowed himself a grin until he saw his colleagues' stony faces and realised that this was malicious and spiteful. But what disciplinary measures could the teachers impose, being prisoners themselves? A firm talking-to, and an extended stand-up at the back of the cave facing the rock were as much as they could do. In a way, the relentless campaign against Adrian almost made Charles feel nostalgic, as if some things had never changed. But Adrian's persecuted face reminded him that Florian was conducting psychological torture, in a most cowardly fashion.

Charles had tried to descend to Florian's level. Once, when an extra roll of blank paper appeared, Charles decided to try and engage their creative side.

'OK boys,' he said with wary enthusiasm. 'This is a bit of a Classical Civilisation question, I suppose, but let's give it a go.'

'Sir, I thought you said you hated Classical Civilisation?' asked a voice at the back.

'I do, Dylan, I do. Even out here, stranded as we are halfway up this mountain, I still think Classical Civilisation is a subject that only the truly dim-witted ever study. Not that this relates to you in any way,' he added quickly, then paused. Sometimes, the only subject on which he felt he could really extemporise was the sheer inadequacy of Classical Civilisation. 'So just for fun, and to show what a silly subject it is, I'd like you to draw a scene from the Colosseum of Rome, in which a gladiator does battle with a lion.'

The boys set to, and for several minutes there was the satisfactory noise of stubby pencils scraping against cardboard-like paper. But then Charles stopped behind a mess of spiral blobs and nothing else.

'And what on earth is this apology for a drawing, Florian?' asked Charles, staring balefully at the work.

'You see, sir, the lion won,' said Florian.

Ten days had gone by. Charles, judging the moment as carefully as he could, decided that the moment had come to reintroduce adjectives, and even adjectival comparison for the brighter ones. This, he felt sure, would allow them to express their emotions more freely, since they might appreciate being able to describe themselves as "frightened" or "brave". So far that morning, the lesson had been proceeding relatively normally. The main set were now comparing *laetus* (happy) with *miser* (wretched) and Charles was beginning to think that his teaching skills had been sharpened by confinement, since he had been able, with relative ease, to transfer his attention to the minuscule top set in order to check that they remembered how to turn *laetus* into *laetior* (happier) and *laetissimus* (happiest). The fact that two 13-year-old armed guards stood outside the locked door was, for the moment, a secondary factor in their compliant behaviour.

'Right, gentlemen!' shouted Charles. He could hear a good deal of shouting outside, and a vehicle's brakes being applied. 'First sentence,' he said, remembering to stay with the lesson, no matter what else was happening. 'Fairly simple: "The boy is happy because the house is big."' He waited but, as usual, no one volunteered, so he wrote down the words needed to translate this short prose masterpiece. Slowly, he scratched the words "*puer, quod villa magna est, laetus est*" onto the wall, then took a step back as if to admire his efforts. 'Now then, see what I've done?'

One or two hands went up in response to this question, but they were saved from further confusion when the door was wrenched open with more vigour than usual, and a man whom they had never seen before appeared in the doorway. Nor had they seen anyone like him before. He was squatter than the two guards who stood with him, but he wore a canary-yellow tweed jacket, a faded check shirt and a striped tie, and he was holding what seemed to be a leather riding crop. He stood with his hands on his hips, tipped his head back, and let out a deep, rumbling laugh.

'Well, well, well,' he said in a strangely cadenced English accent. 'I appear to have interrupted the Latin lesson.'

CHAPTER 9

For a moment, Charles was unable to speak. The stranger clasped his hands together as if acknowledging the applause of a crowd. The teenage guards stood stiffly against the wall, looking galvanised by the appearance of what must be their leader. It was stuffy in the cave, and the draught of warm, late afternoon air suddenly made Charles gulp.

'You are the teacher, yes?' the man said, seizing Charles' hand and pumping it furiously. Charles had always felt that only a psychopath would choose to sport a gold tooth, but he immediately regretted this thought when the man smiled to reveal a glint in his front top-left incisor. He had smooth black skin and a small scar on the left cheek. His hair was short but tightly scrunched and he looked, thought Charles as he tried to realign his knuckles, around 30.

'I am sorry that I could not be here to welcome you,' the stranger said, in near-perfect, African-inflected English. 'Normally I make a point to greet my guests but I had to attend an incident, some way down the coast.' Charles looked at the boys, who were listening with great attention. 'Some common criminals. A very dull execution: nothing to make the blood race. But this is more interesting. Allow me to introduce myself. I have the honour to be your host during your stay in Smilia: Abdi Baadi, BA.'

Charles tried to smile back. 'We were... just looking at adjectives,' he said. 'Words like "happy"...'

'Ah!' shouted Mr Baadi. 'One of my favourite words. Now boys, hands up. Who is happy?' Not a single hand went up. 'Oh now, come come. Why so down in the mouth?'

'I'm happy, sir,' said a voice from the back. Charles thought his insides might be about to tumble out. It could only be Florian.

'One of our more feisty students,' said Charles with a hasty sign to Florian to keep his mouth shut.

'Yeah, really happy,' said Florian. 'We love it here, especially in the cave.' Even now, the giant, one-eyed sneer of sarcasm was his main method of communication.

Mr Baadi seemed impressed. He folded his arms – just as Charles had seen Mrs Hughes-Howard do. 'Ah, but you all know what the ancient Greeks said, don't you? "Call no man unhappy until he is dead." True, eh, gentlemen?'

Mrs Hughes-Howard got up and waved, a little stiltedly. 'And we have been learning all about your beautiful country, sir...'

Mr Baadi snorted. 'Not beautiful, madam. It has been torn apart by power-hungry warlords with big guns and small brains.' He turned and spat on the straw-covered floor. 'But I do not wish to cross words with a lady.' Mrs Hughes-Howard blushed, while also looking terrified.

Then the newcomer saw Dr Ngo.

'And you, sir, do you teach too or have you just come along to complain to my guards? Because from what I have heard...'

'I teach I.T.,' said Dr Ngo quietly, 'And I would have you know that you are in breach of...'

'Thank you, sir, you are a hero to the boys, I am sure,' said Mr Baadi, looking as if he were not of the same view. Dr Ngo, unused to this level of discourtesy, frowned.

'So what do these letters "I.T." stand for?' Baadi went on. 'Or is it E.T.: Easy to Teach? Ha!'

'Information Technology,' Dr Ngo retorted.

'Ah yes,' said Mr Baadi. 'Is that an actual school subject these days? Dear me. I know how important computers are, but really...' He suddenly looked at Charles. 'I am so sorry, I have not yet asked your name. How rude of me.'

'No, it's fine, absolutely fine,' said Charles. Then he realised that Mr Baadi wasn't just staring at him for the view. 'Charles, er, Goldforbes,' he said, wondering if he had just written the first line of his death certificate.

Mr Baadi smiled. 'Mr Goldfork the Latin teacher! Excellent. *Ave magister*, is that right?'

'Excellent, yes, very good, *ave*, er, yes,' Charles said, forced by terror into taking a fresh breath between each word.

'Now, Mr Goldfork, I dare say you and I would not regard "Computah Studies" as a serious subject, am I correct?' Mr Baadi beamed at him.

Charles and Mrs Hughes-Howard did their best to bridle at these charges, although similar views had been voiced, whether seriously or not, back in the comfort of the Rydon Hall staffroom. 'On the contrary...' they both tutted, but Mr Baadi waved their feeble protests away. 'I mean, whatever next after "Computah Studies": Advanced PlayStation Sciences or an A Level in Watching Television?'

He laughed uproariously at his own joke and Charles wondered whether it might extend his lifespan if he joined in.

'May we know for how long you intend to hold us?' asked Dr Ngo, as if interrogating a boy for talking during assembly.

'You may ask, but for organisational reasons I am unable to tell you,' said Mr Baadi. 'I hope you understand.'

'Well, I would prefer it if you would tell us,' said Dr Ngo, not even trying to take the hostility out of his voice.

By way of response, Mr Baadi reached out and yanked Dr Ngo's left ear so hard that the teacher gasped, as did the boys. 'And I would prefer it, sir, if you would stop asking such awkward questions, but unlike you I have the means at my disposal to stop you: for example by ordering my guards to slice this piece of flesh from the side of your head.'

'I... I am sure that Dr Ngo would not want you to go to all that trouble,' said Charles.

'I withdraw the question,' said a chastened Dr Ngo,

rubbing his ear.

'Apology accepted,' said Mr Baadi. This time he was not smiling. 'Sir, I hear you have been very persistent with your pleas about human rights. We will deal with you shortly.'

Dr Ngo was reduced to gawping like a goldfish. Charles was amazed to discover that Mr Baadi could make Dr Ngo seem a less formidable figure than he had ever appeared before.

'You speak English terribly well,' Charles began to say, deciding that sycophancy while under the heel of an oppressor was merely survival by another name.

Again he seemed to have hit the jackpot. 'You must have noticed that I went to a British university,' Mr Baadi declared, as if reciting from memory. Perhaps he had been waiting a long time for an excuse to reminisce. 'My father was an arms dealer, you know. Really, a very bad man, but he could afford to send me to your windy but picturesque island. I studied at the famous West Mercia University, sandwiched between historic Hereford and the cathedral city of Worcester. You have heard of it, I am sure.'

'Oh yes, of course,' said Charles.

'Have you?'

'Yes, well, mainly by reputation,' Charles added, nodding furiously.

'I learnt English there. I reinforce it by listening to the BBC World Service... when my computer connection allows, which sadly, at the moment...'

'Sir, will you be asking for a ransom?' asked Dr Ngo, as if trying to cut through all this small talk.

'Dear me, are you trying again?' said Mr Baadi.

'Dr Ngo is, er, a legendary figure in our school,' said Charles hastily. 'He has been taking school parties on tour for several years now and his concern for their wellbeing is paramount.'

'And is this his first time as a hostage? Not on the school skiing trip to Meribel? You surprise me,' said Mr Baadi in a cutting tone of voice. 'Well, you fall into my hands in conditions of great fortune, and now I must make the most of it, so if you will forgive me, I must interrupt the lesson for a few minutes...'

Perhaps because there had been nothing else to do that morning, there was a flutter of protest at this from the boys. Mr Baadi took a step back. 'Extraordinary: the pupils want the lesson to continue. You must be a very brilliant teacher: where did you study?'

'Well, er, Cambridge,' said Charles, who was as surprised as Mr Baadi at the boys' reaction, 'but, you know, not at one of the more impressive, er...'

Mr Baadi rolled his eyes. 'Oh, er, *so* sorry, *Cambridge, actually,* oh, dear me!' The impersonation sounded so like Charles that some of the boys started to laugh. Baadi smiled even more brilliantly. 'Well it is no surprise they enjoy the lessons: they are benefiting from an Oxford and Cambridge graduate. I enjoyed myself at West Mercia, but of course *any* Cambridge college is preferable to a provincial university, eh, Mr Goldfrap?'

'Well, no, of course not...' said Charles, immediately feeling all the liquid drain from his mouth. Perhaps this was where his luck ran out. He had had to deal with anti-Oxbridge resentment before, but never when his accuser was backed up by four armed guards. 'In fact, these days Oxford and Cambridge are as much a part of the Russell Group of British universities as, I don't know; Bristol, King's College London, possibly Leeds, er...'

Mr Baadi did not reply to this over-long protest. He held his hands behind his back and began to walk round the room. All eyes followed him. He stopped a few paces from where Florian, Dylan and Yedverd stood, hooked his thumbs inside his belt loops and rocked on the soles of his feet for a few moments.

'I hope you found the room acceptable, Mr Goldfobs BA Cantab or is it MA? I am sorry that we could not provide a lady to make your bed here, as you

110

were used to...'

'No, no, please, honestly, it's fine, I wasn't, really...'

'*Bedders*, weren't they?' Mr Baadi continued. Charles did not like the turn this conversation was taking. 'Do women go to Cambridge these days? Have they allowed the ladies in yet? Or are they still just used to clean the students' rooms?'

'Oh no, they're full members of the university these days, in every way, it's all very...'

'I was told that I should have got in, you see, but I had a terrible cold the day I sat the exam. My nose was streaming so badly I could hardly see the paper in front of me.'

Charles nodded sympathetically. There was always a simple explanation.

'But you must have been so happy, bumbling around on your bicycle. How nice to have King's College chapel within walking distance. Still, we had Worcester Cathedral, an hour away by bus.'

'I hardly ever went to King's,' Charles said, really struggling to speak. He was wondering if he was about to go down in history as the first ever Oxbridge-fuelled fatality, and whether the story of his demise would merit a small paragraph in *Cantab*, the magazine for Cambridge alumni.

'Excuse me, sir, what did you study at university?' The question came from one of the boys. Charles looked up. Adrian Purvis' hand was raised into the air.

'Ah yes, now I am glad you asked me that question,' said Mr Baadi and began to smile again. The mood in the room changed instantly. Charles looked at Adrian with amazement. Had Purvis done this for him? Did he really owe his salvation to the boy with the most pungent personal aroma in the school? 'I was lucky enough to study that prince of subjects, an undergraduate course that gave me a solid and lasting love of all the finer things in life: the academic discipline that covers politics, history, philosophy, archaeology, religion, mythology and so much more.'

He turned and stared at Charles. 'Well? Have you guessed?'

Charles trembled. 'I was going to say...'

'Classical Civilisation,' announced Mr Baadi.

'A wise choice,' said Charles, nodding sagely. 'Most wise.'

Florian's hand popped up. 'But sir, I swear you said that people who...'

'Excellent subject,' said Charles. 'Excellent.'

'Not now, Florian...' said Mrs Hughes-Howard, trying to remain calm but, as ever, Florian was not listening.

'People who studied Classical Civilisation were, like...'

'Florian, that will do,' said Dr Ngo in a rising tone.

'They were, like... dummies?'

'*Florian!*' said Charles.

The room filled with a shocked silence.

'But Miss, he said so,' said Florian.

'Aha! Did he?' exclaimed Mr Baadi. The room had frozen, as if midway through a game of Grandmother's Footsteps. 'Well, I shall be most interested to hear your views on Classical Civilisation, Mr Goldpap. In fact, I wonder if you would be so kind as to step outside with me?'

'Um, yes, of course,' said Charles. 'Is there anyone else..?'

'No, just you,' Mr Baadi called, 'If anyone needs us, we will be in the torture chamber.'

Mr Baadi snapped his feet together, turned on one heel, and left the cave. Charles knew he was meant to follow, but on hearing Mr Baadi's last words, he found that his legs seemed reluctant to move. He turned to Mrs Hughes-Howard.

'Did he say *torture chamber*?' he whispered.

'I think so,' she said, hardly able to look Charles in the face.

'Oh my God,' said Dr Ngo. His face, normally impenetrable, now looked openly scared. Charles was sorry that he had been pleased to see Dr Ngo have his ear tugged.

Mr Baadi's head appeared in the doorway. 'Come come, Mr Goldpork, please don't keep us waiting.' Charles was still unable to move his legs but it didn't matter because two of the burlier guards, as if used to this sort of behaviour, were alongside him in seconds to carry him across the floor. Every boy seemed to be staring at him, open-mouthed. Was this the last sight they would ever have of him? He wanted to utter an immortal phrase like, "It is a far, far better thing..." or, "Weep not." He racked his brains for something classical but all he could think of was, "*ave Caesar, nos morituri te salutamus.*" In any case his lips were as paralysed as his feet. Suddenly Florian's face came into view.

'Sir,' the boy said to him. 'It wasn't my fault because you did say that, didn't you, about Classical Civilisation, so I was just...'

Charles heard Dr Ngo tell Florian to stop remonstrating, but it no longer mattered as his legs were whisked off the floor and he was marched down between the ranks of Rydon Hall boys, as if he were being clapped off the pitch after making a century. He was vaguely aware of Dr Ngo still trying to prevent any more of Florian's self-justifying protestations when, uttering the same hideous clang as when they had first arrived at the camp, the door slammed shut and Charles was outside the cave, with Mr Baadi and the guards.

CHAPTER 10

As they stood outside in the warm, clear mountain air, Charles turned his head and looked, for the first and possibly last time, at the cave which had been their classroom, canteen and dormitory for the past ten days. He tried to take in more of it, but the guards were not in a sentimental mood and slipped a cotton mask over his head. Then, allowing no more time for visual inventories, they spun him round several times, first one way, then another, and finally, when he was totally disorientated, marched him in what felt like a circular course, round the corner to whatever squalid death awaited him.

Charles' brain was numb. Unable to think what horrors this beast had in mind for him, he concentrated on the simplest of tasks, such as walking. He took some small comfort from the thought that all those left behind must be rounding on Florian for, in effect, denouncing him to Mr Baadi. If he ever got out of this, Charles told himself, he would make Florian regret having said that. He made a secondary mental note to himself to be less rude in future – if he had a future – about the study of Classical Civilisation.

Mr Baadi was talking to someone else, but Charles could no longer hear him. Within a few paces his frogmarch escort halted, leaving Charles standing, swaying slightly. At first he thought they had entered a metal foundry until he realised that the noise was being made by his own heart. He put a hand to his cheek and it came away drenched with sweat. Then he sniffed the air and wondered what was missing. For the first time in days, he couldn't detect the rancid butter of Adrian Purvis' peculiar skin condition. Yet he felt deprived of it. Trying to control his breathing, Charles let his head hang down low. Perhaps he was about to discover where hundreds of terrified prisoners had been brought, to be beaten senseless and left for dead or hung up and shot. He could hear a metal handle being turned and a rusty hinge squeaking. Charles tried to memorise as much as he could, either for a brave but foolhardy escape plan, or to take with him into the next world.

He wondered if he was going to faint, or be sick. What secrets could they possibly want from him? All he knew were his banking PIN code and the combination lock of the Rydon Hall front gate. What else could they get out of him after battering him for several hours, and what methods would they use? He had always feared having a bright light shone in his face, but what wattage was he about to be exposed to and – for that matter – how could bulbs of such vicious intensity, whether bayonet or screw-in, be acquired in a failed state? Maybe they had other methods in mind. Was it to be electrodes on his – oh God, please no – on his genitals? Or was he about to become the first Rydon Hall teacher ever to suffer the terrifying ordeal of water-boarding? A hand went round his neck and he stiffened, expecting a sharp and possibly final tug, but in fact the mask was pulled off and he could see again. He blinked and shook his head. They were standing in front of the entrance to another cave. Feeling sure that his resistance would not last beyond the first minute, he allowed himself to be pushed limply forward – and stepped into a different world.

It was like a mini-study, smaller than the dormitory cave, but with stronger internal lighting and a thick rug in the centre. To the side was a desk with a marble bust of Julius Caesar. The walls were hung with photographs of a young man, presumably Abdi Baadi, laughing along with a bunch of students at a party. The women were in voluptuously creamy dresses, the men in starched white shirts and mock-Victorian jackets. There were photographs of brutal, 1970s-style concrete courtyards under crisp blue skies and an attractively naïve painting of a mother and father – perhaps Mr Baadi's own – with four or five children climbing all over them. Charles transferred his astonished gaze to the wall opposite, which had a large black and white photograph of a man – still Baadi but no longer an undergraduate – posing with modest pride beside a pile of what looked like half a dozen corpses. But, most unexpected of all, was the sight that greeted Charles as he looked down at a small table, and was astonished to find himself staring into the azure-lidded eyes of the falcon of Helikonopolis.

'Do sit down,' said Mr Baadi, pointing to a wicker chair. 'Glass of water?' He walked round the leather-topped desk and dropped into an elegant, round-backed wooden seat.

'Now, sir,' he said, in a conciliatory tone. 'You seem a little breathless. Has the heat got to you?'

'It's not... it's not that,' Charles gasped as he sat down, 'but did you say we were going to the... the torture chamber?'

Mr Baadi let forth a bleat of laughter. 'Oh, a figure of speech!' he chuckled. 'Just my little joke. You would hardly expect me not to abuse my position of power, would you?'

'So you're not... going to... torture me?' said Charles.

'Fear not,' said Mr Baadi, with redoubled laughter. 'We also have a room called the Bridal Suite but we have not yet had a honeymoon couple sleep in there. We are far from civilisation and must find ways to entertain ourselves. So what do you think of my study?'

Charles took several deep breaths and pointed at the falcon. 'That's an interesting item,' he said cautiously.

'Ah, yes. Our associates were lucky to find it in your rooms. Well, we had your keys, you see, so we took the opportunity to have a little snoop.'

Charles decided, on the basis of two wrongs not making a right, that he should not make excuses about the falcon.

'I thought it was in the safe,' he said.

'Yes,' said Mr Baadi. 'But one of your colleagues provided various numbers to us during the bus journey. Maybe he was trying to… what, negotiate? It's very pretty, isn't it?'

'Yes,' said Charles, surprised at how clearly he was thinking. 'We, um, we got it in Cairo.'

'You can get almost anything there,' said Mr Baadi.

Charles decided not to draw any further attention to it. 'So how, um, how are things in Egypt, if you don't mind my asking?'

'Oh, well, they got rid of the old man, you know, the Pharaoh.'

'Did they? Just after we were there?'

'Were the two events connected?' Mr Baadi let out another bleat of laughter. 'Yes. So now they only have themselves to blame.' He put his hands behind his head and rested one booted leg on the desk, toes almost touching the falcon. 'People power: well, it worked for the Greeks but we shall see. So what do you think of the room?'

'Well, it's very…'

'An exact replica of my first-year room at West Mercia. I know it does not compare with the view over the Cam from, what is it, the Great Court of Trinity College, but we did our best out there.'

'Of course you did,' said Charles, beginning to get his breath back. 'I wish I could say more, but I am afraid I haven't been eating very well lately and…'

'No need,' said Mr Baadi, waving a hand in the air. 'I will do most of the talking. I am a quick thinker and you are nervous, weak with hunger as you say and, if you will forgive me, somewhat smelly. So why have I brought you here: you and your poor, suffering students?'

'I was beginning to wonder,' said Charles.

'Fair question,' said Mr Baadi, patting his forehead with a clean handkerchief. The door creaked. A guard – more like an armed valet – appeared and Charles was presented with a fresh bottle of water. It was the sweetest taste he had ever known. 'So, Mr Goldsap...'

Mr Baadi paused for thought.

'It's actually Goldforbes,' said Charles. 'Not that it matters.'

'I apologise. And first name Charles? Charlie..? Chaz?'

'Charlie doesn't really work... It's always been Charles, I'm afraid.'

'I understand,' said Mr Baadi, as if it really did seem important to get these things right. 'Now, as you know, my country is a mess. It makes the collapse of the Roman Empire look as efficient as the isle of Guernsey. Every tin-pot Caesar in Africa feels they should be number one. Well, they are all wrong. I am the number one fellow round here, hee!' The last syllable was uttered with a little squeak. 'But, like any emperor, I need cash to run my business, or my so-called colleagues will turn on me and – how would one put it: "*et tu, Brute*?" Yes?'

'I'm with you so far,' said Charles.

'Now, I am a simple person,' said Mr Baadi, bringing his second foot to the table and rocking on two legs of his chair, just as Charles was repeatedly telling boys in his class, especially Florian, not to. 'Left to myself, I would be happy just to read quality literature, attend the occasional night club in search of sexual pleasures and listen on headphones to the world's greatest recording artist.'

'Yes,' said Charles, not feeling like second-guessing him.

'Do you know who that is?'

'Who..? N-no,' said Charles.

'Marshall Mathers, better known as..?'

'Better known as, yes...' said Charles dumbly.

'Eminem!' said Mr Baadi. 'Truly a world class act. Try and keep up.'

'Ah,' said Charles, wondering whether to reveal that this was Florian's favourite singer too.

There was a paper bag on the desk, from which Mr Baadi produced a long, green leaf. He proceeded to cram this into his mouth, sucking and swallowing languidly. Then he pulled a pistol from his jacket pocket.

'First,' he said, 'I must inform you that if you try anything silly – though of course, being a graduate of the University of Cambridge, you are far too clever to attempt such a thing – you will have to pick up the pieces of your own head off the floor.' He sat back, continuing to chew.

'But,' said Charles, 'would you want my blood and gore all over your photographs?'

Mr Baadi put the tip of the leaf back in his mouth. His whole body seemed to tremble with pleasure. 'Do you chew qat?'

'I've never really tried it,' said Charles.

'Best not to,' he said. 'It is rather addictive and I hate, absolutely hate, running out of it. But, sir, the photo of myself and my family. Please look behind it.'

Unsure if he wanted to know the answer, Charles slid the photo off its hook to reveal a cherry-sized punctuation mark and a dark black stain. He put it back, shakily.

'So you see, here on my tiny Mount Olympus, I am indeed... a Rock God, you agree?'

Charles nodded.

'And do you know how many people I have shot in this office?' said Baadi.

Charles shook his head.

'Three,' said Mr Baadi. 'This is Africa. Question: Why is running water so scarce? Answer: because we need it to wash the blood away. And my point is? Listen to me, sir: the world economy is going down the tubes thanks to some idiot western bankers.' Charles stared back, but the mini-dictator seemed to be in a qat-induced world of his own. 'This stuff is good,' he said, his lips pursing as if it were too sharp. 'Hurts the stomach though.'

119

'So that's from...?'

'Ethiopia,' he said. 'But it is too dry: on the road too long. That is why we need peace in this country. So you see, I need an injection of funds, but I do not have that much time. I suppose I could go on *Who Wants To Be A Millionaire*? but I might not get through the opening round, hee! And besides, when it comes to phoning a friend, what would I do? Either I have shot most of them or some other madman has...'

He paused. The air hung heavy, and all Charles could hear was Mr Baadi, palpating his qat leaf.

'So why have you taken us all captive?' asked Charles.

'Good question,' said Mr Baadi. 'What on earth was I thinking? That is a lot of mouths to feed, and, believe me, I do not want to starve you. But it is not easy getting food up here.'

'Incidentally, where are we?' asked Charles.

'Oh...' said Mr Baadi. 'I could tell you but... do you know how the rest of the sentence goes?'

'I think so,' said Charles.

'Do you still want to know?'

'I'll think of a different question,' said Charles.

'That is better,' said Mr Baadi. He grinned toothily. Despite the fact that the man was a lunatic who could rub him out with a click of his fingers, Charles felt strangely elated by their dialogue. Perhaps it was the closeness to death that spurred him on.

'How much money are you asking?'

'Ten million. Dollars. Is that such a lot?'

Charles scratched his cheek. They would never get out.

'I am a pirate, yes? I need money to oil my pirate wheels and keep my plates spinning, as it were. Trouble is, I now have 20 of Britain's finest, plus their three inspirational teachers. Woooah... Over-load! That's a lot of hungry mouths to feed.'

Charles nodded. He was wondering how much Baadi could get on the black market for the falcon of

Helikonopolis. But then Mr Baadi interrupted him.

'To lose one hostage... Well I suppose that could be called an accident. But to lose one, two, three...' He was counting on his fingers. 'It does sound like, what was that famous line... carelessness, no?'

'But you can't just get rid of people if you don't need them... That's monstrous!' Charles exclaimed.

'You are calling me a monster? I may burst into tears.'

'But I mean...' Charles was experiencing a strange emotion: the possibility of a single altruistic deed. Had it fallen to him to sacrifice his own life? Did he dare, like Mucius Scaevola, to hold his own hand in the fire to spare the others? Or was this case more like that other story, one he dimly remembered, about ripping up the prophetic books one by one? 'You can't just dispose of people when you don't need them, Mr Baadi. That's even worse than... that horrible story of the Cumaean Sybil.'

'What is that?'

'You know, the old hag who went to see Tarquinius Superbus. Roman mythology. Sorry, I thought you'd...'

'You have lost me,' said Mr Baadi.

Suddenly, Charles remembered how the story ended. He decided that the story would keep for another time. 'Oh, it's nothing.'

'But I am intrigued,' said Baadi. 'Please explain.'

Charles could feel his armpits moistening. 'Actually I've forgotten,' he said.

'Oh, I do not think you have.'

'No, really.'

'Wait. Let me get one of the guards.' Baadi got up and was moving towards the door when Charles' memory came back to him.

'I think I've got it now,' he said, realising with finality that resistance was useless.

'Do you? I am so pleased. My assistants have some very imaginative ways to boost your powers of recollection.'

'This old hag offers Tarquinius nine books of ancient prophecies, for a huge sum. He says forget it, so she burns three and then...'

'Do not tell me, let me guess: she asks double what she asked before!'

'Well, she asks the same amount as before but you've got the idea,' said Charles.

'And does he agree to pay?'

'Well, no,' said Charles. 'So she...'

'Wait, wait! I know this one!' Mr Baadi almost had his arm in the air. 'She burns three more?' Mr Baadi looked genuinely delighted to have second-guessed the ancient legend.

'Yes!' The man was no fool. Had he asked Year Eight the same question, he could easily have allowed ten minutes to pass as they vied to miss the point.

'And then he pays the original price? For just three books? Superb!'

'Mmmm...' said Charles.

'But Mr Boldgut, I wasn't planning to burn any of my dear hostages. Oh dear me no.'

'I'm very glad to hear it,' Charles said. He might still pass out, but what would it achieve?

'But that old lady was right. I don't need all 23 of you to get the ransom. That's too many and I don't have the provisions to keep you all fed. I only need... three?'

'Three?' said Charles. He didn't like that number. 'Three...'

'In fact,' said Baadi. 'Here's my final offer: I just need one.'

'And, how...' Charles' latest battle was with swallowing: he was finding this very difficult. 'How would you reduce our numbers to one?'

'Well, I could play a very nasty game and kill one at a time. But that's so... I don't know, that seems mean, somehow, and a little ungrateful to the country that taught me so much. You see, sir, one day, when this, this war...' For a moment, it almost seemed as if his eyes had misted up. 'You must forgive me,' he said, 'but what else can I get passionate about, apart from the next Eminem album? It is terrible to see your own country being ripped apart by these murderous bullies. I hate bullies: don't you, Mr Godfork?'

'Indeed so,' said Charles.

'It all begins in adolescence, I suppose,' Baadi said. 'You know, my parents separated when I was a teenager, and I am not sure I ever got over it. It really does leave one – what is the word – handicapped.'

'How interesting.' Charles sat forward on his chair. 'As a matter of fact, one of the boys has experienced a very similar...'

'Furthermore, I always took all possible measures to prevent having children of my own, which I now think is a great pity, because I am sure I would have made a good father. Not sure about being a good husband, as I do prefer to chase moving objects, but I have always wanted a son. Or a daughter.'

'You could have both,' said Charles. 'You're still young.'

'Are you mocking me, Mr Goldbore?'

'Good God no!' said Charles. 'That would be insane.'

'I must admit it would have seemed a little eccentric. If not downright suicidal.'

'I meant, you must feel a special bond with children who have been through a similar experience to your own, such as divorce.'

'Well yes, I suppose I do,' said Mr Baadi tenderly. 'The civil war of the bedroom.'

'The failed state of marriage.'

'Ha ha, yes.' He stood for a moment, almost lost in thought. 'I need a hostage, sir. I thought I would hold a handful, but, thanks to your delightful story from ancient Rome, I now see that I need only one. One of the boys. Will you help me choose?'

'I..?' It was the most terrible question he had ever been asked. 'I couldn't possibly. I mean, how could I look any parent in the eye and say we left their son behind..?'

Baadi shrugged. 'You don't have any choice. But when the ransom is paid, they will be so glad to have little Johnny back, they will forget all the pain. And as I say, he will come to no harm. Come, please? I will show you.'

He rose swiftly and Charles struggled to his feet. The door was opened before they reached it. Baadi marched Charles round the corner to a patch of earth, which he began to palpate with his foot. The twigs and leaves parted to reveal a trapdoor, complete with metal ring. Baadi pulled on it and it yawned open, exposing steps down. At the same time, a white light flickered on.

'After you,' said Mr Baadi.

'Oh dear,' said Charles. 'Must I?'

'Please, Mr Goldfork,' said Baadi. 'Where would we be without trust? I will be right behind you.'

Charles grimaced. Tears were pressing against his eyes but, judging from the available firepower grouped around Baadi, he seemed to have no choice. Trying not to whimper, he put one foot on the step and began to descend. Baadi did indeed accompany him.

'See?' said Baadi as they walked into another quite different space. 'Welcome to the Bridal Suite.' It was quite small, but it had a chair, a table, a cupboard and a bed.

'All flat-packed,' said Baadi, wandering around the room, checking the light socket and testing the bed with his knee in a house-proud manner as if he were about to rent it out. 'Sadly there is no *Ikea* in Mombasa but the drive back from the furniture warehouse was one of the longest days of my life, let me tell you.'

'It must have been awful,' said Charles.

'It got worse. When we reached the border we realised they hadn't given us enough of those wooden dowel plugs. Can you picture me in the Returns queue..?'

'Not a happy bunny.'

'Indeed not, sir. But this is where our guest will stay. It is just another cave which happens to be underground.'

'Ingenious.'

'So, much as I would love to keep you all here, I think I must put the rest of you on a bus and send you home. Back to Blighty. Unless you love it so much you want to stay.'

'It's been fascinating, honestly, but we would hate to impose on you,' said Charles.

Baadi placed one leg on the low bed. 'What is the name of your school, by the way?'

'Er, Rydon Hall?' Charles said, without thinking.

'And where is this?'

'Churley. It's south-west London. Sort of suburban London. It's quite middle class but it has, you know, some rough areas.' They were more towards Varley Park, in truth, but Charles did not want to get bogged down in excessive detail.

'How interesting,' said Baadi. 'Have you been there long?'

'This is my first year. I started a bit late.'

'Perhaps one day I shall visit it,' said Mr Baadi, staring beyond Charles. 'I am sure they would make a fuss of me.'

'They would make a much bigger fuss of you if you let us all go...' said Charles, once more pursuing the noble course.

'Ah but you see my hands are tied. Or rather...' Mr Baadi let out a little giggle. 'Yours are, or they will be. But most of you are so lucky! I need only one!'

Charles was doing his best to think fast. They couldn't leave one boy here, could they? Even if they happened to choose the most odious boy of all? He folded his arms. 'I'm sure I speak for my colleagues when I say we will absolutely refuse, under any circumstances, to leave anyone behind. We all leave together or...'

Mr Baadi scratched his head. 'In that case, my dear sir, you leave me with no choice but to slit all your throats with kitchen knives, dump you by the side of a road somewhere, and find some other hostages. Do you understand?'

'Yes, of course I do,' Charles said, nodding very deliberately. 'And could I just rephrase my earlier remarks?'

'You see, sir, this is not the Oxford and Cambridge cricket match. We are not stopping for tea. This is war, and I intend to come out the winner. I have set a trap, and I need a lump of cheese. Who will it be?'

'I... I'm not sure,' said Charles.

'Well, who is the most annoying boy? Who do you want to get rid of, or who would you miss the least? Come on, sir: every school has one.'

'But you can't just choose one boy because he's annoying. Can you?'

'Why not?' said Mr Baadi. 'Take that boy, for example, the one who spoke up in class. He looked a bit of a, what do you call it, a handful, no?'

Charles did not answer straight away. 'He is very good at I.T.,' he said.

'Then he must be very poor at Latin,' said Mr Baadi, as if that settled the matter.

'Perhaps, but that doesn't mean we would leave him behind with you,' said Charles. 'Even if he likes Eminem – which he does, incidentally – and comes from a broken home, which I am sure you would find interesting...' Charles' face assumed a look of great sincerity. 'But I couldn't just leave him with you!'

Mr Baadi's face came closer. Charles could smell his qat-scented breath, could see the perspiration on his brow. 'This boy: do you ever wish you could snap your fingers and be rid of him? I am offering to take him off your hands! I understand that they have examinations later this year. Well then, the others need to concentrate and no doubt he is a distraction.' He smiled at Charles. 'I am trying to help you. Sir.'

'And what will happen to us?' asked Charles.

'In the first place, I have a special entertainment reserved for your colleague up there on the moral high ground who keeps reminding me of my shortcomings. Then, in the morning, after a delicious farewell breakfast, you will all – well, all but one – be escorted to the outskirts of a nearby city, the authorities will be tipped off, and I am sure you will be taken care of. They will probably fly you to the relative safety of Enitenia, although in my opinion the country is a tip with nothing in it to recommend.'

'Do I have your word on that?'

'My word?' Mr Baadi lifted two fingers to his head, in a mock-salute. Then, solemnly, he said, 'The boy scout's honour that you will not be hurt... by us, at least...'

'But how can you keep one child hostage?' said Charles, trying to say the right thing. 'How very cruel, I mean, it's not right...'

Mr Baadi groaned. 'Oh there you go again. Have you ever spent any time in Smilia? Stand on a street corner in our capital Muccatchino for five minutes: you will hear a dozen worse stories. You say that I am unbearably cruel? Are not all great men forced, sometimes, to make tough decisions? You remember the battle of Alesia, I am sure.'

'The... I'm sorry?'

'Alesia.' Baadi flicked his fingers impatiently. One side of his face had developed a small bump from the qat leaves stored in his cheeks. Charles was struggling to remember if it was a stimulant or a relaxant, but his mood didn't seem to have changed too much.

'You might have to remind me of some of the details...' Charles began.

'Julius Caesar... defeating the Gauls, and their leader Vercing... what was his name?'

'Vercingetorix?' said Charles, relieved at last to be of use. Of course: he had been reading about the Battle of Alesia only a few days earlier.

'Thank you: yes, him. The hero of the Gauls, no? But to Caesar, he was just getting in the way. And so he turned him into a slave, yes?'

'I carry the *Gallic Wars* with me all the time,' said Charles, patting his jacket pocket.

'Ah! Good!' said Mr Baadi. 'A nice treat, perhaps, for the boy who stays behind. Lessons in how to be a great leader. You see, Mr Gofor, you are not the only ones to feel pain – far from it. But I give you my solemn word as a Muslim, as an African, as a Smili, that the boy will not suffer any abuse from anyone, while he is under my care.' He spat a gobbet of green liquid from his mouth and picked another leaf. 'Unless, of course, the money does not arrive, in which case we will kill him.'

Mr Baadi slapped the desktop. 'So, sir, our time together is over. The rest of the party are only hours from freedom. When you get home, you will tell your politicians in Whitehall that you have met Abdi Baadi, BA, West Mercia University. Tell them about him. They say of some people, I think, "Such and such, he takes no prisoners." Well, I do! But, in this case, only one.' He held out his hand.

Shakily, Charles took it. Then he said, 'Mr Baadi, may I make a request?'

Mr Baadi smiled back at him serenely. 'Name it, dear sir.'

'I think I may have found a... well, a *modus operandi*, shall we say? But afterwards, I might need a few moments of privacy in the company of your guards.'

As the door of the prison cave opened and Charles' crumpled body was sent flying onto the floor, the boys and staff crowded round.

Water was brought and, after Mrs Hughes-Howard wiped the smears of blood from his lips, Charles took several sips.

'Oh Charles, we're so relieved you're back,' she

said, not trying to stifle her sobs.

'Give him some space,' Dr Ngo ordered. 'He needs air.'

'I'm OK, I'm OK,' Charles panted. The guards had been a little freer with their blows than he would have liked.

'Did they hurt you?' asked a blurred face.

'Not after the first few punches, Josh, but thanks for asking,' croaked Charles.

'It's Duncan actually, sir.'

'Sorry. I meant to say Duncan. I knew that. Ouch, sorry, is there any more water?'

'Did they torture you, sir?' asked a concerned Adrian Purvis. He turned to Florian, baring his teeth. 'Oh sir, I'm so sorry. It's all Florian's fault.'

'Please, please, it's alright,' shouted Charles, grateful if mystified at receiving support from the most detested boy in the class. 'Don't blame Florian.'

'Sir?' It was Florian Bavington. 'My bad...' He might have said more, but, as if even that amount of contrition were too much, he went on, 'But it wasn't my fault they took you away, true dat... I mean, just because you were saying all that stuff about...'

'It's alright, Florian. Mr Goldforbes is back now,' said Dr Ngo.

'You were always so rude about Classical Civilisation and that. I swear...'

'For God's sake, Florian,' said Dr Ngo. 'Can't you see he's been beaten up?' The boy really was unbearable.

'We'll look after Mr Goldforbes,' said Mrs Hughes-Howard in a calming voice. 'And then we should all try and get some sleep. It's been a very difficult day. And Mr Goldforbes, you're an absolute hero.'

'In fact, it wasn't as bad as I thought it would be. I kept saying to them, you know, you can hit me all you like, but you can't break my spirit. You can't take my freedom. And I think, in the end, they realised that that was bigger than any guns or, or any, er...' Charles stopped. Was he overdoing it?

'Go on, Charles,' said Mrs Hughes-Howard, her eyes glistening with emotion. 'Go on.'

'Sir? Florian Bavington was laughing as they took you away,' said Adrian Purvis.

'Don't try and get me in trouble, you neek!' yelled Florian.

'It's fine, it's fine,' said Charles, taking another sip of water. 'Honestly, it's not a problem.' Because it really was not. Or at least, for the first time in months, it soon wouldn't be.

CHAPTER 11

The conversation that sealed Florian's fate came later that night, and in conditions far from conducive to a mature and reflective discussion. As the last of Year Eight fell asleep, their three teachers were pulled from their makeshift beds and taken outside. They were terrified at leaving their teenage charges unattended, the air was cold, and the matter under discussion anything but restful.

Apart from the occasional caw of a distant beast, the night was silent as they tried to discuss the terrible dilemma into which they had been placed. A spray of stars shimmered overhead and they could see, silhouetted against the horizon, tree-tops similar to the jungle effect of the painted walls in the Year Two classroom. Charles and Mrs Hughes-Howard were tied to a post out in the open, a hundred or so metres beyond the cave, so that they could agonise over what few options they had without the boys overhearing. There was wiggle room for their legs but not much else.

This, however, was the height of luxury compared to the obscene punishment which Mr Baadi had devised, close by, for Dr Ngo, and which would impede his walking, and even sitting, for the next few months. It was all very unsettling and, no doubt, intended to be so by Mr Baadi, to "set an example" as he put it - in language that could have been borrowed from the pages of *What A Way To Behave!* - to any who dared try and contradict him.

'If this madman would let us just sit up and talk in reasonable comfort, we might have a proper conversation,' said Mrs Hughes-Howard.

'He doesn't want to make it that easy for us, does he?' said Charles, trying to turn his head to see Dr Ngo's condition. 'He's putting us under pressure.'

Mrs Hughes-Howard flexed her back against the pole.

'I keep wondering what we could have done differently.'

'And..?'

'Well,' said Mrs Hughes-Howard, 'I've only got as far as thinking that if we'd left Florian in London, none of this would have happened.'

A single tone – 'Mmmmmmmngh,' like a cow about to give birth – reached their ears.

'Can you hear us, Dr Ngo?' she chirped. Then, raising her voice fractionally but with a trace of extra tenderness, 'Are you alright over there, dear?'

'Mmmmmmnnnmmm,' came from behind the gag.

Charles and Mrs Hughes-Howard were tied, back-to-back, their limbs secured with plastic gardening bands. By contrast, Dr Ngo had been stripped naked, his slightly podgy body lashed to a pole like booty from a day's hunting. The pole was now suspended horizontally between two uprights.

'You must admit, Mr Goldfor,' Mr Baadi had said sweetly as his guards wound the cord around Dr Ngo's body, 'that in a part of the world known for theatrical gestures, this is unusually, what is the word, *macabre*?'

As if this were not agony enough, two guards were slowly spinning him clockwise by means of a pulley system that produced a regular squeaking noise. Finally, and for extra effect, a dish of coals glowed just beneath his rump area. Each time the orbit of his buttocks came under the influence of the coal pan, he let out a gasp of pain.

Charles closed his eyes. He had no wish to see one of his colleagues naked, preferring to preserve the image of Dr Ngo, fully clothed and sinking into one of the saggy staffroom armchairs, rather than being turned like a pig on a spit.

'I'll never be able to look at those Waitrose rotisserie chickens again,' said Mrs Hughes-Howard. She groaned and pressed her hand to her stomach. 'What's worse is I'm still famished.' They hadn't had more than a few scraps for over two days now, as if to prove that these teenagers really were eating Mr Baadi out of house and home. Charles could only see the brim of Joy's large straw hat but he could hear the distress in her voice. He nodded sadly in agreement.

'Don't hold back, will you, Colin?' said Mrs Hughes-Howard, as ever, doing her best to include everyone in the group. 'We want your tuppenny-worth too.'

'Yerrrr,' said Dr Ngo.

'What a thing to do to us,' said Mrs Hughes-Howard, twiddling her ankles to keep them warm against the cold night air. 'I mean, we'll be carrying this burden around for years.'

'Yyyyyrrrz,' Dr Ngo agreed, followed by a little howl as a spark from the coals blew up onto his lower cheeks.

'So tell me again,' said Mrs Hughes-Howard. 'He said he was going to – I can't even bear to say it – he was threatening to... to kill one boy every week?'

'Well, you know, it was difficult to remember every twist and turn of the conversation because they kept hitting me,' Charles said, 'but that was what he said at first.'

'And you argued him out of it. You are a wonder, Charles. *One a week?* Is the man mad?'

Charles tried to stretch his hips, which were chafing against the dry earth. 'But I'm not sure if what I got from him was much better.'

'But it's an impossible choice, isn't it?' said Mrs Hughes-Howard, which was true. Yet Charles knew that if he could persuade her to adopt his solution, while thinking that she had arrived there herself, the deal was more or less done and they would be on the bus, homeward bound, that morning. 'We can't choose one of the boys ourselves.'

'I know,' said Charles, trying not to sound impatient. 'I know, and that's what's so terrible. We have to, though. He won't do it for us: that would make it too easy.'

'But what has any one boy done to deserve that..?'

133

said Mrs Hughes-Howard with a plaintive gasp.

'Well, exactly...' said Charles. He needed to give her time to catch up with him. 'I mean, let's think about this. Which boy would you – or Colin – say has been the least helpful on the trip so far?'

'Well...' said Mrs Hughes-Howard. 'I mean... I don't know... I suppose it would have to be Florian, wouldn't it?'

'Or look at it this way: who took the least interest in any of the, er, cultural stuff?'

'Mmm, let's see. Well, Florian barely noticed anything we...'

'Oh?' said Charles, in a surprised tone. 'OK, put it this way: who's the biggest bully?'

'Oh... Florian, definitely, the way he goes after that pathetic little snip, Adrian Purvis.'

'Florian again? Hmm,' said Charles. 'But whose behaviour has been so bad, even after we were taken prisoner, that we lost the few liberties we were entitled to?'

'Well Florian's got us into trouble time and again, but...'

'And if you were standing in Cairo Airport and you had to send one boy home, who would it be?'

'Florian, obviously. Many's the time I've wanted to lose him. But I'd send him home: I wouldn't leave him stuck out here.'

'Point taken,' said Charles, graciously. 'On the other hand, who is the most pig-headed member of the group?'

'Flrrrrrrrn,' came from the stricken Dr Ngo.

'Right, Colin,' said Charles. 'I mean, I don't have an opinion either way, I'm just asking the questions. But here's a different one: which of these boys is so thick-skinned that you might put money on him to come out of an ordeal like this less damaged than any of the others?'

Charles could tell by Joy's expression that he had won this point too. 'You know the answer to that as

well as I do, Charles,' she said. 'But even so, I mean...
it's one thing to give someone a good telling-off, but
how could you leave him in a cave with this barbarian?
I mean, it's the difference between punishment and,
well, *retribution*.' This case did seem to fall into the
latter category, even though Charles was not sure that
Mr Baadi could be described as a barbarian.

'I hear what you're saying, but we have to decide
which...'

'I mean, imagine telling his mother?' said Mrs
Hughes-Howard slowly. 'And they did endow the I.C.T.
Room, after all. I'm not sure that was meant to be a
down-payment on a ransom demand.'

Charles' belly, tender after 10 days of irregular
diet, contracted still further.

'I dread to think how Mrs Bavington would react,'
said Mrs Hughes-Howard in a strained whisper. 'And as
for his father...'

'What's he like?' asked Charles.

'Have you not met him? Much worse,' she said.

'I mean,' said Charles, 'I've seen where they're
going to keep Flor... whoever gets left behind. It's not
like we're consigning him to a sort of underground
dungeon. Yes it's underground, but...'

'It might be alright now,' Mrs Hughes-Howard shot
back. 'But are we going to be able to pop over every
few weeks for a health and safety check? I fear not.
What's that? Oh – oh!' She lashed out with her foot,
flicking some type of beetle or scorpion up into the air
and away.

'What else can we do?' asked Charles. 'Could we
offer him someone else?'

'I can't believe we're sitting here, discussing which
boy to hand over to a Smili pirate,' said Mrs Hughes-
Howard. 'To be reduced to this...'

'But you know what I mean...'

'Yes of course I do. Well let's see: Dylan Cristiano?
Yedverd Zygnwycyz?'

'What have they have done to...'

'What has any of them done?' she demanded. 'Roley Yousuf?'

'Nnnnnn!' Dr Ngo called out.

The name hung in the air for a few moments before they shook their heads.

'Politically sensitive,' said Mrs Hughes-Howard.

'Definitely,' said Charles.

'Yyyyyyyyy!' yelled Dr Ngo as a flame reared up above the low glow. He screamed louder than ever, and then fainted.

'How will we break it to... whoever it is?' said Mrs Hughes-Howard, looking concernedly at the groaning Dr Ngo now lying at her feet after the guards had grudgingly taken him down.

'He'll probably think we planned it all just to spite him,' said Charles.

'Well I can't do it; I'm sorry,' she said. 'And I don't think Colin is up to it either, poor thing.'

'Owwwww,' said Dr Ngo weakly.

'Then again...' said Charles slowly, as if he had had a sudden idea. In fact the thought had come to him as soon as Mr Baadi had mentioned it. If they chose someone else and returned home with Mrs Bavington's son, would she be so relieved as to forget all thoughts of Charles' misconduct? Or would she thank him earnestly for a week and then withdraw to rebuild her life with Florian, ignoring all others? That was not ideal at all. Then again, what if Florian stayed behind? Obviously the government would do its best, diplomatic ropes would be pulled, the money scraped together – it wasn't hard to see to which cause the Year Five tombola would be donated, for example – but, in the meantime, Mrs Bavington would be alone and desperate. With no husband to comfort her, she would come to identify strongly with whoever had seen Florian last. If Charles were the one to break the news to Florian, his connection with her missing son would assume totemic significance, which would surely supplant any lingering unease she might still feel over

136

the mortifying poolside strip incident. She would want to see him more and more. He might find himself invited to Churley House for dinner, to be asked endless questions which he would answer while wiping real tears from his eyes. Maybe, at the end of the evening, with a glass of wine inside her, she would decide that it was time to do something selfish, but which brought her a small measure of comfort. Turning to Charles, she might ask – could he only face it – if he would lie beside her in bed that night. It was a desperate tactic, to be sure, but was Charles really so inhumane as to refuse her?

'I suppose one of us has to step forward and do this,' said Charles. 'But...'

The whimper from behind Dr Ngo's gag spoke more eloquently than words of the emotional connection between Year Eight and their form teacher.

'What are you trying to say, dear?' asked Mrs Hughes-Howard.

'Cnnnnnnnttt...'

'I mean...' said Charles, hoping he had interpolated the correct vowels between Dr Ngo's clenched consonants, 'are we really asking the Year Eight class teacher to break the news to... to whoever it is?'

'But you're surely not asking me...' Mrs Hughes-Howard's voice trailed off.

Charles looked up. A shooting star streaked across the sky. Night: Charles dimly recalled something from Ovid to the effect of *curarum maxima nutrix,* "most potent healer of our cares".

'OK,' he said, his voice clearly breaking. 'One of us has to find a way to tell one of the boys that he's staying here. No one wants to do this but I'm the newest member of staff. Obviously it'll be on my conscience forever, but...'

'You mean you'd tell him? Oh, what courage you must have, Charles. And after they beat you, too.'

'Don't, Joy,' said Charles smoothly. 'I'm just trying to do what's best for the school.'

'What do you think, Colin?' Mrs Hughes-Howard said. 'Do you think our Charles is a hero?'

'Oh I wouldn't call it that...' said Charles. For a few seconds, his mind lapsed into a reverie about what he should wear for his first encounter with Natasha Bavington, but then two other guards came over and snipped his and Joy's plastic wrist-ties.

'You come with us. He come back later,' they pointed at Dr Ngo.

'Be brave, Colin!' Mrs Hughes-Howard cried out as they led them back to the compound. Charles tried not to turn round, but when he did, he saw them suspending Dr Ngo back above the coals. He looked a little closer to the flame this time.

Dr Ngo had still not returned when Charles and Mrs Hughes-Howard woke from a snatched few hours of sleep amid their young charges. The door of the cave was being scraped open. Charles immediately felt intense hunger. The first day without food had been bearable but yesterday – save for Mr Baadi's very welcome bottle of mineral water – had been horrible. The night-time conversation had only made things worse. Now two guards brought in a bowl half-filled with what looked like papery feathers and put it down where the teachers lay. The aroma filled their nostrils. It was like bresaola.

'Your friend, he come back soon,' said one of the guards. 'But please, special breakfast from Mr Baadi.'

Mrs Hughes-Howard picked up a strip and laid it cautiously on her tongue. 'I'm starving,' she said. 'What is this?' She sucked slowly.

'Maybe they're feeling bad about last night,' said Charles.

'I wonder where they've been keeping this all these weeks,' she said. 'Must be a local dish: you can't get this at La Dolce Vita in Churley. It's absolutely delicious.' Abandoning her normal etiquette, her jaws pumped as she spoke. 'Smells like hickory barbecue. Try a bit.'

'I'd be happier about eating it if I knew what had happened to Colin,' said Charles.

'I know,' she said. 'But this will give us some strength. *We need to see our colleague*,' she called to the guard between mouthfuls as one or two of the boys stirred. 'Where is he?'

'He is come soon. Please not to worry, madam.'

'We need to see him,' she repeated.

'Miss, can I have some?' The first cries went up and Mrs Hughes-Howard, rather grudgingly, broke some bits off one strand and handed them out. She turned back to Charles. 'I could eat a whole bowl of this, it's delicious. It tastes like…'

Charles picked up a ribbon and inserted it tentatively between his lips. 'Like barbecued beef. It's very smoky. Mmm.' He was still chewing enthusiastically as the door squeaked open. Two guards entered, holding Dr Ngo, and laid him down near Charles and Joy. He looked shockingly dishevelled in a string vest and singed shorts.

'Poor Colin,' said Joy, still chewing. 'It's rather peppery, this, isn't it?'

'It's delicious,' said Roley, which nearly caused a riot until Mrs Hughes-Howard barked at them to form an orderly queue.

'Could do with a dash of mustard,' Charles began, amazed at how a tasty dish could deaden him to the suffering of others. He looked again at Dr Ngo. The I.T. teacher's shorts were spotted with blood.

'Charles…?'

Mrs Hughes-Howard had stopped chewing.

Dr Ngo's hair, normally so spiky, lay matted against his scalp like the pelt of a sick dog. When the guards laid him down, Charles had noted that they were careful not to leave him on his back.

Mrs Hughes-Howard was shedding the contents of her mouth. Her eyebrows had risen to an admonitory V. 'Spit it out,' she said sternly. 'Everyone spit it out!'

'I'm sorry?' said Charles.

'Spit it out,' she said, her voice rising. 'I know what it is.'

'I'm still trying to guess.'

'Do you know what we're eating?' she said, her hand rising to her mouth in disgust.

'It feels like seared tuna.'

'It is not tuna.'

'Smoky bacon?'

'No.'

'Hickory, um..?'

'*We're eating Colin!*' she screamed.

The next few seconds were given over to a lot of coughing and retching while staff and pupils ran to clear their mouths or throats. But as the noise was dying down, the door scraped open and Mr Baadi charged in.

'Good morning, good morning!' he roared. 'And how is Year Eight today?'

Their oppressor was wearing a mustard-coloured waistcoat and a monocle in addition to his riding crop. He greeted a few of the early risers with a crisp, 'Good morning!' but most were still wiping their mouths or spitting, or crying, so he put his hands on his hips and, jutting his chin forward, declared: 'Oh I think we can do better than that. Good morning Year Eight!'

'Good-morning-Mr-Baadi,' the boys chanted back, hypnotically.

'I hope your teachers enjoyed their special breakfast?' Mr Baadi's tone could not have been more considerate. Charles felt his belly. Had they really been eating their colleague's shaved flesh? Nausea and appetite duelled inside him. It was unspeakable, and yet, until the taste had been identified, strangely moreish. Two guards stood in front of Dr Ngo, protecting him from view. 'Well, gentlemen,' said Mr Baadi, addressing the whole room. 'Now that we have all been reunited, I have a very important question for you. Who has heard of Vercingetorix?'

Predictably, no hands went up. Mr Baadi looked

disappointed, a reaction which Charles was keen to prevent. 'I am sure the boys would benefit from a short History lesson,' he said.

'With pleasure,' said Baadi. 'This man, this Vercingetorix, he was, you know, the leader of the Gauls. He stood up to Julius Caesar, is that the right phrase? Yes, he resisted him. He was a fighter. A hero – and the most popular man in his tribe. So now I ask you: who is the most popular boy in this class?'

Further discussion was paused as a green-faced Mrs Hughes-Howard indicated that she needed to go outside. The door scraped open and a guard accompanied her out. Mr Baadi, without changing his expression, continued.

'Who is the most popular? Because whoever that boy is, I have a special job for him. I need a class *rep-re-sent-a-tive*. A *special* representative, for a *special* job, yes? I need a leader! A second Vercingetorix! I shall be back in a few minutes.'

He turned on his heel and was gone.

'Sir?' said Dylan. 'Will we get in trouble for eating Dr Ngo?'

'Don't even think about it,' said Charles.

'But sir…'

'That's enough, Dylan!' said Dr Ngo, perhaps more stridently than he might have wished.

'Shall we move on?' suggested Charles, as casually as he could. 'You heard what he said. Mr Baadi needs a class rep. Any volunteers?'

'Why doesn't the head boy do it?' shouted Josh.

'*Arthur, Arthur,*' the murmur went up.

Of all the people, thought Charles. Arthur Clough: presentable, polite, good at showing parents round the school on an open morning, Arthur was also, in the words of Bill Drummer, as thick as a box of cheese.

Charles tried again. He had to make the job sound irresistible to one candidate in particular.

'Any other offers?' asked Charles. 'Incidentally, while I was being – shall we say – attended to by Mr

Baadi's men, I happened to hear that he is a big fan of the music of Eminem. So I don't know but it might have something to do with that...'

'Yeah I'll do it,' said Florian, as if yielding to popular clamour, like Cincinnatus being dragged out of retirement to save Rome. The cave door opened again, and Mrs Hughes-Howard, still looking somewhat waxy, reappeared.

'Are you OK?' asked Charles under his breath.

She waved a hand in front of her face and sat down cautiously.

'We're picking a class rep for a special job for Mr Baadi.'

For one moment, Mrs Hughes-Howard looked as if she was going to be sick again, but she held her ground. 'I see,' she said at last. 'And how many volunteers do we have?'

'Me,' said Florian. 'I'll do it.' For once, he didn't even sound sarcastic. 'I can talk to the Baadi man. Believe.'

Charles nodded silently. He turned to Mrs Hughes-Howard and said, in an awed voice, 'He's a natural demagogue, isn't he? Give him a whiff of power...'

Charles went and knelt by Dr Ngo's side. 'How are you?' he said in a low voice.

The answer that came back was frank, and in a pained whisper, but not of a sort that could be shared with a younger audience. Charles gave his arm a sympathetic squeeze and left him to recuperate.

Mrs Hughes-Howard took a sip of water. Her face had recovered most of its colour. 'This reminds me of when we were selecting a new secretary at my tennis club. That was brutal. We were very nearly at daggers drawn. Mrs Kenwright said she thought she might wake up with a horse's head in her bed.'

'Any more nominations?' asked Charles, sensing victory. It had to look like the people had spoken.

'Don't even think about it, guys,' said Florian. 'Mr Goldforbes is right: this job's got my name on it.

Serious: don't vote for Arthur, he's not up to it. He only got head boy because his mum works in the library.'

'Now Florian, that is no way to canvass popular support,' said Mrs Hughes-Howard.

'I don't mind,' said Arthur, still smiling. 'It's probably true.'

'No no, Arthur,' said Mrs Hughes-Howard. 'You've done a really good job as head boy, but maybe you should consider having a break.'

'That's fine, Miss, honestly,' smiled Arthur brightly. 'I would have voted for Florian anyway.' He was so agreeable: Charles could have clubbed him over the head.

'Yeah, bruv,' said Florian. 'Come to me.' Arthur presented himself to Florian, who gave him a hug. 'He knows he can't talk in assembly. Best will in the world, he always cocks it up and then it's like, "What the effing tits was all that about?"'

'Florian!' said Mrs Hughes-Howard in her most reproving terms. 'Where did you learn to speak like that?'

'Sorry, Miss,' said Florian.

'We can do without that sort of language here, thank you very much,' said Charles. 'So with Florian standing unopposed, I declare...'

A single hand went up: that of Adrian Purvis. The entire class laughed.

'Yes, Adrian?' said Dr Ngo.

'I am the official opposition,' said Adrian, in his curdled, lisping treble.

'Not that *mong*,' said Florian, with a snort of derision. 'No one's going to vote for you, Mr Fartyhead.'

'Could we raise the level of debate a bit?' asked Charles.

'I am the protest vote,' said Adrian in a tone of voice that could hardly be called presidential. 'A vote for me is a vote against Florian.'

'Come on people, let's vote for change,' said

Florian, closing his eyes and holding up his hands. 'Let's vote for a better future.'

'Don't vote for Florian,' said Adrian, changing tack, 'because he just bullies people.'

'That's not true,' said Florian. 'I bully him because he's a *neek*. No one else suffers.'

'Don't talk like that,' said Charles.

'It's true, sir. His farts smell out the cave; we all know that.'

'Stop it, Florian!' said both teachers, but Florian won the vote by a show of hands.

The door squeaked, and scraped open. All went silent as Mr Baadi stood on the threshold. 'Ah good,' he said, when Florian stood up proudly to declare himself the winner. 'The judgment of Paris, no?'

'I would remind you, sir,' said Mrs Hughes-Howard, adopting Dr Ngo's role in his enforced absence, 'that you are holding captive 20 boys and three qualified teachers...'

'Well,' added Charles, 'strictly speaking, two fully qualified teachers and one...'

'And one teacher who, although not formally qualified at present, will, I am sure, soon be undergoing the necessary steps to becoming an N.Q.T. or Newly Qualified Teacher in the near future, or would, if...'

'Such solidarity!' brayed Mr Baadi. 'I am very impressed. So now I am going to talk to your teachers outside for a few moments, to tell them what the *special* job for that *special* person will be. Now, this room is a little messy, no? A bit of a "dump", as I think you say. Let us see who can impress me by tidying their space in the next few minutes. Eh gentlemen? '

Grinning slightly, he rested one finger against the side of his chin. All the boys seemed to sit up, arms folded, eager to be noticed as his eyes ran along the rows. Really, thought Charles, had he not decided to go into international piracy, Mr Baadi might have become a truly inspirational teacher.

PART FOUR

CHAPTER 12

Doctor Ironsize was fond of saying that when the diving got tough, Rydon Hall got diving, and never was this more true than with the homecoming of the Year Eight Egypt tour party. They had the best possible help, of course. Her Majesty's Government had prepared exemplary rest and recuperation facilities, from the medical team waiting at Heathrow for the flight from Mombasa to the Post Traumatic Stress counselling, which continued well past their return, but the headmaster had lost no time in making himself an alternative emergency service, and he proceeded to emphasise this whenever he had their attention.

In what was possibly a first for diving/warfare mixed metaphors, Dr Ironsize kept insisting that the boys had endured the equivalent of "jumping backwards off a 20-metre board without knowing when they would hit the water", adding that the staff had been in "an ethical air bubble", so he brushed aside any criticism, however mild, of their handling of the situation. What else could they have done?

The school manual contained two pages on school trips, including how to avoid getting an upset stomach, what to do if jostled in the street, and where to report a stolen or lost passport. It did not, however, have anything to say about what to do if one found oneself caught up in a mass movement designed to oust a much-feared tyrannical leader, nor any admonishments against snatching historical relics from besieged museums, or handy hints on how not to be taken hostage, still less on how to choose which of one's pupils should remain behind while the others went home.

All the boys behaved very oddly, in different ways, on their return. There were even times when some teachers, through gritted teeth, uttered the semi-sincere regret that more pupils could not have been left behind.

Having arrived back in the last week before the February half-term break, Dr Ironize had made it clear to all the returning heroes – as he insisted on referring to them – that they should feel under no pressure to turn up for school until they were ready. Rohan Shapcott was allowed, strictly for therapeutic reasons, to attend with his parents the opening of a sailing regatta located on a rapidly-melting Norwegian glacier. All the other boys stayed away for a further week or two, except for Cato Wang, whose parents were of the opinion that the best way to get over a shock was to bury it with homework and piano practice. Dr Ironsize was impressed.

'Get back on that board and plunge in,' he said, as Cato turned up for school the following Monday, white-faced and still trembling. 'That takes guts.'

There had been a nerve-jangling hiccup surrounding their return which, fittingly, was due to Florian. Even though the Falcon of Helikonopolis had been removed from their room at the Blue Turtle by Mr Baadi's henchmen, a note had been found there which read, "Birds head from, Egyption Meuseam, property of Adrian Pervis, Rydon Hall, School, England". Although the handwriting, spelling and distinctive punctuation were immediately recognisable as Florian's, the ensuing bureaucratic tangle nearly led to poor Adrian having to spend an extra night in a prison cell, cooped up with that sub-stratum of Enitenian society which had come to the attention of the ragged state's over-zealous civil police.

Fortunately, on this occasion the British consulate was on hand to argue that surely the poor boy had suffered enough. Even so, the few hours that Adrian was behind bars – given how close the scent of freedom was - were among the most arduous of the whole trip. Adrian's hour of anguish might have drawn more sympathy but, sadly for the Rydon Hall tour party, another member's sufferings were, or were about to be, far greater.

The school had been told to expect side-effects, and these were not long in coming, such as the day when Adrian got stuck inside one of the first-floor toilet cubicles. Luckily his mother had been sitting downstairs, waiting to take him to the open day at Wendlesham's, the boarding school for the bright but error-prone. She was up the stairs like a shot, but her explanation that 'I'd know my son's screams anywhere' only reinforced Mrs Portal's suspicion that Adrian's domestic circumstances were far from ideal. 'He hasn't been sleeping well,' Mrs Purvis said later. But then, which of them had?

There were practical difficulties at every stage, even with the morning roll call.

'Do I put an "N" in the register for "No reason for absence provided"?' asked Mrs Ware the Geography teacher, to the rest of the staffroom. 'That seems a bit harsh, but "A" for "Absent *with* Leave" doesn't feel right. It's not *with* leave. But it's not without leave either.'

'"U" for "Unexplained Absence?" said Madame Allardyce.

'How about "B" for "Educated off-site"?' suggested Ms de Souza. 'He might be learning something.'

'"K"... for Kidnapped,' hissed Dr Ngo, perched awkwardly on his inflatable cushion. Everyone did their best to smile.

After some more discussion they invented a new one: an "A" with a circle around it.

'He'd be thrilled to know he's got his own mark in the register,' said Charles, who was still trying to get used to skipping across Florian's name straight to Rufus Coe-Haine without pausing.

Elsewhere, the signs of Florian's absence were glaring. His hook, in the cloakroom, remained bare, and an eerie silence settled over his desk, such that some teachers had wondered whether to remove it from the classroom. But everyone knew that this could not take place, even though closer examination revealed that the words "PURVIS IS GAY" had been scratched, very deliberately and probably with the point of a compass, into the underside of the lid. This only compounded its fascination for the boys, who were frequently found huddled around it, as if communing with Florian's spirit.

As for the senior members of the tour party, poor Dr Ngo was, as Mrs Hughes-Howard kept saying in a brave bid to sound breezy, "not a happy camper", hobbling around school on a walking stick. There had been little doubt that he had caught something nasty, and the diagnosis of Trichuriasis was only a surprise to anyone who had not heard of the painful but not life-threatening infection of the gut. Charles and Mrs Hughes-Howard had made the tacit decision not to check whether he was aware that some of them had chewed, salivated copiously into and then swallowed (before spitting out) a very finely diced section of the skin around his buttocks on the last morning of their captivity. Dr Ngo's plastic surgeon had assured him that, with the help of skin grafts, the prospects for recovery were excellent and that within a few months no one who came within sight of his buttocks would notice the difference.

Mrs Hughes-Howard, her eyes more sparkly, her lips fuller and redder than ever, had got into the habit of giving little impulsive hugs to the tiniest Reception and Year One boys as if, were the world only filled with children as innocent as these, they might never have had to suffer their recent ordeal. As for Charles, he could not quite believe that, having been a prisoner in the Democratic Republic of Smilia, he could again be waiting for – and occasionally cursing – the fickleness of the H41 bus from Embury Park to Churley. He often thought back to that last morning in Smilia, and to a very different bus journey.

Charles had not been looking forward to breaking the news to Florian that morning. The door of the cave had been opened, and some of the boys had even been let out to play football with, by now, one hemisphere of a plastic football – which was all that had not been eaten by wild beasts after Florian had left it out a few nights earlier. But he was still competing strenuously for a header when Charles caught up with him.

'Well Florian, I've got some good news, and some really rather not so good news,' said Charles when he had pulled him to one side.

'What's the good news?' asked the 13-year-old.

Charles looked at the door to the cave, their old detention room which they were about to share for the last time. 'I must be honest, Florian. This isn't a conversation I had ever expected to have with you,' he said, as if to set the mood. 'The good news, as you know, is that you've been elected class rep, which is great. So well done, that's fantastic...'

'Yeah, I'm chuffed about that. I've got loads of ideas about stuff we could do.'

'Of course you have, and all that enthusiasm is going to come in really handy,' said Charles, 'at some point. Enthusiasm, and physical strength, and of course mental stamina. The bad news, er, and it really is not great...'

'Did I come bottom in the Latin test again?' Florian flashed him a craggy smile.

'No, it's more serious than that,' said Charles. He felt he ought to sound upbeat, however futile it was.

'Are you going to have a go at me for calling Purvis a gaylord?' Florian looked momentarily perturbed.

'I didn't know about that and I wish you hadn't called him a gaylord but it's... Florian, listen. This is terribly important and we don't have much time. You have been picked for a very special job. That's what the class rep means. Mr Baadi has *only just* told me what you will have to do for that special job.'

'Mr Baadi wants me to DJ his next party?'

Charles was finding all this *sangfroid* rather tiresome. 'For goodness' sake, no: look, Mr Baadi was telling us – your teachers – what he saw as the responsibilities of the class rep. You see, it's a bit like being a prefect.'

'Right.'

'Now, you know that prefects have all sorts of extra jobs to do. Extra responsibilities, like, I don't know, laying out the benches for assembly or staying in for lunch duty. And when you do that, you have to *stay in* and see that job through, you see, while everyone else goes out...'

'OK...' said the boy.

'Well, this is a bit like that. You're going to stay in... and do that job *really* well, to the best of your ability, as we all know you can... and, and, meanwhile, we're all going to go out.'

'Oh yeah? Where are you going?'

'England,' said Charles.

'We realise this is a difficult moment for you, dear,' said Mrs Hughes-Howard, who had run over as soon as Florian started howling. 'And obviously, this wasn't the holiday we had promised you.'

'You're going back without me!' screamed Florian, his face red with tears. 'You're abandoning me!'

'Not all of us,' said Mrs Hughes-Howard. 'Part of us will remain here, with you.'

'Which part?' said Florian with an accusatory sneer.

'All these, for a start,' said Charles, pointing to a pile of books that the other boys had left on the floor of the cave. 'And I'd like to add one more.' Fishing around inside his jacket, he pulled out his battered, split-level Loeb Classic.

'This is not just any book, Florian. It's my Latin-English Loeb edition of Caesar's *Gallic Wars*. I have had it for many years, and, unlikely though it might sound, it has become a sort of friend to me. I am going to leave it here with you, Florian. I hope there will come a time when it might, ah, be a friend to you too.'

'I don't think it will, sir,' said Florian.

'Well, it might.'

'I doubt it, sir.'

'Well, you never know, and when that time comes, I hope it brings you comfort.'

'You can take it back, sir. I'm not going to read it.'

'Florian: just take it.' Even now, Charles could feel himself becoming irritated at the boy's intransigence. 'We seem to have hit a little bit of a wall, Mrs Hughes-Howard,' Charles said, turning to his colleague.

'We don't want to leave on a sour note, Florian,' said Mrs Hughes-Howard.

'A sour note? *You're leaving without me!* How do you think that makes me feel?!'

'But we have to, Florian. This is our only chance...'

'Oh yeah, well if it's *your* only chance then obviously...'

'Stop it, I mean it's *your* only chance.'

'How?'

Charles had to admit that was a good question but Mrs Hughes-Howard had taken the decision to move on. 'Florian, we want to give you something that you can take away with you. I mean, not that you can take it away, well not yet anyway, but...'

'The trouble is,' said Charles, leaping in, 'we do have to leave. Quite soon, so...'

'Oh well, don't let me keep you...'

'I didn't mean it like that...' He was so infuriating.

'If you want me to forgive you, sir, I'm not going to,' said Florian. 'Or Dr Ngo, or Mrs 2H.'

'Ouch,' said Dr Ngo, leaning heavily against the table he was resting on for support.

'We're not asking to be forgiven,' said Charles.

'Yes you are.'

'No we're not.'

'Yes you are, and I'm not going to. Why can't Purvis stay? Why does it have to be me?'

'Florian!' Mrs Hughes-Howard looked at him

sternly. 'Are you trying to get another boy into trouble?'

'Into trouble? Like I'm not?!'

Charles hated arguing like this when the moral high ground was stacked so steeply against him.

Florian tried again. 'If you choose Purvis, they'll hate him because he's really boring and he just talks about space rockets, and he'll make the room smell because he does huge farts and then they'll want to let him go.'

Mrs Hughes-Howard's expressive silence somehow managed to combine sympathy for Florian's predicament with disapproval at his latest tactic. 'I cannot volunteer another boy to go in your place, Florian, because...' she began. Then she stopped, unable to take this tone any further.

Florian was not done yet. 'If you choose Cato Wang instead of me, the Chinese army will come in.'

'I'm sorry, Florian, but there's nothing we can do now.'

'This sucks,' said Florian.

'I know it does,' said Charles.

'And so do you, sir. You suck.'

Charles could only bow his head. 'I expect, from your point of view, I probably do, although I can't say I care for the way you expressed yourself.'

'You always did.'

'Well let's have a conversation about that another time.'

'Oh yeah, when? You coming back next week?'

It was worse than the tantrums and sarcastic outbursts that characterised his daily school life, or even his behaviour on holiday until then. But as well as the pity he felt for the boy, Charles was fighting the impulse to look at his newly returned watch. Grim though it was, he suddenly wanted to see the back of Florian. A part of him which he barely dared acknowledge felt a sense of relief that they were about to lose this most vexing of boys. It took a few extra moments to appreciate that Florian was about to be punished more severely than any lunchtime detention.

'You're really, really special, Florian,' said Mrs Hughes-Howard as, behind their backs, the guards moved the bags onto the coach. 'Everyone is special but you're extra-special.'

'You're joking me,' said the tearful boy. 'Is that why I'm staying behind? Thanks but I don't think I want to be that special.'

Dr Ngo gave him the thumbs-up, which was about as much as he could bring himself to do after having had his rump turned into biltong.

'If I had to pick someone who I thought would come through an ordeal like this,' said Charles, 'it would definitely be you.'

There was a pause. Florian had retreated into tearful self-absorption again. Then he shouted, 'You all hate me.'

'No, Florian, we don't. We love you!' said Mrs Hughes-Howard, and began to cry.

'Now look what you've done. You've upset her,' said Charles.

'Have I upset her? Oh, I'm so sorry. I bet she'll be feeling bad about that all the way home.'

'Oh God...' said Charles. He hadn't expected Florian to turn heroic, but even so...

'How do you think I feel? I'm staying behind! You're leaving!'

'That's true,' said Charles. 'We are, and this is going to be very tough. But I know you're strong. You are strong, aren't you? Show me how strong you are.'

'OK. I hate you and I'll never forgive you for this.'

'No, no, Florian. That's not mental toughness. That's just feeling sorry for yourself.' Charles scratched the back of his very grimy neck. 'Maybe you should read a bit of *Gallic Wars*: there are plenty of examples of mental toughness in there.'

'You think I deserve to be left here because I'm crap at Latin.'

'Just because you're crap at Latin – I mean, whether or not you are one of my most able students – has no bearing on whether I think you deserve such a... to go through such a difficult, er, situation, Florian.' Charles scrabbled around desperately: when was the coach leaving? 'Believe me, if I could have swapped with you, I would have. Any of us would have.'

'Go on then.'

'I asked Mr Baadi. He didn't want me to.' Charles felt fairly confident in saying this.

'Try harder.'

'There's no point.'

Charles was saved from further bickering as the cave door was wrenched open and Mr Baadi walked in, his jaws moving up and down furiously, his cheek bubbling outward to accommodate a dense plug of qat leaves.

He smiled and crossed his arms. 'So, who is the lucky individual?'

Florian had begun to whimper, but when he gave himself up to full-pitched keening it was apparent on whom the blow had fallen. Mr Baadi offered his hand to Florian.

'It will be a pleasure to get to know you, young man,' he said. 'We will do our best to make you feel at home. You will eat well and sleep well: the only thing missing will be your liberty. But don't worry! There is a price on your head – and I am sure that, back in Blighty, it will be paid very soon.'

'I do hope so,' Charles found himself saying.

'Is he your top student?' Mr Baadi asked. 'Or is this his punishment for being the worst? Eh?!'

Charles winced. He was in enough trouble with Florian as it was. 'Look after him, Mr Baadi,' he said at last. 'He's worth more than money.'

'And I am sure you are looking forward to writing me an essay on the daily life of a centurion in the Roman army?' said Mr Baadi, grinning at Florian.

Florian stared with unmingled hostility at Charles,

as if blaming him both for introducing the topic and for leaving him ill-prepared. Charles smiled back apologetically.

Mr Baadi turned to the boys, rubbing the tips of his teeth with a single leaf. 'So, what a story you will have to tell, so long as the money is found. In a way, you see...' He ran the top of his riding crop along the side of the wall. 'I too am being held to ransom. I cannot leave my country, and there is a price on my head. So you see, we are none of us in charge of our own destiny. But as the Greeks said, who knows what destiny the fates are spinning for us?' He turned to Charles. 'And the poet's name, Mr Goldfop?'

'I'm afraid I don't quite...'

'Hesiod,' said Mr Baadi.

'Ah yes, typical Hesiod,' said Charles.

'Perhaps the Cambridge examiners left the study of Hesiod to the lesser universities.'

'It wasn't so much that...' Charles began to say but luckily Mr Baadi raised his hand.

'You are captives now, but are not all students held hostage by their teachers? They keep you from going home, they threaten and bully you, they hold you in a small room against your will. True, no?'

Charles shrugged. 'It's a point of view, but...'

'Enough. May I wish you all – well, nearly all – a safe journey, though that is no easy matter in itself. This is a dangerous country; no high fives until you are back on Enitenian territory. The coach will leave in ten minutes.'

Mr Baadi swept out, his jaws chomping furiously. Dr Ngo was helped outside by the other boys. Before he left he reached out to hug Florian, almost collapsed on him, then limped onto the bus, and to the agony of a hard, square seat.

It was a particularly difficult leaving ceremony, because Florian left no one in doubt that each of them should, if their moral compass were properly tuned, have handed themselves over for captivity instead of

155

leaving him behind. And yet, having accused each one of betraying him, he also wanted to give them all a hug. Almost all: even now, he excluded Adrian Purvis. 'I'm not hugging him because he smells of fish,' he said.

'Come on, Florian,' said Adrian. His face had become wrinkled with snuffles: whether through malevolent glee or the general emotion was not yet clear. 'Don't be so nasty.'

'You accusing me of being nasty?! You cock-snogger!'

'Florian! There's no need for that!' said Charles, his impatience finally showing through. 'Just give him a hug or something and then...'

'And then you can all go. Yeah...'

Florian squeezed Adrian's arm, while pointedly holding his fingers over his nose. The biggest hugs were reserved for Dylan and Yedverd. Everyone was in tears.

Charles and Mrs Hughes-Howard were kept back until last. 'I like your room, Florian,' said Mrs Hughes-Howard, still trying to keep the tone upbeat. 'It reminds me of the B & B Ivor and I stayed at in the Lake District.'

'How'm I going to survive?' wailed the boy.

'Florian, this is not going to be easy for us either,' said Mrs Hughes-Howard.

'What, back in London?' he said mockingly. 'Is it going to be a real struggle for you?'

'Yes, in a way, it will, Florian,' said Charles, fighting with himself not to add to the woes of a boy about to be handed over to a bunch of Smili kidnappers.

'Come!' said the teenage guard, jabbing at Mrs Hughes-Howard. Charles thought she was going to slap him, but she merely put her hat down hard on her head, gave Florian a huge kiss on the cheek and a big hug and, blinking back tears, allowed herself to be walked to the bus. Now it was only Charles. On a practical level, he needed a last, snatched conversation with Florian.

'I'd better go,' said Charles.

'Yeah, you don't want to miss the bus, do you, sir?' said the boy but his expression changed from scornful to scared. 'I'm not going into no cave on my own. I'm scared of the dark.'

'Mind over matter, Florian,' said Charles, fighting to stem the tide of panic. 'Imagine! Pick somewhere you feel comfortable, like, I don't know...'

'My mum's bedroom.'

'Exactly,' said Charles.

'Before she put those curtains in.'

'Curtains?'

'It's so dark in there now. But before my dad moved out, their room was really nice... I used to go in there all the time.'

'There you go. Excellent, you see?' said Charles. 'Now you're getting it. And, Florian, one other thing: if there's any message you want me to give your, er, your mother, when I, I mean, when we, er...'

'Tell her you suck,' said the recalcitrant teenager.

'Do you really think that's what she wants to hear?'

'No, wait.' The boy's eyelids started to flicker. 'Tell her... tell her I want her to get back together with my dad.' Then his shoulders began to heave.

'Um, really?' said Charles. This wasn't the sort of message he had in mind at all. 'I mean, do you think there's any, any realistic, er, chance of...'

'Of what, sir? Of me getting out or of them getting together? What's more likely?'

'Now, let's not get ahead of ourselves, eh?' said Charles, his heart charging uphill again. 'But if we get back - and we have a long and difficult journey ahead of us, don't forget - I will make sure that I do my best, ah, to tell her.'

'And tell my mum she's got to keep swimming, yeah?' Florian said, his voice clotted by tears. 'She's got to look after herself. You know we've got our own pool.'

'Oh really? I hadn't, er...'

'She needs someone to keep an eye on her.'

'I will make it my...'

'Have you ever left someone behind before, sir?'

'Oh come on, Florian...'

Even now, a part of Charles wanted to tell Florian to stop milking it. And yet, of course, he was more than entitled to do just that.

'One minute!' said the guard.

'I'm sorry,' said Charles, and his voice caught in his throat as he spoke. He wished they could all be saved, that they didn't have to leave one behind in this beautiful, scarred wilderness. 'You know something?' said Charles, and then stopped. This was just the sort of thing Mrs Bavington would want to hear.

'Know what?'

'One day, when you're back at Rydon Hall, you will put your hand up and say, "Sir, did I ever tell you about the time I was a hostage in Smilia?" And we'll all groan and say, "Oh no, not again, Florian..."'

'Really?' said Florian. He didn't seem that taken with the idea. Perhaps he couldn't think speculatively unless he was linked up to an X-Box or a Wii.

'You see, in a sense, Florian, by remaining here, and by not coming back with us, you are holding us as your hostages.'

'Does it feel like that, sir?' said Florian. Why did he always have to sound so mocking?

'Yes. Well, in a sense.' Charles coughed. The air could get very gritty at times.

'In what sense?' Florian persisted.

'In the sense that we are all being punished for coming back without you. But I know that your mother would want you to behave as a Rydon Hall boy should do, and...'

'Oh please, sir, don't bother.' He was doing it again: not playing the game. This, Charles felt, was why they were where they were now.

'Don't give up on the Latin, will you?' said Florian in that nagging whine which was about to become less familiar. 'And when you're declining your verbs and...'

'Florian, verbs conjugate! For the last time, I mean...'

'OK sir, I'll try and remember,' said the boy, but it was obvious that he wouldn't.

The horn beeped outside. It was time to go. Charles stood up. Then he said, 'All I was going to say was, you know after the Common Entrance exams, when Year Eight get to go on trips, like to the BBC to see *So Local So London!* being recorded...'

'Oh yeah,' said Florian. Charles could tell that he was going to start whimpering again.

'We do those trips to show Year Eight how the real world is and so on. But when we get you back – and we will, Florian, I promise – when we get you back, you'll be so mature that you probably won't even want to come on the trip.'

'Are you saying I can't come on the *So Local So London!* trip?' said Florian in a rising tone, as if this was the ultimate deprivation.

'I didn't say that. You're taking it the wrong way again...' Charles could hear his own voice getting shrill. Why did Florian always have this effect on him?

'That's our big treat after the exams and you won't even let me go!'

'That's not what I meant...' said Charles, but the door was being wrenched open. 'It was a metaphor!'

'Whadyamean?' said the boy. Had he not listened to a word Bill Drummer had said?

'Come!' said the guard. 'Bus going. Come.'

'Of course you can come on the trip, Florian,' Charles shouted.

There was uproar on the bus. Everyone was calling out Florian's name.

'You said I couldn't come!' Florian was shouting back.

'You *can* come!' shouted Charles, his voice vying with the others. 'Of course you can!'

Charles could see the boy's face: eyes wide with

terror. The others all had masks on their faces. Only Charles could see.

'Tell my mum I love her! Tell my dad! Tell him I love him!'

'You'll be OK, Florian! You'll be fine!' Charles was shouting as two hands put a mask over his face and propelled him from the room. The last splash of colour he saw was Florian's orange hoodie, and the last words he heard before the bus door closed with an emphatic click were Florian's frenzied cries, 'Don't go! Don't go!'

As Charles took his seat on the bus, red-eyed and shaking with emotion, he felt almost overwhelmed by the horror of his final conversation with Florian. He would do his best, of course, to keep an eye on Mrs Bavington and ensure she didn't stop swimming. But urging her to reunite with her ex-husband while trying to advance his own interests: not for the first time, Florian's wishes were running completely at odds with his own.

CHAPTER 13

All children, no matter how much they might protest otherwise, need a sense of routine and so, somehow, life at Rydon Hall managed to find a semblance of regularity after the jarring episode of the hostage drama. Year Eight were back in school a week or two into the second half of the Spring term, and were being coaxed, joylessly as ever, to make a serious bid for the Common Entrance exam requirements. Charles no longer even thought of dressing up as a Roman senator, but he couldn't help sensing that some sort of shift had taken place in their collective mindset.

By removing the chief agitator, discipline had returned to the school's senior year, and there was a general sense, during staff meetings, or merely whispered conversations in corridors or the staffroom that, terrible though it was to lose Florian in this way, the academic prospects for the Common Entrance candidates were looking healthier.

The first, packed, staff meeting had about it a terrible sense of unreality. The kettle was on the whole time: a host of tea bags were subsumed beneath boiled water that afternoon. The returning staff members had been greeted not just with joy but also some incomprehension. Charles even felt he saw a trace of disapproval on Madame Allardyce's face, as if implying that, had she been on the trip, none of this nonsense would have occurred.

Dr Ironsize raised a hand for silence. He had insisted that Charles and Mrs Hughes-Howard sit on either side of him. Dr Ngo was down the other end of the room, his ample bottom supported by a very large rubber ring.

'I shall not pretend that the rest of this term is going to be easy,' Dr Ironsize began. 'Nor will it be straightforward, or simple, or effortless.'

He paused. Charles interlaced his fingers. Was the man trying to sound Churchillian?

'But I do know one thing, and it is this,' the head went on. 'The C.E. exams are in June, and they wait for no one. The clock is ticking.'

A small whiteboard had appeared in the secretary's office, on which Mrs Portal had added a vertical stroke each day since the tour party had returned without Florian. The number currently stood at 31. Dr Ironsize also gave out some wristbands. These had been supplied by the *Churley Advertiser*, and were coloured in the topaz and magenta school colours. The inscription read, "Where's Florian?" and was accompanied by a thumbnail photo of his face, as if it were a publicity ploy for a new picture book. The other side gave the numbers both for the news desk and for classified advertising.

'Well,' said Madame Allardyce, 'they can't hold out for long once they realise they're up against the *Churley Advertiser*.'

'It's about keeping it in our minds,' said Dr Ironsize. 'And I won't take it off until that boy returns. It stays with me, even while I'm gardening. Or in the shower.'

'Hear hear,' said Bill Drummer. 'What do we want? Florian! When do we want him? Now! Fuck, yeah.'

Just before the meeting, Dotty had given Charles' right forearm a gentle squeeze, which, in its way, expressed sympathy and support more eloquently than several hours of trauma counselling.

'If you need to step out for a minute, you know you can, Charles, OK?' she said. It was almost the first time that there hadn't been a teasing lilt to her voice and its sincerity made Charles unable to speak for several seconds.

Normally, pictures of every school trip were projected onto the screen at the first assembly back, but the collective will of the staffroom rejected this. Most of the boys' phones, and that of Dr Ngo - the official sharp-shooter of the party - were now being pored over

162

by government security agencies in the hunt to find evidence which could lead them to Florian.

Moving on, the burden of Year Eight homework was reduced to one subject a night, to give the boys more time to re-acclimatise. For the school's termly grudge fixture against the much larger and more aggressive Blagden House, Charles was asked if he would like to accompany the teams. He wasn't sure if his presence was meant to reassure the boys, or whether the school simply felt he needed a day out, but as Bill Drummer reversed gingerly out through the school gates, Charles was jolted back to the moment the coach door had slammed as they left Mr Baadi's compound, with the words 'Don't go!' still ringing in his ears.

His eyes red with tears, Charles had taken his seat on the bus. In a way he was grateful that the world had gone dark as a guard slipped the facemask over his eyes. He felt terrible that possibly his last conversation with Florian had ended on the anti-climactic subject of whether or not the boy would be allowed to go on a trip to the BBC studios in West London to watch *So Local So London!* being recorded, but, as he said to himself repeatedly while the bus toiled across the dry earth, what *was* an appropriate final word at such times?

He wriggled around in his seat trying to get comfortable. Everyone was still shouting Florian's name along with exhortations to hang in there, be strong and not give up, and assurances that they would be back to get him.

Charles had no idea at first who he was sitting next to, but it soon became clear that it was Harry Beamish: not his favourite pupil, and a fool when it came to written work, as well as a bit of a chatterbox when it was least needed. Here, however, where Charles could have done with some frivolous distraction, the boy was virtually mute.

After a while he said, 'Sir, do you think they'll kill him?'

'Of course not, Harry,' said Charles. 'Don't be stupid.' But this was asking too much of Harry, and Charles knew it. They left it at that for a further half-hour.

Making no allowances for the psychological state of the opposition, Blagden House were not feeling merciful, and the Rydon Hall teams returned to the bus with their batting and bowling averages severely dented. Bill Drummer suggested they sing *Jerusalem* on the way back to liven themselves up. That reminded Charles of Smilia too, but whereas the return journey from Blagden House was hindered only by queues of cars waiting to join the M3 at Byfleet, the road journey from the slopes of Smilia to the border with Enitenia had been stiflingly hot and what Mr Drummer would have called "extremely cross-contour". The coach was forever going up or down some minor hill, and there was much twisting, turning and grinding of gears. At first, the main sound that could be heard was of teenage sniffling and weeping. Before long, however, Mrs Hughes-Howard's sobs had taken over. They were lengthy and dignified. Dr Ngo, who had been attempting to kneel so that his scraped bottom did not have to rest on the unforgiving plastic seat following the indignities of the previous night, occasionally let out a piercing cry of 'Shhhhhhht!'

Mrs Hughes-Howard's First Aid skills had been put to good use dressing his wound and her plasterwork just about survived the jolting bus journey. After a while, the masks were removed. Then they drove in virtual silence.

Six hours or so later, the masks were put back on and the coach stopped to allow the driver to stretch his legs, and to give the boys a toilet break. Suddenly the voice of Mrs Hughes-Howard could be heard breaking through the crick-crick of the cicadas.

'Boys, and colleagues,' she said, her voice muffled behind the stiff cotton, 'we have all been through a terrible ordeal. We may be on our way back, but we have left one of our party behind. So I think now might be a good time for us to come together in prayer, no matter whether or what sort of God we believe in...'

'Florian's an atheist,' said a voice, pronouncing the word like "eh-fist".

'I know that, Dylan,' said Mrs Hughes-Howard. Charles was impressed that she had been able to identify Dylan through two layers of calico. 'I'm assuming it was you interrupting, not for the first time: but this is about more than just believing in God. I want us all to hold hands together, and to offer our thoughts – if not our prayers – for Florian. I want him to know, somehow to feel, that we are with him, right now, in his suffering.'

'But we're not, Miss? We're here...'

'I know that, Rohan,' said Mrs Hughes-Howard. 'It *was* Rohan, wasn't it?'

'Yes Miss,' said Rohan. Right again!

'I want us to offer our thoughts for poor Florian.' Suddenly the walls of her throat seemed to contract but she forced herself to carry on. 'I want us to think really hard about this young man, who is about to undergo a very much more severe form of the hardship that we have just been through...'

'Two minutes,' said the driver, who seemed to be smoking a cigarette. 'Then we go.'

'I know,' said Dylan. 'Let's sing one of his party tracks.'

'What a good idea, Dylan,' said Mrs Hughes-Howard. 'What songs does he like?'

'He likes Eminem,' said Josh.

'Well, I don't know an awful lot about him but if you think he's the sort of...'

'He's a rapper, Miss,' said Arthur.

'I know that, Arthur,' said Mrs Hughes-Howard, with the sort of sharpness that all teachers seemed to reserve for the eternally agreeable Arthur. 'I'm not totally senile.'

There then followed some discussion about what his favourite track might be. Yedverd thought it might be *Puke* but Dylan preferred *Big Fat Weenie*. In the end they settled on Dylan's choice, but the group's attempts to connect with the spirit of Eminem led to a rather wan rendition of "You're really just a big weenie," repeated several times but failing to build into the great swell of teenage voices that Mrs Hughes-Howard had been hoping for.

'Stop, stop, this is dreadful,' she yelled. 'What a riot. Can't we sing something with a proper tune that we all know the words to? Like *Jerusalem* or something?' As the bus party retraced its steps from the motorway through Lower Churley, Charles wondered if any of the other boys remembered the last time they had been invited to sing the great patriotic hymn.

On a smaller scale, life moved on, following its habitual pattern. Ms Brundleby, the new Special Needs teacher, announced a few weeks into term that she was "a tiny bit pregnant", and everyone cooed to hear that the baby was due a week before the end of term. Every day, a new number appeared on Mrs Portal's whiteboard and every morning Charles woke up to hear the voice of Florian Bavington sobbing, "How'm I going to survive?"

In the absence of the resident Year Eight bad boy, Dylan Cristiano stepped up to the mark, becoming, by turns, obtuse, intractable, slothful, disrespectful and mouthy. It was not an edifying spectacle, and no one was greatly surprised to hear that Mr and Mrs Cristiano had decided to transfer him, with immediate effect, to Thickett Lodge, where he would be nurtured to realise the potential in the one area at which he really shone: kicking a rugby ball high over a crossbar. (Charles could barely look at a horizontal pole without seeing his colleague Dr Ngo strapped to it.)

'We decided,' said Mrs Cristiano at the school gate one day, 'that what with – with Florian being, you know, away...' She seemed to stumble but then collected herself, 'we thought that a change of scene might do Dylan some good.'

The Thickett Lodge school motto, "*digitis cogitate*" – "Think on your feet" – was considered appropriately supportive, though Dr Ngo, whose sense of low humour was making a slow recovery thanks to a large dose of anti-infection pills, confessed to Charles that he had always assumed it meant "Count with your toes".

'And then there were 18,' said Dr Ironsize at the staff meeting when the news of Dylan's departure was revealed. 'I hope the pool isn't running dry.'

Relations between the three teachers who had had to endure the incarceration proceeded uneasily. Charles and Dr Ngo kept on stopping each other in the playground and saying, 'We really need to have a very long drink together,' as if this would finally nail the whole post-trauma thing, but somehow it never happened. It was the same with the other teachers. Bill Drummer often invited Charles into his office at the back of the hall to sample his espresso machine, but somehow their free periods never overlapped. Even though both Dotty and Charmian claimed to want to hear all about his traumatic experiences, there came to be something slightly last-term about the incident.

In a sense, Charles' shared experiences with Joy and Colin reduced the solidarity that they might have felt, almost making them rivals for the same pot of sympathy. If Charles walked into the staffroom and overheard Mrs Hughes-Howard telling a group of her colleagues about Mr Baadi or his guards, he wondered why they hadn't asked him. Either that, or he would attempt to laugh it off as if it were nothing, even though he didn't feel that way about it at all.

167

Dr Ngo, who had received no end of gaudy cartoon ties - his trademark item of apparel - as presents from the boys under his care, was the clear front-runner in the sympathy stakes, since he had been roasted about the bottom and was still walking with difficulty. Mrs Hughes-Howard, as the only woman present on the trip, had also been in an unusual position. She was now accompanied on the short walk to school by a large grey bull mastiff straining and puffing at the lead. Colleagues who bumped into her very early in the morning, being pulled by the slavering hound across Churley Common, said it was unclear whose eyes were redder, Patch's or his owner's.

Charles wished that more of his colleagues would ask about him, but there was a general sense that the school must try and move on. Everyone was at pains to point out that this was not meant to imply that Florian was forgotten but, as one of the trauma experts put it, they had to "come out of the cave". At least that had a practical application, unlike "You can't swim by looking over your shoulder," which was how Dr Ironsize framed it. Charles wondered how the backstroke fitted in with this analysis, but Dr Ngo discouraged such sniping.

'We all know what he means,' he said, 'even if he is a bit of a tit.'

Charles had been dreading weeks or even months of insomnia, but he never found going to sleep too much of a problem. Staying asleep was harder, as he was assailed by startling and accusatory dreams. These were often futile attempts to rewrite history, with Charles refusing to let Florian stand for the post of class rep, then being profusely thanked and Aristophanically pleasured by Florian's grateful mother. On another occasion, he was on lunch duty in the playground when Florian floated down on falcon wings. As Charles was about to greet him, he turned into Mr Baadi, his entire face contorted by masticated fistfuls of qat leaves. Mr Baadi pointed an AK-47 at Charles, whereupon Adrian Purvis appeared and yelled, 'Don't hurt me, sir!' Dr Ironsize called out 'Just dive in!' and Mrs Bavington squeezed the trigger, snapping Charles awake with a cry.

Florian had said his mother must keep swimming. And then he'd said, 'She needs someone to keep an eye on her.' This double-instruction began to fuse in Charles' mind to a single idea: that he himself should be there while Mrs Bavington was swimming. Of course he was prepared to do that. How could he deny Florian almost his last words before the door of captivity closed about him?

Mrs Portal had bought a large greeting card – the message on the front reading, "Thinking of You" – which had been passed round the staffroom for signatures before being forwarded to Mrs Bavington.

Charles had written his name, and then, after much deliberation, "Do call". He wanted to add, "Florian said I should watch you swimming," but felt that this might not be the best moment to express that thought. He knew, too, that he was meant to tell her to try again with her former husband, but for such wishes, greetings cards didn't quite carry the right emotional charge. He drafted and re-drafted a letter, hinting that he had been the last to speak to Florian, but it sounded so much like an obituary that he held back from sending it. Abandoning this plan for now, but still intent on meeting her, he continued to walk into Churley a couple of times a week but there was no sign of her offensively large Lexus.

'She's a strong woman,' said Dr Ironsize admiringly. 'Very strong: she'll come through.' But come through what? Dr Ironsize assured them that the Foreign Office were doing their utmost to find Florian, but everyone assumed this was a coded way of saying that they had no idea where he was.

Questions were raised in the House of Commons,

and there was a brief flurry of activity when a camera crew turned up to grill Dr Ironsize one day, but he was at his most evasive, padding up to every question from the increasingly shrill interviewer with limply ungrammatical eulogies like 'Florian is a really unique student' or blatant untruths like 'We're just holding our breath until he comes back.' Worst of all for the media, none of the mothers seemed able to burst into tears in front of the cameras, so they soon got bored and moved on.

Eventually, the only regular calls they got were from the *Churley Advertiser*, and even those stopped when Anthony, the other half of the hairdressers *Mark & ...*, was found to have covered Mark's car with hair gel in revenge for an alleged sexual infidelity. The ensuing courtroom battle began to assume greater prominence in the public mind.

After a while it emerged that Emmanuel the lunch attendant was not in fact from Enitenia but Smilia. He was invited to come and address a meeting of Year Eight boys and parents one evening, but despite an eloquent introduction from Dr Ironsize, the poor fellow's English was not terribly good, and when, still wearing his white overalls, he revealed that his parents, brother, sister and most of his cousins had been killed during the fighting of the last 20 years, he subsided into racking sobs and had to be helped from the stage.

Nobly, Mrs Hughes-Howard stepped in, stressing once again that the people of Smilia were a beautiful and peace-loving people, to whom the thought of imprisoning a single human soul – let alone a child – was anathema. At this point, Des Muireadhaigh's father jumped up and asked how much ransom money had been generated. He added that Mr Shapcott had texted him from Shanghai to say that he would double whatever the maximum contribution had been so far. Dr Ironsize responded by saying that he couldn't, "for security reasons", put a figure on the sum raised, whereupon Mr Justice and Mr Wang said that they were prepared to add their next Christmas bonus to the fund. Dr Ironsize said that Foreign Office policy on the payment of this particular ransom was still being formulated, and then Mrs Moyne put up her hand. She said that she was appalled because her stress counsellor had had to cancel their session last week as she was going on holiday to Ibiza. Mrs Zygnwycyz, whose English may not have been up to the cut and thrust of the discussion so far, complained that Yedverd's football shirt had gone missing, and that *Tyler & Everett*, the school outfitters, didn't have his neck size – which was hardly surprising as Yedverd was at least two sizes larger than anyone else. Mrs Coe-Haine countered this point by complaining that there were only two teachers on hand to accompany the boys down to the sports ground.

'Is that not enough?' asked Dr Ironsize.

'Not if someone tries to abduct them,' said Mrs de Burgh. A shiver went up around the room.

'In Churley? In south London?' said Dr Ironsize. 'I hardly think...'

'It happened in Egypt,' insisted Mrs De Burgh. 'In a Red Sea beach resort. You think these people only operate inside their own countries? They're coming over here – and they haven't come to learn cricket!'

At this point, so many others joined in that the meeting made little progress until it was forcibly adjourned by Ms de Souza. It was evident that the Year Eight parents had fallen victim to a mood of collective anxiety. 'If only we could get Florian back,' said Dr Ironsize afterwards in the staffroom. He mopped his brow with a sharply squared white handkerchief. 'Amazing: I never thought I'd hear myself say that.'

Charles' landlady, Mrs Annersley, continued to play host to an unfeasible number of strangers who were ill-equipped to occupy her mind for longer than they occupied her bed. After she kicked them out, not always waiting until they were fully dressed, she would creep back into the kitchen and open a consolatory bottle of wine.

'Good riddance to bad rubbish,' was her usual first comment, followed by an unnecessarily detailed analysis of how she had found them lacking, in between the sheets. In fact, as the wine bottle passed back and forth, Mrs Annersley proved to be a surprisingly sympathetic listener, and Charles was glad to unburden himself. She took a particular interest in the dreadful final night before their release, drawing out further details of Dr Ngo's horrific deprivations, suspended above the coals. 'The poor, poor man,' she kept muttering to herself, though her eyes seemed to shine with a peculiar glow.

One morning in late April, after steering Mrs Annersley through a particularly ruinous post-coital drinking spree the night before, Charles stepped gingerly from the H41 bus onto Churley High Street with a dull ache in his head. Dimly his eyes registered the fascia of the Fire Station and he walked in, thinking of nothing more ambitious than a large black coffee. He had just given his order when a smallish woman with olive-coloured skin and a single plait of hair rushed in and pushed ahead of him. She handed over a ten-pound note and, in what appeared to be a well-rehearsed ritual, was given in return a bulging brown paper bag. Charles was considering how he might confront the woman and have a quiet but firm word with her about pushing in, but then he saw her face.

'Linda?' he said.

The woman looked at him for a second. She clearly had no idea who he was.

'How is Mrs Bavington?'

Linda's face changed. 'Oh, I remember. You teacher? Rydon Hall?'

'That's right,' said Charles. 'How is she?'

'Oh...' said Linda. She waggled her hand. 'So-so. Very lonely. We no see you no more. You come over.'

Suddenly Charles wanted to kiss her. 'Do you think so?'

'You come say hi, she outside in car,' said Linda. 'You see.'

'Really?' said Charles, but as he said this, the coffee trainee yelled, 'Large Americano,' and a car horn could be heard.

'She no like to wait. Must go,' Linda turned and left.

Charles flung two pound coins on the tabletop and told them to keep the change but the trainee barista needed an extra ten pence.

By the time he had run outside, the car bearing Mrs Bavington and Linda had disappeared in a cloud of noxious soot.

When Years Six and Seven prepared a project about life in northern Africa with an emphasis on Egypt and the eastern parts, Year Eight were retained as overall consultants. In this way, the horrific end to the school trip could be recognised without being directly confronted. Before long, several tables were groaning with Ethiopian caps, Enitenian flatbread, metal mini-pyramids, plastic sphinxes and phials of herbs and spices. 'All we need now is some stuff from, like, an Egyptian tomb, yeah!' said Bill Drummer. Charles chose not to point out that, had fate not disposed otherwise, he might have been able to provide one such item himself.

Then came the unsettling day when a French trawler was hijacked off the coast of Smilia and its crew were interrogated on camera. The footage was flashed all over the world, and it took up the whole of an unusually international *So Local So London!* for one particular reason. The ship's crew, who looked as if they might be about to pass out from fear, or lack of sleep, were paraded in front of a single, very low-resolution camera – probably no more than a mobile phone, with sound quality to match. They were in a

173

bare room, with walls too dark to identify as concrete or rock, though Charles felt fairly certain that he had seen them before. The person asking them to confirm their identity was not in shot, but his voice sounded familiar.

'Absolutely appalling French,' said Madame Allardyce. The staff room TV was small and high up, and the smattering of teachers – including Charles – who weren't teaching had gathered in much the same way as an earlier generation would have waited to watch the Moon Landing. Despite the wobbly camera work, they all sat up during the last few seconds of footage when the interviewer, who could not have been French and was almost certainly too young to vote, said, in a dreadful accent, '*Vous savons que je me suis? Je suis Baa... da... vinto!*'

It sounded like a mangled version of either Baadi or Bavington, and it so shocked the staff that Mr Scamage had to be summoned, mop in hand and cursing under his breath, to clean up the mess made by so many spilled cups of tea. The fear was that Florian had somehow been programmed into going into partnership with Mr Baadi, in a pattern familiar from various hostage crises over the years involving heiresses and others.

'If it was Florian,' said Dr Ngo, 'and I do mean "if"... He sounds like he's gone native.'

'They must have brain-washed him,' said Madame Allardyce. 'But they'd have to empty his whole head first.'

Charles frowned. 'Well, the Latin wouldn't have taken long,' he said, hoping for a few sympathetic grins, but from the outbreak of tutting he could see that the remark had not gone down well. 'I just meant, maybe that part would have hurt less...' They were still staring at him. Eventually he was forced to resort to, 'Hey, I was there too, you know!'

The Year Eight parents' evening was always held towards the end of the Spring term. Each parent or set of parents was allotted five minutes with each teacher and, thanks to some skilful shuffling by Mrs Portal, the evening was split in two with a break in the middle, so that parents locked in acrimonious divorce proceedings could avoid each other and ask exactly the same questions while blaming their ex-partner for never telling them anything. (The former Mr and Mrs Shapcott and the former Mr and Mrs Zygnwycyz always attended separately. 'It's about the only thing I can get them to agree on,' said Dr Ironsize ruefully.)

Housed in the Hall, the tables were set up in a circle, with the teachers on the inside and the parents making their way round the outside, as if offering their condolences. There were 18 boys left to talk about – it hardly needed to be said that no representative of the Bavington family would be present – and while the teachers were supplied with a complimentary bottle of mineral water, for most parents the evening was lubricated with a glass of Chilean wine which didn't make too much of a dent in the £2,495 termly bill.

This parents' evening had a rarefied atmosphere. There was a crude painting of an east African elephant in the room, and the efforts of everyone to ignore its significance simply emphasised its presence. Head boy Arthur Clough's mother gave Dr Ironsize an over-lengthy hug, such as she had not given since Curlew Lodge had hinted at a Fencing Scholarship. Mrs Merriman said that Enzo was going to try for Boyson Hall because 'he needs open space. He doesn't like being locked up. Well, who does?' Then, realising what she had said, she spluttered, 'Sorry, I didn't mean...' and ground to a halt. Charles did not try to help her.

Equally unsettling was Mrs Purvis' declaration that Adrian "pretty much worships the ground you walk on, Mr Goldforbes." Charles expressed surprise but it turned out that Adrian had taken it into his head that, had it not been for Charles' intervention, he might

175

have ended up as class rep, and been stuck in Smilia with Mr Baadi. He had been pulling out all the stops ever since and his average mark had increased by very nearly a whole percentage point.

When all the parents had gone, Dr Ironsize breathed a huge sigh of relief and poured the dregs of an open screw-top bottle of wine into a glass.

'That was hard work,' he said as he spun the glass between his fingers. Then he tipped his head back, exclaimed 'Don't drink and *dive*,' and drained it in one gulp.

'Tell you what,' said Bill Drummer. 'Parents' evenings without Mrs Bavington, eh? I don't know why I turned up! Seriously!' Then he made a pint-lifting gesture at Charles. 'Charles, time for a quick one?'

'Oh, right, yes, OK,' Charles said. In fact he had been eyeing Dr Ngo who was limping, quite fast, out of the door. He had been wondering if now might be the night for them to go down the Four Horsemen and chat about the time they had been hostages together.

Dr Ngo looked back and caught Charles' eye. 'Got to get home,' he said. 'Arse killing me. Next week?'

'Sure,' said Charles.

Mrs Hughes-Howard, with Patch beside her, was pushing past him with the shopping trolley she used for ferrying books home.

'I've got that much marking to do: I'm fair glaikit,' she said, suddenly reverting to Scottish dialect. Then she turned around. 'I sometimes think Florian put himself up for class rep on purpose, just so that he could get out of doing homework.'

'I wouldn't be surprised,' said Charles.

'The little devil,' she said. Then she paused, with her hand on the door handle. Suddenly her eyes were swept with tears. 'Oh but I do miss him. Funny how it steals over you.' And then she was gone.

'I'll join you,' said Charles to Charmian and Bill.

'We're going now, yeah,' said Bill. 'Come to my office?'

'I'll see you in the pub,' said Charles. 'Could you get me a pint of Adnam's?'

'Get your own drinks, you freeloading twat,' said Bill, correcting himself a second later as he always did. 'Joking! Tourette's, sorry.'

In the marking room, Charles wondered as he filled his bag with Year Eight books, could he really sit chatting with Charmian and Bill about his experiences of captivity? Still, he could do with a drink.

As he set off up Windrush Avenue towards the Four Horsemen, the air didn't seem as tranquil as it usually was. He turned his head: some idiot in what looked like a cross between a jeep and a tank was slowly revving his engine. Why did big car owners have to show off all the time? Arsehole, thought Charles. Tosser. He considered the matter afresh and added: dick-head. He walked on, but when he turned around, the car was just behind him. His heart did a sort of low dive: he was being followed.

Charles tried to walk and think quickly. There was no one else around, the pub was three streets away, and he was being followed by – Holy Mother of God – had the Egyptian Museum sent an agent to quiz him about the falcon of Helikonopolis? Had CCTV images of the heist come to light? Had Florian, damn his eyes, denounced him under pressure from Mr Baadi? He stopped, and tried to think rationally. It was more likely to be a mugger. Should he phone the police, then? But surely they only wanted his phone. Fling it down and run for it? Or dash for the darkened streets around the pub? The high street was busier but further away. Could he knock on someone's door, throw himself on their mercies, protest that he had been kidnapped in Smilia? He tried to break into a trot, but his bag was weighing him down. Typical: not content with getting him kidnapped in Egypt, Year Eight were going to get him beaten up in south London. But then the car pulled level. Its cold, blue headlights were so sharp that for a few seconds his eyes were helpless.

Then he heard the car window whining downwards. He put a hand up to protect his face, expecting to feel a bullet rupture his skin. Instead, he heard a well-spoken voice.

'Excuse me, are you the Latin teacher?'

Charles took his hand down from his face. He still couldn't see much, except that the driver, who seemed to be on his own, had a sharply receding hairline and dark shades resting on the top of his head as if he were in southern Italy. Charles' heart was still racing like a skipping flea.

The man leaned over: the steering wheel was on the left-hand side. 'Sorry, but are you the Rydon Hall Latin teacher?'

'I... Yes,' said Charles.

'Charles Goldfraud?'

'Goldforbes,' said Charles. 'But who the fuck are you?'

The stranger slid over the black leather seat towards him. He had piercing blue eyes. 'I want to talk to you, and I think you might want to talk to me. I'm Hugh Bavington.'

CHAPTER 14

Hugh Bavington peered into the depths of his pint glass. 'Of course I knew it had to be you,' he said. 'I know what all the other teachers look like.' He sniffed. 'And the parents, too: bunch of cock-snoggers.'

The pub where they were sitting was in a remote and unfamiliar corner of Lower Churley, on the borders with distant Fring. When it was called The Bull, it had been frequented by the staff of a nearby hospital until, in the 1980s, a Thatcherite firebrand had had the brilliant idea of pulling down Fring A & E and hiring a medium-sized firm of architects to give it a "site optimisation" as a housing estate and supermarket. Within the first few weeks of the supermarket's special beer promotion, The Bull had fallen silent. It staged a minor comeback as a wine bar called Yours Grapefully but, when the supermarket threw in a free bottle of wine with any purchase over a fiver, Yours Grapefully's doors were closed within the month. Yet, somehow, it refused to accept that its time had come. In its latest incarnation, it had been re-named and re-branded with what the brewery hoped was a wrily post-modern slant on 21st century masculinity. Yet even that had not brought the numbers they had hoped, and so the Huge Cock was, on this evening, as on most other evenings, some way short of half-full.

Inside its narrow booths, much younger women were expressing forced but voluble delight at whatever their older male companions were saying. Charles didn't put up that much of a struggle when Florian's father insisted on buying the drinks. 'I've kidnapped you, after all, haven't I?' he said brightly, followed immediately by, 'Sorry: bad joke.' Two pints of blonde-crowned Belgian beer were poured into two glasses that seemed to have been modelled on the shape of a tuba. There were no available booths. 'Wait here,' said Bavington. He returned a few seconds later. 'Come on,' he said. 'We're in.' It seemed that whenever he spoke, it was gruffly.

They walked over to a sort of bird table with a square top and a safety rail round the edge. Balanced against it were two high chairs. Bavington was a large man, and about half a head taller than Charles. He wedged himself into one chair: Charles virtually had to vault into his.

'So, Mr Latin teacher,' Hugh said, '*amo, amas, amat*, is that right? Don't ask me any more: that's all I remember.' He picked up his glass and necked half of it in one gulp. The hair on top of his head was thinning, but in compensation he had a curly ponytail which Charles would have told him, had he not been bigger than Charles, and the purchaser of the drinks, and the father of a missing boy, made him look ridiculous. Apart from a rather florid expression to his face, he was still in pretty good physical shape, but his eyes had grey panda circles around them. The cheesily dim lighting couldn't have helped, but it didn't look as if he had been sleeping too well.

'Don't you think you had better call me Charles?' said Charles.

Hugh Bavington grunted.

'Or Mr Goldforbes,' said Charles.

'How about Sir?'

'If you insist,' said Charles.

Bavington took a slurp of lager. 'So what the effing tits went wrong on this tour? I've heard of *Cook's Tours* but this sounded like Cock-up's Tours to me. Getting a whole class taken hostage by some quacking towel-heads? What the bollocks were you playing at?'

'Well, we didn't do it deliberately, Mr Bavington,' said Charles.

'I should hope not,' said Bavington, ripping open a pack of dry roasted peanuts with his teeth. 'And now my son is in some prison cell in the middle of darkest sodding Africa.'

'Not the middle. It's just inside the Horn of Africa,

in fact. Shall I tell you what happened?'

It was a while since Charles had unburdened himself to anyone else apart from his landlady and a by now somewhat jaded trauma counsellor, so he told the story. Bavington listened, or appeared to. He was wearing a pink striped polo shirt and a Golf Club de Monaco V-neck sweater. At one point he got out a gold toothpick and began to scrape the backs of his teeth with more force than could have been good for them.

Charles didn't think Mr Bavington needed excessive detail so he stuck to the basics. He closed his account with a brief but glowing encomium about his son. 'From what I saw of Florian in those last few minutes before we left, I think he is a very brave young man...'

'Scrap all that,' said Bavington sharply. Then his face appeared to tremble, and Charles really thought he might be about to weep, but he mastered it. 'Don't want all that crap,' said Bavington. 'Question is, how do we get him back?'

'I assume you've discussed the ransom demand?' said Charles.

'Ten million?' said Bavington. 'I'm in pretty good shape, Mr Goldforbes, and I know it's dollars, but even my business isn't worth that much. I might be able to sell it for five: seven, tops. From the sound of this guy, I don't think he's into haggling.'

'Have you tried to get in touch?' said Charles.

'Of course,' said Bavington. 'Done everything. Messages, threats, pleas, faxed a list of demands to Lord knows where. The lot. The effing lot.'

'Do you know if they've got through?'

'That's the trouble,' said Bavington. 'No idea. My son could be effing dead for all I know.'

'Let's not contemplate that,' said Charles.

'Mr Golfbore...' said Hugh.

'Goldforbes,' said Charles.

'Whatever,' said Hugh. 'I'm a businessman. I'm not a languages man, and neither is my son. I'm not a bloody intellectual. My father bred racehorses: full stop. If it didn't have four legs and a tail, he wasn't really that interested, and that included me. I don't really give a toss whether Caesar conquered Gaul. If he did, fine: me no interest, very sorry.'

'Just out of interest, he did,' said Charles, marvelling at the bond between father and son.

'You get excited about that sort of thing, that's fine. I import large American cars. I'm in the luxury goods market. I deliver dreams. People who think they deserve the best, or the longest: that's what they get. No one can tell me anything about a stretch Cadillac that I don't know. I get what I want because I knew what I wanted. I wanted to be the best: full bloody stop, chum. But now I want something else.' He suddenly seized Charles' wrist so hard that Charles thought he might never be able to hold a board rubber again. At the same time, one or two other couples stopped smooching with each other, not because Hugh Bavington was shouting – he was not – but because his face had contorted, not violently but pitiably, and the tears that he had been holding back sprang into his eyes. 'I want my boy back. I want the little sod back. I need him: do you hear me?'

'Very, very clearly,' said Charles, as the first stabs of pain died away. 'I completely understand how desperate you must feel.'

'No you don't,' said Bavington, letting go of his hand. 'You can't. Look, Chuck...' No one had ever called Charles "Chuck" before. 'What's Flo like in class? Bit of a handful sometimes?'

Charles considered how best to answer this question. His mind raced back to his first few weeks at Rydon Hall, when Dotty had shown him a teachers' website that contained invaluable euphemisms for parent evenings.

'He's certainly very lively,' he said. Bavington stared at him without speaking. 'He has a very strong personality.' Bavington said nothing. 'He can be... forceful and single-minded at times, when he's trying to get his, um, his way.' Bavington's eyes were burning holes into his, and his slightly mottled cheeks were beginning to quiver. Charles tried to think of some more useful comments. 'He can come across as quite detached, which can unbalance the lesson when his attention isn't...'

Charles stopped talking this time because there was silence in the bar. The reason for this was that Mr Bavington had brought his hand down on the tabletop with an enormous crack. Both their beer glasses frothed up, and Charles felt as if he had been picked up and rattled. Speech, too, became difficult, mostly because Mr Bavington's enormous and hairy hand had stapled his neck to the edge of the table.

'Don't give me that crap,' said Bavington in a disturbingly dulcet tone. 'My son is an annoying little prick. You know that, I know that. For fuck's sake, he's called Florian! Whose bloody idea was that? Not mine, I can assure you. Lost that battle a long time ago. Now stop pretending and just give it to me straight. Is he or is he not an annoying little prick? Tell me!'

'Mr Bavington,' said Charles, speaking through a narrow fissure in his lips, 'your son is an annoying little prick.'

'He's a pain in the arse.'

'He is a total and utter pain in the arse,' said Charles, feeling the pressure on his neck begin to lessen.

'What else is he?'

'He's impossible to teach. He's sly, he's surly, he's unreliable, he's slippery, sarcastic, snide, mendacious...'

'He's a prat.'

'In a way, yes,' said Charles after serious reflection. 'Yes, he's a prat.' Charles was finding this strangely liberating. 'And he's a dickhead.'

Bavington took his hand off Charles' neck. 'He's a little shit.'

'Well, he can be,' said Charles. He celebrated his

183

freedom by straightening his tie.

'Say it.'

'Florian Bavington is a little shit,' said Charles.

'He's all those things,' said Hugh. 'All his teachers agree he is.'

'Yes.'

'Mrs Fucking Two Aitches and that absurd Chinese fellow...'

'I think he's one quarter Vietnamese actually...'

'Fine,' said Hugh. 'Now that we're agreed on that, tell me one thing: was that why you handed him over to them?'

Charles let out a little gasp, as if a spark from some glowing coals had just alighted on one of his buttocks.

'Mr Bavington,' he said, beginning to ease himself off his high chair as if he were about to jump to the floor. 'I think we are going to have to continue this conversation via our lawyers. Because if you think...'

'Shut the fuck up and answer the question,' said Bavington.

'I will thank you not to tell me to shut up,' said Charles. 'I am not one of your limousine drivers: I am the head of the Rydon Hall Latin department.' His hackles were rising. Even now he was wondering, if he got the first blow in, whether he could evade the counter-punch.

'I like your attitude, Chuck,' said Mr Bavington, somehow conjuring a waitress out of the depths and ordering two more drinks. 'I like a fighter. But on this occasion I am simply asking if you would be so kind as to shut up, sit down and listen.'

Charles tipped his head back and drained his glass before the next one arrived. 'Go on then,' he said.

'Florian is my son,' said Hugh, 'which means I can slag him off as much as I want to. But I - thank God - am not the poor sod who has to teach him. I don't have to sit in some wretched classroom with him for eight sodding hours a day, waiting for him to stop talking. I

184

hate his fucking bling attitude and his Eminem songs. You and I know what he really is: he's a skinny white kid from south London: not some rapper from South Central Los Angeles.'

'I could not agree more...'

'But my point is this, Mr Goldorf. Even though there are times when I really do want to kill him, I still maintain that that right should rest with me, not with some tin-pot African dictator.'

'Yes it should,' said Charles. 'Although it would still be a criminal offence if...'

'You're not a parent, Mr Golborne. Perhaps you will be, one day, unless you're a *ho-mo-sexual* and you prefer taking it up the arse.'

'I am not gay, Mr Bavington, and I would like to be a father one day. And could I advise you that language of that nature is...'

'You know, when I became a father...' Bavington spoke as if from inside a reverie. 'That first day, when you see that little just-arrived blob of foetus, it's the proudest, most unbelievable day of your life. You're holding that new-born baby and you would kill anyone who came within a hair's breadth of causing it any discomfort. But here's the incredible thing: two, four or six years later, when your sweet little angel tips a mug of tea over the dashboard of your new Lexus or wakes you up at five instead of letting you lie in for an extra half-hour, for a few moments you genuinely entertain the idea that you could slaughter your own child. Now how is that?'

There was an uneasy pause.

'Strange to think, isn't it,' said Charles hurriedly, 'that the Spartans practised infanticide?'

Mr Bavington's expression suggested that he was not as keen on aspects of Classical Civilisation as his ex-wife. He sighed, long and hard. Then he said, 'I could do with a cigarette. I do wish those effing pussies in the European Parliament hadn't banned smoking everywhere. You know there is literally nowhere... If I want a cigarette in my London office, I have to go onto the fire escape with the effing receptionist.'

'That must be awful.'

Bavington grinned crookedly. 'Actually if you'd seen her tits you probably wouldn't say that. Fantastic top rack. However...' He cracked his finger joints together like dry twigs. 'If anyone is going to hurt my irritating bonehead of a son, only one person gets to do it. Got it?'

'Quite right,' said Charles.

'But there's one thing left we haven't tried.'

'Really? What's that?' said Charles, taking his first sip of the newly-arrived lager.

The father of the missing boy gave him a lopsided grin. There, but for the chip in the front tooth, was Florian's face. Charles didn't like it all that much when Florian grinned, and he wasn't sure if he was going to like it now. 'The nuclear option,' he said.

'The nuclear option,' said Charles. 'Are you sure that might not work out a bit...'

'The nuclear option, Chuck,' said Bavington. He stuck out a hairy finger and jabbed it towards his own neck. 'If nobody else can find my son, I'll have to do it myself.'

'You..? You're going to..?'

'I'm going to go to Smilia to find my son. I'm going to get myself taken hostage, just like what happened to you and Hong Kong Charlie and Mrs Two-Aitches.'

'Well I think that's unbelievably brave and noble of you,' said Charles.

'Do you think I'm mad?'

'Possibly. Slightly,' said Charles, 'but you want your son back and you're willing to try anything, and I don't blame you.'

'And I need your help.'

'Of course you do, Mr Bavington, and you know full well that I'd be willing to help in any way you thought was necessary.'

'You were the last person to see him.'

'It was a very special moment,' said Charles. 'I shall never forget the impression he made on me that morning. In fact, he almost made me promise that as soon as I got back, I would go up to the home of your, ex, er...'

'How much do you want him back?'

'Oh,' said Charles, 'you just can't put it into words.'

'Would you do anything?'

'Absolutely,' said Charles, knocking back some more of his new pint. 'Of course I would: you know that.'

'Good,' said Bavington. 'Because I need someone I can trust.'

'I'm your man,' said Charles.

'And that's why I came to find you.' Bavington sat back.

'Right, so you want me to put you in touch with someone...'

'I want you with me.'

'I'm with you all the way, Mr Bavington. Excellent beer, by the...'

'We're going to find Florian.'

'I'll drink to that.'

'We're going to get him back from Smilia.'

'Right by your side,' said Charles, holding his glass out for a supportive chink. 'I'm there for you, seriously. Call me whenever you...'

'We leave in three weeks.'

'We...?'

'You and me.' Mr Bavington pointed the gold toothpick at Charles. 'You did say you were coming, didn't you?'

Charles looked down: it suddenly seemed a long way from the chair to the floor. He raised his shoulders up towards his ears several times, as if he was considering this matter very carefully. Mr Bavington was still staring at him.

'Can't hear you,' said Bavington.

'I'm just... I'm still thinking,' said Charles.

'I thought Latin teachers were quick thinkers,' said Bavington. 'What is there to think about? Do you want to rescue Florian or not?'

'Of course I do,' said Charles. 'I'm just wondering if this is the most effective...'

'We've tried everything else!' said Hugh. 'I've got to find this Baadi guy, do a deal with him. I'll swap with him. Let Flo go: I'll stay behind.'

'I'm just wondering what actual, you know, specific use I would be?' said Charles, wondering how hard his face would hit the ground if he fainted now.

'Speke!' said Bavington.

'Sorry?' said Charles.

'Speke!'

'That's what I'm trying to...'

'Speke, you idiot. Hanning Speke. Livingstone's companion and trusty sidekick. Me Livingstone, you Speke. You will accompany me, get me in there. You never know, you might end up bringing Florian home if they let you. Or you'd stay with me. Teach me Latin: that'd give me something to do. The main thing is: I want my boy out of there.'

'Have you discussed this with the Foreign Office?'

'The F.O.?' Bavington snorted with derision. 'Eff off to the F.O., that's what I say. Bunch of shirt-lifters. I don't need any help from those public school arse-bandits. I need to retrace my son's steps, and that's where you can help.'

'Ah, small problem,' said Charles, with real pathos in his voice. 'You see, we were blindfolded for most of the journey, so I didn't get to look out of the window that much. It's a real pity that I won't be of any use but...'

'It'll all come back to you, matey, don't you worry,' said Bavington, ramming a fistful of peanuts down his throat. 'Even the smell of the place, or the sound. It's amazing what a difference it makes when you're there. I've done business in Africa: every inch of it's got a different feel to it. I want you to be my bloodhound. That's what these effing school trips are all about, isn't it? What's the point of talking about the bloody Colosseum in Churley when you can go to Rome and walk round it? Do you see? We've got to do it. I can't take that Chinky fellow: he's buggered. And I'm fucked if I'm going out there with Mrs Two-Aitches. You're my man. So here's the plan. We fly to Egypt, head for Hurghada, fanny about a bit, get noticed, head off for Enitenia. At some point, they come for us, same as they went for you: we get captured, meet this guy Baadi. Bingo. It's our only chance. Point is it's *his* only chance. Do you understand? I don't care what happens to me. It's not about me. I'm going to find my son or die trying.'

'I mean...' Charles was conscious that he was rubbing his hands together in a patently nervous way. 'The thing is: those students who are still at Rydon Hall need my – if I may say – my expertise with their Common Entrance examinations: exams which will profoundly influence the course of their lives. Now...'

'Come off it, Chuck,' said Bavington. 'You Latin teachers are ten a penny. Stand outside some Oxbridge quad on a Saturday night and you could fill a truck with 'em in half an hour. But *you've* got the local expertise: that's what I need.'

'Right. I see,' said Charles. 'And you know what? In a way I feel really honoured you've chosen me to be part of your team.'

'Good,' said Bavington.

'And of course, if I were free, I would have considered this trip to be, well, a no-brainer.'

'Which it is,' said Bavington. 'Well spotted.'

'But let me be absolutely straight with you.' Charles licked his lips. 'My landlady is approaching the end of her life. She's an extraordinary woman, I've known her for a long time, she kind of found me in the street after my parents, uh, they were both hopelessly drug-dependent, you see, but...' Charles wondered if he

189

could ever buy Mrs Annersley enough wine to make her stand by this version of events. 'But she's on her last legs, and the nuns have told me that really what's keeping her alive is the prospect of seeing me...'

Once again, Charles stopped speaking. This time it was because Bavington had removed the shades from his pate and was aiming them at him.

'Are you frightened?'

'Frightened? *Me?* No way!' Charles said with excessive fervour. 'Far from it. I'm just... I suppose the truth is I'm worried that if we did get to meet Mr Baadi again, I would be so... angry, I suppose, for having imprisoned your son all these months, that I might just... We're just creeping up behind him and I'd be unable to help myself crying out, "We're coming to get you, Florian!" or something and he turns round, or one of his guards does, and I'd never forgive myself if I cocked up the whole thing...'

Bavington only had to look up, this time, for Charles to grind to a halt. Then he leaned forward. Charles leaned in too, but not quite so far. 'Have you heard what my ex-wife has been up to lately?'

Charles felt his gills jangling. He shook his head.

'She's learning Latin.'

'Oh really?' said Charles. 'With...?'

'Your predecessor.'

Charles sat bolt upright in his extremely high chair. 'Mr Norringham? But I thought he was...'

'He is,' said Bavington. 'He's at an international school in the Gulf. They Skype each other twice a week. She says she wants to be able to coach Florian when he gets back. And Latin was his weakest subject.' Bavington looked with derision at Charles. 'You did know it was his weakest subject, didn't you?'

'Well, I had rather got that impression,' said Charles, weakly. 'But I didn't know... the other thing.'

'I'll be seeing her tomorrow,' said Mr Bavington. 'We've had to meet up a few times over the last few weeks. She's still mad as a pint of bricks.'

'Do you think so?'

'If you'd seen her taste in interior decor,' he said, 'you'd know what I'm talking about. At least I got my way with the swimming pool. So anyway...' Bavington's hairy hand extended itself across the table until it encircled Charles' fingers like a baby partridge. 'So you'll do it? Good man,' he growled.

'And what will you do when you've found Florian?'

'Probably stick him over my knee and thrash his silly arse till it's red,' said Mr Bavington.

Hugh – Charles felt he could refer to him by his first name, since they were about to spend the rest of their lives shut inside a cave in Smilia – gave Charles a lift back home, or at any rate towards a bus stop from which he needed only two night buses to get there. Now that he had revealed his plans, the father of Florian seemed a bit more relaxed, and had stopped swearing all the time, or at least with every other word. Charles thought it worth one more attempt.

'Have you thought,' he said, while they were still driving, 'of what effect it might have on a certain person if you don't..?'

'*Arsehole!*' Hugh nearly ground a solitary cyclist into the kerb. 'Drive me fucking spare, those people. Think they own the bloody road. Who pays road tax?'

'Do you?'

'Not in this country. I pay enough back home, let me tell you.'

'But if you don't succeed in your mission...'

'You mean if *we* don't succeed...'

'Of course, but I mean, how is Mrs Bavington going to react?'

'Oh for God's sake,' said Hugh. 'My dear wife will not lose a night's sleep over *my* passing, I can assure you. If I got locked up in a prison cell in darkest bloody Africa, that's her Christmas come early, that is.'

'Are you sure you're not over-dramatising...'

'Mr Golfdawes...' Hugh pulled the car to the side of

the road so that it more or less filled the bus stop space that they had just reached. 'As you may know, my wife and I are divorced. Do I regret splitting up with her? Well, yes, in terms of its effect on Florian. Do I miss the sex? Yes, but I've made up for that elsewhere. Our marriage simply failed. By the end, there just wasn't any chemistry between my wife and I.'

'Actually it's *me*,' said Charles, unable to resist.

'I'm sorry?' said Hugh.

'I mean, between your wife and you,' Charles added hastily. 'Not I. Me.'

'You've completely lost me,' said Bavington.

'It's just the grammar that's wrong,' said Charles. 'It's an accusative: me, not I.'

'Oh, the grammar,' said Hugh wearily. 'Where would we be without the grammar?'

An N659 bus, which would have conveyed Charles to within two miles of his front door, drew up to the sign and flashed its lights at Hugh. As he was ignoring it, the bus had no option but to cross two lanes of traffic in a bid to get away.

'Was that your bus?' said Hugh.

'Yes, but there'll be another,' said Charles.

'Another bus?'

'Yes.'

'Not another wife,' said Hugh. 'Not making that mistake again. Mind if I drop you here?'

Charles opened the door and negotiated the descent to the roadside. Then, with his hand on the door, he said, 'You know, um, Hugh, there was one other thing I hadn't told you. It's a bit odd, but if we're doing this trip together, I might as well share it. It's something Florian said to me in the last few minutes before we...'

'Left him behind,' said Hugh.

'Er, not quite,' said Charles. 'But it was strange: he looked at me and he said, "Sir, I want you to ask my mum and dad to get married again."'

Even though he had done his best to deaden the message, Charles still expected Hugh to feel some emotional impact. Instead, he merely grunted.

'Tell you what,' Hugh revved the engine. 'Let's get Florian, then we'll plan the wedding. And you can be best man, Charlie.'

'Great!' said Charles, relieved to have got away with it. 'Oh and he asked me to make sure she kept swimming, as well?'

'Good luck with that, Mr Latin teacher,' said Hugh.

Charles slammed the massive, thickened door shut, and Hugh's Hummer skidded away with a dirty, thirsty drone, dusting Charles' face with a shower of gravel pellets. Charles surveyed the timetable. The fragment that had not been vandalised informed him that the next bus would arrive in the next 50 to 70 minutes. As Charles started walking home he felt a mixture of feelings. Abject terror, obviously, at the prospect of returning to the Red Sea with Hugh Bavington, on a mission which might draw the so far not terribly satisfactory threads of his life to a close. And yet, for reasons distantly connected with the smell of chlorine at Churley House, Charles proceeded to do an odd sort of dance all the way up Sparrow's Nest Hill.

CHAPTER 15

Fortified by three pints of Belgian lager – or as much as had not spilled each time Mr Bavington thumped the table – Charles had retired to bed, hoping merely for a passable night's sleep and a not-too-thick head in the morning. But his first thought on waking was to reflect that his time with Mrs Annersley really might be drawing to a close. If Mr Bavington's desperate plan came into effect, he could be out of Embury Park within the month, having volunteered to spend an indefinite period as a pawn in Mr Baadi's game of asymmetric chess. Charles had never been a religious person, but as he lay, sweating coldly, in bed, he did mutter a short prayer to the effect that some minor but disabling accident might befall Hugh Bavington.

Given these apocalyptic musings, Charles could only reflect, some weeks later, on the different turn that events had taken. He was at the shallow end of Mrs Bavington's pool, having decided that two lengths were probably enough. The raisin bush by the side was not yet in flower, but he found its presence there reassuring. The plant was still struggling to establish itself in the steamy atmosphere but that was hardly surprising: the original had been bought by Mrs Hughes-Howard at a combined service station and micro-shopping centre during the one toilet stop they had made in Smilia before barrelling their way towards the border, accompanied by a convoy of police outriders and a truck filled with twitchy soldiers. The plant had been meant as a memento of their trip though it was impounded before they crossed into Enitenia. Ever eager to please, the staff at Close to the Hedge, Churley's garden centre, had found a replacement. Linda, on her way to Paws for Thought to collect Finzi after his latest tooth-whitening expedition, had collected it from school.

Charles had emerged from his Finals exam feeling he hadn't quite done justice to the title "What is Irony?" but he felt fairly sure that he was dealing with a case of it now, given his current situation and the fact that Florian had set him the task of resurrecting his parents' marriage. If there wasn't irony in there, thought Charles, he probably needed to redefine the term.

So far, his resuscitatory efforts hadn't achieved a great deal. His excuse was that it was difficult to discuss matters of the heart during shouted conversations with Mrs Bavington's former husband whenever he rang from Andorra, Liechtenstein, Monaco or some other European principality more famous for its casinos than its heavy industry. He was usually ringing to make some minor but terrifying alteration to their itinerary. Depending on which model he was driving, Charles could sometimes hear Hugh's soft-top roof assembling itself while they spoke, which they continued to do until a tunnel – much to Charles' relief – cut them off.

He had heard that Mrs Bavington was in the habit of dropping into the church of St Botock's on the Hill. A nervous Charles Goldforbes, evidently a man with much on his mind and a pressing need to share it with a trustworthy figure, sought out the Reverend Anne Itkyss, and they both speculated about Florian's requests of Charles – at least those regarding Natasha's swimming and Charles' watching her. He may have forgotten to add the part about resurrecting her failed marriage to Hugh.

He had, however, mentioned, almost in passing, that, out of concern for Florian's safety, he was considering returning to Smilia to track the boy down. The Reverend Itkyss gave his arm a supportive squeeze and asked if she had his permission to say something to Mrs Bavington the next time she came in for Evensong. Charles – the expression on his face all but saying "Oh Lord, take this cup from me" – bowed his head and mumbled the words, 'Thy will be done.'

In fact, Charles' re-emergence at Churley House was not down to his own subterfuges at all but rather to the foibles of his immediate predecessor. It had all been going so well for Geoffrey Norringham in Oman: a warm climate, all the cash he could possibly need and the chance to enjoy what was, in Mr Norringham's own words, "not a conventional Classics teaching post". The problem was that the consumption of alcohol was, of course, a flagrant breach of the Koran's strictures and while everyone – especially all foreigners – flouted the ban, few were so stupid as to get caught. Once Mr Norringham's part in an illegal Moonshine racket had been reported to the authorities, there was, in the words of Dr Ironsize, "a bit of a stink". For a while it even looked as if the poor man might receive several blows in public with a strap, but the British Consulate stepped in and Mr Norringham was allowed to escape as far as Bahrain, where he got a better-paid job in a less impressive school. But as his phone line would take some time to sort out, the connection with Mrs Bavington was the main victim of the cross-Gulf transfer.

He didn't know whether or not it was all thanks to Anne (they were on first-name terms now) but on the Friday after Mr Norringham's enforced departure, Charles was amazed to read an email from Mrs Bavington saying that Mr Norringham was no longer able to teach her Latin and asking if Charles had any spare time.

Charles managed to hold off until Monday afternoon, but his reply – measured, sober, unerotic but not too despondent – was calculated to reassure. Yes, he said, he thought that could be arranged. A meeting was set up for a few days later, and so Charles once more found his feet crunching on the gravel of the looping path. Just ahead of him, a red squirrel – part of a Churley-based scheme to reintroduce the lost species to London – paused with a hazelnut in its mouth. A wood pigeon cooed softly in the Dutch Elm overhead: the scene was softly sylvan.

Linda met him at the front door. 'Hi Mr Gofor, you here for Skeep lesson?' she said. Charles wasn't sure what she meant. She must know that he taught Latin, not physical education. All became clear when she led him into the improvised classroom with the cartoon wallpaper. When he sat down, Charles saw a milkmaid perched shakily on the branch of a tree, a huge exclamation mark suspended like a Damoclean sword over her head. She seemed about to scream but whatever the source of her anxiety was, it had not been included on the roll.

Having expected to see Natasha, Charles felt bemused and disappointed to discover that the room was empty bar a large, flat-screen computer, complete with built-in webcam, which dominated half of one wall.

'Oh, is this Skype?' he said. That explained the confusion. Was he really not going to see her?

'Yeah, is a Skeep. You know, she want lessons but she still feel bad. I say to her you do a Skeep, is better. You can to start straight way: she wait for you. She hear you if you put the headphones.' Linda tapped lightly on the keyboard. 'Meesis Babbington, you there? Is Mr Charles here.'

Charles had imagined some scene out of *Great Expectations*, with Florian's coat still on the floor where he had last flung it, but there were no skeins of cobwebs billowing from the ceiling. Instead, he sat down in front of the screen and waited for the link to open. A window flashed up, asking if he wanted to continue. Charles was not sure if he did but he sat down nevertheless. The screen showed a woman's hand, writing with a pen on a sheet of paper. He thought he recognised the fingers.

A word appeared, then more.

- *Shall we begin?*

'Hello Mrs Bavington,' said Charles as the spongy

ear-pieces reduced all external sounds to a mere hum. 'How, er...?'

He realised he could not finish the sentence. Was he really going to ask her how she was? And what answer would he get back, considering her son had been missing for over two months? He didn't even want to speculate on how she was feeling.

- Chapter 5.

'OK,' he said.

Charles had done a little forward-planning for the lesson, just in case any unfortunate sentences came up. Once they had got beyond "*nauta puellam amat*" (The sailor loves the girl) he could see that the more demanding "*nautae puerum capiunt*" (The sailors capture the boy) should perhaps be excised from the lesson. Another apparently innocent clause – "*filius in villam non venit*" - which could be translated as "The son is not coming into the house" – met the same fate. He didn't know whether she had noticed these sentences in her book or not, but it seemed sensible to avoid references to the imprisonment or liberation of children. Farmers and doctors, on the other hand, were allowed to get away with almost anything, from loving money to carrying horses.

One sentence that he would have liked them to take on was, "I will soon be travelling to Smilia with your ex-husband in order to find your son", but that was still, he hoped, some way off.

- See you next week? She wrote after just under an hour.

'Er, yes,' he said...' The sentence tailed off and a screen message told him that the other person had ended the conversation. Charles stood up. He padded into the corridor, where Linda met him with a brown envelope.

'Here, for you,' said Linda.

'Is it a letter?' said Charles.

'Is money,' she said.

'Oh I couldn't...' he began, but she interrupted.

'Please. She told me. You take it.'

Charles walked out through the massive front door that Linda held open. He walked down the winding path and didn't open the envelope until he was round the corner. It contained two 20-pound notes.

For Charles, it was hard to know which was the worst aspect of Florian's absence. One was his deification *in absentia*. With Florian away, a myth took hold of the school that this spiteful, insincere master of low-level disruption had been charming, modest, sweet, helpful and – strangest of all – intellectually gifted.

It was the wilful falsification of history, the revisionism, that Charles objected to, and it assumed greater impact by the day.

The other aspect, which really was awful, was the absence of news. Moves had been suggested to drum up the required ten million dollars, either by selling off parts of the school playing fields or by taking out a huge loan, but little progress seemed to have been made. The government continued to reassure them, which made everyone feel less reassured than ever. The longer it went on, the more the mood of hysteria, barely confined by the appearance of normality, continued. Service staff, delivery men, even Hari the local postman, found themselves exiting the school at high speed, as if the very air were beating down upon them.

Florian was missed in another sense, since the school had recorded its worst set of sporting figures in years.

'Losing by five goals at home to St Arbuck's,' said Mr Drummer in the staffroom after the first team's particularly heavy defeat. 'It doesn't get much worse than that.'

But then it did of course, when they lost by nine goals, two weeks later, at home again, to the traditional whipping boys of the group, All Scholes.

One area of school life in which Year Eight were,

for once, doing above average seemed to be in the field of Art. Charmian Thirst had encouraged them to try and produce work which reflected their current concerns. Cato Wang and Enzo Merriman, two boys who until then had shown as little talent for Art as any other subject, produced a striking image of a dark, brown, rocky landscape.

'It's very expressive, isn't it?' said Charmian, as she held it up in the staffroom. 'Is that what the cave looked like, Charles?'

Charles stared hard at it. 'Kind of,' he said. 'I mean, it was dark a lot of the time, so...'

'You still look tired, Charles,' said Dotty. 'How are you sleeping?'

'Not bad,' he said. 'I get off OK, but I wake up.'

'Me too,' she said. 'What's the point of waking up early if there's no one else there? Sorry...'

Her voice had suddenly become rather throatier and Charles had an image of the two of them, naked, exhausted and moist with commingled sweat, on the carpet of the staffroom. The image surprised him and he stood up hastily.

Charles continued to walk into and out of classes, but the feeling that he might very soon be plucked from Churley and set adrift in the Gulf of Aden was beginning to make him anxious.

In the circumstances, Mrs Annersley's continuing quest for the ultimate sexual experience was a welcome distraction.

'I'm sorry Charles, but he had to go,' was one typical riposte as some poor student, barely out of his teens, could be heard limping down the stairs one night. 'Doesn't know a G-spot from a hole in the wall, and no imagination, either. All I did was offer to tie him up: he turned as white as a sheet and ran out of the room.'

'You're too much for them, Mrs A.,' said Charles.

'Still, you've got to have a go, eh, dearie?' she said,

pouring herself a large glass of red wine. Charles hadn't told her about Hugh's rescue plot. He wondered if Mrs Annersley knew how much he would miss her when the moment of departure finally arrived.

Charles hated Hugh Bavington for manipulating him into joining his mad trip, and yet, what choice did he have? He felt stupid for claiming to Florian that they would be suffering as well as him, back in the safety of London, and yet, in a sense, was it not easier to be in Smilia and knowing what depredations one was suffering than worrying about the captive back here, at the mercy of the most lurid inventions of one's imagination? It was the not knowing that was so awful. The fate of the trawler crew, along with so many other innocent travellers, was still unknown, but were they soon to be joined by two more – one bumbling, the other strident and foul-mouthed – walking straight into captivity at some point along Smilia's extensive L-shaped coastline? And, if so, how would that development be received at home: with sympathy or fury? Charles had told Dr Ironsize and Dotty de Souza about Hugh's scheme. He didn't want his employers to think that he had lost his marbles, and yet it was vital to show that he would do anything – even to the point of self-sacrifice – to bring back the most thankless, uncooperative and unrewarding student he had ever taught, probably just in time for Florian to be rejected by the few remaining schools which had not already turned down his application.

As summer temperatures at last began to make an impression on Churley, the atmosphere at Rydon Hall became even more oppressive. Dr Ironsize did his best to keep the mood upbeat. He had made much of the opening of a Twitter feed offering instant updates about any developments from Smilia – 'My tweets will ring out like thunder!' he had promised – but there seemed very little news to report. Charles had followed every new one at first, and could see that Dr Ironsize was trying hard to master this new medium. 'Just going into meeting with FO,' read an early one. 'Will have no hesitation in clashing heads if nec (necessary)!' The speed of communication, compared with Dr Ironsize's weekly email letter, meant that procedural misunderstandings occasionally arose. 'FO using CIA drone to find Florian!' read an early one. An hour later there was an update. 'Please ignore earlier message which was a purely personal impression with no factual basis,' he wrote, perhaps after a rap on the knuckles from a Whitehall mandarin.

There was also much excitement that a question had been asked in the House of Commons by Churley's MP, Kay Honez. But she seemed as unable to move the situation on as anyone else. 'MP assures me she is leaving no stone unturned,' wrote Dr Ironsize, though that was surely one of the very activities that she was least able to do. After a few days, the tone of Dr Ironsize's tweets began to take a distinctly parochial turn. 'Tina and self driving back from Close to the Hedge,' he tapped out in a rare reference to his wife on a shopping trip to Churley's favourite garden centre. 'Florian Posters all over, several by DIY gardening tools on special offer.' Charles decided to spend more time with the conventional news servers.

With her son's captivity now extending beyond two months, school terms barely registered for Mrs Bavington, so Latin lessons continued into the Easter break. Charles could have Skyped her from home, but he preferred to maintain that his computer was behaving erratically, so he continued to make the trip to Churley House. He was rewarded with the sound of an occasional exhalation, and the sight of her fingers, the jarringly absent engagement and wedding rings reminding him of her domestic rupture. And then, in the first week of the Summer term, with Florian's absence now measured at 76 days, they started on the imperative.

Charles, dabbing the sweat from his nose in the close air of the little room, did his best to put Mrs Bavington through her paces. Holding his pad up to the camera, he wrote down such forms as "Carry!", "Wound!", "Sit!", "Run!" and "Sleep!" – and, sure enough, within a minute or so, a sheet of paper was being held under the screen on which he could see that all had been translated correctly. Charles didn't need to say anything: they both knew that she had answered the questions correctly, and he simply wrote "5/5" on his pad, underlining it and adding an encouraging double exclamation mark.

Combining infinitive and imperative forms was a further refinement, but Charles felt Mrs Bavington was up to it, so he lost no time in writing "I want" (*cupio*) followed by an infinitive expression like "to sing" *(cantare)*. Accurate as ever, Mrs Bavington grasped quickly the possibilities of this useful construction. But the next sentence Mrs Bavington wrote seemed to suggest that the effort of getting this far had exhausted her. Charles looked at it and his first impulse was to grimace. He spoke into the microphone.

'Mrs Bavington, you've written *"tu ascendere cupis?"* Does the question mark mean that you are trying to say, "Do you want to rise?"'

- *Yes*, wrote Mrs Bavington on the sheet.

'Well,' said Charles blithely, 'the trouble is that you have written down a question but you haven't used the appropriate question form. You can't just stick a question mark at the end of the sentence. You have to add the letters "*ne*". Now the way this works...'

Charles stopped speaking. The pad at the other end had been taken away and then held up again. This time he could see the words "*cupio te ascendere*".

Charles frowned and tapped the page with his finger. 'Mrs Bavington, you mustn't try and run before you can walk. I can see that you are trying to say "I want you to rise or come up" – is that right?'

'Yes, Mr Goldforbes.'

He thought at first that his headpiece was faulty. Then he recognised the voice of Natasha Bavington.

He tried to remain calm.

'You see, if you want *me* to do something, that's an indirect command, which we won't really come to for a while. We haven't yet met the subjunctive, you see, so…'

The writing pad had appeared again, with the word "*ASCENDE*" in capital letters: "Come up".

His head was beginning to ache. 'That's better: the singular imperative means "Arise", "rise", "climb" or simply, um, "come up." Is that what you were trying to say?'

The pad flickered again: she had added the adverb "*NUNC*" – now.

'Mrs Bavington, you have just written the words "Come up now". Is that right?'

Mrs Bavington's ringed hand underlined the two words.

'Yes,' said Charles. 'Really?' he added.

Mrs Bavington's hand made an impatient beckoning motion in the centre of the frame, as if willing a dog to sit up.

'Do you want me to come up, Mrs Bavington?' he said.

– *VENI.* The single word "Come".

'I'll…' he began, then decided not to cloud the issue with superfluous dialogue. He stood up, got as far as the door, raced back to the video monitor and unplugged it. Then he went out and, with his heart battering against his ribcage like a metal door in a high wind, he made the unfamiliar journey from the scrolled foot of the stairs, upwards.

Charles walked along the thick, pink carpet. With no doors open, the corridor got darker as he walked, as if feeling more intensely Florian's absence. One door at the end of the corridor was open. He knew it was her bedroom by the fragrance: the concentrated essence of

Natasha Bavington hit his nostrils as soon as he entered. Apart from the sense of smell, there were no further clues as the curtains were drawn and it was hard to see much on entering. He could just about make out a bed, but that was it. As his fingers brushed against a starched linen top-sheet, his eyes began to adjust. He was aware of a diamond formation of scatter cushions, arranged above the bed cover. A large clothes screen spanned almost half the room on the far side of the bed. For a moment he wondered if he was in the wrong room: then he heard a voice that he recognised from behind the screen.

'Close the door, Mr Goldforbes,' she said.

Charles closed the door. He could see that, liberated from the brasher tastes of her ex-husband, Mrs Bavington had hired a proper interior furnisher: the room was near pitch black.

'Thank you. Please take off your clothes and get into the bed. And try not to speak.'

Amazed and confused, but feeling in no position to object, he kicked off his shoes and wriggled out of his trousers and shirt. He got into the bed. Black shapes arched into his retina which he did his best to dispatch.

'Mr Goldforbes, I regret asking you to do this, but please understand it is purely for my benefit, not yours. Your enjoyment doesn't come into it.' Charles lay there, his five senses all oozing into one another like old Brie. Her voice was still limpid, but edged with even more scar tissue than before. Suddenly a spectral shape flitted out from behind the screen.

'Please don't move,' she said. It was definitely her, even though her voice was barely louder than a whisper. 'I am sorry about this, but for obvious reasons I couldn't ask anyone I like or respect. I'm sure you understand.'

'Of course,' began Charles. A moment later, Natasha Bavington was lying on the bed beside – but not touching – him. He wanted to stretch out a hand towards her, but then he felt something drop onto his stomach. He picked it up: it was a single, wrapped, condom. He waited.

'Put it on,' she said.

As he did so, she pulled the duvet up and over her. Charles turned his head to see that she was wearing a T-shirt. Again, there was total silence in the room. Then, removing what must be her panties and throwing them onto the carpet, she spoke again.

'Mr Goldforbes, please listen. I need to have an orgasm. I suppose I could pay someone but it was less hassle to ask you. Do you have any objections?'

'I... Well, none in particular,' said Charles. 'I mean...'

'Do you feel violated?'

'Not at the moment.'

'I decided to pick someone towards whom I feel absolutely no sexual attraction. You don't mind, do you?'

'I can probably live with it...'

'You can still leave if you want to.' But as she said the words, she slid over and on top of him. He wriggled as he felt her clasp his *membrum virile* and rub it between her legs. He tried to recall the poem in which Catullus mentions nine consecutive copulations, or *novem continuas fututiones*. But she was talking to him again, and her voice was a tone deeper than before.

'Please try not to move against me, Mr Goldforbes. And I would be grateful if you did not attempt to touch my breasts. This is about me, not you. Please nod your head if you agree.'

'Mmmm...' Charles managed to say. She had placed her hands on the bed-sheet beside his shoulders. Then, with a deft flip, she buried his *psōlē* inside her and started to grind up and against him.

He felt her moving against him silently, heavier than he had expected but still lithe from whatever Churley-based yoga regime she had set herself. He wanted to call out but knew he must not speak. He could sense her breasts swinging as she pivoted up and down. Her hair smelt syrupy from the swimming pool. The strands stroked his face as she rose and sank against him, and he could feel her breath begin to thicken. He tried and tried to think about Mrs Portal, in a bid to staunch flood. He wanted more than anything else not to want this woman, but he knew that he could not resist his own desires. He could not kiss her, couldn't tell her that she was beautiful, nor how much he wanted her, but her legs were kissing his knees with each rhythmic descent. Charles tried to force himself to think of all the mug titles in Mrs Hughes-Howard's collection, or Dr Raymond Ironsize delivering an address in Monday morning assembly, but there was nowhere he could think that was not, just then, fraught with sex. Then, suddenly, Mrs Bavington arched her back, tensed, and the tautness drained out of her. He could hold on no longer.

'*Veni, vidi,*' he croaked, at which point a trapdoor inside him flicked open. 'Uh, *veni,*' he said again, and gave up the unequal struggle.

The room was still. She was panting, or sighing quietly, and he could see her head had sunk low over her chest. He longed to touch her, but she pulled away from him and he saw her hand come up to her forehead.

'Have you finished?' she said in a low voice, almost as if she were invigilating in some end-of-year exam.

'Nmmmmmm.'

'The bin is by the door,' she said, in the same balanced tone as before. 'If you need to wash, use the shower by the pool. You remember where it is. And please don't look behind you. Please don't move until I have left.'

The reference to the pool-side disrobing served to embarrass him into detumescence. She was gone in a second. Charles got out of the bed, removed and tied off the condom and pulled his clothes on. As he opened the door, light flooded back into the room.

Forgetting her injunction, he turned, as if, once again, Orpheus might glimpse his Eurydice, but she was nowhere to be seen. He walked unsteadily along the corridor, found his way downstairs and saw an envelope on a small table. When he opened it, he found the usual sum plus an extra five pound coins. Shrugging off the slight, he found the shower room, removed his clothes again and stepped into the shower. A thin gurgle of water came out. After a minute, he turned off the tap. Then, fearing nothing now, for soon he would be back with Mr Baadi in Smilia, he ran out and plunged, naked, into the pool.

PART FIVE

CHAPTER 16

To Charles' surprise, Mrs Annersley was scathing when he told her what had happened.

'Taking advantage of a poor, lonely woman like that,' she tutted. 'Shame on you.'

Charles had protested, as vigorously as he could, that if anyone had been taking advantage of anyone else, he was surely the victim, but Mrs Annersley remained unconvinced. 'Had you a shred of dignity,' she said, her voice rising to a rhetorical flourish, 'you would have wished her a good afternoon, made your apologies and left. Instead of which you pulled your pants down and stuck your…'

'I did not do any such thing,' Charles said. 'She lowered herself onto me like a…'

'Spare me the sordid details,' she said, holding up the hand of outraged decency while taking a mighty swig from her wine glass.

'Well you're a fine one to accuse me,' he said. This was almost sounding like an argument. 'You don't hesitate to talk me through every sexual misadventure you've had, but when it comes to one of my own…'

He thought back to the afternoon's encounter, and to why he had been chosen to provide this service for Mrs Bavington. There had been no shortage of sexual disappointment, humiliation and under-achievement in Charles Goldforbes' life so far, but this one occupied a different place. He had fantasised long, hard and fruitlessly about sex with Mrs Bavington, so to have ended up in bed with her, feeling her roll onto him, cling briefly to him, quiver with erotic ascendancy and then, as the tsunami of her frenzy finally hit the shingle, roll off, should have left him hyperventilating with joy. And yet it felt a strangely hollow victory, like Pyrrhus showing off his war medals. Of course, he was familiar with the argument that there was no such thing as bad sex, if undertaken by two consenting adults, but Mrs Annersley was even questioning Mrs Bavington's consent. Maybe she was a slave to her mental turmoil? Charles was uncomfortably aware of this viewpoint, but he could not yet agree with Mrs Annersley that he had committed a crime against genteel society.

Charles was mulling over these issues as he arrived in school the following day. The source of his anxiety had shifted across the Bavington family, from son to mother, and currently centred around Mr Bavington, who was still determined to fly him away from the comparative safety of Embury Park and Churley and dump him, bleeding, in the Red Sea, where Mr Baadi's sharks could grab them. This insane idea had been declared thoroughly impractical by every governmental and intelligence agency that Mr Bavington had contacted, and yet their refusal had only made him redouble his efforts.

Charles was teaching when his mobile rang. (In these exceptional circumstances, the ban on mobiles had been relaxed for staff.) He had been trying to persuade Year Five that a noun was a name for a person, thing or place, whereas a verb was a kind of doing word. Judging by the serried rows of quizzical stares that confronted him, Year Five were treating this information with the same sort of suspicion that they brought to attempts to make them add or multiply numbers in Maths, find Ordinance Survey coordinates in Geography, or believe that a certain battle had taken place or a certain king or queen crowned in a certain year in History. The trouble with Year Five was that they didn't believe anything any sensible grown-up told them. The trouble with Hugh Bavington was that neither did he.

Charles saw who was phoning him and considered not taking the call. Then he reconsidered. He had no regrets about cuckolding Hugh Bavington, so long as he didn't find out. In a way, now that they were both nearly dead, or dead to the rest of the world for the rest of their lives, he felt the licence to behave with more effrontery than usual. He cupped the phone with his hand and, in a hushed monotone, whispered, '*ave, Caesar, ego moriturus te saluto.*'

There was a momentary pause, and then Hugh, in the same incurious voice that distinguished his son, said, 'Is that you, Goldforbes?'

'Of course it is, Hugh,' said Charles. 'Do you know what I just said?'

'Listen,' he said, not allowing himself to be diverted by the quest for knowledge. 'I've got a departure date.'

'Oh goodie,' said Charles, trying to sound relaxed. 'Let me check my diary to see if I'm free that day.'

'Very funny,' Hugh went on. 'So it's you, me, and a South African psychopath called Piet. Old mate of mine. Used to be in the SAS. Knows how to fight: more importantly, he knows when to walk away. We leave on Friday week.'

Charles felt his insides lurch. There it was, with the cold formality of a calendar entry. All he could say was, 'But I haven't had any jabs.'

Bavington growled. 'Where we're going, they won't do you any good, chum. Piet's taking care of all that, anyway. There'll be a car for you at five o'clock in the evening.'

Charles tried again. 'What time is the plane?'

'Eight. We're going to fly into Aden and then take a boat across.'

'But... Mr Bavington, don't you know that night flights are really bad for the environment?'

Bavington let out a grunt of indifference as to the future of the planet. Charles sensed that neither of his two objections had made much impact so far. 'But what will happen to Year Eight's Latin?'

'Don't be an effing dipstick,' said the ex-husband of Natasha Bavington. 'They'll hire some new egg-head in a corduroy jacket and proceed as normal. It's all there in the book. All you do is tell them which page to read.'

'I was led to believe that there was slightly more to it than that, but…'

'Well there isn't, Chuck, let me tell you.'

'And your friend, this South African. Is he prepared to enter into captivity with us?'

'Course not,' said Mr Bavington. 'He'll get us in there as far as it's safe, and then leave us to toil over to this Baadi fellow.'

Charles tried again. 'Have you had much luck raising the ransom?'

'Sod all,' said Hugh. 'Not even from my sodding bank. They said if he'd been kidnapped a year earlier it might have been different, but these days they've got to be more careful who they lend to.'

'And you're telling me that they consider a Smili warlord a bad risk? What on earth could have driven them to that conclusion?'

Bavington's grunt suggested a disaffection with high street banks' attitudes to ransom demands.

Charles looked at his class of reluctant students. Those not attempting to stuff rulers up their noses seemed to be trying to eavesdrop on the conversation, so he produced a pirated DVD of the film *Spartacus*: the refuge which most of his lessons with Year Five had eventually sought that term. The remainder of their telephone call took place against the background of Kirk Douglas' heroic but ultimately suicidal revolt against his Roman captors and showed, once again, how timeless and relevant a Classical education was.

Charles decided to change tack. 'Hugh,' he whispered, 'has it not occurred to you that – understandable though it might seem for you to try everything in your powers to see Florian again – it is simply mad to proceed with this jaunt, since it cannot possibly succeed?'

The line seemed to go dead for some seconds and Charles wondered if he had driven into a tunnel or, even, better, the wall of a tunnel. But then he heard a low snarl. 'Let me tell you one thing, Mr fucking

Classics teacher. This is not a "jaunt".'

Charles sighed. 'Obviously I didn't mean it like that,' he said.

'A jaunt is a trip to the seaside, or Disneyland Paris.'

'That's not what I meant to say.'

'Let's go ten-pin bowling. That's a jaunt, isn't it?'

'Hugh, believe me when I say that I was under no impression that this was going to be an easy trip…'

'This is not a jaunt, you pipsqueak. This is a trip to find a 13-year-old boy who may very well, for all we know, be dead already. I need some evidence that he is alive – or dead. It's my last throw of the dice, *chum*, and I need you there. Not because I like you. Not so that you can read to me from Caesar's sodding *Gaelic Wars*…'

'*Gallic*, actually, in fact I gave my own copy of…'

'But because you might be the one human being on this earth who might be able to screw up in exactly the same way and the same place as you screwed up last time.'

'How reassuring to know that you have that much faith in my ability.'

'In which case, even if I fail, I will go to my grave knowing that I did my best to free my son.'

'And indirectly leading to his death the Latin teacher who…'

'The Latin teacher who would otherwise have stayed in bloody Churley, teaching the gormless, pampered, spineless offspring of the overpaid cock-snoggers who were stupid enough to send their annoying brats to that trough of a school.'

'Excellent: I think we'll put that on the website,' said Charles. Having received sexual intercourse from Hugh's ex-wife not 24 hours earlier, he felt generous enough to indulge him.

'Listen, you arse,' said Hugh. 'I'm offering you the chance to be a hero. It's the only way out of this and it might be the only chance you'll ever get.'

'Dear me, you do sound grumpy.'

It was a stupid remark, but it came out before he could check it. In fact, Hugh merely grunted. 'Going to see the old lady this afternoon,' he said. 'Never puts me in the best of moods.'

As he said this, right on cue the DVD jammed and the picture went into a thousand hissing stars that reminded Charles, briefly, of the Smili night sky. Charles ejected it and ended his call with Hugh. He switched over, in the last few seconds of the lesson, to a daytime TV programme in which an elderly couple were talking to a slightly older couple on a barge outside a pub near a church. It was drizzling. Dear old England. Dear, damp, run-of-the-mill England: how he would miss it.

The bell went and he dismissed Year Five, or watched in bemused silence as they left the room by creating, as they always did, a creature that was widest at the point it made contact with the door. He had a free period now, and then it was lunch, but he felt over-burdened, almost suffocated, by the imminent disappearance from the developed world of Charles Goldforbes – and all because of one boy: Florian bloody Bavington. Was it really for this that he had been created? Had he studied Greek rhetorical skills for nothing, if he was unable to persuade a brick-built car importer out of such a hare-brained scheme? He was about to walk across the playground to the staffroom, but as he did so, the door to the Year Four classroom creaked open. Mrs Hughes-Howard stood there with Dr Ngo.

'We're going for a drink,' she said, conspiratorially. 'Want to come?'

'Well, this is nice,' said Mrs Hughes-Howard. They were in the Four Horsemen, all trying to remain apart from each other on a sofa whose camber caused the outer two to sag into the middle. The pub used to be of the spit-and-sawdust variety and was packed every night and loved by all, but the brewery closed it for 11 months to convert it into a gastro-bar. It was now half as full but twice as expensive. The walls were decorated with items salvaged from the refurbishment, so it seemed to have been knocked down and rebuilt in order to look like a restored version of itself, prior to the demolition.

'Do Latin teachers prefer Italian wine?' asked Mrs Hughes-Howard, staring warily at a barstool hanging by a wire cable from the ceiling.

'Shall I buy?' Charles said. With only a week or so to go before his departure, possibly forever, from Churley, he thought he might as well buy his round, so that these two, at least, would remember him a bit more fondly. Dr Ngo seemed on the mend and no longer needed his walking stick. Mrs Hughes-Howard's mastiff, Patch, had been left tied to a post by Mr Scamage's shed.

'Good idea,' said Dr Ngo. 'Half a lager?'

'I'll have a Campari and soda,' said Mrs Hughes-Howard. 'Very generous of you, Mr Goldforbes.'

Charles waved and smiled at the Bulgarian barmaid. At that moment, Mrs Hughes-Howard's phone rang. She answered it and pressed it to her ear. As she spoke, a series of expressions ran across her face that Charles could not easily identify.

'Yes?' she said. 'Hello Mrs Portal... Yes. No, no it's OK. No, I haven't heard... What? No... Really? I don't believe it... I do not believe it. He's dead, isn't he? Don't tell me... He got away? How did he get away? Oh my God, but he's dead. I knew it. I knew we should have - He's what? He's... He's... No.... No...' And then one final, drawn-out, disbelieving, 'No...'

Charles and Dr Ngo exchanged bewildered glances. Mrs Hughes-Howard put her phone down and leaned heavily on the armrest.

'Well?' said Dr Ngo.

'He's escaped,' she said. 'He's coming home.'

'Patch?' asked Charles, pointlessly.

'Florian,' she said.

The school was in turmoil when they got back. Boys were running around, shouting, waving bits of paper and comparing mobile phone screens. So were members of staff. Mrs Portal went up to them and gave Dr Ngo a huge body hug that left him panting for several moments. The only exception to the mood of jubilation was Adrian Purvis, who was sitting in the corner of the playground, looking as if the sky had fallen on his head. Any attempt at normal lessons had been abandoned.

Charles had never imagined that it would fall to Harry Beamish to elaborate what had happened, since Harry had not yet said anything of interest to him, but as soon as he saw Charles he rushed up to him, grabbed the sleeve of his jacket and shouted, 'Florian's out, sir!'

Charles took some recourse in confusion. 'I know, but... How?' he felt entitled to ask.

'Yedverd just got a tweet from Dylan. Flo's safe!'

'Yedverd had his phone on in class?' It might not have been the most appropriate response but he needed more time to think.

'He never switches his off, sir,' said Harry.

More boys were gathering round them, eager to share the news. Some wanted to hear it again, others to say what they knew. Only about four facts were known, but each one was pounced on and added to with greater and greater appetite. Mrs Hughes-Howard started cantering around the playground.

'Rejoice!' she shouted, as if announcing a military victory, 'rejoice!' before subsiding into sobs.

With the senior school not yet on lunch break, Dorotea and Emmanuel in the kitchen prevailed on to suspend whatever fate they were planning to inflict on a consignment of pasta, since Dr Ironsize felt that only a whole-school assembly, in hall, could do justice to the immensity of the occasion. The overhead projector was brought down like a portcullis, the words were flashed onto it, and pretty soon the entire school was belting out "Guide Me, Lord, Protect and Guide Me" followed by a spirited version of the Rydon Hall school song, including the rarely-heard third verse, written for an earlier confrontation, in which the author's feelings towards the enemy had led him to commit several crimes against rhyme and scansion. The verse had been suspended ever since emotions towards the defeated Germans had begun to cool in around 1948. But this time they belted it out with full hearts:

"Rydon Hall, Rydon Hall, Rydon Rydon Rydon Hall,
Cross the sea in Flanders wettest, faced with guns and bayonettes,
Smite the Bosch athwart their limbs, awed by British javelins.
Strike them where they like it least, til their Hunnish war cry's ceased,
Up them do they most resent it, where no sun doth shine – present it!
Make our founders truly proud, stand you out amid the crowd."

Mr Drummer accompanied on the piano with a brio that Charles had not heard since the Christmas carol service when he had come straight from a longer-than-usual session in the Four Horsemen.

If more evidence were required that Florian really had turned the tables on his captors, a postcard arrived that afternoon, from Enitenia. It was delivered by courier, but it contained an uninspiring view of a series of sandy beaches, and the slightly inappropriate caption "Missing you already in Enitenia" on the front. Florian's hand was immediately recognisable in the address, on which his home country was presented as "United Kindgom". The message on the other side, punctuation losing out to dramatic vividness, "See you soon I have got out" was immediately put on display under the notice board on which the sports teams were normally presented. The boys were allowed to inspect it in small groups, as when Year Five travelled to Normandy to see the Bayeux Tapestry.

A telephone call to Dr Ironsize from the Foreign Office provided further details. Florian, it seemed, had made himself very useful to his Smili captors. Mr Baadi had taken a shine to him, and, far from punishing him or suspending his freedoms, had entrusted to him various jobs. On one occasion, this did indeed include cross-examining a French trawler crew, for which he had been rewarded with the job of overhauling Mr Baadi's computer network. This had been in tatters before Florian had arrived but, being a boy of 13, Florian knew exactly what was wrong with it and, within a few weeks, he had reinstalled his hard disk, properly backed up his files, flushed a debilitating virus out of his system, created a reliable broadband connection and hooked Mr Baadi up, behind a bristling firewall, to the worldwide web. In recognition of his efforts, Florian was granted sufficient autonomy to roam the compound, going more or less unfettered from cave to cave. What Mr Baadi did not know, and, being a shade over 30, could not know, was that, having located his exact GPS coordinates using Google Earth, Florian had been able to bypass Mr Baadi's cryptic and teasing exchanges with the Foreign Office and make his own overtures to British intelligence by reviving an IsatPhone communication system which had been left for dead. And so one day, when Mr Baadi was away up country, overseeing a punishment beating, a helicopter – filled with elite Enitenian troops and a crack S.A.S. squad – dropped from the skies, covered the area in smoke bombs and swept Florian – easily spotted in his trademark orange hoodie – and the four trawlermen to freedom.

The whole operation had been planned with such nerveless detail, at both ends, that some might have wondered that it went ahead so smoothly in a country in which nothing was straightforward, still less that part of it could have sprung from the mind of a boy who could not negotiate his way from *porto* to *portant* without getting lost twice on the way. And yet Florian had achieved his own freedom.

Having heard the account, which was already on its fifth or sixth retelling and felt more unbelievable each time, Charles wished he could be back in the Four Horsemen finishing his drink. However, they were forbidden to leave school as a rash of reporters was gathering outside. Instead, he found Dr Ngo in the staffroom, wriggling the foil off a bottle of Cava.

'I bought this when we got back. Swore I wouldn't open it until the little toe-rag was released,' he said as Mrs Hughes-Howard stood waiting, holding a mug that read, "Pottery Teachers Aren't Sacked, They're Fired".

Madame Allardyce waltzed in.

'Champagne!' she yelled as the cork was twisted off. 'I always knew he was a creature of low cunning. I hadn't realised how low. Or how cunning.'

'Must have taken a lot of preparation,' said Charles, not even trying to keep the tone of wonder out of his voice.

'If he'd put a tenth of that effort into his homework,' said Madame Allardyce, 'just one tenth, he could have got a scholarship to Wasteminster.'

'I bet they're sorry they turned him down now,' said Dr Ngo. 'Especially with all that building work they've got on.' He filled various mugs with bubbly and then lay with his back on the carpet, resting his ankles on the tip of the sofa in accordance with his physiotherapy programme.

Mrs Allardyce started re-touching her make-up. 'I think, for the first time in my life, that I actually admire Florian Bavington,' she said.

'You never know what qualities life's challenges bring out in you, Elise,' said Mrs Hughes-Howard, with the air of vouchsafing one of life's great secrets. 'My niece Clara was a dab hand with ponies but she couldn't play hockey to save her life. Then one day...'

The door opened and Dr Ironsize entered the staffroom. This was something he did rarely, either because he understood that the staff needed a place to let off steam, or because he was too busy with administrative jobs or, as Dr Ngo had quietly speculated, because he was not absolutely confident that he could find it unaided. Ms de Souza followed a second later. They both sat down and folded their arms.

'I always knew he'd be fine,' said Dr Ironsize. 'I knew he'd do it. You can't chain a Rydon Hall boy: they'll always find a way out.'

'I liked your prayer during the service, Dr Ironsize,' said Charles. 'Though I did wonder at your use of the word "evil".'

'Wrong to call them evil?' said Dr Ironsize, frowning down the length of his nose at Charles. 'Let me remind you, Mr Goldforbes, that these men took an entire class hostage. And then, as if their souls were not in sufficient mortal peril, they released all but one of those children.'

Charles, Dr Ngo and Mrs Hughes-Howard stared back at Dr Ironsize.

'That was what happened, wasn't it?' added Dr Ironsize, less confidently than before.

'Do you know when we can expect to see Florian?' asked Dr Ngo.

'Soon. Very soon,' said Dr Ironsize, who had now taken upon himself the additional role of information czar. 'Although it may be less soon than we would like. He will need to have a significant de-brief with the authorities, and he will then need family time. And personal recovery time. So it might not be too soon. I cannot, at this juncture, give you an exact time. It will be days, though, rather than weeks, or indeed months. Though it might be weeks. Or days.' He broke off to wipe his nose. 'And meanwhile, of course, it's business as usual at Rydon Hall.'

Dr Ironsize backed towards the door, smiling as if this were a new facial expression which he had brought back from an educational seminar and could recommend to all his colleagues. Then he was gone. Mrs Hughes-Howard rocked on her heels, finally bringing her cup down heavily on her saucer.

'What a silly old sausage he is,' she said, with a dismissive shrug.

'Can we go back to the pub after school?' said Dr Ngo. 'I'm sure we can give those reporters the slip.'

'What a good idea,' said Charles.

'Is this survivors only?' asked Madame Allardyce.

'I would have thought anyone who's taught Florian can be called a survivor,' said Mrs Hughes-Howard.

The bell rang for the end of afternoon school, and Charles went downstairs to collect his things. As he did so, he realised, for the first time, with a rush of pure euphoria, that he would not now be revisiting Smilia. He decided that it would be civil to congratulate Hugh Bavington.

Bavington answered his phone with a joyful grunt.

'Ah, Goldfag, you've heard the news?'

'Yes. I'm so happy for you.'

'Thanks Chuck.' Hugh sounded almost happy to hear from him.

'When will you see him?'

'Not sure yet. Not sure where he is. Can't tell you how I feel, really, it's...' there was an inevitable pause as he fought to control his emotions. 'Got time for a quick pint? I'm in the area.'

'Well, why not?' said Charles. He was almost getting to like being called Chuck.

Mr Bavington was waiting outside school in a brand new black Hummer H3, the off-road vehicle for on-road driving. He was looking almost beneficent.

'Running it in for a customer,' he said. 'Be my

221

guest.' The celebrations had started early: an opened bottle of champagne rested in an ice bucket on the back seat. Charles saw a plastic flute in the glove compartment of the back seat as he jumped into the car, but there seemed to be less daylight than was normal. The reason for this, he saw, was an enormous head blocking the rear window.

'And this is Piet,' said Hugh. 'He's from South Africa.'

'Hi buddy,' said the man, in a quavery Boer-tinged accent.

Shaking hands with him brought back painful memories of the *Playdoh* mincing machine from Charles' childhood. The hair on Piet's head had been munched to within a millimetre of his scalp. He had a dapper little triangle of white hairs just under his bottom lip, teeth that looked like they could skin a stoat, and eyes formed by a pencil tip pushed through paper.

Fingers still throbbing, Charles poured some Cristal: the bubbles looked superior to those in Dr Ngo's bottle.

'Whole operation's been hush-hush for days,' said Hugh. 'I didn't have a clue. Those Foreign Office chappies were in on the whole thing: they were just playing Baadi along, keeping him sweet. Buggers: I always said they were smarter than they looked.'

'Just as well we hadn't left for Egypt, I suppose,' said Charles.

Piet let forth a cackle. Then he peered down towards Upper Churley Road and let forth a tremor. 'Traffic's building up down there, buddy.'

'You're right,' said Hugh. He added, 'Piet's a traffic genius. Even when he doesn't know where he is.'

'Which I don't,' said Piet.

It took some time to turn the lumbering beast round but they were off eventually, though as they climbed towards Churley Old Town they were soon stuck there too.

'Shit, piss and effing tits,' said Hugh. 'Those damn reporters, I expect.'

'Still, Hugh,' said Charles, draining his glass at the third sip. 'The traffic's moving slowly, but look on the bright side: your son's alive.'

'That's true,' said Hugh, 'and I suppose I ought to thank you for…'

'Me?' said Charles, waving a self-deprecating forearm. 'Oh I didn't do anything, I just…'

'No, you did, you sort of stayed my hand,' he said. 'I was champing at the bit to get out there and, well, it probably would have been a total effing tits-up.'

'Cut through here,' said Piet.

'Really? OK.'

'This tastes good…' said Charles, enjoying the champagne. He re-filled his glass. 'Hugh?'

'Not while I'm reversing, thanks,' said Hugh.

Charles offered some to Piet.

'I don't drink, but help yourself, buddy,' said Piet. He was chewing something which, to judge from his breath, must have been a sprig of mint.

'Have you spoken to Florian yet?'

'For about ten seconds. Satellite phone from somewhere near the border. "Hi Dad I'm fine. I'll see you in London." Couldn't speak for several minutes.'

'I'm not surprised,' said Charles. Charles was feeling a little emotional himself as he knocked back a second glass.

'And I suppose I should thank the school too,' said Hugh. This was beginning to sound like an awards ceremony.

'Oh, I mean…' Charles was enjoying being the grunt-maker this time.

'No, no, you and your… your colleagues, you must have knocked some sense into him because he came through. I mean, Mrs Two-Aitch and Charlie Chan: I know I've been rude about them but they must have taught him some computing tricks and what-not. And I dare say he learned something from the whole Rydon

223

Hall experience. Don't know what, but...'

'Hey buddy? Better take a right here,' said Piet.

'Near the old lady's pad,' said Hugh. Charles didn't need to be told that they were just round the corner from Churley House. 'Seeing her later.'

'Good for you,' said Charles, taking another sip of Champagne. Perhaps now, for the first time in however many months, he could start relaxing and just enjoy life.

'Beautiful house,' said Piet as it came into view.

'Looks like she's opened those bloody black curtains at last,' said Hugh. 'Let some air in.'

'And some light,' said Charles. 'I couldn't see a thing, er...'

He stopped. Despite the pleasant champagne effervescence in his brain, he knew he shouldn't have said that.

The car slowed down. 'What did you just say?' asked Hugh.

'I... er, er...' said Charles, less confidently than he would have liked.

Hugh stopped the car, bringing the traffic to a complete halt. 'How do you know how dark it is?'

'How do I... how do I know what?' said Charles.

'How do you know what it's like in her fucking bedroom?!' Hugh's voice changed sharply as the car braked.

Charles put his glass down. 'OK, fair question,' he said. The champagne seemed to have muddied his thinking.

'And I want an answer.'

'And I can explain everything, very easily,' said Charles. 'There's a perfectly simple explanation for all this.'

'I hope there is, Mr Goldforbes,' said Hugh, in the old Hugh voice. He and Piet were now staring very hard at Charles.

'Yes,' said Charles, nodding as his fingers fastened round the door release. 'Very, very easy. Nothing simpler. Just give me a second.'

And those would have been his last words to Hugh and Piet before disappearing down the narrow alleys of Churley Old Town, except that, as every potential Hummer owner knows, all vehicles come equipped with a child lock on the rear door as a standard feature.

CHAPTER 17

Charles could see that Hugh was trying not to allow his joy at Florian's escape to be overshadowed by the unwelcome news he had just heard about his son's Latin teacher, but it was clear, after a few minutes, that Natasha's ex-husband still needed time to take in the events of the day.

'I can tell that you're upset, Mr Bavington,' said Charles, speaking in short gasps. 'Of course you are. But you are going to... *oof*... break one of my ribs if you keep shaking me like this.'

'I wish I could hurt you more, Goldforbes, I really do,' said Mr Bavington, between his teeth.

'I've said I'm sorry,' panted Charles, taking a moment to rearrange his collar.

'Sorry for what? For shagging my ex-wife? What have you got to be sorry about?'

'I told you,' said Charles, as his body smacked into the passenger door again. 'I did not have sex with your wife.'

'My ex-wife.'

'Your – ouch! Your *ex*-wife. Exactly! She's your ex!'

Mr Bavington broke off – not for long enough, in Charles' opinion – from bouncing his son's teacher's chest against the toughened glass window. 'And...?' he demanded.

'Well...'

'So she's fair game? Is that why you had sex with her?'

'I did not *have sex* with that woman,' Charles said, trying to sound more presidential than evasive. 'I was "had sex with". It was like when a verb goes into the passive.'

'Don't try the grammar on me, Mr Casa-bloody-nova,' said Hugh, continuing with the punishment beating. 'Don't try and blind me with that crap.' He had driven, very fast, to an isolated stretch of Churley

Common, so that the sound and spectacle of Charles being flung repeatedly against the bodywork of Hugh's gigantic Hummer were absorbed by a sweep of elm trees. It was a lovely late spring afternoon. A family of bunny rabbits was carousing a safe distance away and the air – when not riven by Charles' cries of pain – was full of birdsong.

'If there's any damage to this car, you're paying for it, Goldforbes,' said Hugh.

'She was lonely!' Charles sobbed, feeling a searing pain in his chest.

'If I wasn't so happy, I'd break your legs,' Hugh snarled.

'It was her way of coping!'

Hugh pulled Charles upright and picked him up by his lapels. 'How do you think I coped?!' he roared at him.

Charles tried to move his nose so as not to meet Hugh's forehead, but not before he felt a blurring pain and the taste of his own blood. He thought he might be about to pass out, or cry.

'Take this,' said Bavington. Charles flinched, expecting another blow, but Hugh was holding a paper towel out to him. 'And don't worry, Piet will take care of you after I'm done. Did that hurt?'

'Mmm,' said Charles. 'I dink you boke by dose.'

'Sorry, did I?' said Hugh. 'Right, Piet, he's all yours.'

Whether or not Charles actually fainted he couldn't be sure, but it turned out that when Hugh had vowed to hand Charles over to Piet, it was not for a second round of thrashing. Piet was, it turned out, an army medical officer, and he never left home without his First Aid bag. Apologising profusely, he inserted a needle into the skin alongside Charles' nostrils and realigned the battered classicist's splayed nose with one quick but awful snap. Mr Bavington might have been a bit hazy about the details of South African geography, but Piet turned out to be a Zimbabwean, not an Afrikaner, and, while sticking Charles back together, he spoke movingly of his profound sympathy for the Smili people. He too had known a lot of suffering, having lost several cousins and various old friends to Robert Mugabe's over-assertive approach to crowd-control.

Listening to Piet – talking was unwise, given the state of his jaw – Charles could begin to appreciate that, humiliating and painful though it was, in the long run a slightly realigned nasal passage barely registered on the spectrum of civilian harassment. And that if he had been behaving like a dog, he probably deserved to be whipped. As he limped home, holding his ribs with one hand and a bag stuffed with further supplies of painkillers in the other, Charles reflected that now he could at least look Mrs Annersley in the eye and say that he had taken his punishment standing up or, rather, lying down.

Charles phoned in sick the following day. He blamed it on a collision with his bathroom sink, an accident which seemed to satisfy Mrs Portal.

'Were you celebrating Florian's good news a little too enthusiastically, Mr Goldforbes?' she sniggered.

'Ha ha, you could put it that way, yes,' he said, gratefully. A visit to the Accident and Emergency ward confirmed a mild fracture to one of his less critical ribs. A period of rest was suggested, and Charles went home in a taxi, his pockets crammed with analgesics. Every time the cab hit a sleeping policeman, Charles felt he might pass out.

He stayed home for two days, lying in bed, dozing and reading. Whenever Mrs Annersley knocked on his door, he was either asleep or pretending to be. The punch-up with Bavington had knocked the stuffing out of him, along with any appetite for further updates about Florian's astounding release from captivity. The first few times his phone rang, it was because a journalist had somehow got his number, and wanted to hear his Impressions Of The Real Florian Bavington.

Since Charles was not feeling cooperative, he ended most conversations after the initial remarks and thereafter ignored landline, mobile and emails. On hearing the first hint of the jaunty theme tune for *So Local So London!* or any other Bavington-related news on radio or TV, he could just about raise his arm high enough to switch it off, or over.

So, when he finally struggled into school, he was surprised to find that life at Rydon Hall had not stood still. The entire downstairs area looked as if it had just hosted a week's Mardi Gras. There were photographs, streamers and balloons.

'Oh it was lovely, Charles, what a shame you missed it,' said Mrs Hughes-Howard as he stood marvelling. 'I'm so sorry about your nose. How's your arm?'

'Missed what?' said Charles, resting his left hand on his right shoulder.

'The party for Florian. It was so special. He came here straight after the debrief at Brize Norton. We had the mayor and the TV cameras here. He's going to get the Freedom of Churley: ooh, it was lovely.'

'Party?' Charles said, taking shallow breaths. 'Why wasn't I invited?'

Mrs Hughes-Howard looked shocked. 'We sent you emails and texts, and rang your landline. Were you not picking up messages?'

'I wasn't feeling well,' he said, faintly. 'I hurt my nose.'

'That's funny, because your... was it your landlady...?'

'Mrs Annersley?'

'She was here: she said she was representing you.' Mrs Hughes-Howard's nostrils flared. 'She certainly got the message.'

Charles looked at the spray of photographs on the wall. After the pounding his face had taken, he had to close one eye to focus properly, but the first features he recognised were the red hair and swelling chest of

229

Mrs Annersley, standing close to Dr Ngo and flanked by a group of Year Five boys holding party blowers. In another photograph she was staring admiringly at Dr Ngo and in yet another, she had an arm trailed around his waist. She was in a lot of photos, but she wasn't as ubiquitous as someone else. Charles found him first in a Year Eight group shot, and he recognised the face so readily that he had to take a step back to steady himself. Mrs Hughes-Howard stood on one side of the boys with Dr Ngo, stick in hand, on the other. A caption, in Charmian Thirst's meticulous script, running across the top, read, "The Survivors" with a small Post-it note in the bottom corner that read, "Not present: Mr C Goldforbes." As if this were not bad enough, everyone's eyes were fixed on one boy, in a grimy, grungy orange hoodie, with the familiar mocking look in his eye and the slight chip in the corner of one of his front teeth. To Charles' surprise, he felt his eyes start to swim as he peered into the middle of the frame where he could see, finally, the face of Florian Bavington, back on home soil.

'Oh I can tell you've missed him too,' said Mrs Hughes-Howard, giving him a little pat on the elbow. 'You know, I never realised how big a part of the school he was.'

'Is he in school?'

'No, he had to go off and appear on some TV programme,' she said, removing a strand of confetti from the banister. 'It's important for him to ease in slowly. Funny, really,' she said. 'First it was Colin limping, now he's fine and it's you who's hobbling around. I expect it'll be me next. I was saying to Ivor...'

'How is he?'

'Ivor? Same as ever, really...'

'*Florian.* I don't want to know about Ivor. How's *Florian*?'

'The strange thing is, in a way it's like he never left...'

Mrs Portal darted out and sent Mrs Hughes-Howard

off on some errand, and Charles was left to inspect the rest of the photographs. Florian was in almost every one, being gawped at by various boys or staff members as if he'd come back from the dead. Charles took some time to study them, wondering how the boy's temperament had coped with the confinement. He also wondered why, wherever he came across an image of Dr Ngo, Mrs Annersley was standing nearby.

It was agreed that, in his first week back, Florian would attend morning school only. The next day was Saturday, so it was not until Monday that Charles got to see the returning hero. As he entered the Year Eight form room, he pushed open the door, walked to the front, turned round and looked to the back of the room. The praetorian guard of Yedverd Zygnwycyz and Enzo Merriman took one step forward. Then they turned at right angles to each other and Charles' old tormentor, Florian Bavington, stepped forward. All three boys had their arms folded across their chests, like they were emulating Mr Baadi. Charles walked slowly to the back of the room, trying to look pleasantly surprised to see Florian.

'Well, well,' he said, 'Florian Bavington, I presume.'

Florian shook Charles' extended hand.

'Morning, Mr Goldforbes,' he said.

Charles studied his face. A thin sprouting of hairs had begun to bristle along his upper lip. Other than that, he thought at first, he looked little different from the boy who had – more than anyone – ruined the Egypt party. 'So. It's you. Here you are. Once again.' He stopped, in case he sounded like an extra verse from a 70s disco hit.

'You missed the party, sir,' said Florian. There it was: the first jeer of the summer term. Charles decided to parry it. The boy had suffered terribly, after all.

'I didn't mean to. I'm sorry, I was... As you see, I had an accident.' Charles winced as he spoke.

'It's just not the same when there's one person

231

missing, is it?' said Florian. Now he was baiting him: that had survived Mr Baadi's privations too.

'Ha ha. Yes. Well, how on earth are you?'

'Not bad, thanks. Considering I Was Locked Up On My Own In Smilia For Three And A Half Months.'

'Great. Where's my copy of Caesar's *Gallic Wars*?'

Florian seemed to waver momentarily. Then, looking straight at Charles, he said, 'Do you know where I've been? Do you know what I've been through?'

'Calm down, Florian, I'm kidding!' he cut in. 'Well, it's good to see you haven't changed.' Charles walked, limping slightly, to the front of the classroom and turned around. 'Or have you?'

The next item on the curriculum for the main set should have been imperatives, but Charles felt awkward about re-treading ground which he had covered a few days earlier with his only private student. Instead, as he directed the top set to revise indirect commands, he tried to steer Florian and his peers through the Scylla and Charybdis of second declension neuter nouns and adjectives.

As he paced up and down, he wondered how on earth Florian could have been so ingenious as to secure his own freedom from Mr Baadi. He wondered if the boy had already vouchsafed his secrets to a member of staff. To Dr Ngo in sympathy for his roasted behind? To Mrs Hughes-Howard in gratitude for her sympathetic frown? To Ms de Souza, untouched by any taint of Smilia? He scanned a few examples of their written work. All those in Florian's row had committed sizeable mistakes on the simplest of examples.

'Florian,' he said as if plucking a name at random. 'What does *bellum* mean?'

'"War", sir,' said the boy.

'Correct. Why not have a... have a house-point?' he said casually. 'And how do we say "war*sss*", in the plural?'

'I don't like to think about it really, sir because I was...'

'I know you were in the wars yourself, but just... for the sake of argument, and for two house-points, how would you say "wars", in the plural?'

Florian didn't seem to know this, but he conferred openly with Cato Wang, got the right answer, and was awarded two more house-points for showing initiative. He managed to fill in four more case endings in his book, got three simple sentences very nearly right except for the verb and the nouns, and looked genuinely pleased to be awarded two more house-points.

'Well done, Florian. Welcome back! You deserved those, because, well, you've been off for a few weeks, haven't you?'

'More than that, sir,' said Florian.

'Yes, well we're all very...'

'But sir?' It was Florian again.

'Yes?' Charles said, looking up brightly. 'Was there something you didn't understand?'

'Adrian Purvis has guffed and it's getting a bit pongy: could we open the door?'

'Go back to Smilia!' Purvis screeched.

'Actually,' said Charles, 'I suppose there is a Health and Safety aspect to that, quite right, so...' He turned nonchalantly to the board. 'I think, um, a house-point might be awarded on the grounds that you displayed concern for Adrian's well-being and that of the rest of the class. So, yes, have a house-point, or perhaps two.'

As the bell rang, Charles totted up Florian's haul. It occurred to him that he been a little over-generous in awarding him 25 house-points in one lesson. Perhaps he could raise it with Ms de Souza in one of their mid-week briefings, or discuss it with Florian now.

'Back in the swing of things, eh, Florian?' Charles murmured as the class filed out.

'Yeah, sir. It's great to be back,' said Florian, standing up and taking several deep breaths. He seemed to have grown in height, but looked thinner.

Charles searched for signs of trauma. The boy's

eyes appeared bleaker, as if still adjusting to the sunlight. He also seemed to require more air to speak than he had used before. He kept checking his tie knot as if he wasn't used to having his neck constrained, and every few seconds he turned round, as if looking for available exits, to where Yedverd and Enzo were hovering by the door, unwilling to leave him alone.

Charles felt moved to offer a few conciliatory words. 'Now, you may remember us having a chat about the pros and cons of being the class rep, before you, er, you were... er...'

'Yeah, I do remember that, as a matter of fact, sir,' said Florian, his fingers pulling at a strand of hair, something he never used to do. 'You told me that Mr Baadi had a special job for me...'

'That's right. Obviously, at the time I didn't know what the job was. Well, these people never quite make things clear, do they...'

'He made me stay behind,' said Florian, as if Charles needed to be reminded.

'Which must have been terrible.'

Florian stared at, or slightly beyond, Charles. It was rather disconcerting.

'Must have been really awful...'

The boy nodded his head, apparently unwilling to entertain any further discussion on that point. Charles sighed several times and blew out hard, as if trying even now to soften the blow.

'So, you were locked up in Smilia for three months...'

'98 days,' said the boy. 'I worked it out...'

'So that was the bad news, yes. But now... You're back! Hooray!'

'Yes sir, I know that.'

'And shall I tell you one of the best things about being back?'

'What's that, sir?' asked the boy, with a glassy stare.

'Well, now that you're no longer in a prison cell

being guarded by Mr Baadi's soldiers, you can score a *seriously* large number of house-points for your house.'

'Oh great,' said the boy, not meeting his eyes.

'Which is... Rangeley?'

'Yes sir,' said Florian.

'There you are. How fantastic is that!' gushed Charles helplessly, though he already felt he had lost the argument.

'Right, sir,' said Florian.

'That house-point trophy could be yours on speech day! So let's keep that outlook positive, eh?'

'Right, sir,' said the boy, but his foot had started drumming impatiently against the floor. 'Anyway, I have to go now.'

'Of course. Run around a bit.'

'Actually I'm meant to be doing an interview in a couple of minutes.'

'Great! I look forward to seeing your ugly face in the *Churley Advertiser.*'

'Actually it's, like... *BBC World Services*?'

'Ah, the World Service! Marvellous!' said Charles, aghast that anyone who couldn't pronounce the station's name correctly could still appear on it. 'Well, a splendid organisation, as I'm sure you know. Radio or TV?'

'I think it's just on the phone.'

'How exciting,' said Charles.

'I've got to do quite a lot this afternoon and I'll be very tired afterwards so I won't be able to do any homework.'

'Right. Not any? Not even some? No, I suppose not.'

The boy remained silent, staring through the window.

'Well, I'm glad we've had this chat.'

'Me too, sir,' Florian said, instantly looking more lively.

'And we should probably have a longer chat,' said Charles. 'Nothing too heavy. Just...'

'Yeah. Let's do that some time, Mr Goldforbes,' said

Florian. 'That would be good.' And then he turned and walked out with Yedverd and Enzo, leaving Charles alone in the classroom.

Charles had a lot of marking to do, and it was almost dark by the time he got home. As he opened the door he heard a curious combination of sounds, both ravished and yet strangely muffled. He walked up the stairs and nearly fell over a pair of stiff black leather shoes. He registered that they were male shoes, but no more. He could now hear cooing sounds from behind Mrs Annersley's closed door, interrupted by a series of urgent whimpers, which again reminded him of something, or someone.

Finding stray items of clothing on the floor was not an unfamiliar sight when Mrs Annersley had been doing some last-minute 'shopping', as she called it: some brown trousers, a white shirt, a jacket which he was sure he had seen somewhere. But the sounds were normally a duet of male over-exertion and female under-appreciation. This was something else. It was only when he noticed the Donald Duck tie hanging from the arm of the sofa that he was able to connect it with the crescendo of pleading and satisfied groans coming from Mrs Annersley's bedroom. He began to feel queasy. With a final, triumphant cry, the plangent sobs died down and, a few moments later, the door was forcibly opened by Mrs Annersley, wearing nothing but a pink bra, stilettos and blue panties.

'Oh! Hello Charles,' she said. Charles had not seen her dressed so scantily before. She was still in good shape.

She stood in the doorway, holding a box of matches and what Charles felt sure was a riding crop, similar to that brandished by Mr Baadi. The smell of burning wax wafted out from behind her, as did the image of Charles' colleague, Dr Colin Ngo, bound tightly with what looked like Close to the Hedge garden twine, and with the cotton belt of Mrs

Annersley's bathrobe between his jaws. Dr Ngo registered Charles' presence with a guttural "Hhhharrr," such that Charles had not heard since their last night in Smilia. Even without peeking, Charles could see that his colleague had been suspended diagonally between two walls, with his naked buttocks - shielded by a sizeable but discreet wedge of protective dressing - hanging just above the comforting glow of a reflexology candle.

'I heard the voicemail about the party at your school,' she said, pushing the door shut with the back of her foot. 'They said bring your friends and I kept calling you, so I assumed you were already there. So I... anyway, I turned up. Well he's something of a celebrity, that young man, isn't he? And then guess who I bumped into?' She pointed over her shoulder to the bedroom door. 'He's quite a lad, is your colleague. I'm hopping out for a pee. Honestly, Charles, he doesn't hold back. Luckily, I had the means to restrain him.'

'I'm glad you're happy, Mrs Annersley.'

'Oh, yes,' she said, raising her voice to the most theatrical of whispers. 'And between you and me, *he's got a willy like a baby's arm.* When he got it out, I said, "Colin, we may have to take this in stages". I mean I've seen some big ones but...'

'That's enough detail, thanks very much, Mrs Annersley,' said Charles.

'Well, you know,' she dropped her voice still further. 'The poor man, he's suffered so *terribly*, he really has, so I just feel I'm here to help in any way I can. Now have some wine, dear, and put the telly on, we're not done yet. Colin?' She shouted through the door. 'I'm going to the bathroom. And if you haven't managed to get those knots undone when I return, you are going to be in all *sorts* of trouble.' She winked at Charles, playfully snapping the riding whip against her arm. Charles stood there for a second, then retraced his steps and went out into the cool night air of Embury Park, and a consolatory curry at All The Raj.

CHAPTER 18

Teaching Latin to an adolescent latter-day saint and war hero was not, Charles discovered, an easy task. The experience of being Mr Baadi's captive for three months might have broken a lesser individual, but Florian seemed to have emerged amazingly intact. And yet if the other teachers were amazed at his psychological robustness, Charles began to suspect a more prosaic explanation, that Florian simply lacked the imagination to be traumatised. If he went silent during a lesson, and Charles asked him if he was all right – perhaps suspecting that he was having a flashback – Florian would look a little confused, and then say something like, 'Fine sir, I was just trying to remember Dylan's *Facebook* password,' rather than 'I was thinking back to what a terrible time I had in captivity.'

Having spent so much time left to his own resources, it was anyone's guess whether he would want to bounce back into the school community, or hover on the edges. 'You may find him exhibiting either of those personality traits, or a little of both, or something different that you don't expect,' as one of the trauma counsellors had helpfully advised. This proved to be true. They had also warned the staff – and the rest of Year Eight – to look out for some pretty violent mood shifts. 'He needs *time* to *recover*,' said another adviser. 'And you've got to give him that. We call it "Recovery Time".'

'Ah,' said Bill Drummer. 'Now that reminds me. We're going over *Lord of the Flies* in class, OK?'

The advisor looked slightly alarmed at the literary reference.

'Now, that's all about boys being on their own, so should I worry that it might set Florian off?' Bill asked.

'Well,' said the advisor, 'you might find that a book like that *impacts* him *negatively*.' She paused.

'Right,' said Bill.

'But then again, it might not, or not in the way that you might have thought. Does that help?'

'Kind of,' he said.

Florian seemed to have his own survival toolkit. One day, Charles was about to chastise him for not having brought his homework to school, as well as for not having his textbook open at the right chapter, or open – or even, in fact, with him. But Florian merely dipped his head and lifted a hand. Instantly there was silence in the room.

'You know, sir, this reminds me of this one day, when Mr Baadi got really cross with me? He said he was going to lock me in the cave with the lights off. And he did.' Everyone gasped. Charles felt it best not to interrupt. The counselling team had also stressed that if Florian had "emotions" that he needed to "share", it was necessary to give him the "space" to do so. The term they used seemed to be "Emotional Space Sharing".

'How did you cope?' asked a hush-voiced Enzo Merriman.

'Well,' said Florian, his voice getting ever quieter. 'I made a sort of deal with myself. I sat there in the dark, repeating to myself this phrase, over and over again. It was like, if I could hear myself saying that, I knew I was still alive, and I wasn't scared. But I thought to myself, if I get out, and I, like, come back to school, one day I'll hear that phrase again. But this time, it won't be just me saying it but the rest of the guys. I want to hear them all say it, not just me.'

'What was the phrase?' asked Roley Yousuf.

'Do you really want to hear it?' asked Florian. 'It meant so much to me at the time.'

'Go on,' said Enzo Merriman and the whole class.

'It was: "Adrian Purvis takes it up the arse",' said Florian, with no hint of a smile.

Adrian shrieked in consternation but could only

carry on shrieking as the rest of the class joined in with Florian's mantra. And as Charles explained later during one of the ever-more frequent staff meetings, 'How could I stop them? The way he told the story, it was as if he had been building up to that moment for months...'

'Tricky,' said Dr Ironsize, linking hands behind his knee.

'Tough call,' said Dotty.

'It's as if he's using the whole... situation just to have a swipe at Adrian.'

'Whatever it takes...' said Bill Drummer, who always tended to back Florian.

'Yes but, it's a bit low, isn't it?' Charles insisted. 'I mean... in a strange sort of a way, I think we lost something when he came back.'

'Steady...' Dr Ngo began, but Charles wouldn't be deterred.

'I mean, it was like the Blitz, out there. We were all in it together. But now that he's back, we've...'

'Were you, like, being bombed?' said Charmian. 'Like with Messerschmitt airplanes and sirens going off, and A.R.P. wardens outside, and everyone listening to Vera Lynn...?'

'No, not literally,' said Charles. 'But we were all in it together. We had this sort of Smili spirit, even when we came back. Now it's just about Florian.'

By this reading, those left behind in supposed freedom had a much harder time of it than the captive, which was how Charles saw it. For the fact was that the Common Entrance exams would soon be upon them, and the teachers' supplies of patience were running low.

'It's not as if he came down to earth from heaven,' complained Mrs Hughes-Howard in a tetchy aside. 'I mean, I know he had a difficult time of it, but he wasn't nailed to a cross with a crown of thorns on his head.'

'That's true, I suppose,' said Dr Ironsize. He flexed his elbows restlessly. 'Now, how many schools are we up to so far, Ms de Souza?'

Dotty looked at her pad. 'He's had 47 offers so far,' she said, 'but more are bound to turn up after the postal strike ends.' As well as offers of places, an even greater number of invitations were for personal appearances, from infant schools to sixth form colleges. Just that day, Florian had been invited by Charles' alma mater to address the Cambridge Union Society to debate "This House Believes That Democracy Is Making The World A More Dangerous Place." The fact that the organisation, which had been recognising notable speakers since 1815, chose to dignify a barely literate 13-year-old ahead of one of its own alumni – moreover, one with a fairly respectable Classics degree – made Charles want to throw his hands up – and then place them firmly round Florian's neck. But still the requests came in, on a range of subjects from the straightforward – "Survival Tips" – to the fanciful: "How to Pass Common Entrance".

The interested parties included banks, consultancies, management consultants, financial strategy firms and others. Most were accompanied by discreet bribes like chocolates, computer games and – perhaps to sweeten the boy's mother – flowers. One Sunday, Florian was flown by helicopter to a management conference on Jersey. He arrived back on Monday, just in time to go home at lunchtime, but before he left he handed Charles a sheet of creamy paper, with some indecipherable scribbles below the letterhead "Grand Hotel d'Atlantique".

'I can't read a word of this,' said Charles, handing it back.

'Sorry sir, it's really hard writing in a helicopter?'

'Well, you should have thought of that earlier,' said Charles.

'But you know when you're the special guest at a conference, and there's about five thousand people asking you questions, sir?'

'Er...'

'And you only got there the day before, but you had to do like a personal appearance in this conference room until ten o'clock the night before?'

'I can't say I've...'

'And they said the morning session would only last two hours but it runs over cos there's so many people asking you questions...?'

'I wasn't criticising, Florian,' said Charles, 'all I meant was...'

'And you get this standing ovation as you walk into the hall that lasts about five minutes but it doesn't leave a lot of time for Doing Your Latin Homework: do you know what I mean, sir?'

'Now Florian...'

'And you're so tired from, like, having your picture taken about a hundred times that you can't memorise that much Latin vocabulary, do you know that feeling, sir?'

'Yes, Florian,' said Charles, admitting defeat. 'I know exactly what you mean.'

It was hardly surprising that so many schools were taking Florian seriously. For the first few days after his return, there was a squatter camp opposite the school, made up of camera teams and massive microphones like grey storks' nests. Every time someone approached the solid timber gate, they started to pulsate in a variety of languages and accents, firing off frame after frame and, had they not been kettled behind crowd barriers by the Churley constabulary, they would have been all over the school in seconds. About a week after Florian's return, Mrs Hughes-Howard came across him in the playground, as Charles watched. 'All this attention, Florian!' she said cheerily. 'Do you ever wish you could run away and hide in a cave?'

Florian didn't answer right away. 'I was joking about the cave, obviously,' she said hurriedly, but

Florian just grinned and moved away. He evidently did not consider himself to be a hostage to the world's media.

The following day, Charles spotted Florian sitting quietly on a bench during mid-morning break. He was reading avidly from a pile of papers. Charles asked him what he was doing.

'Revising,' said the boy.

'Excellent,' said Charles, satisfied that he was at last feeling the urgency of the oncoming Common Entrance exam week. 'What subject?'

'*Newsnight*,' he said, and indeed, later that evening, Charles switched on his TV to find one of the BBC's most famously truculent interviewers lobbing a few easy passes to the nation's most recent escapee.

'Can Smilia do it?' asked the dreaded grey-haired interlocutor. 'I mean, can it rise from the ashes?'

'Well, I reckon if they're lucky they'll be able to do it, but it might take some time,' said Florian, with the floundering earnestness of a football pundit.

'What does the country need?' the Rottweiler tried again. The man was smiling and looking nervous: Charles had never seen such a transformation.

'I would say... they need a government with, you know...'

'Teeth?' offered the feared inquisitor.

'Yeah,' said Florian, 'definitely.'

Charles switched off: it was hardly a Chatham House briefing.

Florian's behaviour showed no sign of improvement, but conventional methods of discipline were discouraged by the Home Office post-traumatic stress counsellors. Any form of detention, be it at break or lunchtime, was felt to be 'unhelpful' if it reminded Florian of his previous circumstances. Nor was his attendance record that bad: the problem was not in getting to school, more that he could never be relied on to remain in the class once he was there. Florian's timetable was largely of his own devising: if he walked from the room in the middle of a lesson, or more likely at the start of a vocabulary test, protesting that he 'needed to get away', what teacher could oppose him?

Whereas, in the previous term, swearing at or in the presence of a teacher was an offence instantly punished by exclusion, the scale of Florian's hardships made such reactions appear somewhat knee-jerk. He was allowed some time to cool down outside (known as "Cooling Down Time" in the jargon), perhaps by sprawling on a beanbag in the library, "helping" Ms Thirst in the Art room or chatting to Dorotea and in particular to Emmanuel in the kitchen. He could read in Ms de Souza's office, but he also liked to visit Dr Ngo in the Bavington I.T. Suite, which really meant spending a few minutes each day responding to emails and checking references to himself – a practice to which the school had decided to turn a blind eye.

Florian's worst behaviour was still reserved for Adrian Purvis who, having survived a brief but unwelcome extra period of captivity, had reacted very badly to Florian's release. It was easy to see why. Florian was victimising him with, if anything, more energy than ever. The previous week, a vast quantity of pornography had been detected in Purvis' computer files, perhaps copied from a USB stick, and it was obvious from Adrian's protestations – and from the fact that the folder had been called "Hardcowre Porn" – that he had not placed the images there himself.

'It can't have been me, sir,' said Florian, pointing to the Date Created tag. 'I was on Five Live then.' They knew it was him, but they couldn't prove it without extensive reference to that week's media schedule. But what if they could?

The problem was that the disciplinary system at a small prep school in south-west London could hardly be said to hold many fears for a boy who had been held at gun-point by Smili kidnappers. Florian knew better than anyone what an asset he was to the school, and he showed no signs of playing down his role, nor of trying harder at Latin. Charles hoped he might come to respect the school ethos, but it was time wasted, especially when he was boasting about how many schools had offered him a place. On one occasion, right in the middle of Charles' brief but catchy PowerPoint exposition of the workings of the imperfect tense, Florian's hand rose into the air. Charles decided to accentuate the positive.

'Yes, Florian?' he smiled, ringing the occasion by adding, 'And may I say what a pleasure it is to be able to say that to you.'

'Sir, I just thought you might like to know that Thickett Lodge have offered me a one hundred per cent scholarship.'

The whole class cooed in astonishment, except for Adrian Purvis, who made a frenzied clucking sound.

'Delighted to hear it,' said Charles. 'Whichever school you go to will be as lucky to have you as we will be sad to lose you.'

'I won't be sad to lose you,' said Adrian.

'Thank you, Adrian,' said Charles.

'And they don't teach Latin there so I don't need to do the exam.' Florian informed him.

'That will be the classical world's loss,' said Charles, sensing strongly that his supplies of generosity were becoming strained. 'Do let us know when you have made a firm decision.'

'Actually I'll probably go to Thickett, because that's where Dylan is,' said Florian.

'Good. Let's move on.'

'He's my main man.'

'Let's turn back to the translation,' said Charles, determinedly.

'My honky.'

'I want you to look hard at these endings,' said Charles, feeling the blood racing to his cheeks.

'Hey Dylan, love you bro.'

As Florian spoke, there came into Charles' head a jarring image of himself with his hands around the boy's neck, shaking him until he ceased to quiver. He decided not to share this unpleasant fantasy with any of his colleagues as he was beginning to worry that his only ally against Florian was Adrian Purvis. He didn't particularly want to be on the same side as this universally derided figure. In fact, he didn't even want to be in the same room as him, unless the windows were lowered or there was a good ventilation system.

Then, of course, there were the book offers. Florian had been taken to tea by several book agents within a few days of his return, but was eventually wooed by Letitia Throbisher, of the nakedly commercial firm Thrumm and Hewson. The matter of assembling the words might take a little time, but it was assumed that these would flow as soon as a ghostwriter was appointed. The other teachers revelled in the attention, a little like Perseus, dazzled by the glint of the Medusa's reflection.

'I wonder what they'll call it,' said Madame Allardyce.

'It needs an exclamation, like *I Made It!*' declared Bill Drummer.

'Or how about *Alone In Mr Baadi's Cave?*' suggested Madame Allardyce.

'I'd go for something a bit arty, well that's me isn't it, the Art teacher,' said Charmian Thirst. 'Something like *I'm A Schoolboy, Get Me Out Of Here!*'

Madame Allardyce asked Charles if he had a title.

'*My Struggle?*' he said, without hesitation. There was a pause.

'Wasn't that... Didn't someone else use that?' said Charmian.

'I think it was Hitler,' said Bill. 'Steady, Charlie boy!'

'Oh, that's not very nice,' Charmian looked put out.

'I think he's joking, dear,' said Madame Allardyce.

But he wasn't. Not really.

Another source of vexation for Charles was the photograph of the "survivors", taken during the enormous swell of emotion that had accompanied Florian's return. He wanted it re-taken with him in it. Charmian Thirst kept promising to help but, being an art teacher, she kept forgetting, and without that photographic evidence, Charles felt marginalised. He also longed for an opportunity to see Natasha, and to say whatever was on his mind. So when Year Eight's average test scores, which had shown a cautious rise while Florian was away, showed a marked descent, it was decided that the gauntlet must be thrown down and Florian's parents – divorced or not – had to be invited to come and meet Dr Ironsize and Ms de Souza.

Natasha Bavington arrived first, and Charles happened to be hanging around in the playground when she walked in. It was the first time he had seen her since her darkened bedroom – not that he had seen her then.

'Hello, Mrs... Bavington,' said Charles to Natasha. He wished he could glimpse her eyes, but she was wearing a pair of sunglasses that covered most of the top half of her head.

'Hello, Mr Goldforbes,' she said.

'Are you, er... all right?' he started to say, but just then, Charmian drifted over.

'Hello Mrs Bavington!' she said, kissing Natasha. 'It's so nice to see you. Isn't she gorgeous?!' she said to Charles.

'Lovely to see you, Charmian,' said Natasha.

'I bet there were times when you thought you'd never see Florian again!' said Charmian.

'There were times, yes,' Natasha allowed herself a tiny smile.

'I don't know how you coped. I mean, I don't have kids of my own but I'd have gone mad.'

'I think I did, a little,' said Natasha. 'At times I'm sure I went quite mad.'

'Me too,' said Charles, feeling his throat contract.

'Oh look, he's welling!' Charmian put a hand on Charles' arm. 'Stop it, or you'll set me off too! Aaah..!'

'I just wanted to say...' Charles tried again. 'I'm so sorry, about what happened.'

'Yes, I'm sorry too,' said Natasha.

'You don't have to say sorry to each other,' said Charmian with a big wide grin. 'You haven't done anything to each other!'

'No, we haven't,' said Natasha.

'I know,' said Charles. 'But I just wanted to say... I wish I could have done more. Or something else.'

'You did quite enough,' said Natasha. 'But it's over now.'

'Oh listen to you two!' said Charmian, the unconscious diplomat. She broke off for a moment. 'It's all so emotional, isn't it? Too much for me. When it gets like that, I just want to go and lie down in a darkened room, do you know what I mean?'

'Yes,' said Charles, too quickly to catch Natasha's response.

'Isn't he lovely?' said Charmian. 'He's a dark horse.'

The gate pinged again and Hugh entered. 'Hail Caesar,' he said, stretching out a hand to Charles and instinctively ignoring his ex-wife. 'I hear Florian's still crap at Latin.'

'Er, unreliable,' said Charles, glad in a way for the change in tone. It was the first time the two had met since Charles had been sent colliding forcibly against Hugh's body-work.

'Handed out many detentions?' asked Hugh.

'Not to Florian,' he said. 'Quite a lot of house-points though.'

'Hello Mr Bavington,' said Charmian. 'Isn't Florian amazing, the way he came out of that cave and just got on with his life?'

'Yup,' said Hugh. 'And now he's giving a few others a taste of it, from what I've heard.'

'He'll be fine,' said Charmian. 'He'll have forgotten all about it in a few months.'

'It might take a bit longer than that,' said Natasha.

'But *we* won't forget him, will we, Charles?' Charmian said.

'No we won't, and we won't forget... his parents, either.'

'Oh isn't he a charmer?!' said Charmian. 'Now in you go or I'll get a detention for making you late.'

'Goodbye, Mr Goldforbes,' said Natasha.

'So you *are* human, after all,' said Charmian, putting her arm through Charles' as they walked back across the playground.

'What?'

'You've gone all goggly-eyed.'

'Don't be daft,' said Charles, but he was glad she'd said it.

At the staff meeting that afternoon – they were coming thick and fast now – Dr Ironsize explained that he had "read the riot act out" to Mr and Mrs Bavington, but that he had agreed to give Florian a raft of new responsibilities, including making him a prefect, which was, in Dr Ironsize's view, a significant gesture of appreciation for his privations abroad. There was a general rumble of approval around the staff room.

The headmaster looked at Charles. 'We didn't discuss individual teachers, but I wanted to involve you, Charles, too. Have you thought of resuscitating the Debating Society?'

Charles learned that the Debating Society, once a prominent feature of school lunchtimes, had been lying dormant ever since an overwhelming majority of boys had voted in favour of the motion "Nobody Cares About The Debating Society", some years earlier.

'It never really recovered after that,' said Mrs Hughes-Howard, passing the tea round. 'Even with the debating award. So there's a challenge for you, Charles: you could restart the club!'

Whatever its chequered history, given Florian's increased tendency to make his views heard, it was felt that this might help him and the school to let off some steam. As for Charles, since his aching ribs still made walking difficult at times, a more sedentary activity might suit him.

The first meeting was scheduled for the next day, and Charles had chalked up various debating society favourites which he thought might trigger a response from the boy who had evidently carried all before him in a question and answer session at the Cambridge Union the previous week. Topics included "Truth Is Stranger Than Fiction", "Democracy Is On Its Last Legs", "Slavery is Dead", "Greeks Are Better Than Romans", "Capital Punishment Should Be Re-Introduced" and – in lighter mode – "English Football Needs Foreign Managers". These, though, were all ignored in favour of Josh De Burgh's suggestion that "GameBoy Is Way Better Than Power Rangers", which put paid to Charles' invocation, in his introductory remarks, of the spirit of Demosthenes and Cicero.

Florian appeared for about a minute, with half the school trailing behind him, but he walked in, sat down and was gone a minute later, leaving the meeting as sparsely attended as it had been before. From the way his work was going, he was going to last about as long in the upcoming examinations.

'I gave them a past paper just now,' said Mrs Hughes-Howard in the staffroom one afternoon. 'Question five was "Can you name angle D?" Florian wrote, "Donald."' She flicked the switch of the kettle crossly. 'We've only got a few weeks left before the exams. Sometimes, I don't know why I bother.'

The problem for Charles was that, apart from the top set, much of the progress made in Smilia had unravelled since the journey home. Worse, Latin – which had responded so well to the enforced privations of Mr Baadi's prison cell – had come to be associated, negatively in their minds, with captivity. And yet every day brought fresh offers from schools to which Florian had never applied and of which no one had even heard.

'Before this,' said Ms de Souza, during another staff meeting, 'he was never going to get into any local school without an unconditional offer, unless the only condition was performing very badly in the exams.'

'Or unless they needed any building work done,' added Dr Ngo quietly.

'But… given all this excitement,' Ms de Souza continued, 'we have to admit that Florian has presented us with something of a problem. Or an opportunity. May I, er, Dr Ironsize..?'

Dr Ironsize rounded his eyes. 'Please do,' he said. He suddenly looked exhausted.

'The thing is, as you all know, Mrs Portal has a sore throat from the number of calls we've been getting.'

'Lots of parents want to see the school that produced Florian Bavington,' said Dr Ironsize.

'Exactly,' said Dotty.

'So, having put up with Florian for so many years, we have finally been presented with the chance to capitalise on his memory,' said Dr Ironsize.

'I thought we were going to use the word "Legacy",' said Ms de Souza hastily.

Dr Ironsize agreed, stressing the point that they should strike while the iron was hot, or, as he put it, 'Dive in while the water is still warm'. Exams were nearly upon them, the end of term would arrive before they knew it, and then Florian would be gone, together with any attendant publicity opportunities. It was agreed, therefore, that Speech Day, the last day of the school year, should be combined with an extended Open Day.

'This will be a private occasion, on which outsiders are invited to eavesdrop,' said Ms de Souza. 'And it will be a chance for them to see the school doing what it does best.'

'Giving prizes to boys who don't really deserve them,' said a voice.

'Thank you, Dr Ngo,' said Ms de Souza.

The publicity windfall had evidently been on the minds of the senior management team for longer than they had been letting on. The very next day, a murrain of photographers descended on the school, their brief being to encapsulate the experience of being at Rydon Hall. This amounted to taking photographs of Florian Bavington in as many different settings as possible. The accompanying brochure, produced too quickly to erase the dozen or so spelling mistakes that so dismayed Charles, bore the predictably over-inflated cover line, "Rydon Hall: The Freedom To Learn". If anyone had missed the smiling face of Florian Bavington, prominently displayed on the front cover amid a clump of Year Eight boys, he also appeared on pages three, five, six, seven, eight, nine and 11, always amongst other boys but always recognisable as Florian. Dr Ngo and Mrs Hughes-Howard's faces could be seen towards the front. Charles was included somewhere near the back, on a page marked "Think Latins Dead? Think Again!" Charles howled when he saw the missing apostrophe but several thousand had already been printed.

'Sorry Mr Goldforbes. It was all a bit of a rush,' said Dotty.

Charles could only nod and sigh.

He kept meaning to talk to Dr Ngo about his new relationship with Mrs Annersley, but events inside school were moving forward so fast that they rarely had time to chat.

As for Hugh Bavington, he was spending more time in London, to be with his son. He even turned up at school one day to collect Florian, and when he saw Charles he thumped him warmly on the back as if they were old mates. Charles braced himself before the blow landed: the left side of his chest was still causing him pain, and he had started wheezing when climbing up stairs.

Apart from not seeing Mrs Bavington any more, the most painful aspect of Florian's return, for Charles, was that his own anguish was put into the shade. Florian was now the supreme embodiment of suffering: also of resistance, endurance, ingenuity, survival, even – to the amazement of all who taught him – of raw intelligence. Charles felt like Florian's prisoner, and unlike Mr Baadi, the captor did not seem to value his hostage in the least.

'It's not fair,' said Charles to a few others one afternoon. 'It's as if the rest of us just had an extended holiday in Benidorm.'

'Don't be a stupid prick,' said Mr Drummer. 'Kidding! Only kidding. Tourette's, sorry. No, but don't be...'

'But that's how it feels,' said Charles, ignoring Bill. 'It's as if we just over-stayed our welcome, whereas Florian's been through this Daniel in the Lions' Den experience.'

'Well, dear, just look at his age. I mean, he's only a child,' said Mrs Hughes-Howard. 'No wonder the school is making a fuss of him.'

Charles wondered if she knew about Dr Ngo's after-school activities with Mrs Annersley. 'It's good to see Colin looking so much better,' he said.

'I know, dear,' she said, thumbing through her marks book.

'Do you think there's a special reason why he's so happy?'

'Sorry, dear?'

'Why he's in such a good mood?'

'Well,' she said, 'no, but I imagine the skin graft operations are helping. He's a survivor, is Colin.'

'I know,' said Charles, a little spitefully. 'I saw the caption on the photograph.'

Mrs Hughes-Howard's apparent indifference made Charles feel that no one felt like he did, or had suffered as he had done, or could sympathise with him. He must therefore be a self-obsessed meanie who was suffering from a bad case of sour grapes. Charles had to admit that he also felt sore because – barring one letter forwarded by the *Churley Advertiser* inquiring about Latin tutoring for senior citizens - no fame of any sort had come his way. Mrs Annersley had encouraged him to believe that his route home would be blocked by young women desperate to ask about his experiences, and to nurse him patiently back to health. Nothing had come of this, however, and he was forced to conclude that no one cared.

Florian had attempted to duck his first exam – English Comprehension – on the thoroughly specious grounds that the *GQ* photo shoot he was lined up for simply could not wait, but even he was not allowed to opt out of Exam Week. An enforced silence clung to the school like hairspray. The sight of Year Eight, legs splayed under the narrow desks as they chewed their pen tops in the main hall, was arresting. The juniors did not at first understand that they were effectively being asked to mime their mid-morning break routine, but they eventually got the hang of it and pottered about, building low walls from *Brio* bricks and then, for once, not knocking them over straight away.

When the marks came in, there were few surprises. Dr Ironsize was a master of examination tactics, and his teaching staff had been able to predict – pretty much to the grade – what scores their students would achieve. If anything, Rufus Coe-Haine marginally over-performed, getting more Bs than Cs. Rohan Shapcott – who left shortly after for an indoor skiing tournament in the Seychelles – did spectacularly well.

It appeared that almost everyone's hard work had paid off, and that all the Year Eight students would be going to the rash of perfectly decent but far from brilliant schools that they had applied to. Dr Ironsize did his best to position himself so that all the reflected glory fell on himself, while claiming that any bounce was generated by a diver's legs, not the board itself.

Staff were unsure if he was aligning himself with the diver, the legs, the board or the water.

'He loses me sometimes,' confessed Dr Ngo, rubbing the side of his still very tender neck.

Florian scored either a D or an E for every subject except a triumphant C at I.T., whereupon word reached the staffroom that, after a difficult meeting with Dr Ironsize, it had been agreed that he would not be taking up the offered place at Thickett Lodge. Mrs Bavington wanted him to go to a small boarding school on the Cornwall-Devon borders, where every child had their own farm animal, the Headmaster's wife cooked lunch, and there was an emphasis on self-exploration through tree-house construction and charcoal drawing.

Mr Bavington preferred l'Ecole Olympique de Monaco, the school which had equipped France with virtually its entire winter Olympic squad – and a shelf-ful of French *Vogue* cover stars – for the past 50 years. This was where the water temperature in the showers never rose above 15 degrees Celsius, sports training proceeded seven afternoons a week and the school uniform consisted of a tracksuit and trainers.

Mr Bavington got to pay the fees and so won the argument: Florian would be receiving extra French tuition to keep up.

'And I hope he does a better job with his next trawler crew,' Madame Allardyce observed.

Passing by Churley House one day, Charles saw a Plunkett-Hastie & Carnegie-Doyle "For Sale" sign outside, and he realised that Mrs Bavington must be preparing to move closer to her son's new school.

With exams over, it was time for the Year Eight post-exam programme to kick off. The school strove to provide an exhilarating schedule of uplifting and character-moulding outings for the boys – all strictly Home Counties-based this year, for obvious reasons – on their way from academically under-achieving childhood into mediocre adolescence. They had a paintballing afternoon with real soldiers, all of whom crowded round Florian for a photo. They went to Newmarket for a day of horse-racing: Florian's lopsided grin dominated *The Racing Post*, *Racing News*, and every other Course tabloid the following day. They spent a day in a field building hayricks, although Adrian Purvis, whose allergies had returned in strength, had to wait in the farmhouse, where he sneezed on just about every in-breath. They even travelled, under lowering and eventually spitting grey skies, to Villa Podmore, once one of the biggest and most lavish Roman baths in Britain, now reduced to about three dozen large stones on the edge of a dual carriageway outside Carshalton, during which Charles could think of very little to do apart from positioning himself in the gift shop and shooing boys away. The trip to the BBC studios went ahead as planned, and Charles joined them for that too. The party were meant to be watching the news, but Florian ended up being the subject of the main report.

'Did you always think you'd get out?' asked the *So Local So London!* interviewer, who looked only a year or two older than her interviewee.

'Yeah, basically,' said Florian.

'What gave you the strength to keep going?' she asked, sweeping her hair to one side.

'Cos I thought, like, if I got out, I'd be on TV?' said Florian.

The interviewer giggled with delight at what she took to be his understated humour, but Charles knew he was simply telling the truth. He could have pointed out that he too had been "Lost in Africa" – the title of the report – but he knew he was wasting his time. Still, at least he wasn't the only person who was affronted by all this lionising of Florian. Looking at the boys, he noticed that Adrian Purvis had begun to gnaw at the skin of one of his fingers as Florian spoke.

CHAPTER 19

And then it was speech day, and the last day of term. The red bricks and copper turrets of Rydon Hall had never looked lovelier. Mr Scamage the caretaker had taken to telling anyone who would listen that if he had to paint any more walls he would start to resemble a pot of paint, and it was true that the school did smell eerily fresh, especially in Year Eight, which also helped to lessen the clinging residue of Adrian Purvis.

Blue skies, flecked with Rubenesque clouds, smiled down on the Bavington Computer Suite, and the whole school seemed irradiated with goodwill.

The theme of new beginnings was reflected in the bundle clutched by Ms Brundleby. Every time the tiny baby coughed, she had to step out of the hall.

Rydon Hall was a generous school, and one way or another, every boy in Year Eight received an award for effort or achievement, no matter how strained those definitions had to be. Art, Music, Drama and all the academic subjects were recognised, together with Football, Rugby and Cricket, and even though Florian had scooped the lion's share of nominations, it should have been easy to spread the praise across the year. The staff meeting at which these were allocated did not normally take long. But at the end, as Ms de Souza was totting up the totals, she tapped her pen against her brow.

'Hold on,' she said. 'Haven't we missed someone out? Y-yes, I'm afraid it's Purvis.'

That floored everyone. There was no subject, no discipline, at which he emitted anything other than a pallid glow.

'Poor lad,' said Mrs Hughes-Howard. 'What can we give him?'

'A deodorant?' suggested Madame Allardyce.

After a lengthy examination of the back of the trophy cupboard, Ms de Souza emerged with a small, square, Perspex trophy called the Honora Cleremont Award for Special Effort. No one could identify Mrs Cleremont, still less the most recent winner who had obviously strived fairly hard but to little effect: just the thing for Adrian Purvis, in other words.

On the afternoon of Speech Day, an armada of trophies stood on the table beside the grand piano. Charles had gasped when Dotty told him who had won the Sir Emerick Rydon Debating award. He picked it up and squinted at it. The brass base supported a coiled fist from which a slender index finger emerged, jabbing, into the air. 'Why does it have to be Florian?' Charles sighed. When talking to Dotty, he felt unable to dissimulate. 'Why does he have to win everything?'

'I think you know the answer to that, Charles, and please don't re-arrange the prizes. I've been here since six this morning, setting them out.'

'But he barely even made a speech.'

'Well, be fair: he did speak once or twice.' Ms de Souza was looking a bit shifty. 'And there was that time he went to the Students' Union at Cambridge, wasn't there?'

'Don't remind me,' said Charles. 'From what you told me, he just went off on some rant about how Eminem gave him the strength to survive three months of captivity.'

'I thought it was very passionate,' she said.

'No way! How about Adrian Purvis on school uniform? He really spoke from the heart.'

'Charles,' said Ms de Souza. 'This is Florian's year, hundred per cent. Look: why don't you say a few words to him when you hand him the prize? That would go down well with the parents.'

Charles nodded wearily. If nothing else, at least he would finally be sharing the stage with a celebrity.

The open day had lasted three hours before the speeches even began. Mrs Portal looked like her knees were about to give way by the end, as more and more people swept past her at the gates. Prospective parents were shown around the school with over-elaborate care by Year Eight students, from the boys' toilets on the first floor to Mr Scamage's suspiciously tidy carpentry shed. Six parents were assigned to one pair of boys. These included Dylan who, as a favour to Florian, had been invited back for the final day, and who, as a gesture of thanks to Thickett Lodge, had instantly grown two inches so that he now had to bend his knees to shake Charles' hand.

Obviously the group of six parents that most enjoyed themselves were the ones being shepherded by Dylan and the school's repatriated Odysseus, Florian Bavington. By the end of the tour, many of the parents had all but paid the deposit for the first term's bill. All had requested to stay to hear the speeches, and everyone fell silent as Dr Ironsize approached the microphone. The parents inside the hall sat up. So, Charles could see, did Mrs Annersley, looking uncomfortably formal in a floral blouse and tight blue skirt. So did the 500 potential parents crammed into the playground outside, watching on a hired video screen. Dr Ironsize, his hands trembling as he said they would, stepped forward.

In the first part of his speech he singled out some of the junior school's achievements, such as the successful construction, for charity, of a cornflakes tower and its "really plucky" staging, thanks to Mr Drummer, of *Von Ryan's Express*. Everyone nodded, a few smiled, and some parents glanced slyly at their phones. Dr Ironsize also thanked the staff for what had been, "even by Rydon Hall standards", an eventful year.

But it was when he said, 'Every year, in January, for the past eight years, Year Eight have gone on a trip to Egypt,' that everyone sat up. 'We normally see this as a chance for the boys to stretch themselves,' said Dr Ironsize, with a dull resonance to his voice. 'We had

259

not meant to stretch them that far.' There was an uneasy giggle in the hall. 'But by a most unfortunate series of misadventures, and nothing to do with the organisation or planning of our tours, which is always absolutely one hundred per cent water-tight and regulated by the Independent Schools' Association of Tour Operators, our 20 brave students and three members of staff fell into the hands of a criminal gang where they were forced to confront evil, pure and simple, for the first, and - we hope – last, time.'

He adjusted his tie and went on, 'These villains released all but one of their captives. They kept one behind. Just one. They might have thought that they could subdue that one prisoner more easily. They did not know Florian Bavington.'

Nor do you, thought Charles to himself. Dr Ironsize looked out proudly at the Year Eight boys, all sitting at the front of the stage with their feet resting on the wooden floor, including Dylan, sitting next to Florian, his eyes hidden behind his improbably low-slung fringe. Dr Ironsize heaped praise on Florian's courage in overcoming fear, loneliness, uncertainty, anxiety and doubt. Florian had had to "dig deep" during his three-month captivity, and it was a tribute to the boy's resilience that – permitting himself a little cough – "his personality seemed unaffected by his ordeal". (The parents outside missed the wry smiles that wreathed the lips of the staff as the headmaster spoke.)

Charles looked across to the other side of the room, where Adrian Purvis seemed to be about to bite through the skin round his index finger. He looked back at Mrs Annersley, whose eyes had caught Dr Ngo's in a soft beam of love. He noticed, at the back, that the imposing figure of Zimbabwean Piet had inserted itself like a human buffer between Mr and Mrs Bavington.

As Charles listened, he experienced once again a painful tug of emotions. Obviously it was wonderful to be back, and obviously Mr Baadi was very bad. But in a way he was honest. He was not insincere. He had a reasonable sense of humour. Apart from being guilty of unlawful imprisonment, he seemed not to have committed any other forms of abuse towards a boy who had thanked him by giving him the slip and who had been, ever since his return, utterly graceless. Charles was unable to prevent his shoulders writhing in discomfort as Dr Ironsize droned on. He wriggled, fidgeted and let out little snorts of disgust, like emissions from a smoke outlet, so much so that Bill Drummer looked at him and hissed, 'You OK, you arsehole? Kidding! Sorry.' But Charles was not OK. He missed that united front which had arisen during Florian's absence, and which, since his return, the school had conspired to demolish in its bid to beatify the unspeakable.

Dr Ironsize ended with the observation that education was like jumping off a diving board. 'We start by going up, then we plunge downwards for a while,' he wittered. (Some parents exchanged quizzical glances.) 'But if we keep our heads up, we will always surface.' And with that he asked Florian to come forward and receive a medal "For Valour", which had been carved from Perspex in the shape of a diving board. Florian stood up from his position at the front of the low stage, from where, as Dotty had explained, he would be able to move back and forth more easily to collect his many awards. Charles thrashed about on his chair: the day before, Florian had openly referred to Dr Ironsize as "an effing muppet".

Various more awards were given out, in between which the school orchestra scythed its way through some classics – from *Amazing Grace* to an extract from the *New World Symphony* and a timorous version of *I Believe I Can Fly* – in a variety of tempos, many of them within the same piece.

Ms de Souza handed Florian the Craddock Trophy for Sporting Excellence, despite the fact that Florian had phoned in sick on the day of the vital last match of the term against St Arbuck's, but was spotted by Mrs Portal coming out of the Varley Park Odeon with Dylan and a trail of autograph seekers that same afternoon. 'And when I confronted him, he offered me some popcorn – the nerve!' she had exclaimed.

Arthur and Des received their awards, and then Dr Ngo – "one of our brave survivors", Dr Ironsize explained – presented Florian with the Hewlitt Lee I.T. Trophy, which he said proved that being good at I.T. really could save your life. (This occasioned a light chuckle from the audience.)

Every time Florian stood up, the movement instigated what looked like a North Korean salute, as every parent held their mobile phone with one cocked arm to record the moment. Florian and Dr Ngo's handshake lasted several seconds, and there was an affectionate exchange of words between them. Charles noted that Dr Ngo chose not to refer to the day when Adrian claimed Florian had made him spill *Ribena* over two of the computer keyboards in the Bavington Suite.

Nor did Mrs Hughes-Howard – "another brave survivor" – escape. She presented Florian with the "One To Watch" award, which was sponsored by the area's most prominent high-street optician, Visions of Churley. She left a tiny lipstick mark on his cheek and immediately tried to dab it away. Florian's wrinkled nose drew a fresh burst of laughter from the audience. She made no reference to the incident the previous week in which Florian had terrified Des Muireadhaigh's tiny brother Cathal, by telling him his big brother had been kidnapped by Mr Baadi.

'And now,' said Dr Ironsize, in his sonorous voice, 'it is time to announce the winner of the Sir Emerick Rydon Debating Trophy, named after our founder. And I am going to ask Mr Charles Goldhorse – Goodforbes, sorry, Mr Charles Goldforbes – ah, to hand this over.'

Charles waited for the headmaster to remind the assembled crowd that he too had been a survivor, but evidently the discomfort of getting his name wrong twice had derailed him. Charles approached the dais. The trophy, with its oddly conical index finger held aloft in the manner of an orator driving home an emphatic point, was almost the last object left on the table to be given away.

'Thank you Dr Ironsize,' said Charles. He could hear the echo in the playground. 'This award has not been, er, awarded for some years but after quite a vigorous... quite a vigorous, debate, ha ha...' – he had been hoping for a ripple of laughter but the room remained disappointingly still - '... we have decided to award it to a student with a lively, outgoing personality, who is very, ah, strong-willed...' He thought back to his first ever conversation with Hugh. 'Very single-minded, um, always speaks his mind. But...' Ms de Souza was almost glaring at him. He had to do the right thing, for her. 'And so the Sir Emerick Rydon Debating Trophy goes to – yes – Florian Bavington.'

As a round of relieved applause crackled through the room, he knew that he had lost his last opportunity to tell the waiting audience the truth about Florian.

'Congratulations, Florian,' he said in an undertone as Florian robotically held out his hand to receive the latest trophy. 'I bet you weren't expecting that.'

'Very nice, sir,' said Florian, barely glancing at him.

'So...' said Charles, but the unfortunately-named Archie Neeples, looking tiny and anxious, was approaching the grand piano. As the boy began a tentative piano adaptation of Flo Rida's *Club Can't Handle Me*, Charles put his hand to the side of his mouth.

'Amazing, isn't it?' he said. 'Just amazing.'

'What is, sir?' asked Florian.

'Well, you know, to think that, a few months ago, there we all were, sitting in Mr Baadi's cave.'

'Oh yeah,' said the boy. 'I'd forgotten.'

'Forgotten?' said Charles. 'Forgotten you were there?!'

'No,' the boy said, and suddenly his mouth twisted with contempt. 'Forgotten *you* were there.'

Then he picked up his trophy and, with Archie Neeples' error-decked notes still ringing out across the hall, slouched back to where he had been sitting, surrounded by his afternoon haul.

'And I turn one final time to Mr, er, Goldforbes,' Dr Ironsize carried on, though Charles probably could not have moved if he had wanted to. He stared at Florian's back in disbelief. 'Because, last but not least, ha ha, we have one more very important award to hand out.' Charles hardly heard what the headmaster was saying: he was too shocked by Florian's calculated insult. Was this the ultimate humiliation: to be excluded from the collective experience of captivity? He had come back from the trip feeling better-disposed towards most of Year Eight, but Florian, despite his lip-quivering antics whenever disciplinary measures threatened, was simply a bully. It seemed that Charles – or the school, or captivity – had failed to teach Florian anything useful or meaningful at Rydon Hall. Was there not time for one final lesson?

'Mr Goldforbes,' croaked Dr Ironsize in a stage-whisper, flapping his hand towards the Perspex slab as he stepped away from the microphone.

Charles turned, and picked up the trophy as Florian returned to his place on the stage. 'This award,' he said, still trying to catch his breath, 'is the Honora Cleremont Award for Special Effort, and it goes to...' He was suddenly aware of a smell like a petrol refinery. 'It goes to Adrian Purvis.'

Purvis had stood up, to tepid applause from an audience now looking forward to going home. He stepped forward. Adrian Purvis smelt pretty ripe at the best of times, but today there was an even stronger whiff emanating from him which, had he not still been reacting to Florian's deliberate snub, might have made more of an impression on Charles.

The Latin teacher handed him the award and tried

to smile. He knew that teenagers were surly and ungrateful. He knew that they said things for effect and that they could be glib, coarse and thoughtless. He knew he must not take these things personally, and he certainly wasn't trying to make friends with any of his students, but still he felt singled out. Not just for disrespect: he had been written out of history. Mechanically, Charles held his hand out to shake Adrian's. The boy's skin felt alive with a kind of oiliness, but his eyes looked as if they were focussing on a considerably more distant object.

'Congratulations, Adrian,' he heard himself say. 'I'm sure, er...' But Charles' diffidence got no further. Adrian grabbed his award and, instead of returning to his place, set off across the hall, and with each step he took, the elaborate choreographing of the day began to fall apart.

'Arsehole!' he screamed as he strode with his unathletically lunar tread. 'Wanker! Tosser! *Cunt!*' Waking from the bad dream of Florian's affront, Charles wondered if Adrian had chosen this day to unburden himself of all the pent-up rage which he had amassed during seven years of being picked on by Florian. The North Korean salute had become more selective now as parents decided not to record this moment, but as Adrian arrived opposite Florian, he took something from his pocket which prevented anyone from confronting him head on. It was a disposable cigarette lighter, and – Charles realised at the same time – his school blazer must have been marinated for several hours, possibly over-night, in a liquid such as Turpentine Solution.

'Wanker! Tosser! Cunt!' The banned words were still echoing round the playground through the sound system as Adrian, brandishing his lighter, planted his large flat feet in front of Florian. Charles, not really thinking, tried to move closer but Adrian held up his hand.

'Now, no one move except Mr Goldforbes. If anyone

moves, I'm striking this, and then – *whoof*! Please bring the microphone over here, sir,' he panted, grabbing Florian's arm. 'I want you to tell these people what Florian is really like...' As he spoke, he pointed towards the microphone.

'Well, Adrian...' said Charles, for once feeling that a measure of hesitancy was an advantage. He looked at Dotty and Dr Ironsize. They looked scandalised but had wisely kept their places.

Adrian held his lighter against his arm, threatening not just himself but the school's most famous student. 'Tell them he's not a hero. He's an arsehole, isn't he, sir – say it!'

Charles fiddled with the switch on the stem of the microphone. 'Ladies and gentlemen,' he said, trying to keep his voice calm but conscious that it was ricocheting off the walls outside. 'I have been asked to tell you that Florian Bavington is an arsehole.'

'He's a tosser,' said Adrian. 'Tell them.'

'He is also... a tosser,' said Charles, trying to sound sincere and credible. He felt a sort of freedom at last. This might be under duress, but these were the words he longed to hear. Maybe today was going to turn out alright after all.

'Tell them!' screamed Adrian, producing a Close to the Edge wrist-tie from his pocket and, with surprising agility, attaching himself to Florian. 'Tell them!'

'He's a... he's a little prick,' said Charles, smiling at Florian who, gripped by Adrian, was looking, for the first time in a long time, unsure of himself. 'He's dreadful. He's loathsome. He's really smug and he's just... He's totally self-centred. I mean, I know he's suffered and all that but, really...'

'And if anyone comes near me,' said Adrian huskily, waving the lighter, 'I'll blow us both up.'

'Adrian...' said Charles. 'That's not necessary.'

'There's nothing else to say, sir,' Adrian said, which, in a way, was oddly prophetic.

'Leave me alone, you fucking freak,' said Florian,

rising to his feet. He picked up the Debating Trophy, perhaps planning to assault Adrian with it and win his liberty but he stopped when Adrian began rolling his finger over the lighter's flint. They both knew that one spark meant trouble. Out of the corner of his eye, Charles saw that Zimbabwean Piet had climbed over the tiered seating to the front of the hall and was waiting for his chance to strike.

'Put the trophy down, Florian,' said Charles, 'and just... behave yourself.'

'He's going to set fire to us!' Florian screamed. He looked, if anything, even more terrified than when they were about to hand him over to Mr Baadi.

'Florian! Sit down!' commanded Adrian.

'But he's got a...'

'Florian! Sit! Down!' shouted Charles, aware that with Adrian dangerously out of control, the moment had come to show that he, Charles Goldforbes, was the only person who could save them all. He turned, placed his hands on Florian's shoulders and then, with sudden force, heaved him down into a seating position on the stage as if he were closing a sash window. The boy's legs gave way and he fell heavily, but in the last moments of his descent, his expression changed dramatically. His eyes started to flicker and his face turned bright red. When he stood up again, very slowly, Charles peered down and wondered how the base of the debating trophy could have become affixed to the seat of Florian's trousers. Then he realised that Adrian must have acted with exceptional speed – repaying Florian for what he had done in the cave with a pencil – by placing the trophy in the entry position for the anal corridor.

While Charles was forcing him to sit down, the trophy, named in honour of the school's founder, with its tapered, probing index finger, was being rammed up the inside of Florian Bavington's back passage.

Events now became confused. As Florian's screams began to ring out around the hall, the winner of the debating trophy – having now semi-internalised it – sprang at Adrian and, in his rage, seemed to be trying to bite his ear-lobe, but Adrian moved the lighter even closer to his jacket and tried rolling the flint. Just that one spark was all it needed. The adults prepared for a counter-attack. An impromptu Tai Chi circle of crouching teachers – as well as Hugh Bavington and Piet – materialised around them, and might very well have succeeded in liberating both boys, had Florian been somewhat less encumbered by school trophies, and Adrian more athletically gifted.

Florian tried to snatch his arm away from Adrian, who reacted by, at last, losing control of the lighter. It looped in the air and Charles, seeing his moment to do something heroic, to be admired and talked about, stepped forward to intercept it. Unfortunately, though, it fell among the many trophies which now littered the area around Florian as he writhed in pain. Charles got his finger-tips to it first, but Adrian arrived a second later, and they both pulled at it, from different ends, which was almost certainly the wrong thing to do with an object which depended, for its function, on friction.

A moment later a flame popped up and, with a surprisingly quiet *whoof!*, Adrian's jacket blossomed with flames, like an ill-smelling sacrifice to appease some angry gods.

Charles ducked back from the sudden heat, but he could see that Florian, having been held close by his persecutor, must have picked up some fuel too as he was waving his arm around to deaden the flames which, of course, only made them rear up higher. Now that he was fighting a different type of pain, Florian's buttocks finally lost the shocked rigidity with which they had clamped the trophy and it rolled onto the floor with a mournful clang.

Charles had known for some time that Adrian hated Florian, but it was not until now that he saw how far Adrian was prepared to go – the very act of self-immolation – to make his feelings clear. It was a supreme gesture of heroic resistance, deserving of much praise, but he could only watch now as Mrs Hughes-Howard, springing into action, grabbed a fire extinguisher and advanced, side-stepping as if in a dance-off, towards both boys, squirting and dousing as she went. The next thing he knew was the feeling that his legs had been hit by a truck, which, since Piet had just rugby tackled him, would have been about right.

The ambulance took longer to arrive than it should have done, since there were so many now not-quite-so prospective parents creeping away from Rydon Hall in a tortoise formation of unhealthily large family cars. Had the Fire Station been true to its name, and not just an over-priced coffee bar, a team might have been on site within minutes, but they were no longer able to provide that service, unless it had been baristas dousing the boys with cafe latté or a selection of frappuccinos. Eventually, the boys were taken away in two ambulances, each containing both sets of parents. A shame, too, that Fring General had been replaced by a housing estate. The nearest hospital was that bit further away, in Varley Park, and it was from there that an over-worked medical orderly, still sweating and visibly moved, emerged, a few hours later, to break the news to the parents that, six hours after they were admitted, and despite every effort having been made to save both boys' lives by two teams working with the utmost dedication and care, while they had been able to save the life of one of the boys, they had not managed to do so with his 'friend', who had succumbed to his injuries.

To the disbelief of all present, it was the sad duty of the hospital staff to report to the assembled media that, due to a combination of smoke inhalation and skin burns, Adrian Purvis, aged 13, had lost his fight to stay alive.

It was particularly cruel, as Dr Ironsize made clear in a

specially produced black-edged school newsletter later that week, that a year which had already contained such drama, and from which the school had bounced back so remarkably, should end on such a tragic note. He devoted several paragraphs to a tribute towards Adrian which, if read with a less sympathetic eye, painted a graphic picture of what little impact he had made while at Rydon Hall. He praised the boy's "potential", his "individuality", his "unforgettable" forest creature cameo in a school play performed six years earlier, and even his attendance record, which was said to be "truly exceptional". Adrian, he said, would never be forgotten, and, adopting an unfortunate phrase which would surely never have got through if he had shown it to Dotty first, ended with the line: "Adrian Purvis had the scent of a boy who you knew would go far."

Charles was allowed to read the school newsletter from the very limited comfort of his poky prison cell. His lawyer made clear in court that, obviously, he had never intended to plunge a metal object up Florian Bavington's back passage, let alone set fire to Adrian Purvis, but he was advised not to deny that, in the first place, his actions counted as Assault, while in the second case...

Whenever Charles was driven from his home to court by his mother, as they approached the courtroom he would brace himself for the crowds that he knew would be gathered outside. Luckily for the nation's most loved and recently released captive, the flames had only done surface damage which, combined with a little smoke inhalation, was cleared up in a few days by the country's finest nursing teams. In a sense, the damage done to Adrian was superficial, because he was dead. It was the assault on Florian that really angered the public.

Charles had not realised how many sections of the various Protection of Children Acts there were until all the charges were read out to him. He was surprised, however, by the speed with which an apparently innocent citizen can, in the space of mere seconds, descend into the lowest depths of the criminal underworld. In the fraught moments after he had lowered the golden boy of Rydon Hall onto the taut symbol of debating excellence, Charles had been so swept up in the atmosphere of anarchy – this was the Defence's opening remarks – that he had committed an uncharacteristic act, and his fingers had slipped.

Charles was told that he could not expect to find himself back on the streets for months, if not years. The charge sheet listed aggravated child abuse against two minors on the grounds of attempted physical harm, psychological damage, lack of due care and attention, inappropriate physical contact and unprofessional behaviour. Almost the only aspect of the Act which he had not offended against was that of starvation, but he could hardly claim that it was consideration for Florian that had stayed his hand.

As the hall had emptied, Charles was frogmarched off the stage by Bill Drummer and out to the back of the building. The one advantage of this was that he could hear little of Dr Ironsize's unscripted and somewhat post-apocalyptic attempts to wind up the afternoon. Charles blinked, rubbed his head a few times and tried to work out where he was. It turned out that he was, for the first time, inside Bill Drummer's small, backstage office. Its walls were crammed with posters and photographs of previous school productions. Recognising some colour stills, Charles wished he could ask him about them, but Bill didn't seem in the mood for a chat. Not for the first time in his life, Charles felt a great weight upon himself. In fact, it was Bill Drummer, sitting on his legs and swearing at him.

'We'll stay here a few moments, shall we? Wait for the police,' said Mr Drummer, baring his teeth at him. 'You fuckwit.'

'That's not you being Tourette's, is it?' said Charles. 'That's what you really think.'

'Fuckwit... What the fuck did you... Don't tell me, I don't even want to know.'

'Bill, I didn't mean to do anything,' said Charles. 'It just, sort of, happened.'

'You just crapped on our end-of-year party, you fuckwit,' said Mr Drummer.

'You weren't there, Bill,' said Charles. 'You weren't in Smilia. You don't know what it was like.'

'Oh don't give me that...'

Charles ran his eyes along the walls, which were crammed with pictures of boys trying to look like actors. 'Was that *War of the Worlds*?' he asked.

'That one? No that was *Robin Hood*, two years ago. Good production, that. Eh!' He snapped back into severity. 'Don't try anything, right? You're a disgrace. Absolute disgrace.'

Then the door was flung open, and Mrs Hughes-Howard rushed in, followed by Dr Ngo. They closed the door, then hovered by it, as if reluctant to get too close.

'Hi Colin, hi Joy,' said Charles. 'Did I ever tell you about the time I was a hostage in Smilia...?'

'Oh Charles...' said Mrs Hughes-Howard in a tone of utter bafflement. 'What on earth were you thinking?'

'How are they?' he said. 'Don't tell me they're dead. Not both of them.'

'Too early to tell,' said Dr Ngo, 'but if they're alive, it's thanks to Joy.'

'That Adrian, he was such a hero,' said Charles. 'I'm really sorry I nearly killed him. I didn't mean to. He did it for the school, you know. It wasn't about him.'

'Save it for the judge, mate,' said Bill.

The door was thrust open again, this time by Ms de Souza, who looked in a state of almost total shock. She was accompanied by Charmian Thirst and three police officers: two large, one much smaller. 'Is that him?' said one of them.

'That's...' said Ms de Souza. She glanced at Charles as if hoping she had made a mistake but then straightened up. 'Yeah, that's him,' she said.

'Dotty,' said Charles, trying to get out from under Bill Drummer's body-hold. 'I'm sorry, I really am. And you've got such pretty eyes. Did I ever tell you that?'

'How could you have *done* that?' she asked, despairingly.

'Charles?' said Charmian. 'You, like, assaulted Florian, and then you, like, set fire to Adrian. I mean...'

'Charmian, I know, I do know,' said Charles. 'But I think you're so nice. You're a bit long-winded but you're a really lovely person.'

'Oh, right,' she said. 'Love you too.'

'Incidentally,' said Charles, 'did you know that the word "pyromania" comes from the Greek words...'

'What were you thinking?' cried Dotty.

'Well, perhaps I could just set those actions in context? Yes?' pleaded Charles. 'And I realise this isn't going to look good on my Continuing Professional Development, but...'

'You can forget about CPD, mate,' said Bill. 'CPD? Fuck that. More like Continuing Prison Development. That's the only CPD that's coming your way.'

Bill's tongue flicked out, licking the back of his hand as if his mouth were dry.

'I just wanted to get back at Florian, I suppose, said Charles.

'Don't make it worse,' said Bill.

'But he was such a little prick. Even in the cave. That's why I wanted to make sure he stayed with Mr Baadi...'

'No!!!'

'I just wanted to teach him a lesson.'

Dotty de Souza stood over him. She looked as if she wanted to pull his hair out. 'We're teachers, Charles. We're all trying to teach him a lesson: that's what we do. But not like that!'

'Is this worse than my having sex with Mrs

Bavington?'

'You what?' said Dotty at last.

'Well, that's not quite like what happened. Bit of a long story, but since we're having this chat I thought I'd throw it in.'

'You had...?' Bill looked like he could throttle Charles.

'No. Other way round. She had me. But let's not get hung up on the grammar. But, Colin, could I say this to you? Because, well – I feel I can call you Colin now - if I don't get the chance, I just wanted to wish you all the best with Mrs Annersley. She's a magnificent woman and I'm very happy for the two of you.'

He couldn't see if Dr Ngo's face had registered the remark, because Ms de Souza turned to the policemen. 'Take him away,' she said, and walked out.

POSTSCRIPT

Charles' period of confinement at H.M.P. Dinsmore was not as long as it might have been, and at least he wasn't in a cold and draughty cave, but it was an extremely unwelcome feeling, finding himself back under lock and key. The sentence, which might have been much longer, was reduced to three years, with extenuating circumstances. His Defence lawyer amassed a pile of mitigating factors to show that Charles' behaviour had been entirely uncharacteristic. He had suffered a great deal, had been having difficulty adapting to normal life on his return from Smilia, it was a one-off, he had never lost control before: Charles' grasp of proceedings was greatly assisted by his not needing to have terms like "*mens rea*" and "*prima facie*" translated.

Charles had hoped that, as the facts emerged, Florian's reputation might appear somewhat besmirched, but, in the dock, the hero of Smilia and star Prosecution witness looked like a choirboy whose childlike trust had been ruthlessly violated. Charles might have known, too, that both he and Adrian would barely feature in what some newspapers were calling "The Trial of the Century", before downgrading it to "Trial of the Decade", and then, as a sense of proportion took hold, "Trial of the Month: Florian B To Give Evidence Today." Inevitably, it was about Florian: even though Charles was the defendant, he was only an extra in the greater drama of Florian Bavington's advance towards the godhead.

It was, of course, terrible what had happened to Adrian. Charles had heard that the school had decided to re-consign Honora Cleremont to oblivion and rename the Award for Special Effort after Adrian Purvis, and doubtless there would be other opportunities to remember him, which would never have taken place had he survived.

275

At the trial, Charles had been touched to find that both Milo and Penny, back from their travels and with a baby on the way, took time out from furnishing their second bedroom to speak up on his behalf. Mrs Annersley, speaking, for the most part, in Charles' defence, registered her extreme disapproval of his actions, but at least she conceded that he had never displayed any pyromaniacal or violent tendencies to her. (And she looked in better shape than ever.) Dotty de Souza's evidence was harder to interpret, and in a way more painful for Charles. She just looked betrayed.

Charles realised that he craved Dotty's approval, and that she had perhaps felt an attraction to him, and her look of scorn was very difficult for him to accept.

There was one significant improvement in the prison conditions: each cell had its own TV set and, being a low-ish security sort of prison, he even had limited access to the internet. When Charles was not side-stepping his pills and pot-crazy fellow inmates, he spent a lot of time watching international news programmes. Somehow – or because, like all wrongdoers, guilt made him return to the scene of his crimes – he paid particular attention to events in Smilia, which seemed to be making a concerted effort to turn its back on its violent past. It was amazing and impressive, said one reporter after another, that under the temporary shelter of a United Nations truce guaranteeing their safe passage, some of the country's most brutal warlords – Charles felt a pricking of his thumbs - could sit down opposite each other at a conference in New York, holding "talks about talks" and committing themselves to the objective of making their country merely "the fourth or fifth most corrupt country in the world". Even a year earlier, this had been an unthinkable prospect.

Now that he had the time to reflect on his actions,

Charles had to admit that what he had done was, if not completely reprehensible, then at least very naughty. If he hadn't learnt this lesson properly, the presence every other week, across a glass partition, of Mrs Annersley, was a reminder that he had committed a mortal sin.

'That innocent young boy,' she said, as another prisoner's girlfriend or daughter hurled abuse at a man a few cubicles away. 'Alright, the way you set fire to that poor Purvis was an accident, but the way you went for that dear, sweet Florian...'

'He is not dear, and he is not sweet!' protested Charles, before falling into the habit, so common among criminals, both major and minor, of endless *post-hoc* rationalisation. 'I was sick of his attitude. He thought he could get away with anything.'

'So did you, when you were that age,' she said, jabbing a finger at him. 'But how would you feel if some man tried to stuff a corkscrew up your jacksie and then set you on fire?'

Charles breathed out noisily. 'How's Colin?' he asked, changing the subject.

'Lovely,' she said, smiling at last. 'Very imaginative. Making himself at home.'

'Has he moved all his stuff into my room?'

'We're taking it slowly. Mostly it's just my equipment and so on. You know: all that hoisting equipment takes up a lot of space.'

'I was so happy there,' said Charles, his eyes filling with tears.

'Embury Park?' she said.

'Smilia,' said Charles.

Charles kept in touch with Geoffrey Norringham. They had never met, but he felt a bond with his predecessor, perhaps because of the technophobia that both men shared towards the teaching of Classics. And then, by good fortune as much as bad, Geoff's fondness for a late-night whisky got the better of him again, and his

Gulf hosts decided that they had made allowances for him once too often. Charles was allowed to read the *Times Educational Supplement*, even in his new base, and so he drew Geoff's attention, by letter, to the job advertised in it one week for the "Head of Latin Department" at Rydon Hall. He was less happy to read, in small lettering directly below, "The actual prep school of Florian Bavington". The wording, which both Geoff and Charles immediately recognised as that of Dr Ironsize, invited interested parties "to immediately apply". Both teachers winced at the split infinitive.

"Typical bloody Ironsize," Geoffrey wrote back, but he applied for the job nonetheless. Rydon Hall, with Florian Bavington absent, was much the same prospect as it had been before: the second or third best prep school in a very small area of south-west London. They needed someone to steady the ship, and Mr Norringham's familiar, if somewhat florid, face was deemed to be the most appropriate.

Florian Bavington, now schooled – as his mother was housed – in France, was beginning to become a disturbingly frequent fixture of the media. His *YouTube* appearances were racking up hundreds of thousands of viewers as he re-told his survivor's story over a rap backing track. There was no trace of the sulk, the mope or the leer that normally accompanied him. He smiled, looked healthy, flicked his hair over his white T-shirt and seemed delighted, relieved in fact, to be in front of a camera. Charles wished he could drench the television in paraffin and set fire to it, but with his parole only a few days away, he thought better of it.

Charles was released after two years, with time off for good behaviour and the shelves of the H.M.P. Dinsmore library unrecognisable from the sorry state they had been in before his arrival. He knew that, with his reputation officially tarnished, he would have to spread his net wider than the United Kingdom for teaching jobs, and so he felt very lucky, having moved back to his parents' house on the outskirts of north London, to come across an advert in the *TES* for a teaching post in a brand new academy in "one of the most challenging, unexplored and exciting territories in the world". He applied immediately. The website was lavishly coloured, and featured a very sharp-eyed bird's head, prominently displayed.

Interviews were taking place in London, Paris and Rome. Applicants were advised, "no experience necessary but enthusiasm and bags of energy a must". He revised harder than he had ever revised before. He didn't know any of the three-person interviewing panel, and he admitted that the college's educational syllabus did not quite conform to what he had studied as an undergraduate, but he urged them not to be put off by that. The panel laughed a great deal, and spoke in glowing terms about the new principal, whose ambition and vision were shaping the college – and whose money, however acquired, was funding it.

After an interminable four-week wait, Charles heard the unbelievable news that the job was his, and that he should turn up as soon as convenient to begin planning for the new term. Charles felt almost berserk with joy. A few days before his departure he went to see Milo and Penny in their lovely cottage, a former crack den in the East End of London. He had hardly expected them to ask him to be a godfather, after collecting a criminal record for involuntary manslaughter, but it was good to see them, and the courageously-named Lesbia was very sweet. On his last morning in London, he paid a sentimental journey to Mrs Annersley's house with a large parcel. She unwrapped the Bedroom Bondage Advanced Kit (amazing what one could get on the internet) and threw up her hands with pleasure. After consuming an elevenses bottle of wine - Colin was having his latest skin grafts checked in hospital but he appeared to have

279

made a near-perfect recovery - they held each other and wept as he said goodbye.

Then he set off for Heathrow.

At the end of a very long aeroplane journey, enlivened by his brand new English-only copy of Caesar's *Gallic Wars*, Charles arrived at Muccatchino International Airport and queued up at Customs underneath a sign that read, "Smilia Greets You With A Happy Smile". The August heat was so fierce it took him several seconds to gather his first lungful of air, and the tarmac was still thicker with military helicopters than civilian aircraft. He took a taxi and the driver, whose English was passable but whose knowledge of the Barclay's Premier League extensive, drove for several miles past gutted houses, occasionally diving down smaller roads when yellow triangular signs advised that the landmine clearance team still had some sweeping to do. Finally they arrived at the edge of a jungle, out of which a huge five-storey mass of steel and glass had been built. Charles couldn't tell if it was a bomb-site or a building site – he was told it had been the former and was now the latter – with the words "International Humanities Academy of Smilia", together with its principal and proud owner's name displayed in ostentatiously grand lettering and the bird's head outside the top floor, two storeys up. He could hear exotic cheeping in the trees, too. It was a beautiful day.

Charles was greeted by an immense, faultlessly polite gun-toting security guard wearing shades and a crew cut. He was shown first to his living quarters – accommodation was provided for staff and some students – which were small but comfortable. He wasn't too thrilled, at first, at being one floor underground, but he understood the explanation that, since the odd missile did occasionally still crash through the air, it was better not to build too high. Back in the main building, he was delighted to discover the canteen area, which, he noted excitedly, included a pool table. He wondered if he would recognise any of the chalky cubes, and hoped that this was a presentiment – like the ancients planting olive trees – of a peaceful future. There was a generous view of the car park, and of some distant mountains, which he promised to make time to get to know, if he didn't know parts of them already. Then he was shown to his classroom, or rather to the suite of corridors that constituted the department of which he was now chief. He had brought with him several posters showing famous dates, faces and buildings, but he was excited to see that he would need many more.

The tour ended outside the principal's office. As Charles waited, enjoying the faint background tinkle of Eminem tunes (he had taken the chance, while in prison, to broaden his musical tastes), he spent several moments refamiliarising himself with a jaw-droppingly beautiful bird's head, encased behind very thick glass. The secretary noticed that he was admiring it, and seemed impressed when he asked her if it might be a falcon. She told him that she imagined it to be pretty old, and Charles hazarded the guess that, from what he remembered of his university days, it looked about 4,300 years old, from around 2,300 BC. Then he dropped into a sofa and re-read the college's brochure.

He gathered from the names of the prospective students that most of their parents must have played a prominent part in the country's previous administrations (or lack of them) or armies (or abundance of them), but that they had somehow squirreled away just enough to pay the astronomically high fees. The other applicants were the sons and daughters of the Chinese industrialists who were taking a keen interest in renovating the country's shattered infrastructure.

As Charles read, his eyes began to glaze over and he must have dozed off for several minutes. Eventually, though, he woke up to hear the scrape of machine-pressed wood on hand-sewn carpet as the door opened and Senator Abdi Baadi, recently returned from "some unpleasant but necessary blood-letting – in a strictly metaphorical sense!" stood facing, and just a little down from, Charles Goldforbes.

'So, Mr Goodfork, we meet again!' shouted Senator Baadi above the sound of an electric battering ram. Charles pumped his boss's hand reverently. The recently-appointed Education Minister of the New Democratic Republic of Smilia was smiling warmly at him. Charles looked for the gold filling and was pleased to see that it had been replaced by porcelain.

'Senator Baadi, I am so happy to be here.'

'Please, call me Abdi, except in staff meetings,' said Senator Baadi, his beard neatly clipped. 'I had hoped that our paths would cross again. Take this?' He reached over to a plastic wall unit marked "STAFF", with more spaces than name badges. He removed one and handed it to Charles. 'Now, as you know, term starts in three weeks. Have some water or you will die of thirst. Then we will begin our tour. Oh, and please pin your badge on and keep it with you at all times. The security guards get a little skittish when they bump into someone they do not know.'

Charles pointed at the cabinet containing the small but priceless treasure. 'I hadn't expected to see that again,' he said.

'Oh,' said the senator. 'Isn't she lovely? I keep meaning to hand her back. But, you know, couriers are so expensive these days...'

Senator Baadi strode towards the lift shaft - no lift had been inserted yet, but there were over three weeks to go before term began - and Charles hurried to catch him up. As he did so, he looked down at the shirt-badge which he would have to wear from now on. "Chuck Goldforbes", it read: "Head of Department, Classical Civilization". He sighed, shook his head and then shrugged. Not perfect, he thought to himself. But then, as Mrs Hughes-Howard would probably have said, Rome wasn't built in a day.

APOLOGIA

This novel sets out to make people laugh, but most readers will, I am sure, be able to identify the real country which I have renamed "Smilia". They might also suspect that the situation on the ground is quite unlike the farcical scenes which I have presented here. I did my best to create a "beautiful, scarred wilderness", as I'm sure it is, in many places, but otherwise I played it safe and limited my research to books and other products of the media.

I did, though, speak to one or two of its natives, whose stories were truly harrowing. For them, I dared to imagine a happier future. My hope for the people of that extraordinary country is that they will soon be able to achieve what most regard as their right: tranquillity, security and the luxury of optimism. And perhaps one day I'll be able to attend a book-signing out there.

ACKNOWLEDGEMENTS

Most of this book was written in the British Library, St Pancras: I am very grateful to its reading-room, cloakroom and catering staff. Other parts were written in the London Library, the Institute of Classical Studies Library (UCL) and Marylebone Library. Thanks, long ago, for Peter Vansittart's advice, Lesley Robertshaw's hospitality and, more recently, Tony Sharp's answers to a lot of questions. Also to James Bourne, Christabelle Dilks, Christopher Phipps, Cressida Downing and Jennifer Warner for being such incisive readers. To Adam Freudenheim for encouragement and sympathy and to Archie Baron for some crucial editorial interventions.

This book is an unofficial leaving present to the students, parents and most especially staff members of Tower House School, south-west London, where I taught very happily for six years. I will miss them, in their diverse and splendid originality, very much.

Huge thanks to Katharine Smith of Heddon Publishing for running an extremely tight ship. Thanks also to Catherine Clarke for producing a really eye-catching cover. And to E, f and e... Just thanks.

BG

If you have enjoyed this book, we would be very grateful if you would take the time to review it on the Amazon website. A positive review is invaluable and will be greatly appreciated by the author.

Please also visit the Heddon Publishing website to find out about our other titles:
www.heddonpublishing.com

Heddon Publishing was established in 2012 and is a publishing house with a difference. We work with independent authors to get their work out into the real world, by-passing the traditional slog through 'slush piles'.

Please contact us by email in the first instance to find out more: enquiries@heddonpublishing.com

Like us on Facebook and receive all our news at:
www.facebook.com/heddonpublishing

Join our mailing list by emailing:
mailinglist@heddonpublishing.com

Follow us on Twitter: @PublishHeddon

Printed in Great Britain
by Amazon